TIMMY

TIMMY

Dewey L Douglas

ISBN: 9798733730745
Imprint: Independently published

For my daughter, Jessica,

who taught me to see the

monsters... again.

In memory of my father

who lived his life in

Crystal Springs.

Dewey Lee Douglas

April 25, 1920 - April 28, 1988

I love you, Pappy.

TIMMY

Prologue

1

It was a chilly night in January when Timmy was born. That type of night that the old back-woods hunters used to call a pricknipper. After one too many slugs of homemade hooch got their blood running thin, they'd build a fire and one of them would invariably comment, "Yep. Gonna be a real pricknipper t'night." Then they'd bundle themselves against the wind, take another good shot of rotgut, and pray to God Almighty that a deer didn't wander through because none of them were in any condition to be aiming a gun.

On that late January pricknipper in 1973, there were, most likely, many of those campfires around which were huddled many more of those drunken hunters. But Gerald White was not one of them. Not that night. His wife went into labor just before six o'clock that evening. And, of course, the doctor was nowhere to be found. Since the contractions were nearly a half-hour apart, any rational person would assume that there was no reason to panic. But an expectant father can be a very irrational animal.

"Where the hell is he?"

"Jerry, would you sit down? You're making me a nervous wreck." Pamela White, Gerald's loving and longsuffering wife. She was the model of patience and calm consideration. At least on the outside. Inside, she was a mass of quivering flesh, dealing as best she could with the alien invasion of her body.

She had started to show early, and at three months had to start wearing maternity clothes. Immediately afterward came the period of ugliness: *Oh, God, I'm so fat and ugly how can you stand to look at me I know you don't love me any more I wish I were dead.* Of course, Gerald didn't help the situation, looking so smug and strutting alongside his elephantine wife as if to say, "Look at what I did! Whoopee! I'm a man!" At least that's the way it seemed. It also seemed that he stared for a considerable length of time at any beautiful young lady who happened to stray into his field of vision. But before long, people began to talk about "the glow," that bright-eyed, rosy-cheeked radiance that, sooner or later, infects every pregnant woman. It took a little doing, but as soon as she managed to convince herself that The Glow was with her, she found that things were not nearly as bad as she thought, and that life was once again worth living -- except for one relatively minor problem. For at least the last 200 days, her morning routine consisted of leaping out of bed, throwing up all her vital body fluids, crawling back into bed, and waiting with one hand over her mouth for the alarm clock to ring. Not a pleasant way to start the day, but through it all (except for the days of ugliness) she managed to maintain the appearance of calm, the attitude of total control. Even when the first contraction crept up on her and brought along a dull, throbbing pain to settle in the small of her back.

"But he's supposed to be close by! Where the hell is he?"

"For God's sake, Jerry, I'm already two weeks overdue. We can't expect him to sit around waiting for me to bust open. He probably went to spend the weekend with his sister in Jackson."

"But why *this* weekend?"

"Jerry, for cryin' out loud, sit down!"

Jerry sat, but he kept looking at his watch, running a hand through his hair, and twisting his shirttail. Pamela shook her head.

"That's a little better... I guess. Now I'm gonna tell you something and I want you to listen very carefully. Do you think you can to that?"

"What? Oh, yeah, yeah." Another glance at the watch.

"It really doesn't matter that the doctor's not here. Do you know why?"

"No. No, I don't." A hand through the hair.

"You're not listening to me."

"I heard every word you said. 'It doesn't matter that the doctor's not here.'"

"Very good. And now I'll tell you why. Because if the doctor were here, all he'd do is look at me and say, 'Yep, those are contractions, all right,' and then call the hospital to tell them we're on our way."

"Where could he be?"

That was all she could take. She clenched her fists, her nostrils flared, and her face became a very distinct shade of red. Her composure was shot to hell.

"Gerald White! You stop it right this minute or, I swear to

God, I'll go to the goddamn hospital without you!"

Jerry's mouth hung open and for a long time he had the incredulous look of a little boy whose favorite slingshot had been taken away because he kept shooting his sister in the head with it. "You wouldn't dare."

"Try me." Her jaw was set in sheer determination, but only for a moment. The words were scarcely out of her mouth when she clutched simultaneously at her belly and her back and leaned back stiffly onto the sofa. The contraction was a strong one, lasting a full forty-five seconds. When it subsided, it was Pamela who looked at the watch.

"Twenty-three minutes. Jerry, call the hospital and tell them we're coming."

"But shouldn't we..."

"Jerry, we still have time to do a lot of things but arguing about this is not one of them. Call." Without waiting for an answer, she went into the bedroom to get the overnight bag that she had packed a month ago. When she returned, Jerry was finishing the call.

"It's all set. They'll be waiting for us."

"Good. Will you get my coat, please?"

The drive from Crystal Springs to the hospital in Hazlehurst was not a long one, ten or twelve miles at the most, but it was along one of Mississippi's notorious, twisting, hilly, two-lane roads that somebody had insisted upon calling a highway. Jerry made some quick calculations. Even though the road was narrow, there wouldn't be any traffic after dark. No chance of getting stuck behind a slow-moving log truck or a tractor. If they timed it just right, they could be at the hospital before the next contraction. And that was good. Jerry wasn't exactly sure how many more of those gut-wrenching contractions he could stand.

"Do you want to lay in the back seat?"

"No, I'd rather sit up front. Right now, I'm more comfortable sitting up."

Climbing into the driver's seat, Jerry was suddenly struck with the fear that he would do something really stupid, like flood the carburetor and have to sit in the driveway with his wife doubled up in pain until the engine would start.

But he didn't. The starter turned over twice, the engine caught, and they were on their way.

For the first time in their married life, they were both silent while riding through town. Usually there was some comment about how nice Mrs. Wiley's yard looked or how the Hawkins girl should close the curtains in her room *before* she took off her clothes instead of *after*. But there was none of that discussion tonight. They were on an urgent mission that would increase the population of Crystal Springs, and their own family, by a total of one.

They had gone out of the city limits and were well down the highway when Pamela noticed that Jerry's knuckles were white from his grip of the steering wheel. A little diversion was in order.

"You know, I think I've changed my mind. I think I will breast feed the baby after all." He cast her a puzzled glance and then looked back at the road. "Well, I might as well. I've got the tits for it... finally."

There was a moment of silence, and Pamela was beginning to

think her little joke had fallen on deaf ears. Then Jerry, as straight-faced as he possibly could, said softly, "But did you have to get pregnant to get tits?"

"Jerry!" She punched him playfully on the arm and they burst into laughter. The tension was broken, at least for the time being. That was all she could ask. For the next couple of minutes, they talked and laughed about the pros and cons of breast-feeding, but underlying their light conversation was the feeling of urgency. Pamela was determined to remain calm, no matter how scared she was. Jerry was determined to get them to the hospital before the next contraction. He was driving just a little faster than he should have been. The fog was just a little thicker than he thought it was. And he just didn't see that small patch of ice on the bridge.

2

Tommy Bishop was one pissed off deputy sheriff. The job was all right. It had its advantages, and it had its disadvantages. Occupational hazards, so to speak. Night duty was one of the hazards; Billy Joe was another.

Billy Joe was a nice enough guy. There wasn't a thing that he wouldn't do for you. He was kind and considerate, a great guy to know if you ever needed help. He had even been known to literally give another person the shirt off his back. But there were times when Billy Joe didn't have his mind on what he was doing. Like tonight. He was more than an hour late taking over the midnight shift. At about one-fifteen, Bishop decided that he had had enough and picked up the telephone.

Billy Joe's phone rang seven times before the receiver was

lifted from the cradle and then dropped to the floor.

"Hello?" The sound of his disturbed sleep drifted through the phone lines.

"Billy Joe, where the hell are you?"

"I'm at home. Who is this?"

"Boy, you better git your butt to this office right now or I'll be reamin' you a new asshole!"

That was all Bishop had to say. Now he just sat back and listened to Billy Joe stumbling out of his sleep.

"Bishop, is that you?"

(*rustle, rustle*)

"Am I supposed to be on duty tonight?"

(*tromp, tromp, tromp*)

"Hey, man, I'm sor...

(*THUD!*)

"Sorry. The phone slipped outta my hand.

(*rustle, rustle*)

"I guess my alarm clock..."

(*rustle, rustle*)

"... must be broke. How long have you been waitin' for me?"

(*ziiiiiiiip!*)

"Hey, I'm real sorry, Bishop. I'm on my way right now."

"You have your ass in here in fifteen minutes or I'm loadin' this shotgun with bird shot."

Bishop didn't wait for an answer. He knew damn well that Billy Joe couldn't make it to the office in fifteen minutes. He also knew that with ice on the roads Billy Joe had better sense than to try.

The shotgun stayed in the gun case, and Bishop settled back with an old issue of Playboy.

Some time between a half-hour and forty-five minutes later, Billy Joe ran through the office door.

"Hey, Bishop, I'm really sorry, man. I had to scrape ice off my windows and..."

"Don't grovel. It looks bad."

"Right. Well, how's it been tonight?"

"Slow." Dead would have been a better word, but Bishop didn't care. He wasn't interested in conversation, he just wanted to put on his coat and get out of the office. "Hold it down."

"Right. You take it easy."

"Take it any way I can get it."

"Oh, and you be careful on that old highway. The roads are..."

Bishop pulled the office door shut with a slam, cutting Billy Joe off in mid-warning. The night air bit into the back of his neck, and he turned up his collar to block the icy rain that was falling. Across the street, the neon sign of the A-1 Cafe blinked slowly, rhythmically, cutting through the fog and drawing his attention like a hypnotist's gold watch. His subconscious mind went to work on his conscious mind, and before he knew it, he was standing in front of the cafe with the remembered taste and smell of hot coffee tempting his taste buds. Behind the counter, Ester, with her wide grin and wider hips, was waving him inside.

"Come on in, you idgit. Whatcha doin' standin' out there in the cold?"

"Hi, Ester. How's business?"

"Ain't took in a dime for nearly three hours now. I don't know why George makes us stay open all night. Just a damned waste of good money, if ya askt me."

"But if you weren't open, who'd take care of all us hard workin' peace officers?"

She burst into laughter. "Is that P-E-A-C-E or P-I-E-C-E?" A long-standing joke.

Bishop played along. "I don't know. What kind of mood are you in tonight?"

"Shit! Now I heard everything! Okay, Mister Piss Officer, what'll you have?"

The coffee was as good as he had remembered, and by the time he left the cafe he had put away three cups. Outside again, he silently cursed himself. Even as tired as he was, he would be wide-awake for hours and would probably make ten trips to the john. He slid into the seat of his patrol car and thought about ways to fill those long hours.

The old highway between Hazlehurst and Crystal Springs was even worse than Billy Joe had tried to warn him. The temperature was dropping fast, and the rain was falling harder and freezing as soon as it hit the pavement. A hell of a night to be driving. He slowed to a good safe speed.

In another three miles, Bishop would be glad that he was full of coffee.

3

Pamela wasn't sure how long she had been unconscious.

There was a moment of confusion, of disorientation, before she understood that she was still in the car, but the car wasn't moving. Slowly the memories came to her. The skidding car, the crash, the blackness.

Jerry!

Where was Jerry! In the total dark of the night, she reached out and waved her hands in front of her like a blind person.

"Jerry?" She was trying not to panic, but her voice betrayed her good intentions. Before she knew it, she was shouting, nearly screaming.

"Jerry, where are you?"

Jerry's dead.

"No, Jerry! Answer me! Oh, God, please! Let him be alive!"

She felt Jerry's coat. Grabbing it, she pulled as hard as she could, and he fell limply across the seat.

"Jerry?" Her voice was thin now and frightened. "Jerry, are you okay?" Through his heavy coat she felt his back rise and fall with his breathing. At least he was alive. Pulling off one of her gloves, she ran her hand over his head. She felt a large lump on his forehead and slivers of glass sticking in the skin of his face. Something sticky had traced one long wide path down the side of his head and another out of the corner of his mouth. She started to cry. She was cold, she had glass imbedded in her own skin, and her left leg felt as if it were broken. And she was in labor.

The contractions. She had to time the contractions. She reached for Jerry's arm to look at the luminous dial on his watch, but her movement was restricted by the dashboard that had been forced back by the collision. She pulled at his coat sleeve and twisted his arm until she could see the watch. Its crystal was smashed, and the sweep second hand had stopped in mid-sweep. The hands were frozen at 7:55. No help. In the total darkness, time passes as quickly, or as slowly, as the mind allows. Pamela knew that it was a contraction that had forced her back to her senses, and she had no idea how long ago that was. But she had a gut feeling, no pun intended, that she wouldn't have long to wait for the next one. She sat in the car clenching Jerry's arm in one hand, supporting her swollen abdomen with the other. Her tears mingled with her blood and ran between her lips, leaving a salty copper taste in her mouth.

The next contraction didn't build slowly like her last conscious one had. It came fast and hard and did not feel familiar at all. The pain shot into her stomach and sent a stream of fire through her broken leg. A wave of nausea swept over her. The stretched muscles of her abdomen tightened and pushed downward. She bit hard on her bottom lip to stop the scream she felt building inside her. Fresh blood trickled down her chin. In the freezing cold, she felt beads of sweat breaking out on her forehead.

Pamela tried to remember the breathing exercises they had learned in the childbirth classes. Breathing was the key. She knew it was easy, but Jerry…

Poor Jerry. He's dying.

Stop it! He's not dying! He can't *be!*

… was her coach, her helper. Without him, it was nearly impossible. She struggled against the pain and the pushing muscles and tried to remember.

Breathe in, breathe out. Faster. Breathe in, breathe out.

Poor Jerry...

Faster, faster. In, out, in, out. Through the mouth. In, out.

Jerry's dying...

Faster, HARDER! Stop the pain! Breathe, breathe, breathe! It's not working!

Jerry's dying and you're killing the baby...

She screamed. She threw her head back and sobbed and screamed and reached out for anything she could hold on to. All she found was Jerry's limp arm, and she clung to it desperately.

When the contraction finally subsided, she was exhausted. She was drenched in sweat which the cold air immediately turned into a blanket of ice water. For the first time she realized that the seat below her was cold and wet. The amniotic sac had broken, but when? She folded her arms tightly across her chest and shivered, her teeth chattering loudly between her broken sobs.

4

Bishop would have probably made it through the fog and all the way home without ever knowing there had been an accident if he hadn't run over a piece of the bridge guardrail that had been thrown out onto the road. When it hit, it sounded like the whole bottom of his patrol car was falling out from under him. That more or less got his attention. A couple of seconds later, he came to the hole in the guardrail. Bishop slowed his car and, after crossing the bridge, stopped on the shoulder of the road. He flipped the switch that started the red and blues flashing, just in case there was some other idgit out tonight. Under the driver's seat, he carried a long flashlight. One of those that take four batteries and shines like an airplane's landing lights. He clicked the flashlight on, slapped it twice against his palm to make the light come on, and walked back onto the bridge.

Shining through the gaping guardrail, the flashlight's beam fell upon a monstrous old oak, its trunk marred by deep gouges and its bark peeling away from the fresh wounds. On the ground at the base of the oak was an automobile, its rear wheels sinking in mud and its back end suspended over the stream. Bishop shook his head and whistled softly, his breath swirling like smoke in front of his face. It didn't take an expert in law enforcement to figure out what had happened here. The car went off the bridge and dropped about four or five feet before it centered the tree. It must have been going pretty fast because the front end was squashed like an accordion. Then it dropped straight down seven or eight more feet to the ground. Caught the driver by surprise, too. There weren't any skid marks on the bridge. Hell, if anybody in that car had any luck at all, the Good Lord snatched them up as soon as it happened and never let them know what hit them.

Besides notifying the next of kin, this was the part of his job that Bishop hated the most: Looking for the bodies. He had thought that after a while he would get used to it, especially after what he had seen a couple of years ago. Three high school boys in a jacked-up Chevelle, doing well over a hundred miles per hour, topped a hill just south of Hazlehurst and ran under the back of a flat-bed semi. It took damn near four hours to get the wreckage untangled. And the only way they knew there were three boys was because they found six legs on what was left of the floorboard of the car. The undertaker did the best he could, which wasn't much. Even the relatives didn't view the remains. It was a mess. This was a mess. It never got any easier.

Bishop made his way carefully down the steep embankment. He was getting too old for this and he had one too many beers, or cases of beers, in his lifetime. The extra weight made the downhill climb a struggle. About halfway down, his feet slipped in the soggy clay and he slid on his butt to the edge of the stream. In the slide, his flashlight went out again. Just as he slammed it against his palm, he heard a scream from inside the car.

"Holy Mother of God!" He was beside the car in an instant. The damage looked much worse from here than it did from the bridge. The front of the car was completely demolished. The hood had jack-knifed up instead of being pushed straight back through the front window. (Jayne Mansfield lost her head like that, or so he had heard.) The windshield, little more than a shattered mass of safety glass, was spattered with blood and leaning out against the hood. In the passenger's seat was a very pregnant young lady holding her stomach and screaming at the top of her lungs.

"Help me! Please! Oh, God, help me! Jerry! Ahhhhhh!"

"Ma'am, it's okay. We're here now."

"Can you help me, please! My baby! Jerry!"

"Ma'am, just try to be still. I'll have help here in just a few minutes."

"Oh, God, it hurts! Help me!"

He left her still holding her belly and still screaming. His immediate problem was how to get up the slick embankment to reach the radio in his patrol car. If he side-stepped and dug his heels in, he shouldn't have any trouble. After a few brief seconds of planning, he started the climb.

Bishop wasn't sure how to handle the woman. He wasn't sure how much of the

(*slip!*)

screaming was labor pains and how much was hysteria. He had been known to

(*sliiiip!*)

slap hysterical women on occasion, but a pregnant woman? He wasn't sure he could slap her if he had to.

(*SLIIIIIP!*)

"Shit!" In a flash, he was on his butt at the bottom of the bank. He shined his flashlight back toward the car. The woman had stopped screaming but still appeared to be in considerable pain. She was breathing heavily through her mouth and rolling her head back and forth on the headrest built into the seat. She could be in shock. She could be hemorrhaging. Hell, she could be drawing her last breath for all he knew. He had to get up that hill.

Behind the oak tree there seemed to be a small path that led up into the woods. Probably a deer or cow trail. The ground would be soft and slippery there too, but there was a scattering of bare shrubs that he could hold. Once up the path it would be just a matter of going through the woods to the road.

The path proved to be a little easier than the steep bank. Still, with the unsure footing and the flashlight going on and off, it took

Bishop almost five minutes to get back to the highway. He ran as fast as he could, and by the time he reached the car he was panting like a mad bull. He snatched the radio microphone and pressed the "send" button on the side.

"S.O. One to Base. S.O. One to Base. Over." There was a long pause filled with grating static.

"S.O. One to Base. S.O. One to Base. Do you read me? Over."

Come on, Billy Joe. Where are you?

"S.O. One to Base. Come in, please. Over."

Answer, you son of a...

"Base to S.O. One. I read you. Is that you, Bishop? I figured you'd be at home with the old lady by now. Over."

"Cut the chatter, Billy Joe, and write this down. I need an ambulance... make that two ambulances, about four, five miles north on the old highway. And full rescue gear. Pronto. Over."

"Two ambulances, rescue gear, four miles north. Got it. Sounds like a bad one. Over."

"Bad enough." In the distance, Bishop could hear the woman starting to cry out. His stomach rolled. A tear formed in the corner of his eye. His heart went out to this woman, and for the first time in his life he felt grossly inadequate. "I got things to do. Get that stuff out here quick. Over and out."

From the trunk of his patrol car, Bishop took the blankets that he always carried in the winter, a coil of rope, and a tire tool. He wasn't equipped for full-scale lifesaving, but he was going to do whatever he could.

He tied one end of the rope to the mangled guardrail of the bridge and, with the blankets secured under one arm and the tire tool stuffed in the front of his pants, he more or less rappelled down the embankment. As soon as his feet hit the wet clay, they slid, and Bishop hit the ground again. The end of the tire tool popped up and smacked him in the chin. For just a second, everything went white. He opened his mouth to say "shit," but a pain like electricity surged through his jaw…

Probably broke the motherfucker in twenty places.

… and stopped the word on his lips. He fought the urge to throw the tool in the dark stream. Gathering up the blankets, he slipped and slid to the car.

He immediately went to the passenger's door and tried to pull it open. The impact had jammed it tight, and all Bishop accomplished was to pull the handle off. He checked out the windshield. Even though it was leaning forward, there was only a gap of an inch or two because the crumpled hood held it up. He had to go through the side window.

"Get down." The pain was excruciating. He tried desperately not to move his mouth while he spoke. "I've got to break the window."

Pamela just looked up at him hopelessly. He tapped the glass with the tire tool.

"Get down."

She looked around, her breath coming in short gasps, and after a moment bent into a position that would shield her face.

It took three good blows with the tire tool to make the window collapse. Bishop stuffed the blankets through the hole and, with some difficulty, said, "Wrap up in these. It won't be long now." He heard the distant sirens of assistance.

Pamela spread the first of the blankets over Jerry, tucking it in close to his body. The second, she wrapped around herself. With one hand, she smoothed the hair away from Jerry's forehead. His skin felt so cold. She held his hand and waited. Another contraction was on its way.

Bishop was working on the jammed door when the first ambulance stopped on the bridge. Within a matter of minutes, both ambulance crews and the rescue team were swarming around the wreck. Bishop stood out of the way, listening and waiting to be of service.

"Man looks to be in pretty bad shape. Help me with the door."

"We got a pregnant lady here. Real pregnant. You ever delivered a baby?"

"Not me. I skipped class that day."

"I delivered a couple in 'Nam."

"She's yours. And it looks like you better hurry over here."

There was a loud *pop!* and the sharp *screeech* of metal as the door of the driver's side was forced open.

"The man's in shock. Possible hypothermia."

"Jerry?"

"Don't worry about your husband, lady. He's in good hands. We got our own problems to take care of. Get this door open."

"Got to get his temp up. Respiration?"

"Twenty-five and shallow."

"Head injuries. Lacerations. Probable severe concussion.

And he took a hell of a shot in the chest."

Another *pop!* and *screeech.*

"Okay, Ma'am, can you slide back just a little? We're gonna try to get you onto this stretcher."

"Jerry..."

"Jerry's all right. They're taking him to the hospital, and we'll be right behind them. Now slide..."

"Oh, God! It's coming!"

"What?"

"It's coming, and I can't stop it!"

"Calm down just a little and let me take a look. By golly, you're right. Dale, can you give me a hand here? It's a breech."

"Yeah. What can I do?"

"Hand me the scissors out of the bag. Okay, Ma'am. Everything's fine. Just take a few deep breaths. That's right. Now it seems like your little kidlet can't wait until we get up the hill, so we'll do it here. Dale, douse some alcohol on those scissors. Now, Ma'am, if we're gonna be this intimate, we should at least know each other's name. What's your first name?"

"P...P... Pamela."

"I'm Bob. Now, Pamela, we have a little problem..."

"Is my baby okay?" She tried to sit up, but Bob stopped her with a hand to the chest.

"The baby just got itself turned around and right now its tiny little ass is poking out at the world." She tried to smile and felt a shard of glass in the corner of her mouth. "We can handle it, it's just gonna be a little harder than normal. Is this your first baby?"

She nodded.

"Scissors. Okay, now, here's what we're gonna do. Dale's gonna go around there and hold your hands. Dale's a pretty good guy. You can squeeze his hands until his fingers turn blue and he won't let go. Right, Dale?"

"You bet."

"I need you to spread your legs just a little bit more..."

"Ooooow! No, no! Please!"

"What's the matter? Oh, shit, Dale, we got a bad fracture. Okay, Pamela, we'll be careful. Now I'm gonna make a little cut right here. Can you feel that?"

"Uh huh."

"It'll probably sting, but believe me, it'll make things a hell of a lot easier. You ready?"

"Don't hurt my baby."

"Wouldn't dream of it. Here we go. Now that wasn't so bad, was it? Now, Dale, you hold on tight because, Pamela, when that next contraction comes you have to..."

"Here it comes! Here it comes!"

"Push! Push down as hard as you can!"

Pamela's screams chilled Bishop more than the night air. He didn't know how long they had been here, but this poor woman and her husband had been in that wreck for a long time. He couldn't help thinking that if he had gotten here sooner things would be different. The woman would be having her baby in a nice warm hospital. She would be surrounded by doctors and nurses all rushing about, doing whatever they do when babies are born. Her husband would be recovering nicely from minor surgery since prompt rescue action would have minimized the risk of complications. If only Billy Joe had been on time for work. But he couldn't blame Billy Joe. Not completely. He, himself, had spent a good forty-five minutes in the cafe. Fate's a cruel bitch.

"That's good. Keep pushing. We got his legs and buttocks. Keep her pushing, Dale. We've got to get the shoulders and head before they pinch the umbilical. Push. Push. Here they come. Here they come. There! You can rest now."

Bob worked frantically clearing mucus from the nose and mouth of the baby. Pamela raised her head and watched the scene between her legs.

"Is my baby okay?"

"He'll be fine. We've just got to get him going."

"Him?"

"Dale, do we have a clamp or something in the bag?"

"Here's a forceps."

"That'll work for now."

Bob clamped the umbilical cord and snipped it with the scissors. Holding the baby upside-down by its feet, Bob felt the little body getting cold. He slapped it twice on the rump.

Bishop heard the resounding slaps, but they were not followed by a baby's crying. There was only silence. His wounded jaw barely moved when he said, "Come on, kid. Fight."

"What's wrong with my baby! Why isn't he crying!"

There were two more slaps. Then two more. Then a sound that made Bishop force his mouth open to shout. The baby cried. Not much, and not very loudly, but at least it tried.

Bob put the baby beside Pamela on the stretcher. "Hold him close. Maybe give him something to eat. He deserves that. Just keep him warm. That's the important thing right now. Dale, y'all get her up to the ambulance. We'll deliver the placenta *en* route."

"Right."

Bob absently rubbed his hands on his pants as he walked toward Bishop.

"Not bad, Doc."

"That was too close. I guess I'm a little out of practice."

"He's alive. And any birthin' you can walk away from..." Bishop's hand went to his jaw.

"What happened to you? You look like somebody used your face for a punching bag."

"Just clumsy."

"Well, come on to the hospital and we'll take a look at it."

"Can't. Got to get this mess cleaned up."

"It's too cold to argue about it, and besides, this wreck isn't going anywhere before tomorrow. Come on."

Bishop watched for a moment as the rescue men hauled the stretcher by ropes up to the bridge. He had just witnessed a damned miracle: The birth of Timothy Peter White. Of course, he had no way of knowing that's what the baby's name would be, but he had witnessed the birth and all in all he felt pretty good. Sure, let the work wait until tomorrow. What the hell. The hospital would be warm. And he could call his wife from there and let her know what had happened. He walked with Bob to the embankment. When Bishop reached for the rope to pull himself up, he slipped and fell on his ass.

5

Within a matter of minutes, all the fear, all the tension, all the raw-nerve energy of the crisis was contained within the fading siren of the ambulance. The people were all gone; the flashing lights were all gone. The twisted metal of the automobile beneath the bridge sat silently marking the spot for tomorrow's clean-up crew. Soon, even the sound of the siren was gone, and the darkness and silence ruled over the scene. Tiny snowflakes mingled with the icy rain, but they would be gone before morning. Nobody would ever know they were there because nobody was there to see them.

And nobody was there to hear the slight rustle in the bushes beside the car. Not a loud shaking of the limbs, but a stirring that might have been caused by the wind if the wind had not already stopped blowing. Gradually a mist emerged and swirled lightly around the wreckage.

Tonight's little episode under the bridge was only one link – one loose link. In California, a young woman was being raped at gunpoint. In Georgia, a teenager was fighting for his life in a hospital emergency room. In Kansas, a high-school junior was staring out across an open field of wheat, unaware of how he got there. Loose links that would eventually, inevitably, become a chain.

Now, the mist drifted upward and moved toward Crystal Springs. It was time to rest for a while; it had done its job. It had made its presence known to the newborn child.

6

Years later when he would think back on it (if a ten-year-old ever seriously thinks back about anything), Timmy would not remember the trauma that surrounded his birth. He wouldn't remember the crash and the screaming. He wouldn't remember the fact that he drew his first breath, or almost *didn't* draw his first breath, in the icy rain underneath a bridge. Of course, his parents would tell him the whole story time and time again, but he wouldn't really remember anything about it. Still, whenever he would hear the story, he would know, deep in his most secret thoughts, that his whole life went sour on that night. Something had wormed its way into his subconscious and had begun to slowly turn his world to shit. Something that he probably would never fully understand, even years later when he would think back on it. And even though he wouldn't understand or remember that first night, there were some things that he would never be able to forget.

Rule Number One: When the room is dark, keep your feet under the covers.

Chapter One

May, 1983

1

"Eight, one."

"What?"

"You heard me. Eight, one."

"Serve it."

The enclosed room echoed with the sound of the racquet smacking the ball. It bounced off two walls and the floor before a backhand swing sent the ball again into the wall. A sidearm smash into the corner, and the ball rolled lifelessly across the floor.

"Ten, one."

"Now wait a minute! It was eight, one after the last play!"

"Really?"

"If you weren't a priest, I might think you were trying to cheat me."

"What's being a priest got to do with anything?" With a laugh, Father Francis served the ball. His opponent was the Reverend James Milford, pastor of the local Baptist congregation. And this game was their weekly ritual. Every Saturday afternoon they played racquetball, every Saturday afternoon Reverend Milford accused Father Francis of trying to cheat him, and every Saturday afternoon the bond between the two religious leaders grew tighter despite their theological differences.

"Eleven, two."

"Ten, two."

"Whatever."

Milford watched the priest with fondness. Father Francis was one of the first people to welcome Milford to Crystal Springs. "Checking out the enemy camp," as Francis so delicately put it. During the last two years, the two men found that they had much in common. They were both about the same age, thirty-two or thereabouts. (They had joked several times about starting out at the same age Jesus did and hoping their careers lasted a little longer than his did.) They both remembered where they were when President John Kennedy was assassinated. They were weaned on Elvis and they were shocked when the Beatles broke up. They both turned down student deferments to serve non-combat duty in Vietnam. The similarities ended when the subjects turned to politics (Father Francis, pro-Reagan; Milford, pro-anybody else), football (Francis, the Dallas Cowboys; Milford, the L.A. Raiders), and alcohol (not whether to drink, but what to drink). Of course, the latter topic was strictly confidential. In the Bible Belt, tossing back a few brews was pretty common among the laymen and the deacons, but for Men of the Cloth it was taboo. After all, they were sent by God to be the example for the rest of the world. Milford and Francis had mutually decided that the responsibility of setting an example for some of these people was too much of a burden to put on anybody's shoulders. Sometimes a little drink was definitely in order.

All of these things combined to create a special relationship. Very seldom did the two men lack a topic for conversation.

"Fourteen, three."

"Wait a minute. Something's wrong."

"What is it?"

"That's the right score. You didn't try to add a point."

"Preacher, I'm shocked. It really hurts my feelings that you'd think I'd stoop that low. Don't you know by now that I don't need to cheat to beat you?"

"You're a real snot, you know that?"

"You bet. Fifteen, three. My serve."

Francis served the ball and backed into playing position. The current score was a good indication of how their games usually went. Francis played the game with ease while Milford had to work up quite a sweat. But he was improving. The volley was fast. Both men kept the ball low and close to the corners. Milford made four returns and was running to make the fifth when the pain struck. It stabbed into his left leg and surged like electricity through the rest of his body. His knees buckled and Milford collapsed face-first into the hardwood wall.

"Jesus Christ, Jimmy, are you okay?"

Milford managed to sit up and, with a drop of blood slowly rolling from the corner of his mouth, smile weakly. "You shouldn't swear like that, Francis. Somebody might hear you."

"I don't care who hears me. Are you okay?" Francis took hold of Milford's chin and turned his face up to look at the knot that was beginning to rise on the forehead. Milford softly rubbed the ugly scar on his left thigh. For years it had been just dead white tissue, but lately it showed signs of inflammation and there was an occasional twinge of pain.

"Yeah. I'm okay. Just my old war wound acting up."

"War wound, my butt. You didn't any more get shot in the war than I got laid in the cathedral. You better get somebody to look at that thing. Scars aren't supposed to do that, I tell you."

"Don't start that again. I just need to rest for a few minutes. That's all."

Francis retrieved the ball which had finished ricocheting off the walls and was bouncing in the center of the room. He sat beside Milford and shook his head. "That's a shame, too. You were doing exceptionally well today."

"It's a fluke. Must be my nerves."

Francis chuckled. "What have you got to be nervous about? Just because you're responsible for the spiritual well-being of every Baptist in the city..."

"The series starts tomorrow."

"The sermons you were working on?"

Milford nodded.

"Are you sure they're ready for this?"

"Probably not."

"Are you sure *you're* ready for this?"

"I hope so."

"That's not good enough."

"I know."

The two men sat in silence staring at the blank walls of the room. It wasn't the awkward silence that usually fills the voids in conversation. It was a comfortable silence. A contemplative, sinking-in type silence. After a moment, the men looked at each other and Francis put his arm around Milford's shoulders.

"Good luck tomorrow."

"Thanks."

"Hey, listen. It's almost five o'clock. Why don't we shower and take in an early movie."

"R-rated?"

"You're cruel, Jimmy. You know that?"

"I've been celibate just as long as you have."

"Yeah, but mine's by choice."

"Well, Father Francis, it's like my daddy used to say: It ain't a matter of how it happens, celibate is celibate."

"Your daddy was a truly wise man. Sure. R-rated. Let's treat ourselves. We deserve it."

Francis stood up and reached down to help Milford to his feet. When he rose, Milford noticed a very definite lack of pain in his leg. There was not a throb, not a sting. When he looked at his thigh, the redness had completely vanished. He shrugged, hoping the miraculous healing was normal. But deep in his gut he knew that it wasn't.

2

"Shhhh!"

Three figures dressed in black crept silently through the undergrowth. All black. Black shirt, black pants, black gloves, black knit hats. They had smeared their faces with coal. They were invisible in the darkness amid the towering pines. Each knew his job. Everything had been carefully planned in advance so that there was no need for talking. Silence was imperative.

After several long discussions during the afternoon, the trio had trimmed their list of necessary equipment down to the machetes strapped to their legs, the blowguns slung over their shoulders, and a small handsaw wrapped in canvas. Without heavy packs, they moved quickly; but without a light, even small tree roots became major obstacles. One of them stumbled.

"Shhhh!"

The leader lifted his right hand and the others stopped and squatted low in the honeysuckle vines around them. They listened for sounds, and there were sounds.

Not more than five yards away to their right was a car parked in a little gravel drive just off the road. That was not unusual. This whole area was a favorite place for teenagers to park after movies and carry on their private affairs. And this was Saturday night. Soon there would be more cars and more people. They had to work quickly... and quietly.

One at a time they made their way deeper into the woods away from the car. Straight ahead was the lake. Around the lake, the woods were less dense. A narrow gravel road followed the outline of the water and ran just seven or eight yards from the shore. That was the best place for parking. A nice romantic view of the lake with the moonlight reflecting on the ripples and the submarines speeding by. That was the rumor, anyway. Almost every young lady in Crystal Springs had been convinced by one young man or another that Lost Lake was the site of the weekly Athletic Cup Competition, the most prestigious of the submarine races, held only at night. Of course, the girls never caught so much as a glimpse of a submarine (it was too dark) but by the end of the night they usually didn't care.

The narrow road by the lake was the place. The Black Figures knew. They had watched before. Soon there would be many cars turning onto the gravel road. The shoreline would be crowded. The Black Figures had to be there first.

They moved cautiously. After a minute, the leader held up his hand and signaled the others to stop. He examined the pile of cut wood that lay at his feet. Obviously, someone had been here to chop firewood. There were short pieces of pine about a foot thick scattered on the ground. He pointed to them and nodded. "This'll save us a lot of work," he thought as the group moved again through the brush. They went only a few more feet and the leader sat on the ground. This was where they would wait. They were well hidden, and they could see the entrance. They all sat and waited.

About ten o'clock their waiting ended. They saw the car, an old '67 or '68 green Buick with the right front hubcap missing. It turned onto the road and stopped just before it reached the Black Figures.

"Piece o' cake," thought the leader, and they returned to the pile of cut wood.

Inside the car, Michael was making his move.

"I swear t'God, Sandra, it happened right over there."

"You're lyin. I know you are."

"No, honest. It was just a few years ago. This guy an' girl come out here parkin' in th' middle o'winter. Things musta been gettin purty hot 'cause they fogged up all th' windows in th' car. But anyway, after a few minutes they hear this knock on th' trunk o'th'car. Real slow, like this: Ka-thump... ka-thump... ka-thump..."

"Mike, stop it."

"No, listen. Th' guy was really wonderin' what th' hell was goin' on an' th' girl was about to wet 'er pants. Anyway, th' guy tells th' girl, 'Hey, I'm gonna find out what's goin' on, an' no matter whatcha hear, don't open th' door till ya see me at th' window.' So he gets out an th' girl locks all th' doors and scrunches down on th' floorboard. So she waits a long time an' after a while she hears these noises: Scraaatch, plop... scraaatch, plop... scraaatch, plop..."

"Mike, I don't want to hear any more! Stop it!"

"Well, if ya don't wanna hear th' rest of it... But I was just comin' to th' best part. Okay, if ya don't wanna know..."

There was a long silence. Michael propped his elbow on the car door and looked out the window.

"Okay. If you're gonna pout, go ahead and tell me what happened. But if it's scary, I swear..."

"Well, th' girl starts hearin' these noises, but she remembers what th' guy told 'er. So she stays down on th' floor an' waits an' waits. She musta waited for hours list'nin' to these noises. Then there was this light in 'er eyes an' a policeman was at th' window tellin 'er t'open th' door. When she opened it, he grabbed 'er arm an' told 'er t'go straight t'th' police car an' not t'look back. Well, 'bout half-way t'th' car, 'er cur'osity got th' best of 'er an' she turned around. There was 'er boyfriend, hangin' upside-down over th' car with his throat slashed. Th' noises were his blood drippin' out an' his fingernails scrapin' on th' top o'th' car."

Sandra clamped her hands over her ears and closed her eyes tightly. "Oh, gross!"

But Michael wasn't finished yet. "Th' girl flipped out an' they hadta put 'er away someplace. An' they say..." He leaned closer and whispered slowly. "They say th' killer wadn't ever caught."

Sandra felt the chill run down her spine. "That's sick, Mike. Do you know that? That's really sick."

There was a noise outside. Sandra screamed and flew into Michael's arms. He didn't know where the noise came from, but he was sure glad it came. Things were working out much better than he had expected.

One of the Black Figures had dropped the small log he was carrying. When the girl in the car screamed, he fell to his stomach and remained motionless, watching the car closely. When the two heads disappeared below the back of the car seat, he picked up his piece of wood and continued his job. He knew now that the windows of the car were open. It would be tricky, but not impossible. He was at the back of the car. He lay on his back and, dragging his log, inched his way under the back end of the car. Within seconds he had placed the log firmly behind the tire and wedged it into place. As soon as he crawled from under the car, another of the Black Figures proceeded, with another log, toward the car. And so it progressed, one Black

Figure after another, until all four tires were blocked front and back with small logs.

Back in the bushes, the leader signaled that it was time. The blowguns were distributed, and the Black Figures separated a little. Then, loading the blowguns with acorns, they proceeded to bombard the car. Almost immediately, the two heads were back above the seat and the ignition was turned on. There was a click as the car was put into gear and a whine as the accelerator was pressed. The car did not move. The Black Figures ran to the back of the car and pounded on the trunk. Then the motor was turned off, and they dived back into the bushes.

Michael was scared. That little story he had told Sandra was beginning to sound more and more real. After all, he didn't have any first-hand knowledge that it wasn't true. Just because he had heard it from somebody who had heard it from somebody else who had heard it somewhere didn't mean that there wasn't some grain of truth in the tale. He reached into the back seat and picked up his shotgun. Sandra was hanging all over him.

"Mike, let's get out of here!"

He snarled. "Th' damn car won't move! Git over! Gimme some room!"

He stuck the barrel of the shotgun out the window and pumped a shell into the chamber. He fired. Sandra held her ears and shouted a string of obscenities. Firing a shotgun inside a closed car wasn't one of Michael's smarter moves. With his ears still ringing, Michael opened his door and fired two more times into the woods.

"Jesus Christ! You stupid shit! You almost blew my head

off!" The leader of the Black Figures was on his feet shouting.

Michael's heart was pumping wildly. "Who's that?" His voice shook a little.

"It's me, stupid! Point that thing somewhere else!"

"Jim? 'S that you?"

"Yes, it's me." The leader was walking toward the car. The other Black Figures ran to catch up with him.

"You didn't tell us he had a shotgun!"

"Hell, if I'd aknown he had a shotgun, do you think I'd be out here beatin' on his car in the dark?"

Michael still held the shotgun, a fresh shell pumped into the chamber, pointed at Jim's chest. "Who's that with ya?"

"It's Charles and Timmy. Will you put that thing down before you kill somebody?" Jim had changed his tone. He was almost pleading. Michael had been known to do some stupid things and maybe, just maybe...

Michael pointed the shotgun toward the ground and eased the hammer to rest on the firing pin. Sandra's ears were still ringing so she hadn't heard most of the conversation. "Who is it, Michael?"

"It's my shit-ass little brother. What the hell're y'all doin out here? Momma'd skin your ass if she knew."

"You aren't gonna tell, are ya?"

"I oughtta. It'd serve ya right. And what's that shit all over your face?" Michael ran two fingers down the side of Jim's face leaving white streaks in the coal dust. "Goddamn, if that don't beat all I ever seen."

"We saw it in a war movie. They smeared stuff on their faces so they'd blend in with the shadows." Charles was shaking. He had just come within inches of having his insides scattered in the woods, so he was a bit nervous. When he grinned a trembling grin, his teeth shone white in the black face.

"Hell, I shoulda shot all o'y'all and claimed self-defense. But I got somethin' better in mind."

Timmy was almost crying. "Please don't tell your mother! She'd tell my mother and... and... and I don't know what she'd do to me!"

"I ain't tellin' nobody shit, but you'll wish you'd never heard o'this place before..." He was cut off by the sound of howling in the distance.

Jim's eyes widened and he fumbled at the chain around his neck which held a small silver crucifix. From the pocket of his pants, he brought a large caliber bullet shiny enough to reflect the moonlight. His silver bullet. He carried it with him wherever he went, and even though he didn't have a gun to shoot it from, he felt relatively safe as long as it was in his hand. He was firmly convinced that if he had to, he could *push* that damned bullet -- with his bare hands -- through any werewolf that tried to attack him.

Timmy was the only one in the group who noticed Jim's actions. Michael had turned towards the woods with the shotgun raised, Sandra was clutching his arm, and Charles was still trying desperately not to wet his pants. But Timmy saw Jim grab for the cross and the bullet, and he couldn't help but smile. It wasn't that he didn't believe. On the contrary, he had seen all the movies, read all the books. He believed in vampires, and werewolves, and monsters under the bed, and zombies. After all, he believed in God and some of the things he had been taught in Sunday School seemed much more farfetched than a man turning into a wolf. Oh, yes. He believed. But he had told Jim at least a million times that werewolves only come out at the full moon. Jim's reply was always, "You can't be too careful."

"Sounds like dogs over in th' gravel pits. Mangy things. Gives me th' shivers just thinkin' 'bout em." Michael lowered his shotgun and turned back to the others. "Now, I'm gonna fix y'all..." This time he was interrupted by Sandra who pulled him aside and whispered into his ear. When he turned back to the boys, he looked a little disappointed, but not much. "How'd y'all git down here?"

"We got our bicycles up in the woods."

"Okay then. As soon as y'all fix my car so's it'll move, git on them damn bicycles and fly your asses back to th' house."

It didn't take nearly as long for them to remove the logs as it had taken to put them in place. When they finished, they ran towards the woods with Michael shouting after them.

"I ain't forgettin' this, damnit!"

In the darkness of the woods, the three boys stopped running and watched as Michael and Sandra got back into the car, put their faces together, and sank slowly from view. With a burst of laughter, the Black Figures raced toward home.

3

To be afraid of the dark was childish. To sleep with the lights on was stupid. But to run from the monsters -- to actually move to another town because you were afraid of what lurked in the darkness of your house -- was a sure sign of insanity, yes?

Ma was tired of running. She had been running for damn near fifty of her seventy years and she was tired. On this late Saturday evening/early Sunday morning, she lay on her bed, her perpetual light shining on the nightstand, and stared out her window. The lateness of the hour was no stranger to her. Over the years she had faced many nights when the fear of sleeping overwhelmed the needs of a tired body.

As she watched the sky and listened to a distant howling, slowly -- ever so slowly -- her thoughts drifted to things she had tried so hard to forget.

She was born in the year 1913, somewhere in the bayous of Plaquemines Parish south of New Orleans. Voodoo was practiced in her family as it was in all the families she knew of. She was awed by the rituals and the chants, but she was frightened by the power she felt coursing through her during the ceremonies. She was consumed by the costumes and the makeup, but she was pursued in her dreams by the demons they conjured up. She learned the spells and incantations. She drew the magical signs and symbols. She watched the animal sacrifices.

Then one day, a little boy disappeared from one of the nearby towns. He was never found. It was as though he had vanished from the face of the earth. Nobody ever spoke of it, but Ma, even though she was only twelve years old then, knew deep in her heart what had happened to the little boy. The sacrifices weren't just animals anymore.

She got scared and never went to any more of the ceremonies. A year later, after two more small children had disappeared, she packed all her belongings in a pillowcase and sneaked out of the house while her folks were asleep.

She knew the dangers of the swamps. She had learned them as a baby. But when fear and loathing overcame her, all the rules of safety became nothing more than faraway words in her subconscious.

It wasn't until she lost sight of the house that she actually thought about what she was doing. The swamps stretched for miles in all directions, and they were full of all kinds of creatures. The tall trees were a favorite refuge of the water moccasins. The low-hanging branches made a nice perch from which the snakes could drop onto their unsuspecting prey. From not too far away, the low bellow of a bull alligator reached her ears. He was probably hungry. And she was out there. Mosquitoes buzzed around her and bit into the tender parts of her body. There were soft spots in the ground where a person could probably sink forever unless someone was there to pull them out. And, on top of all that, there was something peculiar about the night. Not just any night, but this one in particular. It wasn't right. It was... it was Evil. To her young mind, it felt as if this night had been infected by all the Evil of all the people who lived in the bayous.

She stopped at the edge of the deep woods and looked around her. It was time to make the decision. If she went back now, no one would ever know she had been gone. But the people were going crazy. They were out of control. How much longer would it be before they stopped going to neighboring towns and started to sacrifice their own children to their evil gods? How much longer until it was her turn? The Evil was winning. She could feel it. The skin on the back of her neck prickled and she rushed blindly into the maw of the deep woods.

For several minutes she ran through the thick undergrowth in a trance, her eyes fixed straight ahead. A million thoughts ran through her head, thoughts of home and her family and dolls with pins sticking in them. She pushed the thoughts out of her mind and ran faster. She could have run like that forever if she had not stepped in the hole.

Her ankle snapped and she was thrown headlong into the brambles. Her left arm was smashed into the trunk of an old tree and she felt the bones as they broke. The pain registered immediately. Reality slammed into her from all sides. The darkness closed around her. Her ankle swelled rapidly. Blood from her forehead dripped into her eyes. Pain, fear, Evil.

She couldn't stay here. There were bad things in the swamp. Things that wanted her.

She ran. Her broken ankle clicked loudly with every step, but she ran without limping. She ran like a person possessed, and she *was* possessed by the most powerful emotions of human existence. Pain, fear...

The moon blinked on and off behind the passing treetops. It offered no comfort.

(*Bad things pray to the moon.*)

Branches reached out for her. They tore at her dress and pulled her hair. Blood and tears filled her eyes. All around her were the noises of the swamp: The snakes slithering through the dead leaves, the gators splashing in the murky water, the sucking sound of the mud as it tried to hold her feet down. These sounds were amplified in her mind. She was scared and she ran.

Behind her, the footsteps started. Panic took over. Her little chest heaved, and pain shot through her body. But she couldn't stop running now. They were after her. She dared not look back for fear of what she might see. She had heard horrible stories about the things that could be conjured up, the creatures that could be summoned from some vast supernatural warehouse of creepy-crawlies. Or maybe they didn't have to be conjured up or summoned. Maybe they were free to wander in the swamp after dark. Maybe they were here every night, just waiting for someone to stumble in. Maybe all those other little children hadn't been sacrificed after all.

"Our Fodder, who are in Hebbin..." She screamed the words at the top of her voice. Maybe God would help. Maybe He would keep her running just a little bit longer.

"Our Fodder, who are in Hebbin..." She didn't remember the rest of the words. She knew them once, but somewhere along the line they got mixed up with all the magic voodoo words and now she couldn't remember them. Now, when she needed them most.

"Our Fodder, who are in Hebbin... Our Fodder, who are in Hebbin... *Help meeeee*!"

The woods disappeared. Whatever relief she might have felt was overshadowed by the fact that she was now in the open, vulnerable. There was no place to hide. And the footsteps were getting closer.

She didn't make it far into the clearing before her broken ankle gave out and she fell onto her shattered arm. Her heart sank and she screamed, knowing deep down inside that it would be her last act. But the scream, instead of dying out in the darkness, bounced back as if someone across the clearing was mimicking her. She covered her head with her right arm and cried, waiting for whatever her fate might be.

The footsteps stopped. There was no sound behind her. No heavy hand or evil claw clamped down on her throat. As far as she could tell, she was alone in the night with only the gentle breeze blowing through her hair.

Mustering up her courage, she looked up. She was confused. The landscape that met her eyes was not familiar at all. She was lying in coarse sand, not the tall grass of the marshy flatlands. Instead of a clearing bordered by tall trees, she was in a huge barren hole surrounded on all sides by sheer cliffs. Pulling her injured foot in front of her, she sat up and cradled her left arm. Her tears turned cold on her cheeks. She knew that it would only take a few minutes to adjust to her new surroundings. As soon as she did, the pain would go away.

She had been here many times before. Not to this particular place, but to others just as strange to her. She felt a little ashamed of having been frightened. She should have known what was happening. Every time the thoughts came, the events were pretty much the same but the places she ended up at were always different. She was manipulated like a marionette into becoming the unwilling audience for some bizarre theatrical ritual. Once, she had sat in the soft grass of a ranch and had watched a man being trampled by fire-breathing horses with razor sharp metal hooves and black-robed skeletons for riders. Another time, she had watched a little girl shoot flames from her eyes and burn her own mother alive, and then the little girl herself exploded into a ball of fire. Before that, she had ended up sitting on the carpet of some lady's fancy dining room and watching a séance where the medium's eyes turned bright green and the medium tortured the participants until some unseen force peeled her face away from her skull and nailed her to the ceiling where she screamed the most godawful screams until she finally died.

Each time she went on one of these little trips, she got scared. But every time, the pain stopped as soon as the "show" started and when it was over, there were no broken bones in her ankle and arm. Another show was about to begin. The pain was already going away. At least the sand beneath her was soft. She settled back and waited. It wouldn't be long now.

Around her, the wind blew harder and howled along the cliffs. Clouds raced across the sky, obliterating the moon. A bolt of lightning zipped through the darkness. Then another, and another. Soon the wind was tearing across the sand like a hurricane. Carried along in its wake was the baying of nearby dogs. Around the top of the cliffs, great trees stood like spectators at the arena.

On the sand to her right, a Man of God appeared. He shouted his religious incantations and they sounded very much like the chants of the high priestess at the voodoo ceremonies. The lightning's flash sent his shadow scurrying along the ground and the crash of thunder drowned out his words. Large drops of rain began to fall over him. He struggled to raise his voice above the noise of the elements, but it seemed to be a losing battle. The rain began to eat away pieces of his flesh until his skin hung in shreds over his skeleton. But he would not die. He could not die. The bony figure of a man sank to his knees and lifted his hands toward Heaven. Bolts of lightning streaked down to devour the man in flames, but they were deflected by the power of the hands and exploded into the cliffs.

From the dust of these explosions there sprang forth a man-child brandishing a sword of fire against unseen enemies. The sword hummed and crackled and vibrated with enormous energy. Flaming balls shot from the tip of the sword with each swing. The Warrior Child stood beside the Man of God and shouted defiance. His shouts echoed back like the voice of a great chorus.

"There is nothing that can stand against the sword!"

"Amen!"

And the battle raged. Lightning bolts were absorbed by the sword and spit back at the invisible foes. The Man of God shouted his incantations and the Blue Light of Destruction leaped from the bony fingers. Great boulders rose from the ground and flew across the arena only to be met by fireballs from the sword which exploded them into a million tiny sparkling suns.

"There is nothing that can stand against the sword!"

"Amen!"

But suddenly, the power of the sword began to fade, and the flames of the blade grew smaller and smaller until they died completely. The sword became an ash which crumbled and blew away in the wind. The young Warrior was reduced to a frightened child. The Man of God lost the Blue Light of Destruction and his incantations became nothing more than the rattling of skinless bones.

From above the arena, the arboreal spectators flung their fruit down at the frightened child and the skeletal man in protest of their dismal performance. The air was filled with the booming laughter of the vicious invisible foe, and the laughter echoed from wall to wall to wall...

Ma jerked upright in her bed and held her eyes tightly closed, covering them with her hands. As the laughter faded away, she heard Captain Jack squawking excitedly and flapping his great wings in his cage. When she opened her eyes, an involuntary cry escaped from her lips. The light beside her bed -- her perpetual light -- had gone out. Her hand trembled slightly as she reached in the darkness to find the switch. There was a *click*, and the light blinked on as if everything were in order. She shivered and hurried out of the room.

In the living room, Captain Jack was still squawking and biting at the bars of the cage. The cage door was closed and locked and Jack couldn't get out. But Ma always left that door open. When Ma entered, the huge macaw began to grow calm.

"It be awright, Jack-boy. Dey wuz here but now dey be gone."

Ma unlocked the cage door and swung it open. The old parrot climbed out and stood on the table while Ma rubbed his head.

"I t'ought fer shur we wuz shed ob dem, but dey be back stronger dan ebber. Yeah, Jack-boy, sumthin bad be goin' on here, an I t'ink we oughtta find out whut."

Ma went to the entry-way closet and shivered again, this time from the night wind that leaked through the cracks in the walls. From the shelf, she removed a battered old box and took it to the table.

When Jack saw the box, he bobbed his head like a cork in rippling water and let out a series of soft, high-pitched *meows* (something he learned from a neighborhood cat).

"You gonna hep me, Jack-boy?"

"Jack help, Jack help!"

The parrot shifted his weight rapidly back and forth, back and forth, from one foot to the other. He was getting excited.

"You be patient now. I be goin' fast as I can."

"Jack help, Jack help!"

From the dusty box, Ma removed a conjure board and placed it carefully in the center of the table. Jack turned his head sideways and with one eye stared at the board as if he expected it to do something interesting. When it didn't move, Jack lowered his head and picked at one battered edge of the board with his beak.

"Okay, Jack-boy, we be ready." Ma placed her fingertips lightly on the planchette which sat in the middle of the board. Jack moved closer and hooked one bony claw over her hands. For several minutes, they waited silently in that position. Ma thought about the dream that was still fresh in her mind. It meant something. They always did. And something always happened soon after. She whispered, "Dis be de question we need to know. Is dey somebody who be in danejur?" Again, they waited in silence.

Even though it was homemade, and she had had it for as long as she could remember, Ma never used the conjure board except in an emergency. Her philosophy, learned the hard way, was that you don't toy with things that you don't understand. So the conjure board stayed in the closet until it was needed. Of course, everyone who knew she had the board laughed at her and told her time and again that it wouldn't work with just one person. But Ma had never had any problems. Maybe Jack counted as another person. He had always helped her, and it had always worked before. And, regardless of what her friends said, the planchette was beginning to move. It moved slowly at first, jerking in short leaps across the board, but smoothed its flow gradually and was soon gliding as if on glass.

The planchette moved to "Yes" and stopped. Jack bobbed his head and meowed again.

"Is it fer us to hep dem?"

The planchette circled the board and again stopped at "Yes."

"Who?"

There was a full minute during which nothing happened. Ma and Jack sat silently. Then the planchette began to shake. Ma wasn't sure, but it might have been her own hands shaking. Before she had time to worry too much about it, it was moving again.

T... I...

4

In Mississippi, summer doesn't wait for the calendar; it comes when it pleases. Its arrival is usually heralded by the tropical wind that swings up from the Gulf of Mexico. Outsiders call this warm wind the "first breath of spring," and the natives just smile. In the Deep South, the ignorance of the tourists is more an amusement than an annoyance.

Take, for example, the man from Wisconsin who, with his

wife, visited a small Southern town for a "relaxing, fun-filled vacation in the sun and surf of the Mississippi Gulf Coast." One morning, in the local restaurant, the man and his wife ordered breakfast and when the wife commented, "I've never eaten grits before," the husband rather loudly and proudly replied, "You put lots of catsup and honey on them." The waitress almost threw up all over him, but the other diners got a good laugh out of it.

Or the Illinois salesman on his first trip through the South. He had gone through South Carolina, Georgia, Alabama, and halfway through Mississippi before he concluded, to his great relief, that the people there (or at least *most* of them) weren't still pissed about losing the Civil War, even if the Yankees did cheat.

Or the couple from New York who visited one of the fine plantations in Natchez and were disappointed at not finding all the women in hoop skirts sipping mint juleps and all the Negroes toiling away in the cotton fields.

Dealing with the misconceptions of outsiders has become an enjoyable pastime, and when mention is made of the "first breath of spring," the natives just consider the source. They know that spring is that time in late February or early March when the North Wind ceases and the ground thaws out, the grass grows almost overnight, and the trees sprout their different shades of green. When the wind starts to blow from the Gulf, summer has begun.

This year, summer was already in full swing before May rolled around. And on this particular Sunday morning, the temperature was almost eighty degrees at five-thirty in the morning.

Toby Lee owned a farm just south of Crystal Springs. Before

he could get dressed for church, there were chores to be done; chickens to be fed, hogs to be slopped, cows to be milked, and an inspection of the fields to be made. What he didn't know, as he leisurely ate his breakfast, was that before he could milk the cows, he had to chase them down. They broke through one of the fences during the night.

At Carter's Egg Farm, there were probably twenty thousand eggs to be gathered and sorted before eight o'clock. The inspectors showed up at six, looking a little worn from their Saturday night pleasures, and took their places at the conveyors. Hunk Carter shook his head. "It's gonna be a long morning."

At the Baptist Church parsonage, Reverend James Milford climbed wearily out of bed a full thirty minutes before his alarm clock, set for seven, went off. Several times during the night he had awoken, the victim of unpleasant dreams. No, not dreams. Nightmares was a more fitting description. He had read somewhere that such dreams were caused by anxiety, and that made sense. The dreams had started soon after he had begun the research for his new series of sermons. And this morning's sermon, being the first of the series, was definitely the cause of some anxiety. He had told Father Francis yesterday that he hoped he was ready for it. And that hope was all he had because he wasn't at all sure how the congregation would react. As he sat on the edge of the bed, he felt a twinge in his chest. There was a faint red ring around the scar there, a scar that matched the one on his leg. He rubbed it lightly and went into the bathroom to splash water on his face. As he poured milk over his bowl of corn flakes, Milford thought briefly about how nice it might be to look up and see a wife sitting across the table.

By six forty-five, old man Hill had nearly completed his morning tour through the orchard. The peaches were just beginning to ripen and since his orchard bordered the gravel pit, a popular teen-age lover's lane, a survey of the damage became a morning routine. And he found the half-eaten peaches that he knew would be there. "I'll get those fuckers," he fumed, and his knuckles turned white on the shotgun stock.

At seven o'clock, Toby Lee screamed "Shit!" and his wife looked out the kitchen window in time to see him race through the gaping hole in the fence, his beer belly bouncing in front of him.

Timmy White ate his breakfast in silence. He was still half asleep, but he did catch the wink from his father and the frown from his mother. There had been another fight last night. When Timmy returned from his escapade, well after eleven o'clock, Mother was waiting up for him. She woke Father and said, "A ten-year-old has no business being out that late," and Father said, "Hell, when I was ten, I was driving a tractor," and Timmy was sent to bed before the real shouting started. Evidently, Father had won, but at what cost? Mothers have a strange way of always evening the score.

By nine-thirty, the parking lot at the church was nearly full. There were small groups of people talking and laughing. There were men, with rivulets of sweat running down their faces, who refused to remove their coats. This was the only time they had to display their Sunday finest and they weren't about to destroy the illusion of affluence because of some heat. Little girls with short, puffy dresses skipped down the sidewalk or ran from mischievous little boys.

Ladies "ooh"-ed and "aah"-ed at the display of fashion they presented. A typical Sunday morning.

As cigarettes were crushed out and the groups began to migrate toward their respective Sunday School rooms, someone yelled out, "Hey, Michael! Hear you had a little problem out at the lake last night!" to which Michael responded, "Yeah? Well, at least my little problem ain't as little as your little problem, if ya catch my drift." A chorus of teen-age boys said, "Ooooo, gotcha!" and Jim was at Michael's side in a second saying, "I didn't tell anybody! I swear t'God I didn't!" Then the bell rang, and Sunday School began.

At ten-forty-five, all those people who stayed for the sermon (and they were considerably fewer than the ones who came to Sunday School) took their seats in the sanctuary. The organist played a variation of a familiar hymn as background music to whispered conversation. At ten fifty-five, the choir entered in their burgundy robes and long white collars. Reverend Milford, his stomach in knots, took his place on the platform at eleven o'clock.

There was no turning back now.

5

Excerpts from the Sermon of

Reverend James Milford

(Audio recording)

Sunday, May 8, 1983

Would you turn in your Bibles now to two passages: The first is in the book of Galations, chapter five; the second is the book of Deuteronomy, chapter eighteen. While you are finding those scriptures let me say that this is the first in a series of sermons I will be delivering on the subject of Satan, his powers and his followers. I began the research on this series over a year ago hoping to present the sermons only a few weeks later. However, the more deeply I probed, the more startling and disturbing were the conclusions I reached. I waited because I was afraid of the reactions that the series would draw. But now, regardless of the consequences, it must be done. I can wait no longer...

We have just bowed our heads and, in an attitude of great reverence, uttered a prayer to "Our Most Gracious Heavenly Father." But is there really a God to hear our prayer, or are we just vainly babbling into open space? And if, indeed, there is a God, can we be sure that the book we call the Holy Bible is really His word or, for that matter, that He had anything at all to do with the Book? What, in fact, can we actually prove about this entity which we insist upon calling God?

(A rumble of murmurs from the congregation)

These questions must be dealt with from the very beginning before we go any further. Either you believe, or you do not. There is no in-between. I cannot stand here today and prove to you that there is a God. And I cannot prove to you that this Book is not the product of some early science fiction writer's vivid imagination. These are things that only you can decide for yourself...

The two scriptures we read just a few moments ago have one thing in common: They both make reference to witches and witchcraft...

The earliest reference to witches that I found in my research was in the Bible, in the book of Exodus, written by Moses sometime around 1400 B.C., chapter twenty-two, verse eighteen. The children of Israel were in the wilderness after leaving their captivity in Egypt. At that time, the Lord had only one thing to say about witches: Thou shalt not suffer a witch to live.

Why?...

It is my opinion, and the opinion of many people who are much more learned than I am, that every belief, whether superstition or religion, is based on some amount of fact. And the more I learn of the myths and legends of witches, the more I am convinced that our ancestors knew something that we don't know or, worse, that we refuse to recognize: Perhaps there is another source of power that may be tapped for use besides the power of God.

Legends make a lot of claims about the power of witches, none of which I can prove or disprove. However, I would like to call you attention to another passage in the Bible. It's in the book of I Samuel, written sometime around 1100 B.C., in chapter twenty-eight. Samuel has died, David has fled the country, and Saul, the king, has been abandoned by God. If we begin with verse fifteen, *where most sermons dealing with this passage begin*, we find that Saul has a conversation with the deceased Samuel. Not really unusual for the

Bible. It contains numerous accounts of visitations by the dead through the power of God. However, if we begin with verse seven instead of verse fifteen, we find that this visitation was not through the power of God. It was through the power of "a woman that hath a familiar spirit." A witch. Samuel was summoned from the dead by a witch. Some of my distinguished colleagues still argue that it was God's message that Samuel carried to Saul. But think back to Exodus: Thou shalt not suffer a witch to live. Why would God use as His instrument a woman whom He had condemned to death three hundred years earlier? No. In His own Word, God has given us a glimpse of the power of witchcraft...

In our great wisdom and our deep concern for our fellowman, we made "improvements" on God's law. That is why today, in the gravel pits outside of our town, there is a group of young people practicing the ancient rites of witchcraft.

(A murmur rushes through the congregation)

I have it on very reliable authority that there are thirteen of them. A full coven. I have a partial list of names, some of which are familiar to me. That hurts me deeply. But what hurts even more is that with all our "improvements" to the law, they cannot be stopped. They can only be fined for trespassing... and that only if the owner of the land ever decides to press charges.

Think about these things. Think about what we have done. In our up-to-date, enlightened society we have led ourselves to believe that evil only exists in the form of bank robbers, terrorists, and assassins and we have thereby made ourselves powerless to act against the very roots of evil. But in the end... In the end, there will be no more Equal Rights. There will be no more Civil Rights. There will be no more Human Rights. There will be no more Freedom of Religion. There will be only God's Law. Just like in the beginning.

6

Reverend Milford closed the door to his office/study with a solid slam and stood very still, his eyes closed and his heart pumping rapidly. Something had happened out there today. It was the first time in the pulpit that he had been really scared.

About half-way through the sermon, his left leg started to hurt right around the area where the bullet had gone in years before. Then his chest. They were small pains at first, but as he continued with the sermon the pains became unbearable. At one point, he almost passed out. Then, as if he weren't having enough trouble concentrating on his sermon, he began to hallucinate. In the back of the auditorium, hovering over the congregation, were several small clouds, almost like a mist hanging in the air. They would come toward him and then back away. He tried to hide his concern, but he must not have done too good a job. Right at the end of the sermon he heard several small children giggling. Probably the kids sitting on the back pew. And if they could see it all the way in the back, what did it look like to the deacons? They sat on the front row.

"Any minute now," he thought, and he waited for the knock on the door that he knew would come.

Standard Church Procedure had been greatly violated today.

And he had to be very careful about that. Even though he had been here for two years, he was still the "new preacher" and he had to watch his step. The people here were leery of young men just out of the seminary.

Church Procedure.

Twenty-five years was a long time, but that's how long the old preacher, Brother Mason, had stayed. Perhaps the Church Procedure had been established even before Brother Mason arrived, but at any rate, it was still going full force when Milford was selected as the replacement. And the Board of Deacons made very sure that he understood and followed, to the letter, the Standard Church Procedure:

After a sizzling hellfire and brimstone sermon, the preacher would introduce the Invitational Hymn and step down to the floor in front of the pulpit. Then, while the choir and congregation sang eleven verses of "*Just As I Am*," the preacher would stand with his arms raised toward Heaven and wait for the sinners to walk down the aisles, repent of their sins, and accept Jesus Christ into their lives. After this emotional ten minutes, he would feel the "moving of the Holy Spirit" and ask that the choir sing "one more verse." While the choir sang (very softly) eleven more verses, he would wipe his brow and beg for sinners to repent and for back-sliding Christians to rededicate their lives. Finally, when it was obvious that no one was going to make the long walk, he would call on someone to offer a closing prayer (preferable someone long-winded to give the preacher time to go to the back of the auditorium and open the doors). He would then stand at the open doors shaking hands with his congregation and listening to three hundred or more of them telling him what a great sermon he had preached.

Church Procedure.

It had been *violated* today. At the end of what could have been an inspired sermon, during which he had acted like a possessed madman and had all but advocated the vigilante lynching of a group of young people in the town's gravel pits, he had simply said, "You may go," and had walked straight back to his study.

He stood there now, his hands trembling, his eyes closed.

There was a light tapping at the door. He jumped a little and hurried to the chair behind his desk.

"Come in." His throat was dry, and his voice cracked, sounding very similar to a mouse with its tail caught in a trap.

The door opened... just a bit.

In that split second, before anyone was visible in the doorway, he wanted to rush across the room and fall on his knees and beg the forgiveness of the Deacons and plead to keep his job and promise faithfully to never break the rules again, and at the same time he wanted to ask God to overlook his inability to stand his ground against this handful of pious, self-righteous bastards (was that the word he used?).

That's what he wanted to do in that eternal split second. But he didn't. Instead, he waited for the door to open.

"Brother Milford?"

The head that peeked through the crack was not the head of Roy Wilson, the Chairman of the Deacons. In fact, it wasn't the head of *any* of the deacons. It was the head of a young lady.

"Melanie..." There was an obvious tone of great relief. "Please come in."

"Golly, Brother Milford, I've never seen your office before."

Melanie Davis was a senior in high school. Cheerleader type. She was beautiful and she knew it. She was smart enough to be dumb if it would be to her advantage. Also, rumor had it that she was a great manipulator of persons. Melanie Davis was seventeen going on twenty-five.

She looked at the room carefully as if she were memorizing every detail.

"Have you really read all those books?" She pointed toward the west wall which Milford so fondly referred to as the "library." The whole wall was built-in bookshelves, but only about half of them held books.

He smiled, a little embarrassed. "I've tried. And on some of them I'm still trying." He laughed, and she giggled convincingly at his stupid reply. Great exercise in the finer (and more useless) points of common courtesy.

Then, quite suddenly, there were no more unnecessary questions and no more cute comments. They smiled dumbly at each other while an awkward silence filled the room.

"Well... what can I do for you, Melanie?"

"Oh! Jesus Christ... Oops! I mean, I'm sorry... I mean... I just wanted to tell you that I really liked the sermon today. I mean, I didn't daydream or fall asleep or anything. And it was so short! I mean... well, you know. I really don't like those long endings. They get really boring. No, wait. I don't mean *you're* boring. I mean... Oh, jeez. Do you know what I mean?"

"Yes, Melanie, I think I know exactly what you mean, and I'll accept it as a compliment."

"Oh, good. That's what I meant it to be. It's just that..."

"I understand, and I appreciate it."

"Oh."

Again, the awkward silence. Milford did not give it a chance to set in.

"Is there anything else?"

"No. No, that's all. I guess I'd better get home for dinner." She hurried to the door and then looked around the room once more. "You sure have a nice office." She closed the door behind her as she left.

That was not exactly the conversation he had been expecting, and he was glad. The exchange with Melanie had definitely settled his nerves some. Now he could wait more easily for the attack of the deacons. (A great name for a horror movie.)

The sermon had been over for almost ten minutes and there was not a sound from the deacons. Maybe he would give them just five more minutes, and then he too would "get home for dinner."

Nervous energy kept his hands busy. He rearranged a few papers on his desk. He bent paper clips into different shapes. He scribbled with the pens from his desk set to see if they still worked (of course, they didn't -- those things never do). He fiddled with his letter opener, balancing and twirling it.

When the phone rang, he jumped and somehow managed to sink the point of the letter opener deep into his left palm. He snatched a Kleenex from the box, placed it over the wound, and answered the phone. The caller was Mrs. Simms, who loved to talk, and during the course of her chatter he replaced the bloody Kleenex with a new one several times. After a couple of minutes, he finally realized that she was trying to ask him, "Would you be free to have Sunday dinner with my family today?" Dinner, of course, being the noon meal; the evening meal was supper.

"Mrs. Simms, I would love to, and I don't want to be rude, but I've just had an accident... No, no. Nothing critical, but I do want to put something on it... Yes, I have some. Just let me get it taken care of and I'll be there in just a few minutes. Okay? Great. See you then."

He kept his first-aid kit on one of the library bookshelves. He fished around in the cigar box until he found the bottle labeled Merthiolate. On an open cut, that stuff would burn like fire, but it would also kill anything that was crawling around in there. Clenching his teeth, he touched the glass rod applicator to the hole in his hand. After he screamed, blew on the cut, waved his hand wildly, and finally cut off the circulation at the wrist, the burning gradually subsided.

While he was wrapping a clean bandage around his hand, Milford thought back over the sermon and his paranoia. Maybe it was uncalled for. The pain and hallucinations were probably from his anxiety. Besides that, the deacons five minutes were up. Maybe he had actually gotten away with it. Maybe he could do it again.

Maybe you shouldn't push your luck.

"Right."

He walked out of his office and closed the door, but he didn't lock it. He never locked his door. He knew it was a bad habit and he would probably have to start locking up some day.

Maybe he should have started today.

7

At the corner, Timmy sat on his bicycle under the huge oak tree. Lunch had been the same as breakfast. The silent treatment from Mother. He knew he would have to be more careful from now on. Next time, Father might not win.

Timmy leaned over and scratched Doobie between the ears. Doobie was the strangest dog that anyone in town had ever seen. He looked very much like a Labrador Retriever that got cut off at the knees. His fur was deep auburn, and his nose was pink. In the summer he loved to nap on the front porch, but at night or at the first sign of rain or a cold front, he would be inside, usually under the covers of Timmy's bed. He went with Timmy everywhere, or at least everywhere he could.

When Doobie barked and started to wag his tail, Timmy knew that Charles was riding up the street. They met at this corner every Sunday after church, every weekday after school, and every Saturday after the morning cartoons. Timmy flipped up the kickstand on his bike and rode to meet Charles. "How did it go?" he called out.

"Not good. I have to be home every night at five o'clock for a whole week. How about you?"

"Mom's not talking to me, so I guess I'd better take it easy for a few days."

They rode together down the narrow streets with Doobie

running along behind them. Houston and Dallas streets were rough and littered with loose gravel from many patch jobs done by the city and, best of all, they didn't carry much traffic. These streets were a proving ground for bicycle and rider. A two-wheel, pedal-power Grand Prix. A place to laugh in the face of disaster.

Charles and Timmy had practiced the maneuvers for weeks, even months. They started by racing, full speed, into the grassy ditch alongside the road and tumbling onto the yard beyond. The trick was to leap from the bicycle at the precise moment that it went into the ditch. If you didn't, the bike flipped over, and you got a handlebar up your butt. Next came the Surfer's Ride. Going as fast as they could, they stood on the seats and let go of the handlebars. Naturally, the first one to fall was the loser, in more ways than one. Today it was Timmy. As the bicycle slipped out from under his feet, Timmy let out a war whoop that Geronimo would have been proud of and then did about four somersaults down the street before he slid to a stop on his stomach. The damage was surprisingly minor. His elbows and knees were bleeding, but what the hell. Nothing was broken. That, in itself, was quite an accomplishment. After assuring Charles that he was okay, all things considered, it was time for the Figure Eight. They learned this one by watching the demolition derby in Jackson. If they traveled in the same direction and kept a somewhat equal speed, they should pass within a hair of each other at the center of the pattern. They made four perfect passes before Charles' bare foot slipped off the pedal and smashed into the rough asphalt. He crashed into Timmy who plunged to the pavement a second time. By mutual consent, it was time to stop. Timmy was bleeding from at least one spot on every limb of his body, and Charles was in "*mucho paino*." When his foot slipped off the pedal, his balls stopped at the support bar.

Together, and in varying degrees of pain and suffering, they walked their bicycles back to the old oak tree at their favorite corner. They sat in the shade, Doobie on the grass between them, and waved at the people in the passing cars. After a few minutes, they began to talk. They speculated about what kind of person would design a boy's bike with a support bar down the middle. It had to be either a woman, a sadist, a woman sadist, or someone who had never had the inimitable experience of being kicked in the balls.

After a few more minutes, they talked about how strange the church service had been. It was short, no complaints there. There weren't a lot of big words. That was good, too. But they both noticed that Brother Milford looked... weird. He was constantly wiping his forehead with his handkerchief. Every time he pointed, his hand shook. And every once in a while, his voice sounded a little tense. They had never seen him like that.

After a while, there was nothing else to say. Charles threw small stones across the street slowly and carefully, aiming for the open trash can on the other side. Timmy doodled in the dirt with a short stick. Doobie flicked his tongue up and across his nose and then lay his head on a tree root. All was quiet.

"Do you think it's true?"

"What?" Charles aimed and tossed. Off to the right.

"Do you think there really are witches out there?"

Charles looked at Timmy and Timmy looked up from his drawing. There was a moment of silence as they stared into each other's eyes. Then they both looked eastward along the street in front of them.

It led to the gravel pit.

8

After lunch, Rev. Milford sat in the Simms' living room drinking coffee and having an engaging conversation about the pros and cons of the current administration under President Reagan. They decided that there were more cons than pros, probably due to the fact that everyone in the house was as adamant about the Democratic Party as they were about the Baptist Doctrine. Very little had been said about the sermon, which probably meant that Mr. Simms had fallen asleep while Mrs. Simms decided what would go good with her pot roast, so Milford did not feel an urgent need to rush away.

That was too bad.

Across town, the door to Milford's study was being cautiously pushed open. Melanie Davis was back, but this time she wasn't looking for the preacher. She was looking for something he had mentioned in his sermon. A list. Being the type of person that he was, Milford had probably felt no need to hide the list so it should be with the notes for the sermon. She found the notes, complete with list, in a folder on top of his filing cabinet. He was so damned predictable.

With the list tucked safely in the pocket of her jeans, Melanie was about to leave the study when she saw the tissues on the desk. Tissues covered with blood. Her eyes widened and her tongue ran quickly across her lips. She snatched the tissues off the desk, hurried to the bookshelf and picked out the photo album she had seen there earlier. Thumbing through it, she found a photograph of the preacher (college graduation picture) which she removed from its corner holders and then stuck the tissues and the photo into her pocket with the list.

When she left the study, she was quite pleased with her success. She was sure the others would be also.

9

"Timmy White..."

No answer.

"Timmy White..." Leapin' Lena moved silently down the aisle between the rows of giggling youngsters. With a quick snap of her wrist, she slammed her report book on Timmy's desk. His eyes shot open, and his feet hit the desk of the girl in front of him.

"Since you don't answer the roll call, then I can only assume that you are not in class. Would you like to tell us where you are?"

Leapin' Lena Green was the old maid of the grammar school faculty. This year the kids held a contest to guess her age, and they narrowed it down to somewhere between sixty and five hundred. She was born with one leg shorter than the other and her parents, being staunch fundamental religionists, refused to let anything like corrective shoes or braces interfere with the healing power of God. When she taught her first class (in whatever century that was), one of her more observant pupils commented to his pals that when she walked, she looked like a crippled rabbit leaping sideways. The nickname stuck. It was preserved and handed down from generation to generation, behind her back, of course. The years had turned her into a gnarly old bitch. She yelled a lot, swung a mean paddle, and called the roll five times a day.

Timmy looked up into her ugly-as-a-mud-fence face and cringed. He had just come inside from recess and Lena was doing her fourth roll call of the day.

"Well?"

"Yes, Ma'am." His brain kicked into high gear. "I was just thinking about the math homework."

"Is that so?" Timmy nodded and Lena peered at him over the top of her cat's-eye spectacles. "Very commendable. Now, Master White, I would suggest that you glance -- very quickly, mind you -- at the clock behind my desk. Math was before lunch. It is now 2:05 and time for the English lesson. You can see the clock?"

"Yes, Ma'am."

"Good. Now, are you answering the roll or am I marking you absent for the rest of the day?"

"Yes, Ma'am. I'm here."

"That's very good of you. See that you don't drift away again."

"Yes, Ma'am."

She bounced back to the front of the class, beginning her lesson along the way. "English is probably the most difficult language to learn if it is not your native language. Even so, I have met very few natives who speak it properly. Our best examples of proper English usage are preserved in volumes of literature which have earned the distinction of being called classics. These books are more than just good stories. They are, and will remain, the standard by which the English language is measured. The classics represent..."

Timmy felt his mind drifting again. He didn't care about the classics. After all, this was only the fifth grade. What ever happened to Dick and Jane and Spot? They disappeared overnight! Anyway, after recess was a hell of a time to have a lesson, and it had been like that the whole school year. A hot meal, the hot sun, and Lena's monotonous voice spouting long meaningless words (Timmy swore that she invented most of them herself) could play hell on a kid's nerves. Timmy had to be very careful not to let his eyelids slide shut.

"... Even with the introduction of his protagonist, Stevenson establishes..."

Lena didn't cut anybody any slack. To her, recess was an occupational hazard. She could care less that her students were all hot and tired and sweaty. They were in school "to be educated, not entertained." And she had told them repeatedly how lucky they were to be in her class instead of one of the others where the teachers were so lax that the students were as stupid when they left the class as they were when they went in. She knew they didn't appreciate her, but they would. When (if) they made it into high school, they would be glad she had them read "*Macbeth.*" They would thank her for teaching them how to do book reports.

"... That is the reason you will be reading one of the classics for your final book report..."

Timmy's head nodded and he made an extra-special effort to sit upright. Springtime was the worst. As soon as the air started warming, the recess games became more hectic. Football, baseball, and dodgeball were the standards with a spattering of Frisbee, tag, and squirrel (a charming little game of grabbing a handful of somebody else's nuts).

"... In reviewing your book report choices, I have found some duplications..."

And naturally, Rev. Milford's sermon inspired the creation of new games like Torture the Witch. Several of the boys abducted one of the girls, tied her to the Jungle Gym, and tortured her by taking turns kissing her. It was all very exhausting. Timmy found himself longing for the good old days of Dick and Jane and nap time after recess.

"... Linda, Jeff, and Todd, you have all chosen *The Count of Monte Cristo*. Linda will keep that one. Jeff will take *The Three Musketeers* and Todd, *The Man in the Iron Mask*. Alexandre Dumas wrote all three, they are all classics, and they have equal levels of excitement.

"Timmy, I see that you have chosen a book entitled *'Salem's Lot*. I'm not familiar with that one. Do you have it with you?"

"Yes, Ma'am." Timmy reached into his desk and pulled out the dog-eared paperback that lay on top of his other books. He had found the book on his father's bookshelf about three weeks earlier and the cover immediately caught his attention. It was black with highlights that formed the face of a little girl who had a bright red drop of blood coming out the corner of her mouth. As soon as he had looked at that ominously depressing cover, he had felt the faintest trace of a chill at the nape of his neck, and he had been reading about twenty pages a night since then.

Now Lena looked at the same black cover and her forehead creased drawing her eyebrows very close together. She turned the book over and read the publisher's blurb with a deep I-must-be-patient type sigh. After checking the title page for the copyright date (1975), she dropped the book onto Timmy's desk and looked over her book report list before speaking.

"I'm sure that Mr. King would be flattered, but an eight-year-old book cannot be considered a classic in the strictest sense of the word. You will report on *The Scarlet Pimpernel* by Baroness Orczy. Class, for the next few minutes, you may work on your homework assignments or you may begin reading for your book reports. Timmy, come with me." Lena picked up the heavy wooden meter stick that she kept on the chalkboard tray. She stood at the door holding it open for Timmy to go out.

In the brief time it took to go from his desk to the door, a flood of feelings, thoughts, and emotions swept over Timmy. He was really disappointed; he wanted to report on *'Salem's Lot*. It was a damned good book, and it made him mad that old Lena Lardbutt would dismiss it without even knowing what the book was about. Besides that, he was almost finished with it. But then, maybe *The Scarlet Pimpernel* wouldn't be too bad. He remembered Daffy Duck playing The Scarlet something-or-other on the Saturday morning cartoons, and it was pretty funny. More than anything else, though, Timmy was confused. As far as he knew he hadn't done anything wrong. Yet here he was, being dragged out of the room to be sent to the principal's office or, worse, to have his butt mangled by Lena's meter stick. He felt his stomach tightening. This was really embarrassing.

When they went into the hallway and Lena did not walk towards the office, Timmy naturally assumed the worse and bent over until he could grasp his ankles. Lena just stood there tapping the palm of her hand with the stick.

"Stand up."

Timmy breathed a silent sigh of relief, but his stomach was still in knots.

"Now, I don't know what your problem is, boy, but you'd better straighten it out. And I mean right now. Do you understand me?"

"Ma'am?"

"Don't play the fool with me, young man. Do you think I can't see what you've been doing? Do you think I'm blind?" She was shouting now. "Do you think I'm getting senile? Is that it?"

"No, Ma'am..."

"Shut up! I know very well what's been going on! I've heard the giggles and the whispers behind my back! And you're the ringleader!"

"What have I done?"

"You're trying to turn my class into the laughingstock of the whole school, and don't try to deny it!"

"Me? I don't know what you're talking about."

"Don't lie to me, boy! I can tolerate a lot of things but lying is not one of them! You may have your parents convinced that you're a perfect little angel, but I want you to know that you're not fooling me in the least. I've watched it from the day the class had the poetry writing assignment. I thought there wouldn't be any harm in having the students read their poems to the class. I could grade them then and it would be done. We had some very good poems. We had poems about pirates, we had poems about flowers, we had poems about dogs and cats. Do you remember?"

Timmy nodded.

"Then you stand up and read us your poem about an eight-year-old girl who is forced to drink the blood of her murdered mother while a group of naked half-human, half-animal spectators cheer her on. What did you call it? Ah, yes. I believe it was 'Fear the Dark.' Is that right? I know your little classmates thought it was amusing, but it was not. It was sick and disgusting. And do you remember what I told you that day while you stood at the front of the class with that trash in your hands?"

"Yes, Ma'am. You told me I should set my sights higher." Whatever that meant.

"Exactly. And not a month later you bring me a short story, another class assignment, about a four-year-old boy who is devoured in his bed by a stuffed teddy bear which is under the control of the boogeyman who resides in his closet. Can you see any change between the poem and the short story?"

Timmy looked at the floor. If she weren't so mad, it might have been funny. "No, Ma'am."

"Of course you don't, because there was no change. And now this whole episode with the book report... This time you've gone too far. I know what's going on, and I will stop it one way or another."

From the minute Timmy opened his mouth to speak, he knew

he was headed for big trouble. But he didn't care. "I don't know what you think is going on, but I picked *'Salem's Lot* because it's a good book."

"It's not a classic."

"Is *Dracula* a classic?"

"*Dracula* has nothing to do with this."

"But it does. They're almost exactly alike."

"So you've read *Dracula*?"

"Yes, Ma'am."

"Then why didn't you report on that?"

"Because *'Salem's Lot* is better."

"So now you fancy yourself to be a literary critic."

"No, Ma'am, but I know what I like."

Lena glared at him, and for several long seconds neither of them spoke. Timmy stared into her eyes trying hard not to blink. Eye contact made him very uncomfortable, but he was determined that she would not stare him down.

"You're just like your father was at this age, but I straightened him out and, by God, I can straighten you out. Bend over and hold your ankles."

10

The mass exodus which occurred at the end of every school day was quite an interesting phenomenon. first, there was the hordes of grammar schoolers, running and screaming from the building. They were followed a few moments later by the junior high and younger high schoolers who walked briskly away from the building. They were followed closely by the royalty of the school, the UPPERCLASSMEN, who strolled casually, nonchalantly toward *their* AUTOMOBILES. Not that the UPPERCLASSMEN weren't just as excited about leaving as even the youngest of the students, but there was, after all, an attitude of cool to be maintained. And so, they left the hallowed halls of learning, each in his own way and in the established order.

Timmy and Charles were among the first group to come bursting through the school building doors. They almost flattened old Ned, the school janitor, but he just smiled and shook his head when they shouted, "Sorry," and kept running. Near the end of the sidewalk, their bicycles were lined up in the parking rack and waiting for them like horses tethered to a hitching post. Theirs were not locked to the rack; in fact, there were no locks on any of the bikes. There were two reasons for this: First, a lock severely hindered a quick getaway; second, a lock wasn't necessary. Crystal Springs was still a very small, safe town.

"Do you have much homework?" The standard first question on the way off the school grounds. Today Timmy asked it.

"No. Do you?"

"Yeah. Lena didn't like the book I picked for my report, so I gotta start reading another one."

"Bummer."

"Yeah."

"Who was Lena pounding on after recess?"

"How did you know she pounded somebody?"

"Shit, you could hear it all the way down the hall."

"Guess."

Charles looked at him suspiciously. "You?"

Timmy nodded and then flipped the bird back toward the school building.

"What'd you do this time?"

"Hell, I don't know."

The boys looked quickly at the intersection and then turned their bikes onto Georgetown street.

"Come on, Timmy. Why'd she beatcha?"

Timmy thought about what Lena had said to him in the hallway. He remembered every word, and he felt his anger boiling up. "Let's talk about something else, okay?"

"Sure. How 'bout those Mets?"

"What?"

"You said to talk about something else, so how 'bout those Mets?"

"I meant something interesting." Timmy didn't really have a subject in mind when he started talking, but it only took a split second to come up with one. "Like witches."

"What about 'em?"

"You wanna go find some?"

Charles slammed on his brakes and his bicycle skidded to a halt. Timmy made a wide slow turn in the street and stopped facing Charles, their front tires touching.

"Are you outta your mind?"

"What's the matter?"

"Shit, Timmy, you heard what Brother Milford said. They're in the gravel pits."

"So? We've been in the gravel pits before, hundreds of times."

"But not while there were witches there."

"How do you know? We've camped out in there an awful lot. How do you know they weren't right up there on top, watching us?"

"Stop it, Timmy. That ain't funny. What if they catch us?"

"We're not even gonna get close enough for them to know we're there. We'll just get a look and leave. Nothing to it."

From not too far away, Timmy and Charles heard a familiar voice. "Hey! Wait up, you guys!" Jim slid his bicycle to a stop and grinned at the other two boys. "Hey, Charles, did you hear Timmy got a beatin' today?"

Timmy turned his bicycle around and started to pedal away. "That's old news, Jim."

"So, what 's the new news?"

The three rode single file on the edge of the street with Timmy in the lead, Jim close behind, and Charles bringing up the rear. Timmy signaled to turn onto a small gravel side street out of the flow of traffic. When they had all stopped and were side by side, Timmy looked straight into Jim's eyes and said, "We're going on a witch hunt."

Jim's eyes sparkled. "No shit?"

"No shit."

"The ones in the gravel pit?"

"Yep."

"Wow. When are you going?"

"Next full moon. You can come too if you want, but this time I'm the leader and we're not doing anything stupid that'll get us shot at."

As the three boys made their way back onto the main street, Timmy and Charles turned right and Jim went in the opposite direction, yelling out, "Give me a call when you get ready to go."

Timmy and Charles waved over their shoulders and rode on toward their homes. Charles was being unusually silent.

"What's the matter?"

Charles shrugged his shoulders and didn't say anything for several seconds. When he did speak it was almost too softly for Timmy to hear. "I'm not sure it's such a good idea."

"You don't have to go if you don't want to. I can go with Jim, or I can go by myself." It was an honest comment, not a backhanded slam. Charles and Timmy never pulled that peer pressure shit on each other.

"No, I'll go. It's just that... Hell, I don't know. What if those people are weird?"

" They probably are weird, that's why they're in the gravel pits doing whatever. And I want to find out what 'whatever' is. I promise you we're going to be so damned careful there's no way they'll know we're watching."

At the next intersection, Charles turned left. He looked back over his shoulder. "You coming to the corner after supper?"

Timmy shouted, "I don't think so. I have to start reading that damn book."

The two exchanged waves and parted company.

11

When Timmy turned into the driveway at his home and saw his father's car there, his stomach tightened a little. His father was home early and that usually meant something was wrong. He heard the shouting even before his bicycle rolled to a stop beside the house. He sat on the porch and listened.

"Gerald, calm down! Did he actually say you were fired?"

"No, but he might as well have."

"Why? You didn't hit him, did you?"

"No, but..."

"But nothing. They've got no reason to fire you and they know it. Except that you walked off the job. You didn't say you quit or anything like that, did you?"

"No." Gerald was talking softly now, and Timmy had to strain to hear his answers.

"Then go back and talk to Mr. Lankford. I'm sure when he hears your side of the story, he'll just have a talk with you about losing your temper and tell you to get back to work."

"Fuck 'em."

There was a slight pause before Pamela spoke, and she sounded mad. "What'd you say?"

"I said, fuck 'em." All hell was about to break loose. It always did at about this point in the argument. "I don't want to work in that stinking shirt factory! I never have wanted to work in that... I've got a fucking master's degree, for God's sake! And what good is it? I should be able to teach anywhere in the country, but I can't even get a job at the goddamn high school!"

"You haven't even applied at the goddamn high school!"

"Maybe I should! I'm more qualified than anybody who's teaching there now!"

"And how do you know that?"

"Because they were all teaching there when I was in school and they didn't teach me a goddamn thing!"

"I'm beginning to think that's true."

Gerald ignored her sarcasm and flew straight into a subject that he knew would hit Pamela close to home. "Look at what they're doing to Timmy!"

And Pamela stepped right in with that sharp, suspicious edge in her voice that all protective mothers acquire. "What about Timmy?"

"Just how well do you think he's doing in school?"

From his position on the front porch, Timmy would almost swear that he could hear the explosion that went off inside his mother's head. He knew them all just as well as his father did, all the things that would send Pamela into a rage, and Dad had managed to hit one that was at the top of the list.

"I *know* how well he's doing! He's doing just fine, thank you! He's making damn near all A's!"

"But can he add and subtract?"

"You've got the fucking master's degree! You tell *me*!" She didn't give him time to reply. She was on a roll. "Yes, as a matter of fact, he can! And quite well, I might add! You might start noticing little things like that if you can ever stop feeling sorry for yourself for being such a fucking failure!"

No holds barred. Show no mercy. Time for Timmy to make like a cow pie and hit the trail. The fight would be over soon. They never lasted very long, probably, Timmy suspected, because his parents were still young and horny enough that they enjoyed the making-up process. He would just go next door to Ma's house while they did whatever it was that they did to end the quarrel.

The fights used to bother Timmy a lot more than they did now. For a long time, he thought he was the cause of all the arguments. That was only logical since his name was always brought up, no matter what the problem was.

(*Oh, so you wrecked the car. No wonder Timmy's fucking up in school.*)

(*You forgot to get peanut butter? No wonder Timmy stays out so late.*)

(*The fucking house is a mess! No wonder Timmy doesn't get his hair cut!*)

But when he got a little older, it didn't take long for him to realize that the problem was much deeper than it seemed. He was just a pawn in their arguments, to be played whenever one wanted a psychological advantage over the other. Of course, he didn't think about it in those exact words, but he came up with something that meant about the same thing.

Personally, he thought a lot of it had to do with the accident on the night he was born. They had told him about it over and over and had even shown him photographs that the sheriff had taken the next day of the smashed automobile still clinging to the tree at the bottom of the bridge. The story itself always sounded like a warped version of a fairy tale about a beautiful princess who had to endure the horrible ordeal alone because the handsome prince got himself cold-cocked at the very start. The whole thing was just too strange. Something about the wreck and the photographs chilled him. The accident. That's what he thought was at the root of all their problems. He just wished they would let it drop. But he wasn't sure they could.

Timmy walked across the yard toward the house next door.

12

"Come in."

That would be Captain Jack, Ma's enormous parrot. Jack always answered when someone knocked on the door. That was his job, at least it was one that he took upon himself.

Timmy pushed the front door open and called out, "Is anybody home?"

"Come in."

Timmy went straight across the room to the steel cage that was Jack's home. Jack was sitting where he usually sat, on a free-standing perch just outside the open cage door. He seldom went into the cage except at night when he was sleeping or in the afternoon when he was napping. He was quite content to spend the rest of the time on the porch. Ma explained that to Timmy once. She told him that the man who owned Jack before kept him locked up all the time because Jack was always trying to escape. The man didn't understand that Jack was only trying to escape because he was locked up. When Ma got Jack, the first thing she did was open the cage and go into the other room. When Jack jumped out of the cage and saw that he could get away any time he pleased, he stopped trying. And it was a long time before he got back into the cage on his own.

Timmy reached toward Jack's bowl of seeds, being very careful not to move too quickly. As soon as Timmy's hand got close to the bowl, Jack stretched his neck so that his beak, slightly opened, was within an inch of the boy's hand. Jack's head followed the hand all the way to the bowl and all the way back out, just in case Timmy tried to do something stupid like steal a handful of food.

Timmy opened his hand, picked a sunflower seed out of the assortment, and, holding it loosely between his thumb and forefinger, offered it to Jack. Jack took the seed in his beak and popped it open with a loud *snap!*. Everything was okay now. Timmy tossed another sunflower seed into his own mouth and dropped the rest of the seeds back into the bowl.

"Is Ma home?"

"Downtown. Downtown."

Timmy spoke softly and began nodding his head up and down. It was a game he played with Jack.

"What's Ma doing downtown? Is she getting stuff for dinner? Huh?"

Jack started bobbing his body in rhythm with Timmy's nodding and shifting his weight from one foot to the other.

"What are you having for dinner? I'll bet you're having steak and potatoes. Maybe even *smashed* potatoes."

Jack slowly spread his long wings and his bobbing turned to short leaps.

"Oooo, and *gravy*. How does that sound, huh? *Smashed* potatoes and *GRAVY*."

"Awwwrrrrk! Awwwrrrrk!" Jack was flapping his wings and jumping up and down on his perch. "Awwwrrrrk!" Timmy was laughing so hard that his sides were starting to hurt, and the harder he laughed the more Jack squawked and that made him laugh even harder.

"Timmy? Is dat you pickin' at de bird?" Ma peeked around the corner from the kitchen. She held a brown grocery bag in one arm and her coin purse in her other hand. "Shit, boy, I come in an' hear de racket an' I know dat must be Timmy pickin' at de bird. You laughin' now, but one day Jack gonna bit de nose right offa yo face, and den I'm gonna do *me* some laughin'."

Timmy left Jack bouncing on the perch and went into the kitchen with tears streaming down his face. "You shoulda seen him! He was great today!"

"I seen him plenty. Here." She shoved two cans of tomato soup into his hands, and he put them in the cabinet. The soup was followed by a small bag of rice (the kind you actually have to cook), a box of frozen field peas, and a one-pound package of ground beef. When the groceries were all put away and the paper bag neatly folded and stashed in the cupboard, Ma turned to Timmy and smiled.

He had seen that smile before, many times. It was the same smile that she had flashed him on the day several years ago when they first met. It was a warm friendly smile, a smile that showed many spaces where teeth had once been. But Timmy saw much more than that. He saw a smile that suggested a deep, mysterious secret shared between them, even from the beginning. Timmy liked that. He often found himself wondering what that secret might be.

"So, boy, what bring you over here to pester me an' Jack?"

"My folks are at it again."

Ma's smile faded just a bit and she shook her head sympathetically. "One day dey'll wish dey not spent all dat time fightin'. 'Till den, dey ain't nothin you can do."

"Yep, that's the way I see it, too. Just stay out of the way."

"Don't eber start feelin' like you in de way, Timmy."

"Oh, you know what I mean."

"Yep, an' you know what *I* mean."

Timmy smiled at the old woman and nodded. She clapped her hands once and rubbed them together.

"Good. Wanna play gin rummy?"

"Naw, I don't think so."

"You tired ob me beatin' de shit outta you, eh?"

"I gotta get home. I just wanted to give my folks time to get through yelling at each other. I gotta do a book report next week so I guess I better start reading the book."

Timmy went back into the living room and rubbed his hand down Jack's back. Jack stretched his wings and flapped them twice. "See ya later, Jack."

Just as Timmy was opening the front door, Ma called from the kitchen, "Timmy, boy."

"Yeah, Ma?"

"Tonight, eleben o'clock, a show for you to watch on telebision."

"What is it?"

"*De Wolf Man*."

"I'll be watching."

"Me, too." She waved to Timmy and went back into the kitchen. Timmy closed the door and headed back toward home.

13

As Timmy approached the house, he listened for any signs that the argument was still in progress. He heard nothing and assumed that all was clear.

His father was in the living room reading the newspaper and his mother was in the kitchen starting supper. They weren't talking. They weren't smiling. At least they weren't yelling, that was all Timmy cared about for the moment.

"Hi, sport," Timmy's father said as he folded the paper and tried to act as if nothing had happened.

"Hi, Dad. You're home early."

"You're home late." A clever dodge. Timmy stored that one away for future use.

"I stopped in at Ma's."

"How was school?"

"Okay." Timmy went to the refrigerator and poured himself a glass of milk. He was trying to avoid all the polite conversation. It just didn't fit with what he had heard earlier.

"Okay? Is that all? Okay?"

"Yep." He started toward his room with an armload of books and his glass of milk. "Mom, I have a lot of homework. Just call me when supper's ready, okay?"

Pamela answered him without looking up from the stove. "It'll be about an hour."

Timmy went into his room and closed the door behind him. He hated days like this, and it seemed like they were coming closer and closer together. He dropped his books on his desk and sat on the edge of the bed.

The Scarlet Pimpernel.

From the size of the book, it looked as if he were in for quite a week of reading. He took a giant slug of milk, kicked off his shoes, settled back against his pillow, and opened the book to page one.

"Chapter One. Paris: September 1792. A surging, seething, murmuring crowd of beings that are human only in name, for to the eye and ear they seem naught but savage creatures, animated by vile passions and by the lust of vengeance and of hate."

Good God!

Timmy looked at the clock on the desk.

Only seven more hours until the movie starts.

"Yippee."

14

At ten fifty-eight, the house was dark. Gerald and Pamela had called it a night early, maybe nine or so. If they made up successfully, they were now in the same bed and asleep from exhaustion. If the make-up had *not* been successful, there was a good chance that Pamela was crying in the bedroom alone and Gerald was on the sofa staring up into the darkness and wishing he had married his eighth-grade sweetheart, what's her name.

Timmy glanced at his clock. It was time to get up. When he had gone to bed, he had taken the precaution of rolling up in a light blanket on top of the sheets. Now, even in the dark, it was safe for him to get out of bed and go into the living room. Doobie followed him, breathing loudly with his tongue hanging out one side of his snout.

Timmy stepped carefully through the black room. He didn't *have* to, but he didn't want to take the chance of waking his dad in case things hadn't gone too well. He reached out his hand and very lightly touched the sofa. No body. He quickly ran his hand back and forth to make sure his father hadn't shrunk or something. Still no body. The coast was clear.

Rolled in the blanket, Timmy had to take small steps, but he made it across the room to the TV amazingly fast and with no trouble at all. He turned the volume all the way off before he pushed the on/off switch. As soon as the picture began to fade in, he found the brightness control knob and turned it to black. Then, very slowly, he turned it back up until the picture was clear but dark -- that way no unnecessary attention was drawn to the room. As soon as he had the picture adjusted, he turned up the volume until it was barely audible from three feet away, his regular viewing distance for late night, unauthorized TV.

Timmy lay on the floor, his head propped on one elbow, and pulled at the blanket until it was comfortable. When Timmy was settled in, Doobie nosed his way under the blanket and turned until his head rested on the floor just under Timmy's chin. He raised his head just once, to give Timmy a long, wet lick across the face.

After a short Honda commercial, a sultry female voice came on and spoke to her unseen audience.

"Come on in and spend the night with me. Kick off your shoes and relax. It's time for Insomnia Theater."

Even though he had never seen her, Timmy had developed his own vision of his late-night hostess. She was tall and had long legs. Her coal black hair hung to her waist and her dark eyes sparkled. And he always pictured her in one of those black lacy things he had seen when he sneaked a peek at his mom's fancy underwear catalog.

Sigh!

Doobie snorted once and fell fast asleep. *The Wolfman* started and Timmy was up for the duration. School tomorrow would be hell.

15

Thursday night.

Full moon.

The Black Figures ride again.

Timmy, as leader, was responsible for formulating the master plan and sorting out all the details. The plan was simple. Since it was a school night, camping out was out of the question. So, it was decided that the three boys would find reasons to retire early. Then, when the coast was clear, they would sneak away from their homes and meet under the big oak at the corner. That was the plan; the details weren't quite so easy to work out.

Crystal Springs was almost completely surrounded by gravel pits. With the exception of due north, any route you traveled to get out of town led you around or through one of these excavations. That meant there were an awful lot of holes for people to hide in. In his sermon, Brother Milford had not given any clue as to which of the gravel pits the witches favored. It could have been any one of them. Or all of them, each on a different full moon. It had taken Timmy two days, but he was sure he had the answer. At least he was ninety-nine percent sure.

Witches loved midnight; Timmy knew that from the books and movies. Witches also did chants and made lots of noise and had a fire, also from the movies. Since their fire, combined with the light of the full moon, would make them highly visible, they would have to be far enough away from any houses that they couldn't be seen, and their chanting couldn't be heard. Also, since their meeting place would be like sacred ground, it would have to be in an area where there was no danger of it being disturbed. As far as Timmy could tell, there was only one place that fit the entire description: The gravel pit east of town. That had been his first hunch after Milford's sermon and now it seemed to be correct. That pit was by far the largest one around. And back away from the road was a huge section that had been abandoned because the machines were dangerously close to the water table.

There were two small roads that came in from opposite directions and curved around the upper edge of the pit. Earlier in the week, Timmy had checked out both of them. Neither showed signs of fresh tire tracks, but one of them was so badly eroded that, in places, the center of the road dropped off into the pit. A hundred and fifty feet, straight down. No way a car could pass, so the other road was the most logical entry.

The plan was complete. At ten-thirty, the three would be concealed alongside the road leading into the gravel pit. When/if the witches began to arrive, they would do their ninja routine, carefully stalking their prey until they discovered the meeting place. They would watch the ceremony in silence, wait until all the witches were gone, and then sneak back to their homes and into their beds. Simple.

The plan raced through Timmy's mind as he popped the screen off his bedroom window. He patted Doobie on the head. "You wait here. And be quiet." Doobie licked his hand.

It was ten o'clock.

16

It was eleven-fifteen when the first car turned onto the dirt road.

At eleven o'clock, Charles had decided that they were at the wrong gravel pit and that it was too late to try to get to another one before midnight so they might as well all go on back home. Now, Timmy just looked at Charles and grinned. They were almost definitely in the right place. Besides witches, the only others who might possibly come out to this gravel pit were lovers looking for a quiet place to do whatever lovers do for hours in a parked car. But it was Thursday night, a school night, and almost midnight. Not exactly the ideal time for a tumble in the back seat. By the time the third car slowed down and turned onto the little road, all three of the boys were convinced but they were not all equally enthusiastic. Charles still thought they should go home; it was too dangerous. Jim was just out for a good time and as long as no one started shooting at them it would be a load of laughs. Timmy, on the other hand, was near the point of being rabid. After watching all the movies, reading all the stories, and hearing all the legends, here was his chance to see real witches in action. It looked to be a very promising night.

The full moon was already high in the night sky, so the whole landscape was clearly visible in the blue-white light. The boys would have to be extra, extra careful not to be spotted when they made their way toward the meeting place. Of course, they wore their standard out-at-night-when-we're-not-supposed-to-be uniform: Black shirt, black pants, black gloves. But there was something else to be considered. When the plans were made, Timmy hadn't counted on the wind. There was a slight breeze blowing out of the south. It felt very good, but the boys were directly upwind of the place where the cars were stopping. Even the faintest of noises would be carried with crystal clarity. They might as well stand up and scream *Don't worry, witches. It's just some stupid kids coming to spy on you. Go ahead with what you're doing and pretend we're not here.*

First order of business: Get on the downwind side.

Making a wide circle around the meeting place would be the safest way to get by them without being seen. The east side was definitely out -- it was a steep cliff that dropped right off into the pit. They would have to go around to the west. Timmy pointed toward their proposed route and the others nodded.

It was now twenty-five minutes until midnight. If they were going to be in position before the ceremony began, they would have to hurry. If they were going to get there without being seen, they would have to take their time. Timmy decided on the latter and the three boys proceeded, staying as close to the ground as possible. Timmy led the way. Crouched low, he stepped softly onto the edge of the road.

He was only half-way across when the headlights flashed on him.

Timmy jumped as far as he could and rolled into the ditch on the other side of the road. He lay on his back in the tall grass and looked out past the stars and thought of all kinds of bad things. He knew that whoever was driving that car saw him when he jumped. He just *knew* it. They couldn't *help* but see him. And now they would just drive that car down that little dirt road until they came to the spot where he had jumped into the ditch and without even slowing down they would very casually turn the steering wheel a little to the left, just enough so that the car would swerve into the ditch and squish little Timmy like a bug. His breath was coming in short, quick bursts. He was scared to death (poor choice of words). And so he lay there looking at the stars, listening to the gravel crunch beneath the weight of the approaching car. As it got closer, he closed his eyes and waited for the tire to hit his head and pop it open like a watermelon walloped with a sledge hammer. For just a brief moment, he wondered what it would feel like. He never found out. The car passed him by. When he tried to lift himself out of the ditch, his knees were like rubber. He dropped back into the ditch and lay still.

After two more cars passed, Charles and Jim made their way across the road and into the ditch. They looked at one another and in unison released an almost inaudible *whew!*.

Only a few feet from the ditch was the barbed wire fence that separated old man Hill's peach orchard from the rest of the world. Once they got out of the open and into the orchard, the peach trees would offer more shadows for them to blend into. It would be easier to move without being seen. Then it would be just a matter of going parallel to the road until they were well past the parked cars, recrossing the road downwind of the meeting place, and sneaking up on the witches from behind. They would never suspect a thing.

Piece o'cake.

For what seemed like hours, the three boys crawled with painful slowness. First, they crossed the short distance to the fence -- there was tall grass to conceal them, but the grass was dry and rustled loudly. When they reached the fence, they lay on their backs and scooted headfirst under the bottom strand of barbed wire. On the other side of the fence, the first peach tree was ten or twelve yards away. In between there was nothing. Zero. Zilch. There were no shrubs, no undergrowth, even the grass was short. One at a time, with Timmy still in the lead, the boys crossed the open ground slithering on their bellies like snakes. Assholes and elbows, as an old marine DI used to say.

Safe behind the first tree, Timmy pulled up his right sleeve and looked at the watch on his arm. It was his mom's watch. There was a little button you could push, and the dial would light up, really handy in the dark. He had very casually lifted the watch off the kitchen counter while his mom was washing the supper dishes. When he got back home, he would put the watch back on the counter but maybe behind the sugar bowl or someplace else out of direct sight. Then it wouldn't look so suspicious when it turned up again and Mom would feel just a little bit stupid for misplacing it.

He pushed the button; it was five minutes until twelve. Things were taking much longer than he had planned. The ceremony, whatever it was, would surely start before they could get into position. But Timmy had had no way of knowing that they would have to go around to the other side of the meeting place. He had thought they could just walk right up, sit themselves down, and watch the evening's entertainment. Now, it was entirely possible that they could get caught and *become* the evening's entertainment. Live and learn.

Timmy looked toward the parked cars. He saw no signs of life, which was good; that meant nobody had seen them yet. Then he looked in the opposite direction, deeper into the orchard. He had an uneasy feeling in the pit of his stomach. He had heard stories about how old man Hill sometimes spent the night in his orchard just waiting for somebody to reach up into one of the trees. Timmy thought about cautioning Charles and Jim about the peaches, but he knew they had heard the same stories he had. Besides, there was no sign of old man Hill.

They made good time moving between the trees and in just a couple of minutes they were even with the parked cars. Although they still saw nothing, they could hear some laughter in the deeper bushes on the other side of the road. In a couple of more minutes, they were far enough away that Timmy thought they could safely cross the road. He looked at the watch.

Midnight.

He was getting anxious, but he took deep breaths, forcing himself to calm down. Rushing things was a good way to screw up, and they couldn't afford any screw ups. Jim was still grinning, having a wonderful time. Charles was still wishing they would call it quits and go home, but he knew there was no chance of that.

The laughter was coming from a small, thick stand of trees near the edge of the pit and as the boys got closer, they could see the glow of a big fire. Slowly, carefully, they picked their way through the thickening undergrowth until they were less than five yards away and had a clear view.

In the center of the trees was a large clearing. The thick bushes on all sides made the meeting place all but invisible from the outside. There were two, maybe three, paths (tunnels) going through the bushes and into the clearing. The altar was in the middle of the clearing. It was only an old orange crate, but with black candles on wither end and the large gold-colored bowl between them, it looked pretty sinister. What the boys had thought was a big fire was actually two smaller fires placed, like the candles, at either end of the altar.

The ceremony hadn't started yet, but the festivities certainly had. Whiskey bottles were passed from hand to hand and empty beer cans were tossed to the side. The laughter wasn't the kind you hear after a good joke; it was more like *Ha, ha, I'm so drunk tell me anything and I'll laugh at it.* Timmy didn't think all these people could have gotten so drunk in so short a time. He remembered watching the guests get plowed at his parents' New Year's Eve parties, and it took at least an hour for them to get as drunk as these witches were. Obviously, this party had started long before it was moved to the gravel pit.

Jim silently counted heads and motioned to Timmy that, yes, indeed, there were thirteen of them and they were all wearing black hooded robes. Just the thing for a nighttime outing. Timmy nodded.

There were four males and nine females gathered around the two fires. Some of them must have been from out of town because there were some faces unfamiliar to the three boys in the bushes. But there were some very familiar ones, too, just like Brother Milford had said. There were Penny Jenson, Patricia Tanner, and Melanie Davis -- the boys saw them almost every day on the school campus. Allison Blower (that name was always good for a laugh) was in the process of blowing Mr. Jim Beam, the slick glass bottle gleaming in the fire light. Glen Peters was a photographer for the local newspaper, but not tonight. There were others that Timmy recognized but couldn't connect a name to. And all of these people were sitting around getting shitfaced in the woods at the gravel pit. Big deal. Timmy was feeling disappointed. It seemed that the whole witch meeting was nothing but an excuse for a bunch of drunks to get together and party. He was just about to motion to the other guys that they should leave.

It was just about that same instant that the black cape slid off Patricia Tanner's naked body and lay in a pile at her feet.

The thought of leaving immediately fled from Timmy's mind. In no time at all, every one of the black capes were tossed to the side and thirteen naked people were dancing around the fires. The females were all nice looking, and of course they looked even better with no clothes, but there was one that kept Timmy spellbound. He had often watched Melanie Davis as she led cheers at the football games or as she walked across campus and he had just as often wondered what she would look like underneath those sexy things she wore. Now he watched her dance, her breasts bouncing slightly. At first, her nipples were just a few shades darker than the surrounding skin, but as they began to get erect and pull tight, they changed to a bright red. She rubbed a cold beer can back and forth, from one breast to the other. Her free hand traced a line from between her breasts, down past her bellybutton (an innie), toward the thin line of pubic hair that disappeared between her legs. The tightness in Timmy's underwear became unbearable. When one of the naked men grabbed Melanie's tit and kissed her, Timmy came in his pants.

Gradually, the dancing stopped, and they divided themselves into smaller groups, a male and two females in each. It was unlike any orgy the three hidden boys could have ever dreamed up in their imaginations. There was passionate kissing, hands exploring bodies, and Allison Blower demonstrating why the jokes about her name were not unjustified.

The thirteenth person, an unfamiliar woman, walked from

group to group and watched. she looked to be just a little bit older than the rest of her cohorts. There was just a hint of sag in her breasts, but she either wasn't aware of it or she didn't care. Probably the latter. She seemed to be quite comfortable with her beauty and her nudity, and she carried herself with an air of confidence that the others didn't have. Lingering at each group, she sometimes reached out to stroke an exposed body part or leaned down to kiss a waiting mouth. She wasn't in a hurry, but she was definitely making her way toward the altar. When she finally reached it, she placed her hands on her hips and looked around her, smiling, like a farmer well satisfied with the day's planting.

Moving with deliberate, almost exaggerated, motions, the watcher turned toward the altar and grasped the two candlesticks. Holding them at eye level, she stared into the tiny flames for a second before raising them high above her head.

"Father Darkness, we are come..."

Timmy felt his face flush; if she only knew how true that was. The amorous activities slowed to a stop and the groups looked toward the woman waiting for her to continue. After a moment, she blew out the candles and placed them on the ground beside the altar. Next, she took the gold bowl, kissed the side of it, and held it high.

"We approach the high altar to give and receive pleasure in you name."

The bowl joined the candlesticks on the ground. From some secret place, probably inside her discarded robe, she brought a long black cloth which she reverently spread over the orange crate/altar. She held her empty hands toward the full moon which was peering down into the clearing. Bringing her hands together, she sat on the altar and lowered her hands until they were even with her face. She stared at the moon with a strange, far-away look.

"Your High Priestess has prepared herself, a human altar at which your faithful may worship and offer the fullness of their pleasure."

She clapped her hands twice in front of her face and the followers approached the altar. Then, with the muscles in her stomach struggling to maintain control, she bent herself backwards until her head rested on the ground behind the altar and her pubic mound was arched upward, straining toward the moon. The girls in the group knelt around the altar and placed their hands on the body stretched before them. One of them squeezed a breast, another let her fingers dart between the spread legs, another rubbed a thigh. Soon the touching turned into an arousing, erotic massage. The air was filled with moaning and sighing, and the human altar twitched with increasing frequency as someone touched a magic spot. As if on cue, the four males took their positions, one at each corner of the altar, and began to masturbate. The girls followed their lead and, keeping one hand on the body in front of them, moved one of their hands to the soft warm place between their own legs. The human altar writhed under their touch and great drops of sweat broke out all over her body. She spread her legs a little wider and groped blindly around her, trying desperately to make contact with hot flesh. Her moans became faster, each one louder than the one before it. Her breathing was reduced to short gasps. She climaxed in a series of spasmodic jerks emphasized by a shattering scream. This set off a chain reaction of orgasms. The men ejaculated onto the human altar while the women rubbed and moaned and screamed and cried. At the end, they were all drained.

Timmy, Charles, and Jim sat in the bushes with their mouths hanging down to their kneecaps. When they had decided to hunt witches, they never imagined they would stumble onto a sexual marathon. There had never been anything like this in any of the movies they had seen. The nakedness, the sounds, and now the clear smell of sex drifting toward them on the breeze. Timmy felt that he had no reason to be embarrassed anymore; he was pretty sure that by now Charles and Jim had creamed their jeans, too.

For about fifteen minutes there was no movement around the altar and no sound except heavy breathing. The High Priestess, when she finally moved, sat up and again surveyed her surroundings. It had been a great time, one of the best. She folded the black cloth and placed it aside. With the same deliberate movements as before, the High Priestess replaced the gold bowl, relit the black candles, and stood the candlesticks on the altar. She clapped her hands twice and again had the attention of the group.

"Father Darkness, we bring a petition." She pointed one finger at Melanie Davis, and Melanie ran to the pile of black robes. After a second, Melanie handed the High Priestess a brown envelope.

"There is one in the community, an enemy who would do us harm and stop our faithful worship of you. We demand a curse on him, and in return we offer his blood." She reached into the envelope and pulled out several tissues with large spots of blood on them. These she dropped into the gold bowl. "This, along with the likeness of your enemy." Again, from the envelope, she took a photograph and dropped it on top of the tissues. "Milford... Milford..."

The rest of the group joined in the chant *Milford! Milford! Milford!* as the High Priestess took one of the candles and held it to one corner of the photograph.

17

James Milford awoke with a start. He was breathing as if he had just run the hundred-yard dash and his pillow was soaked with sweat. His leg and chest were throbbing, and his head felt like the little man inside there was using a sledgehammer to try to break out of the skull. He didn't know exactly what it was, but deep in his gut he knew it wasn't just the pain that woke him up.

At twelve fifty-five in the morning, Milford went into the kitchen to make a cup of coffee, maybe even a whole pot. He had some heavy thinking to do.

18

Milford! Milford! Milford!

Timmy, Charles, and Jim looked at one another with wide eyes. This was a genuine, honest-to-God witches' curse and they were watching it happen!

Milford! Milford! Milford!

The High Priestess had her hands raised and was looking at the moon, so she didn't see the gold bowl when it started to shake. But Patricia saw it. So did Glen and Allison and several of the unknowns. The chanting stopped and the High Priestess looked down to see why.

The photo and the tissues which had been in the bowl were completely burned, but smoke continued to pour over the lip of the bowl. It was a bright red smoke and it spread over the altar and down onto the ground. Slowly it rolled and crept across the dirt and gravel toward the witches who backed away from it as if it would bite them. And maybe it would; this had never happened before in any of their rituals. The silence that filled the meeting place was accentuated by the soft rustling of the leaves in the trees surrounding the clearing.

The small flickering flames on the black candles began to grow brighter. It was an imperceptible change at first, but in a matter of seconds the pinpoints of light became like miniature suns shining bright white. The witches and the three boys in the bushes all had to shield their eyes against the brilliant light. With a great roar, the two fires beside the altar shot burst after burst of flames high into the air. Clouds of smoke and the smell of burning sulfur hung in the air, threatening to suffocate anyone in the area. By now, no one was watching the gold bowl, but its shaking had turned to violent bouncing.

From out of the sky, a thin mist descended through the top of the clearing. It wasn't a mass like a fog; it was more like a delicate white finger spiraling down. The finger mist made large circles around the High Priestess and then tightened the airy rings quickly like the attack of a boa constrictor. The High Priestess screamed, and this scream sounded nothing at all like her screams of orgasm. She clawed at the bands of mist, but as soon as her hand would pass through it, the mist would rejoin itself. The tip of the finger mist disappeared into the top of the bouncing bowl and when it emerged seconds later, the bowl sat still on the altar. And the bowl was empty. No ashes, no smoke, not even a ring of soot. The finger mist unwound itself and released the High Priestess. In a blind panic, she snatched up her robe and ran out of the clearing.

For several long seconds, there was utter chaos as the rest of the group tried to follow their leader. They were pushing and shoving and crying and running into each other and trying to crowd onto the two narrow paths that led out. Soon the clearing was empty except for the two fires, the altar, the candles, the bowl, and the weird finger mist that just kept spiraling in the air.

Jim was the first to speak, and all he could manage was, "Shit!"

Charles tugged at Timmy's sleeve. "Timmy, I'm scared! Let's get out of here!"

If Timmy had had time to speak, he would have said, "Hell, yes!" but before he could even get his mouth open, the finger mist stopped dead still and a deep, booming laugh started in the clearing and echoed through the gravel pit. It went on and on, and the finger mist moved slowly toward the bushes where the boys were hiding.

They ran like hell.

19

Back at the street corner, under the protective branches of the old oak tree, Timmy, Charles, and Jim made a solemn oath not to tell anyone what they had seen that night.

All too soon that oath would have to be broken, but one of the three wouldn't be around to see it happen.

20

It was almost two o'clock in the morning when the knock came on James Milford's front door. He was still in his kitchen just about to brew his second pot of coffee. He looked at the clock on the wall.

"Jesus Christ, who is that?" A visit or a phone call at this time of night usually meant that somebody had died. "Just a minute!" he called, pulling his robe tighter and tying the sash. The knocking continued. "I'm coming, I'm coming!" he shouted, and opened the door.

"Melanie! What are you..."

"I was riding around and saw your light on. Brother Milford, I've got to talk to you." She walked past him without waiting to be invited in.

Milford looked after her for a second, stunned. Then he closed the door and followed her into the living room. Unconsciously, he pulled his robe just a little closer.

"I was just making coffee. Would you like a cup?"

She was already pacing the floor looking distracted and biting one of her long fingernails.

"Melanie?"

"What? Oh, yeah, some coffee would be real nice. Thanks."

She continued to pace. Milford returned to the kitchen, his mind going ninety miles an hour. What was a young girl doing out alone at this time of night? Never mind alone, what was she doing out *at all*? Why was she wearing that strange black robe? And what was so urgent that she couldn't wait until daylight to discuss it? He thought maybe he knew the answer, and it caught him completely off guard. Her name hadn't been on the list.

Milford went back into the living room bearing the coffee and utensils on a serving tray. Melanie was still pacing.

"Please have a seat."

She stopped abruptly in front of the sofa. When she sat, her robe fell open and revealed naked flesh all the way up to where she clutched it closed at her neck. She didn't seem to notice the exposure, but Milford mentally slapped his own face. This was going to be one interesting and trying meeting; self-control had never been one of his strong points. When he had deposited the tray on the coffee table, he cleared his throat and pointed to her open robe.

"Oh." That was all; no surprise, no embarrassment. It was as if he had told her an earring was missing. She nonchalantly pulled the edges of the robe together and went back to biting her fingernail.

Milford poured the coffee. "Cream or sugar?"

"No, black."

She took the cup and saucer, balanced them on her knee, and then completely ignored them. Coffee was obviously the farthest thing from her mind.

Milford leisurely sipped his coffee and watched her. This was not the flighty, bubbly, shy teenager who visited his office last Sunday. Not at all. Something had stripped away the facade, and what he was seeing was the real Melanie Davis (literally and figuratively). She was disturbed and he didn't want to rush her.

Anything she had to say would have to be said in her own due time. Otherwise, she might feel pressured and decide not to tell exactly what was on her mind. Personal counseling was a very delicate mental operation. Even though it was coincidental -- at least he *assumed* it was a coincidence -- it was probably a good thing that he had gotten up and was wide awake before she got there. A foggy mind and dragon breath do not make for good personal counseling. The two, Milford and Melanie, both wearing robes and nothing else, both feeling somewhat uncomfortable but for different reasons, both wondering what the outcome of this meeting would be, sat in silence for several long minutes.

Melanie took a deep breath and let it out slowly through pursed lips. She moved her full coffee cup to the serving tray and, for the first time, looked straight into Milford's eyes.

"Brother Milford, you remember those witches out in the gravel pit?"

"Yes."

"You know that list you said you had?"

"Yes."

"Have you noticed that the list is missing?"

"Yes, I have."

"Well, I took it."

After that, the words came in a flood. During the next hour, Melanie told stories of animal sacrifices, of drinking blood, of orgies and sexual encounters that made Milford blush. Sometimes she was intense, sometimes she cried, but never once did she crack a smile. From her first involvement with the witches right up through tonight's fiasco, she told him everything.

Almost.

When she came to the part about the photograph, the bloody tissues, and *Milford! Milford! Milford!*, she cut it down to, "We were doing one of our stupid chants and all of a sudden..." Neat, clean, and nobody gets their feelings hurt. Right? You bet.

Then there was nothing else to tell. She picked up her cup of cold coffee and it shook in her trembling hand. She took a big mouthful and her face twisted into a grimace.

"Let me get you some fresh coffee."

"No, that's okay. I don't drink coffee very much." When she returned the cup to the tray, her hands were still shaking. She folded them in her lap and again sat silently for a long time. Milford watched and waited.

"Brother Milford, I'm scared." Tears were forming in the corners of her eyes. Milford crossed the room and sat beside her on the sofa. She buried her face in his robe and wept. "Please help me! I don't want to go to hell!"

So here it was, the culmination of all the years of pounding hellfire-and-brimstone fear into the minds of innocent young people. That Old Time Religion, rah rah rah! Okay, so Melanie probably would end up in hell if she didn't change. But Milford couldn't help but believe that it was the emphasis on the *fear* of God instead of the *love* of God that had caused her to rebel in the first place. Religion was turning out to be its own worst enemy. He would have to remember that; it would make quite an interesting sermon one day.

Milford put his arm around her and stroked her long hair. He felt a fluttering in his stomach and his knees turned to jelly. At this very moment, it could be awfully easy for him to be in love with the girl he held in his arms.

"It's okay." He couldn't think of much else to say. "It's okay."

When she was able to stop crying, she dried her tears on her sleeve and looked again at Milford. What he saw was a look of peace and an honest sparkle in her eyes. It made him feel a little more fulfilled, even though he hadn't really done much except listen. Melanie took Milford's hand and squeezed it. Smiling a mankiller smile she asked, "Shouldn't we pray or something?"

"Of course, we should. Of course."

Together, they turned and knelt facing the sofa. When Melanie clasped her hands in front of her, the top of her robe opened, and her right breast lay exposed on the cushion. Milford looked at her breast and then at her smile. After a long minute he closed his eyes.

They prayed, Melanie for her immortal soul and Milford for the strength to make it through the night without doing something stupid.

21

"Today, we will continue the study of Satan, his powers and his followers, a study which we began last Sunday. If you will take your Bibles and turn with me now..."

It started almost as soon as he stepped up to the pulpit. He felt the tiny beads of sweat break out on his forehead, and he fished his handkerchief out of his breast pocket. He felt all the stares, all those people out there wondering what kind of strange service they would have this week. He fought to keep his breathing steady. That was the only hope he had of staying in control.

"... Then saith Jesus unto him, Get thee hence, Satan; for it is written, Thou shalt worship the Lord thy God, and Him only shalt thou serve..."

He looked up from his Bible and quickly scanned the congregation. He was looking for one face in particular, and he soon found it. Melanie was sitting on the third pew, looking up at him and smiling. He smiled back. Seeing her there gave him a feeling of confidence he hadn't had since he left the seminary. After all, they had just recently been through a very emotional experience together, and in the end her soul had been saved from the bottomless pit burning with Hellfire and Brimstone Hallelujah and Amen! Several times during the last few days he found himself thinking about Melanie and wondering if their talking and their praying had done any good. From his own experience he knew that it was very easy in the darkness of the late-night hours to believe in God and the miracles and the mysteries of Christ and to cry and beg and plead for forgiveness of sins, real or imagined. But in the daylight... in the cold, cynical daylight of the real world, "God" was followed by a curse, "Christ" was followed by an "!," and crying, begging, and pleading were things that only happened in soap operas. Milford was afraid that in the days following their night together, she would think about what happened, get embarrassed, and let it all go. Maybe that hadn't happened. She was sitting there, not in her usual back-row seat, but in the third row. She was watching him and not filing her fingernails. And she was smiling. Maybe – just maybe – it hadn't happened. Yet.

"The evil of Satan was made evident early on, in the Garden of Eden. In early scriptures, he is referred to as a serpent and is described as 'more subtle than any beast of the field which the Lord God had made'..."

He reached down and scratched absently at his left thigh.

"Satan is sly in his temptation of man. He knows that man was given a choice. In the beginning of time, God understood that worshipers who had no choice were not worshipers at all, but merely slaves of a tyrant. So, God gave man the choice of following good or evil. Good or evil. It was that simple. I think it's safe to assume that most people, when given that simple choice, would not hesitate to choose the good. Despite what sociologists and psychologists might say, I like to think that mankind is basically good. But this is where Satan does his best work. He takes the simplicity out of the choice. He very subtly glamorizes the evil by making the good look bad or somehow less desirable. Just take a look at what he did to Eve in the Garden of Eden. Genesis three, verses one through six..."

Without even knowing it, Milford unbuttoned his coat and tossed it onto his chair. He loosened his tie and popped open the top button of his shirt. The handkerchief went back and forth across his face. To the senior members of the congregation, this probably looked like old-time religion, the kind they saw in the tiny churches of their youth. The younger generation probably thought the man had taken a few acting lessons and was practicing on them. As for Milford himself, he just went on preaching. Maybe once the thought crossed his mind that someone must have turned on the heat in the building, but it was a fleeting thought at most. His voice rang through the church, a near shout. He stabbed his finger at the air for emphasis. The words were coming in a steady stream. And this wasn't even the good part of the sermon.

"... and that's what he does to you and to me every single day of our lives! He makes the wicked and evil things of this world look more appealing than the good things!"

A quick picture of Melanie flashed (literally) through his mind. He smiled. He wiped his brow. He rubbed his thigh. He glanced at his notes to find his place. He felt a sharp pain in his chest. He saw the strange clouds forming again over the congregation.

For almost a full minute he just stood and stared at the little clouds. They floated and glided through the church, swooping down now and again to settle on a deacon's head or a young woman's lap. He wasn't quite sure, but he thought their shapes were becoming more defined than the first time. They actually looked like they might have arms.

He blinked his eyes and realized that he had just stopped abruptly. He flipped through the note cards on the pulpit and fumbled with his Bible.

"Uh... Satan's main job... here on earth... uh... is to, uh, distract us... the Christians, I mean... from..."

He had been doing so well, but now his train of thought was completely shot to hell. He pressed the fingers of one hand to his forehead and tried to concentrate. He heard giggling, but when he opened his eyes there was not a smile in the whole church. His chest hurt and he held his breath against the pain. He searched for Melanie, and she was there. Her smile had become a look of concern. He straightened himself and held his head high. Concentration.

"Satan doesn't even waste his time tempting the lost, because they already belong to him. He concentrates his efforts on the Christians. He makes life for the Christians as difficult as he possibly can. He throws up one temptation after ano..."

He hit the floor before he was even aware that he was falling. His left leg just gave out. No warning, no pain, no nothing. It just turned to Jell-O and dropped him on his face.

Matt Wilson, the Music Director, was at Milford's side in no time and helped him to his feet.

"Are you okay?" Matt whispered. "Do you want us to just go right into the Invitational?"

"No, no. I'm fine," he lied. The whispers of the congregation sounded like a swarm of bees on a spring day.

"I'm sorry. I guess my foot just went to sleep," he told the group and they turned to look at their holy man once more.

Even the clouds were still. And then they vanished. The pain in his chest went away and he felt the strength returning to his leg. The cool breeze of the air conditioning hit him square in the face.

His hands started shaking and then he got scared.

22

The nights were becoming unbearably hot. There was no breeze. The humidity was high, and the air hung like a damp towel, smothering everything underneath.

Timmy closed his books and stretched. He had heard somewhere (but not from a teacher or a parent) that there was such a thing as overdoing the studies, and he felt as if he had probably done that tonight. His eyes were sore, his head ached, and his back was stiff from leaning over the table. It was time to stop; in fact, it was getting late. The only thing that kept him from jumping straight into bed was the thought of how nice a cold bath would feel on a hot night.

Bath, not shower. Mother told him over and over that it wasn't good for him to sit in a tub full of his own scum and that he really should take showers. But he saw *Psycho*.

He stretched out in the tub so that the water covered the back of his head and filled his ears. It gave him the feeling of being far away from everything. No crickets chirping, no tree frogs calling for rain, no cars roaring down the street. The only sounds that reached his eardrums were footsteps in another room or water rushing through the kitchen pipes. The cool water with its gentle ripples surrounded his body and filled his ears and relaxed him like no massage possibly could. He closed his eyes.

Some strange things had been happening around him lately. The witches -- now, *THAT* was strange. And scary. When he got home from the gravel pit that night, and after he stashed Mom's watch neatly on the kitchen counter behind the box of corn flakes, he wrote down everything he had seen and heard that night. He took great care to be as exact as he could. None of the books and movies had prepared him for that night. Who knows, maybe he witnessed an historic event. It was almost four in the morning when he closed the spiral notebook and stashed it under his mattress. It would be safe there, Mom always made him change his own sheets.

School the next day was sheer hell. He kept falling asleep at his desk. Recess was exhausting, lunch was nauseating (as usual), the lessons dragged on forever, and Lena was doing her damnedest to "straighten him out." She even smacked him across the back with her wooden pointer when he nodded off after lunch. That was when he told her he didn't feel good and he thought he was getting a fever. Guilt trip. Sometimes it worked, sometimes it didn't. And if *this* one worked, it would be a doozie. It would make her feel like a heel for days. She put her hand on his forehead -- none too gently -- and held it there for five or ten seconds. After that, she didn't pick on him for the rest of the day. Maybe he did have a fever. It was hard for him to really tell at the time.

Brother Milford. To paraphrase an old introductory line, what could you say about Brother Milford that hasn't already been said a hundred times? Answer -- he was acting weird. Timmy noticed it again in church Sunday and he heard several people talking about it and scratching their heads trying to figure it out. Timmy knew what it was. Timmy knew a lot more than he wanted to. It was a real, honest-to-God witch curse and he had seen the whole thing and he was honor bound not to tell *any*body. What a pisser.

Even Doobie was getting into the act. Doobie, the ever-faithful man's best friend who never left Timmy's side, had, in the last few days, refused to go into Timmy's bedroom under his own power. The first night, Doobie was following Timmy like he usually did, and he suddenly stopped at the door and whined until Timmy picked him up and carried him to the bed. The second night, the same thing happened. The third night, Tuesday night (last night), Timmy decided to see what would happen if he didn't pick Doobie up, so at bedtime he walked straight into his room and ignored Doobie's whines. About ten or fifteen minutes later, Doobie lay down in front of the gas heater in the living room. (But Timmy couldn't stand it and went out to get the poor whimpering dog.)

Strange things. Things that didn't make a whole lot of sense. Things that you would never suspect in a million years. But there was one thing that he was quite sure of: No one would come sneaking into the bathroom, whisk aside the shower curtain, and stab him a hundred and fifty times with a butcher knife while he was showering -- because he was smart enough to say, "You go to hell. I'm taking a BATH!" He found himself thinking how nice it would be to sleep in the tub.

"Timmy." Mother was calling. She had already called a couple of times but he hadn't heard. The water in his ears made sure of that -- and the fact that he had been dozing.

"Timmy." She knocked once and then heard the splash as he sat up in the tub.

"What?"

"Don't you think you've been in there long enough?"

"What time is it?"

"It's ten-thirty."

An hour. He had been in the tub for an hour.

"Okay."

When he tried to stand up all his joints hurt. His skin had been drained of moisture. It was wrinkled and tight. He didn't have fingertips anymore; they had become tiny prunes on the little prongs that stuck out from his hands. Every part of his body that he tried to move felt as if it were splitting wide open. Suddenly the idea of sleeping in the tub lost all its appeal.

I'd have probably drowned anyway.

Timmy stepped out of the bathroom with one towel wrapped around his waist and another thrown over his wet hair. "Where's Dad?" Timmy towel-dried his hair briskly.

"He's in the den." Then she lowered her voice as if the next part were a big secret. "I think he's writing letters, sending out applications for teaching jobs."

"I was wondering how long it would take. I heard the fight."

"Which one?" She smiled, but Timmy could tell that she was only half joking.

"Which one? Aren't they all the same?" This time *he* smiled and was only half joking.

"Tell your dad goodnight."

"Goodnight, Dad," he called out.

"Goodnight, Kiddo," came the distant reply.

"Goodnight, Mom."

"Goodnight, Son."

Timmy started to walk toward his room. "Goodnight, John-Boy. Goodnight, Jimbob. Goodnight, Mary Ellen. Goodnight, Grandpa..."

"Are you going to bed with wet hair?" Mother Pamela. The ever-watchful eyes. Sees all, knows all. Fortunes told While-U-Wait."

"Yes, Ma'am."

"You know what I've told you about that."

"Yes, Ma'am." It was one of her most popular fortunes, passed down from generation to generation. One night a young man would go to bed with wet hair and wake up with pee-new-monia and expect the whole world to feel sorry for him but he would be really surprised because everyone would just say "told ya so" and let the young man suffer for not listening to his mother.

Three fortunes for a dime! That's one down and two to go! Come on, young feller! What else would ya like t'know!

She had told him countless times about going to bed with wet hair, but pee-new-monia or not, he was going to bed with wet hair. Doobie was sitting at the door whining.

Timmy shook his head and spoke quietly to his pet. "You puss."

"What'd you say?" Mother also had ears like a bat. She could hear things that were well out of the human range of hearing. Timmy was firmly convinced of that.

"I was talking to Doobie."

"I hope so, or you'd be in deep shitski, m'man."

"I know." He picked up Doobie and went into his room.

On nights like this one, Timmy would open the window at the head of his bed and sleep with the top of his head against the screen and his neck resting on the windowsill. Just in case the wind decided to blow or something. That's the way he decided to sleep tonight.

Timmy deposited Doobie on the bed and climbed over to raise the window as high as it would go. He pulled the sheet back to the *ready* position and took his place beside the light switch. He hesitated there and took several deep breaths. This was a nightly ritual, the preparation for the observance of Rule Number Two. He carefully noted where Doobie lay and how close he was to the foot of the bed. He took a deep breath. He flipped off the light.

One-one-thousand...

He took three running steps toward the bed. He leaped

two-one-thousand...

to what he thought was the left side of the bed, because he had put Doobie on the right side of the bed, but he miscalculated and his hand came down on Doobie's foot. Doobie jumped with a soft yelp and Timmy scrambled to get his feet

three...

under the covers and

one...

pull the covers up to his neck as he

thousand!

flopped his head toward the pillow. He miscalculated again and his head crashed on the windowsill.

"Shit!" He immediately pulled the covers over his mouth and waited for Ears to burst into the room. She didn't.

Doobie crawled up to chest level and licked Timmy's shoulder. Timmy could feel the dog's tail wagging and slapping his leg through the thin sheet.

"We made it again, Doobie."

Doobie stretched his neck and gave Timmy a great long lick across the face. Timmy slid himself up on the pillow until his head was against the window screen.

Through half-opened eyes, Timmy watched, but did not really see, the thin clouds drifting across the moon.

Bad things pray to the moon.

Timmy opened his eyes wide. Where had that come from? Too many horror movies, he finally decided, and he let his eyes slip closed. His mind floated in that Twilight Zone between consciousness and sleep. And in that state of semi-awareness, he started to dream...

He was in France. He had never seen France, but he knew it was France. He was dressed like an old woman, a disguise of some sort, and he was driving a horse-drawn wagon. But under the long, loose dress was a sword of the finest steel money could buy. It was 1792, and he was The Scarlet Pimpernel! In disguise and on another daring, though somewhat routine, mission: Rescue a small party of aristocrats from the mob of revolutionaries and leave behind the symbolic red flower as a clue for his archenemy Chevalin.

Under a cover in the back of the wagon were the three aristocrats, trusting their very lives to the old woman with the man's voice and the long sword. The street was narrow and the wagon had to move slowly.

But alas! Something had gone wrong! Soldiers all around! Soldiers of the Revolution, brandishing swords and coming for him! But he was not afraid. The Scarlet Pimpernel knew not the meaning of the word Fear. He flipped away the cover and told the aristocrats, "You make your escape. I'll hold them here." Then, with one swift, smooth motion, he ripped away the disguise, drew his sword, and turned to face the rush of soldiers. For several minutes he fought brilliantly. Twenty or more of the soldiers would force him onto a balcony and he would swing away on a conveniently placed rope. Then thirty or more of them would force him backwards up a long staircase where he would pick up a suit of armor and toss it down on them, sending all thirty of them tumbling down, and then he would swing away on a conveniently placed, and amazingly strong, tapestry. Finally, a hundred and fifty of them backed him into a corner where he fought the best fight of his life. With each thrust of his sword, three or four of the enemy fell. And even though there were so many of them and his sword was getting dull, he knew in his strong, noble, hero-pure heart that he could take them all.

That was his last thought just before everything went black. The rotten bastards cheated and dropped a piece of firewood out of the second story window and knocked him cold.

When he came to, he saw that he was chained to the dungeon wall and that he was not alone. The aristocrats that he was sent to rescue were all there; not a single one had escaped. Hanging there on that wall, he realized that they were all doomed. There was no one left to save them. There was only one Scarlet Pimpernel, and he was it. And he was chained to the dungeon wall.

It was nearing dawn. Execution time. A crowd was gathering in the square. As the first rays of light stretched across the countryside, what began as an isolated shout soon became a mass chant: *Off with their heads! Off with their heads!*

He heard a key turn in the door lock. It was time. For some reason he knew that he would be first. The aristocrats were an everyday thing, but now the revolutionaries had a real main attraction.

He set his jaw and waited to look into his executioner's face.

Off with their heads! Off with their heads!

But his executioner had no face! The dungeon door swung open and there was no one there, only a strange swirling mist that changed colors from blue to red to green and back to blue. The mist held a huge key in the shape of a crucifix, and it moved slowly toward The Scarlet Pimpernel.

From the distance came the faint sound of a marching cadence being pounded out on the drums. As it drew closer it was greeted by cheers from the crowd. It was a high school marching band, complete with drum major and majorettes. Behind the band came the cheerleaders, with Melanie Davis out in front. They were followed by the football team, all dressed in shoulder pads, helmets, and black robes. The band, cheerleaders, and football team took their places in a special roped off section of the town square.

Melanie, in her short cheerleader skirt and her too-tight letter sweater, walked slowly and seductively up the long stairs to the execution platform. When she reached the top, she stood glaring out at the crowd with her legs spread and her hands on her hips.

Take it off!

In a matter of seconds, this new chant replaced the old one as the crowd watched the girl on the platform. The band struck up its version of "The Stripper," and Melanie Davis began peeling off her clothes.

The misty jailer pulled The Scarlet Pimpernel out of the dungeon and dragged him through the narrow hallways toward the outside doors. The crowd was ready. They had a band, they had a stripper, they had a criminal to execute, and afterwards they would have a football game. Who could ask for anything more?

When they saw their victim being dragged out into the street, they cleared a path to the execution platform. They reached out to touch him. They spit on him. An old woman grabbed his nuts and squeezed as hard as she could. The chant became a bastard child.

Take it off!

Take a little off the top!

Take it off the top of his head!

Take off his head!

Off with his head!

As they reached the stairs, Melanie took off the last bit of her clothing and winked at The Scarlet Pimpernel. She smiled her wicked smile and crooked her finger, beckoning him to come to her. She licked her lips and winked again. Teasing, taunting. He looked at her and wanted to climb the stairs and lose himself in her arms.

But a shadow loomed behind her. It stretched upward as far as the eye could see. It frightened him.

He started up the stairs. His feet were like lead and he walked like he was in a trance. One step, two steps, three steps.

Melanie rubbed her hands on her body. He moved faster. Seven steps, eight steps.

He was almost to the top. He ran to meet her. Eleven steps, twelve steps, Top!

She jumped up and he caught her in his arms. She clamped her legs around his waist and kissed him. It was a long kiss, a deep kiss. Not at all the way his mother kissed him goodnight. When they broke away, she took his hand and led him to a bed in the center of the platform. It was a hard bed, made of wood. She unbuttoned his shirt and pushed him back gently onto that bed. She lay on top of him and kissed him again.

Then there was a deep, echoing, evil sounding laugh, and she was gone. He opened his eyes to look for her, but all he could see was the swirling mist. He tried to move, but the soft naked female body had been replaced by strong leather straps. He looked up and saw the glint of steel.

And it was moving. He was on the... the...

GUILLOTINE!

Timmy's eyes opened wide and he saw the steel blade falling toward him. He jerked upright in bed just as the window slammed shut behind him. Maybe he screamed, he couldn't remember. His whole body was trembling. Cold sweat dripped off his chin. It was even possible that he wet the bed.

Doobie was standing at the foot of the bed with his tail between his legs. Whining loudly, he looked at Timmy and then at the door and then at Timmy and then at the door. After a couple of hesitant false starts, Doobie finally leaped off the bed and ran into the living room as fast as his short little legs would carry him.

"I don't blame you," Timmy said softly and clutched the sheet tightly at his neck.

That was when Timmy first noticed the sounds. They were faint, almost inaudible. Scratching, that's what they were. Or gnawing, like mice at the woodwork. That's probably what it was, mice.

Mice. Check it out.

Go to hell! I ain't stickin' my head under the bed!

Timmy lay back down and pulled his knees as close to his chest as he could get them. For the rest of the night, he slept curled in a tight ball in the center of his bed and Doobie slept on the floor in front of the living room heater.

Chapter Two

1

News of Jim Ingram's death was telegraphed through the party-line grape vine and a crowd had already gathered in the woods north of Georgetown before the ambulance from Hazlehurst could get there.

Sheriff Tommy Bishop had some of his men cordon off the accident scene to keep the spectators back. At first there was some pushing and shoving, the human animal trying to get a closer look, but Bishop's men, and a shotgun fired into the air, brought that shit to a halt. In all his years with the Sheriff's Department, Bishop had never been able to understand the attraction, the magnetism of an accident that drew people like flies are drawn to shit. Maybe if they had seen as much blood and guts as he had they wouldn't be in such a rush to stand and watch a man die with his intestines snaking through his fingers, or stare at a woman who had been impaled on the steering column of her car and had spent the last seconds of her life clawing desperately at the metal spear until her fingernails were peeled back from her fingers. Why did people want to watch that shit? Bishop had asked himself that question hundreds of times, but he never came up with an answer. All he knew was the more gory and gruesome the accident, the more the spectators seemed to enjoy it.

Yeah, boy, Bishop had seen more stomach turners than most of the people around him combined. Probably the worst was twelve or thirteen years ago. Some high school kids ran under the back of a flatbed semi at over a hundred miles per hour. Yes siree, *that* one drew a crowd, you can bet your ass. And then there was that car wreck the Whites had back in '73. If it hadn't been so late at night, that one would have drawn a hell of a crowd, because it had SUFFERING -- that's even better than death. But it was his role in the rescue of that poor woman and her husband that endeared him to the people of the county and won him the election when the old sheriff got killed. And that was another good one. A kid got high on acid or some shit like that and went berserk with a high-power rifle. He was hiding on top of the movie theatre and taking pot shots at cars. The then-sheriff knew the kid and was trying to talk the rifle away from him when the kid gut-shot him. The sheriff lay in the road, tried to hold his organs in with his hands, and screamed at the top of his lungs while the kid shot at anyone who tried to help. The sheriff lasted for nearly three hours, and when he stopped screaming the kid did a swan dive off the top of the building. The whole police force and all the deputy sheriffs opened fire, and the kid was turned to so much hamburger even before his head hit the pavement and splattered. Bishop himself had emptied his revolver into the flying kid, but when it was over, he didn't feel a compulsion to go over and look at the body. But the Crowd did.

Maybe we should bring back the gladiator fights.

When the ambulance arrived, Bishop was waiting at the highway. He led them as far into the woods as they could go by car.

The attendants took a stretcher and a body bag from the back of the ambulance and followed Bishop into the thick woods.

Bishop spoke to a man holding a camera. He was from the coroner's office.

"Got all the pictures you need?"

"One more." The flash flashed and the man looked up. "He's all yours."

Bishop nodded toward the little body and the ambulance attendants went to work. Jim Ingram, with only half his head attached, was zipped into the body bag and out of sight of the audience, many of whom were standing on tiptoes to get one last glimpse -- in the funeral home he wouldn't look anything like *this*.

Hey, hey! What a great show! Worth the price! Lots of blood, that's the part I liked the best! It was good for me, was it good for you?

"Fuckin'... perverts," Bishop said quietly and turned from the crowd in disgust. He walked to one side where Jim's brother Michael sat with his head buried in his hands. On either side of him was a deputy.

"You think you can talk now, Mike?"

Michael didn't answer him for a few seconds, then he nodded without looking up.

"You wanna tell me exactly what happened here?"

Michael raised his head and tried to bring the world into focus through the tears that filled his eyes. He looked backwards where the river flowed quietly by. He looked at the barbed wire fence and saw a scrap of fabric from Jim's shirt clinging to a barb. A droplet of snot formed on the end of his nose and he wiped it away with his sleeve.

"I ain't sure what happened."

"Well, let's just start at the first, okay?"

Michael nodded.

"Okay. What were you boys doin' out here?"

Michael sniffed back another droplet and wiped at his nose again. "We came out here to go huntin', but we weren't really gonna shoot anything. Just target practice. Jim said he wanted to learn so he wouldn't be afraid of guns but he didn't wanna kill anything." Michael stopped as a new wave of tears overflowed. "I'm sorry," he managed to say between broken sobs. He was trying hard to BE A MAN.

"That's okay, son. Just take your time. We got all day."

Bishop sat on the ground beside Michael and took a snuff can from the circular leather pouch that hung from his belt. The pouch had been a present from his wife so he would stop wearing big holes in the back pockets of his pants. He pulled out his lower lip with his left hand, stuffed a big pinch of the tobacco into his lip with his right thumb and forefinger, and then offered the can to Michael. Michael hesitated, but then decided that, yes, a dip was probably what he needed right now -- at least it would calm his nerves. He took a pinch and, with an expertise that even impressed an old pro like Bishop, stuffed it neatly into his lip one-handed and packed it down with his tongue.

"Thanks."

"You bet." Bishop returned the can to its pouch and waited for Michael to feel like talking again. It only took a couple of minutes.

"We went down to th' river, y'know. Shoot at logs and other shi... things that float by. I only took one box o'shells with us. I left th' others up in th' car."

"Up by th' highway?"

"Yessir."

"I only see one gun here."

"Yessir. It's mine. It's th' only one we brought."

"Okay. Then what happened?"

"Well, a coupl'a times Jim let the shotgun slide down off his shoulder and when it kicked it was on this big muscle here," he tapped the biceps of his right arm, "and that hurts like hel... hurts real bad. We still had 'bout half a box of shells left when we decided to call it quits for th' day." He dug in his pants pockets and brought out two handfuls of live shells. He looked at them and then dropped them on the ground between himself and Bishop. Then he started to sob again. "I swear I took 'em all out! I emptied that goddamn chamber before we started back up!" Michael again lowered his face into his hands and his shoulders heaved and jerked while he cried. Bishop looked away to let Michael have his cry in private.

Since the ambulance had hauled away the star of the show -- without even so much as a flash of the lights or a howl of the siren -- things had begun to get boring for the spectators. Now several of them were inching their way closer to where Bishop and Michael were sitting. Trying to hear what was going on. Getting more grist for the rumor mill. Bishop turned to his deputy.

"Billy Joe, get those bloodsuckers back. There ain't nothin' for 'em here."

"You got it."

Billy Joe strode toward the people shouting through his cupped hands. "Okay, let's break it up. Show's over. You might as well go on home and read about it in th' papers. Let's go..."

Bishop put a hand on Michael's shoulder. "You okay? Think you can go on?"

"Yessir. I'm okay." *Sniff!* Wipe. "We come up to th' fence there and Jim was complainin' 'bout how his arm was sore. I laid th' shotgun down on that big rock over there. I almost propped it up against th' fence, but I remembered how that ain't... ain't... safe. I was holdin' th' fence so Jim could go through and..."

Michael hesitated. It was only for a split second, but Bishop picked it up. It was almost as if Michael had something else that he wanted to say but thought better of it at the last minute. A split second.

"... and the gun just went off. All by itself. I think Jim didn't even know what happened. I hope not."

"Me, too." Bishop was sincere. "Listen, I sent a car to pick up your folks and they're gonna meet us at the hospital. You ready?"

"I don't know."

Bishop stood up and extended his hand to Michael. Michael took it, and Bishop pulled him to his feet. Together the two men walked to the Sheriff's car.

2

It was Saturday afternoon, and Charles was at Timmy's house when the phone call came. The two boys were discussing the possibility of building a tree house in the old Silver Leaf Maple that occupied one corner of the White's front yard. The tree was definitely sturdy enough. It very seldom lost any of its limbs when a hurricane would blow through, and it had seen quite a few of those in its lifetime. Timmy had been up that tree more times than anyone could count, and he knew where the biggest and strongest limbs were. He pointed them out to Charles as they lay on the grass with Doobie on his back between them hoping one or the other of them would scratch his belly. Of course, a tree house would have to be a summer project, but there were only two more weeks of school. If they made the plans now, they could start as soon as they were home on that last day.

"Timmy." It was his mother. She was standing in the doorway wiping her hands on her apron. She looked serious and Timmy and Charles both wondered aloud what they had done this time.

"Timmy, I need you inside. Charles, I think you'd better go on home. I think your mother wants to talk to you."

Charles looked at Timmy and they each saw fear in the other's eyes. Charles whispered, "Damn, Timmy, I know we didn't do anything *that* bad."

"Somebody thinks we did."

"Do you think they found out about us going to the gravel pit the other night?"

"Did you tell anybody?"

Charles shook his head.

Mom was getting impatient. "Timmy, right now."

"Yes, Ma'am." He sat up and rubbed the soft fur on Doobie's stomach. The dog wagged his tail twice and closed his eyes. Timmy whispered to Charles, "Well, I didn't tell either, so unless Jim did, that's not it. I'll see you later."

"Okay."

When Timmy reached the front porch, he saw that his mother had been crying. Her eyes were red and her nose was running just a little. Now he was really worried. He had never done anything to make her cry before.

She followed him into the living room and told him to sit down. She was still holding the apron, but now she was wringing it and twisting it into a tight ball. When she sat on the sofa beside her son, it was obvious that she was fighting back tears. But she lost the fight, and she buried her face in her hands and the tears flowed down her cheeks.

Timmy opened his mouth to ask, "What's the matter?" but stopped himself because he was not quite sure he wanted to hear the answer.

When she was able to control her crying, Pamela wiped her eyes on the twisted apron and folded her hands on her lap. "Timmy, I just got a call from your father. He was down at the barber shop and he heard..." The tears threatened but she fought them back again. "He heard that Jim Ingram got killed today. Jim got shot, and that's all they've heard so far. He's going to try to find out more before he comes home."

Timmy didn't know what to say. That was the last thing in the whole world he had expected to hear. He just sat there and looked dumbly at his mother.

"Did you hear me?"

"Yes, Ma'am." He looked at her.

"I called Charles's mother and told her about it. She said she'd just heard it." Pamela leaned toward Timmy and swooped her son into her arms. "Oh, baby, I'm so sorry."

Timmy felt his mother's warm tears falling onto his face. He did not resist her hugs, but he did not return them. He remained limp and let her vent her sorrow and grief. After a few minutes, he pulled away from her gently.

"I think I want to go to my room now."

She nodded, and he left her sobbing on the sofa.

For a long time, Timmy lay on his bed and stared at the ceiling. He didn't really think about anything in particular. Now and then a snatch of a song or a melody would go through his head, but it never stayed long. With his eyes he followed the seams in the sheetrock. They always looked like seams, but as long as they were taped and plastered, polite people just ignored them and pretended they weren't there. He traced these seams and counted the cracks in the paint. He watched a spider make the long trek all the way across from one corner to the other, and he watched it start its precision web building just above his closet door. And at the end of all this, when his mind finally decided to try and deal with what had happened, Timmy found that he had a hard time remembering exactly what Jim had looked like.

Why don't I cry?

Timmy blinked his eyes and there were no tears there. He sniffed, but his nose was not running. People were supposed to cry when someone they knew or loved died. That's what he had always assumed, that's what he had gathered from all the movies and from the actions of the people around him. People were supposed to break out in great sobs, the louder the better. But Timmy didn't feel choked up at all. He would never see one of his best friends again -- *never* -- and he couldn't even muster up one medium sized tear. Something must be wrong with him.

He closed his eyes and waited for his father to come home with the rest of the story.

3

It was Sunday, just a little after noon, and James Milford had no idea what the hell was going on. Like the rest of the town, he had heard about Jim Ingram and the shooting accident. Like any normal pastor would do, he had changed the topic of his morning sermon to reflect the situation. Instead of the third in the series on the devil, he pulled out one of the several that he had written, in seminary during the lectures on how to console the bereaved loved ones, on the subject of death and the afterlife. Of all of them, this one was his favorite. He called it "Ashes to Ashes." Not a very original title, but it reached a deeper emotional level than the others.

"For none of us liveth to himself, and no man dieth to himself. For whether we live, we live unto the Lord; and whether we die, we die unto the Lord: whether we live therefore or die, we are the Lord's...

"He that heareth my word, and believeth on him that sent me, hath everlasting life, and shall not come into condemnation; but is passed from death unto life...

"To the victim, death is a passing from one existence to another. But for the family and friends, death is a cold hand that reaches into the heart and squeezes and pulls without mercy...

"And in our grief, multitudes of tears are shed. But as the Apostle John wrote in his Revelation: And God shall wipe away all tears from their eyes; and there shall be no more death, neither sorrow, nor crying, neither shall there be any more pain: for the former things are passed away...

"I cannot tell you not to cry for you loved ones. I cannot tell you not to grieve for your lost friends. Take the time for mourning, but do not let the grief linger in your life. Put it away, and rejoice in the new life that your loved one has found..."

He had only used this sermon once before. It was in a small church in his hometown of Atlanta. The pastor of the church had died during the week, stroke or old age or something like that, and he had been called upon to preach the morning service the following Sunday. This was the sermon he had chosen, and by the end of it there had been an emotional atmosphere so thick that even he had shed his share of tears. And today's performance almost reached the same level as that first one.

Almost.

There was sorrow in the auditorium. That much was for sure. The sobs went unchecked. Handkerchiefs and tissues were soaked with salty tears. Entire families sat together, for a change, and they cried together. Almost all of them knew Jim Ingram, and almost all of them liked him. But even those who didn't know or like him were overwhelmed and swept up in the flow.

But there were no tears from James Milford. Not that he didn't feel the same sorrow as everyone else. On the contrary, before the service he had sat quietly in his study and gone over the entire incident in his mind until he was in the emotional state necessary for the preaching of this sermon. Everything was fine until he rose from his seat and approached the podium. Then he saw the mists, the clouds, the ghosts, or whatever they were, and his stomach started to churn.

There they were, just like on the previous two Sundays, but they weren't moving as they usually did. Instead, they hovered over a few certain individuals in the congregation. Milford looked at the faces of these people and he shivered from the base of his spine. He had never seen the people before, but even in the midst of all the grief and sorrow, these people stared up at Milford and grinned wide, horrible grins. He spent the entire sermon looking from one of these clown faces to another and clenching his hands to keep them from shaking. He consciously shifted his weight to his right foot and, even though it eventually became very uncomfortable, he kept it there. And sure enough, about half-way through the sermon, he felt an explosion of pain and his left leg went limp. This time he stayed on his feet, and when the pain hit his chest, he managed to cover it well enough. At least he made it to the end of his sermon and back into his study.

He had no idea what the hell was going on, but it was driving him crazy. He opened the bottom drawer of his desk and took out a bottle of Scotch, or an empty bottle that used to be Scotch. There was barely enough left to wet the bottom of a shot glass.

Until recently, the liquor was strictly an at-home, once-in-a-while, usually-with-Father-Francis thing. But then all the crazy shit started happening. First the scars started looking weird, and then the spooks in the church, and then the dreams.

Oh, yes. The dreams. They were a new development, and boy, they were real doozies. Faceless bodies and headless skeletons coming to life and chasing him toward the bottomless pit that burned with fire and brimstone. When he reached the edge of the pit and turned to face them, they overwhelmed him. Wherever they touched him, his skin rotted and fell off in big chunks. Finally, they lifted him above their heads (those that had heads) and they all leaped into the pit, dragging him screaming with them. It was the same dream every night, sometimes three or four times a night. A couple of times he had woken himself up screaming. It was when the dreams started, about three days ago, that he first took a bottle into his study.

He turned the bottle upside-down and stuck out his tongue under the open top to catch the few drops that trickled out. Satisfied that the soldier was indeed dead, he returned the bottle to the desk drawer and made a mental note to sneak it out to the garbage later.

Leaning over his desk, he propped his head up with his hands. He was a wreck. He had to talk to someone. He picked up the phone and dialed the number from memory.

"Francis, this is Jimmy. I... Some things..." He found it very hard to say what he wanted to say. No matter how he tried to phrase it, it sounded strange. He paused for a long time.

"Jimmy? Are you still there?"

"Yeah... Yeah, I'm still here."

"What is it?"

"Listen, it's awfully hard to talk about this on the phone and besides that, it sounds crazy. Are we still on for racquetball Tuesday?"

"Jimmy, we've never played on Tuesday. Are you all right?"

Milford held the receiver away from his ear and stared at it. What was happening to him?

ShitshitshitshitshitshitSHIT!

Of course they didn't play on Tuesday! They played on Saturdays! What could he say? How could he cover it?

"Jimmy?"

"Yeah, Francis." He tried to laugh and was convinced that it sounded fake. "What I meant was, are you busy Tuesday afternoon?"

"No, not that I know of."

"Would you mind if I came to your house? I really have some things that I need to talk out."

"Jimmy, you don't have to make an appointment to come to my house. You're always welcome, you know that. Is there something specific that I should prepare for?"

"No. Nothing specific. I just need to talk."

As Milford hung up the phone, he started to think of different ways to approach the subject when he was sitting face to face with Father Francis. It was a delicate subject, to say the least, and he was absolutely right: It sounded crazy. At least they were close friends. That would make it easier.

There was a tapping on the door and Melanie Davis stepped into the study. "Brother Milford, I noticed that you looked upset in church. Is there anything I can do to help?"

Milford looked into her face and saw the red of her eyes. She had been crying, too. Everyone had been crying except him and those damned clown faces. He didn't say anything, he just looked at her and felt the stirring of butterflies in his stomach.

"Brother Milford? Can I help? Please?"

He shook his head slowly, as if in a trance. Then he blinked his eyes and cocked his head in thought. "Maybe there is something. Now please don't take this the wrong way. I'm not trying to imply anything, but do you know where I could get a bottle of some kind of whiskey?"

Her mouth fell open and then she laughed out loud. "I didn't know what you were going to say, but that was the last thing I expected to hear."

He suddenly felt ashamed for what he had just said. "I'm sorry. I don't know what I was thinking about. It's just that it's Sunday and the liquor stores are all closed and... I'm sorry."

"No, no! Don't apologize. I just wasn't ready for that. As a matter of fact, I do know where I can get my hands on a bottle or two. What do you want it for... if you don't mind my asking?"

He felt his face flush and he looked down at the top of his desk. Melanie walked across the room until she stood beside him. He didn't look up.

"Were you going to get drunk?"

He nodded, still without looking up. She gently took his face in her hands and turned his head towards hers.

"I'll stay with you. If you're upset, you shouldn't get drunk alone."

4

The argument had started earlier at church. Timmy had wanted to sit with Charles, like he always did, but his mother and father demanded that he sit with them. It had something to do with "families should be together, and it always takes a tragedy to make people realize it." He didn't understand all the details and he didn't want to. All he wanted to do was sit with Charles in the church service. It did make him feel a little better when he saw that Charles was sitting with his parents in church. Evidently, they had demanded the same thing. Timmy couldn't help but think that the whole thing was planned. Sometimes it seemed that the parents were involved in a gigantic conspiracy against the kids in the world because all the parents demanded the same senseless things at the same time, just like they had a conference and decided "Okay, here's how we fuck with the kids today. On the count of three... One... two... three... FUCKUP!" Or maybe, when you got to be a parent, they hooked you up to a big Parent-Brain that sucked all your good brains out and filled your head with all the shit that parents come up with from out of nowhere, like "wear clean underwear in case you're in an accident and you have to go to the hospital." An oldie, but a goodie.

The argument continued through lunch and when Timmy called Charles and told him they would meet at the corner, Pamela flew into a rage. She was screaming things like, "Doesn't this family mean anything to you?" and "Don't you have any respect for the dead?" and "Maybe you should just go to your room and sit until you learn how to be a human being." The whole time, Gerald sat in his rocker and nodded his agreement. Very little of this made any sense to Timmy. Hell, it was *his* friend that got killed, not theirs. *He* was the one who played with Jim every day at school. *He* was the one who rode bicycles with Jim. *He* was the one who was with Jim when they got scared shitless at the gravel pit. Not them. But they acted like the loss was all theirs. They only knew Jim's face and Jim's name, but Timmy was Jim's pal. It was *his* loss, and he wanted to meet his other friend and sit and think about this thing. Couldn't they understand that? Hell no. That was another thing that got sucked out of your brain when you became a parent. Instead of sitting and thinking, you cried and moaned and felt guilty because you didn't appreciate or spend enough time with your own family.

After about three hours, Timmy slung his bedroom door open and announced loudly, "I'm going crazy in here!"

"If your friends don't mean any more to you than that, then get out of here!" Pamela sniffed back a tear and turned away from Timmy. "I'm just glad I don't have any friends like you."

"C'mon, Doobie." Timmy and his dog left the house with Pamela in tears and Gerald watching them from the door.

Charles was sitting alone on the street corner when they got there. He looked up when Doobie licked him on the face. "Hey, fella. How ya doin', huh?" He rubbed Doobie's head and Doobie licked him again. "I thought you weren't gonna come out today."

"So did my folks."

That was all they could find to say to each other. For the rest of the day, Charles and Timmy sat on the grass and thought and Doobie slept between them.

5

Reverend Milford cancelled the Sunday night service so that anyone who wanted to would be free to go to the funeral home. It was the first time anybody could remember not having a regular church service. It was for a good cause, bit it definitely did not go over big with the deacons. According to them, it was times like these -- times of mourning and crisis -- when the Children of God *needed* a church service. They *needed* to be in their church praying for God's mercy. Milford made the announcement at the start of the morning service and it caused quite a stir among the men on the front pew.

Monday morning in school was pretty strange. Two of the fifth-grade teachers bought cards for their classes to sign and sent them to the funeral home with a wreath. On the other hand, Jim's teacher, Lena Green, seemed unaware of the entire incident. Timmy would have thought that she didn't know about the accident if she hadn't simply omitted Jim's name from the morning roll call. She really was a cold-hearted bitch.

At recess there wasn't much play going on. There was a half-hearted game of kick ball, but other than that the kids just sat around the playground.

"I heard it wasn't no accident."

"Yeah? Who told you that shit?"

"I heard my dad say that some of the men in the barber shop

heard from one of the police that it wasn't no accident."

"That's bullshit, and you know it."

"Yeah, and if you don't shut your mouth I'll shut it for ya."

But there weren't any fights and the day trudged on.

At the shirt factory, the same rumor was going around. Gerald White heard it and shook his head. "That's a load of horseshit. I was at the barber shop and I didn't hear any of that."

"Well, you mighta been at the barber shop, but were you there all day?"

"Listen, I've known Mike Ingram for a helluva long time..."

"Yeah, me too, and I've known him to do some pretty stupid things."

And so it went all day long all over town. Nothing like a good personal tragedy to stir up some juicy gossip. The telephone lines were burning with the latest hot flashes.

When Timmy got home from school, Pamela was waiting for him. "Take a bath and get dressed. As soon as your father gets home, we're going to the funeral home."

It always amazed Timmy how long a mother could carry a grudge. She was still pissed off about yesterday and, from the way she was acting, she wasn't going to forget this one very soon. Timmy thought about this and other things as he sat in the bathtub. Lately it seemed that all he did was complain about his parents and how they didn't understand and how rotten they were to him. Maybe the old saying was true; the bad things linger in the mind much longer than the good. That was a real pity, too, because when he took the time to think about it, he remembered some very good, fun times he had with his parents. They weren't complete dorks.

He remembered trips to the zoo in Jackson, one trip in particular. It was supposed to be some kind of family outing and there were a couple of aunts and uncles and several cousins who were going with Timmy and his parents. One of the kids decided that it would be great fun to ride to the zoo in the trunk of the car. Timmy's dad thought about it for a minute or two and then rigged up a rope and a stick to hold the trunk open without letting the top fly up. It was a great trip.

He remembered water fights with his mother. It used to take the two of them hours to wash the car because they ended up fighting for control of the garden hose. "He who controls the water, controls the battle." The philosophy of a great Water Warrior.

He remembered picnics at the lake and endless games of Go-Fish. He remembered both his parents taking turns reading to him at bedtime. They started out with *Tarzan of the Apes*, one of Gerald's favorite books when he was a boy, and read a chapter every night. He was the only kid around who didn't have a strict curfew and a set time to go to bed. His parents weren't nearly as bad as he made them out to be.

"Timothy, you've been in there long enough. Hurry up. Your father's home and he has to bathe before we go."

They were just having a tiny setback right now, that's all. Nothing major.

Timmy dressed quickly and went out to wait for his parents.

"You stay in the yard. I don't want to have to go looking for you when we're ready to go."

"Yes, Ma'am. Come on, Doobie."

In the yard next door, Ma was making a feeble attempt to weed her flower beds. They were hopeless, but she was out there nearly every day. Timmy and Doobie wandered over.

"Hi, Ma. How's it going?"

"You tell me," she said without looking up.

"Not very good."

"And why not?"

"I gotta go to the funeral home."

The old woman stopped her work and forced herself to her feet. Wiping the dirt from her hands onto her apron, she looked at Timmy squarely in the eyes. "And what de matter, boy? You not wanna go?"

"No, that's not it. My folks are being weird again. They think just because Jim had that freak accident that they have to protect me now... I guess."

"It weren't no accident, boy."

"I heard that same thing, but I don't believe it."

"You hear it? Where, boy? Where did you hear?"

"I heard it at school, but there's no way Mike shot Jim on purpose."

"Mike? No, no, no, no, no. Mike have nothin' to do wid it. It weren't no accident. Dey got Jim fer a reason."

"I don't know what you're talking about."

When Timmy heard the back door slam he knew there wasn't much time left. "Who got Jim?"

Gerald called for him. "Okay, Timmy, let's go."

"Yes, sir."

"I studied de signs and de conjure board, and I know it was dem."

"Who?"

"Right now, Timmy. Let's go."

"Yes, sir."

"Listen, boy, we needs to talk. Not now. Mebbe in de next few days. Dere are tings what you gotta know, but we got no time now. You go. We talk later."

The old woman watched as Timmy and his parents drove down the street toward town. She frowned. Things were not going at all the way she had thought they would, and even the conjure board didn't seem to be working right. It wouldn't tell her what she needed to know. She probably would have never noticed it if she hadn't asked what had happened to Jim. For a long time nothing happened, the damned thing didn't even stir. Then, all of a sudden, the planchette zoomed across the board and spelled out a message so vague that it was of no use to her at all. Three times it spelled out "Jim is dead. Eat shit old bitch." It had never done anything like that before. She had made the board with her own hands when she was still in her teens. She had slept with it under her head for seven nights in a row, the last seven nights before the full moon. On the next night, the night of the full moon, she had taken off her clothes in the clearing deep in the swamp, laid the conjure board on an old cypress stump so that the light of the moon shone fully upon it, and chanted the chant of the mystics while dancing around the board. It was *her* board, and now it was calling her an old bitch.

Something was being deliberately hidden from her, that much was painfully obvious. She was almost one hundred percent sure of who was doing it; they were the ones who got Jim, but she didn't think they had enough power to affect the workings of a conjure board, especially one that was so filled with the owner's personal energy. Still, she learned something new every time she ran into them.

She watched until the Whites' car was out of sight and then she went back to weeding her flower beds.

6

The funeral home was dark, lighted only by four candles. There was one at each end of the coffin and two in the back of the room. The lovely pale blue wallpaper that must have cost a fortune was completely lost in the darkness. The red carnations and the white lilies and the countless chrysanthemums sent by friends and neighbors were only dark silhouettes casting giant shadows that leapt with every flicker of the candles. The whole room might well have been the castle cellar in some Dracula movie. The yellow glow of torchlight, the cold, forbidding silence. And in the midst of the gloom... THE COFFIN.

That was the first thing Timmy noticed when he entered the small viewing room. It was full of the darkness that evokes fear. It was a staple in every horror movie. Timmy hesitated in the doorway waiting for the scary organ music to start.

"It's perfect," Timmy muttered to himself.

"What did you say?" Pamela whispered, leaning closer to her

son.

"Nothing. I was just talking to myself." He went slowly to one corner of the room to sit and observe the people around him.

Mr. and Mrs. Fuller were in the foyer talking to Mr. Thornhill, the funeral director. The Fullers had just arrived and were in the process of signing the Guest Register -- a morbid little practice supposedly designed to give the bereaved relatives something besides an expensive granite or marble tombstone to remember their loved one's funeral by. In reality (though the bereaved relatives probably didn't think so) it was just another way to cash in on someone else's tragedy; the cost of that little memento was usually tripled and then tacked onto the rest of the funeral expenses. That's what Timmy had heard, and he heard it from someone who had a friend who knew someone... et cetera.

His own parents stopped to talk with Janet Mayfield. Draped like a rag doll over one arm, Janet held little Billy, her bouncing baby boy. And bouncing was a pretty damn good description. Both arms and legs flailed; the kid *always* flailed everything he could move at the time. His little head rolled and bobbed as if it were on a spring like one of those little toy dogs in the back window of so many cars. Hyperactive, that's what Timmy's parents had called him. In fact, that's what a *lot* of people had called him, among other things. But little Billy didn't give much of a shit about any of what they had to say. He was nine, ten, eleven months old, somewhere in there, and all he knew to be fact was A) he always got fed when he was hungry and B) he went with his mother *everywhere*. It didn't make any difference to him where they went. When she went to the grocery store, he went. When she went to the beauty parlor, he went. Tonight, she had brought him here, and that was fine. There were lots of really pretty flowers around the room, and boy, would he ever like to get down and play in them. He decided to tell his mother just that, so he opened his mouth and spoke to her in tenmontholdian. He must have spoken too loudly because Mommy clamped her hand over his mouth. But that was fine, too. He was used to it by now, so he kept talking. The words came out as a muted "mmmmmmm" from between her fingers.

Debra Hawkins was there talking in solemn whispers to several young men. Debra was now twenty-three and she still undressed in front of her open bedroom window. Some things never change.

Six more people were sitting with Jim's mom and dad. They were all crying and nodding and hugging and sympathizing and comforting.

Michael was conspicuously absent.

Michael was at home dialing the telephone.

Timmy looked to the other end of the room. The lid of the coffin was open, and after what he had heard about the accident, he was surprised that anyone would get to see Jim. He saw one couple go to the coffin and look in. The man shook his head sadly, the woman wept into her handkerchief, and they went back to their seats. Timmy knew that he had to look. Oh, no one would force him to. It would be a strictly voluntary thing, and even his mother wouldn't accuse him of being heartless for not peeking into the coffin. But Timmy would look. He *knew* he would. That was Jim in there, for

Christ's sake. *Jim!* Shit, yeah, he'd look. Once more for old time's sake. Once more for The Black Figures.

When Timmy stood, he felt his stomach do a somersault and he thought for a second that he was going to blow his groceries all over the room. He took a few deep breaths and stepped away from his seat. The folding chairs had been arranged in rows with an aisle down each side of the room and one down the middle. He didn't want to go down the middle aisle; he thought everyone would be watching him. He made his way down one of the side aisles, stopping now and then to smell the flowers that lined the walls. About ten minutes after he left his seat, Timmy found himself at the foot of the coffin. He was scared. His hands were trembling.

He looked over the edge, into the open coffin.

Jim was there, looking like he had just fallen asleep except that he wasn't wearing pajamas. Timmy relaxed a little. Either the accident wasn't as bad as he had heard, or the mortician was a helluva makeup artist. Of course, in candlelight it would be easy to hide a lot of things.

"Shit, Jim," Timmy whispered and reached out to touch his friend on the cheek. He stopped, embarrassed, before his hand could get to Jim and looked around to see if anyone had been watching. They hadn't. He looked back at Jim and, like so many others before him, shook his head. A glimmer of light reflected off the silver chain around Jim's neck. It was the crucifix.

"You poor, dumb shit. It didn't do you any good, did it? I bet you didn't get to use your silver bullet either." Timmy wondered, and then somehow knew, that the prized bullet was in one of the pockets of that navy blue suit they had dressed Jim in. After all, he never went anywhere without it.

Timmy stood there for a long time. People stepped around him to view the body and then stepped around him to go back to their seats. He just ignored them. He was having an experience that was totally new to him. He was remembering everything that he and Jim had ever done together; all the bike rides, all the campouts, all the school days. All the memories were in living color, and in them all Jim wore his navy blue suit with no shoes and socks.

In the eerie darkness of the room Timmy didn't notice the changes right away. They were subtle at first, and very slow in coming, but after several minutes Timmy saw a small red blotch on the side of Jim's face. It hadn't been there before; he was sure of it. He squinted his eyes and leaned closer to the open coffin. It was there, all right.

And it's getting bigger!

Timmy jerked his head back. "That's stupid!" he said, a little louder than he wanted to. He again looked around sheepishly and saw that several of the people in the room were now watching him. He looked down at his shoes until he knew that they had gone back to their talking and he was no longer the main attraction.

When he looked back over the edge of the coffin, his breath caught in his throat. Jim's face was caving in! The red blotch had spread to cover the whole left side, and the skin on that side was pulling away from the skull. It was actually sliding like loose mud down a hillside and white spots of bone were starting to show through. A ball of modelling clay rolled out of the eye socket -- the eyeball was probably mush out in the woods someplace. A long blackish tongue slid through a big hole in the jawbone and lay on the puddle of facial skin. When Timmy started breathing again, it was harsh and fast.

And when Jim's right eyelid fluttered and slowly started to open, Timmy screamed... and ran.

7

Michael was pacing the floor and running his hands through his hair. Tears were on his cheeks and a droplet of watery snot hung on the end of his nose. He stopped and slammed his fist into the wall. Chunks of paneling and sheetrock fell to the floor. He paced again. He stopped beside the telephone, looked in the open directory, and dialed the number. It rang twice and a man's voice said, "Hello?" Michael listened and the voice said, "Hello? Who is this?" Michael hung up the phone. He paced again.

He went to the gun cabinet and took a double-barreled twelve gauge from the rack. He took the cleaning kit and went into the den. He looked at all the trophies on the walls. There were five deer heads, there was a mountain goat head from Montana, there was an antelope head from Wyoming, there were numerous 'coon skins, and there was even a skunk skin.

Michael stared at the trophies and started to clean the shotgun.

8

Timmy stopped running at the foot of the long stairway in front of the funeral home. Most of the people in the building had followed him out, but they stayed on the front porch while Timmy's father went down to talk to his son.

Gerald put his hand on Timmy's shoulder. "You okay, sport?"

Timmy nodded. He was breathing deeply through his mouth.

"You sure?"

Timmy nodded again. Gerald turned and waved slightly to the crowd on the porch, and they went back inside to continue their mourning. Pamela remained at the top of the stairs to watch her husband and son.

"You want to talk about it?"

Timmy hesitated and then looked up at his father. "Dad, he was horrible. Did you see him?"

"No, I haven't been up to look yet."

"Don't go, Dad! Don't go! It's gross!"

"Timmy, I know he's probably not exactly the way you remember him, but it was a bad accident. I'm sure they did the best they could."

"No, Dad, it's not that! He started... falling apart!"

"Now, Timmy..."

"Honest to God, Dad! It was horrible! And then his eye started..." Timmy thought about how crazy he would have sounded if he had finished what he started to say. He shut his mouth and looked out across the parking lot.

Gerald lightly shook his son's shoulder and then patted him on the back. "Why don't we just go check it out. Okay?"

"No! I don't want to go back in there! Please!"

"You don't have to go all the way in. Just wait for me at the door. How 'bout it?"

Timmy looked at his mother waiting at the top of the stairs and wondered if this little scene was going to make her even madder at him. He looked across the parking lot again and briefly entertained the thought of trying to outrun his father. It wouldn't be that hard, if he broke away real fast...

"How 'bout it, son?"

Timmy nodded, very slightly, and turned to go up the stairs. He stopped at the open doorway and saw another couple making their way to the coffin. He wanted to shout out to them, but it was too late; they were looking in. The man shook his head sadly and the woman cried into a handkerchief and they went back to their seats. Timmy just stood at the door with his mouth open.

Gerald was on his way to the coffin. Several people stopped him to say a few words, and once Timmy read his father's lips as he said, "No, no, he's fine. Just a little" something. Timmy was getting tense. He held his arms stiffly by his sides and gathered his pants legs with his fingers. And the closer Gerald got to the Big Bad Box, the tighter Timmy wadded his pants. When Gerald looked in, Timmy sucked in a breath and held it.

Gerald looked at the body for what seemed like an eternity, and then he turned and crooked his finger at Timmy. Timmy's eyes went wide, and he shook his head with great determination. Gerald's face immediately turned to granite. He mouthed the words "come here" very slowly and very clearly and he pointed to the floor beside his feet for emphasis.

Timmy walked as normally as he possibly could because he

knew everyone was watching him this time. He stopped beside his father and stared straight ahead. Leaning down until his lips almost touched Timmy's ear, Gerald whispered, "Look."

"No!"

"He's not falling apart, Timmy. Look for yourself."

"I don't want to."

"Look, damnit!"

Timmy looked quickly, just long enough to see that, sure enough, Jim was not falling apart, and then he stared straight ahead again.

"Okay?" Gerald asked, holding Timmy's shoulder.

Timmy nodded and walked back to the door. He had decided to spend the rest of their visit sitting in the hallway by the door.

When Gerald sat beside Pamela she asked, "Are you sure that was a good idea, forcing him to look like that?"

"Hell, I don't know. He told me that he saw something horrible in that coffin, and I figured that if he didn't look in again and see his buddy in there, he would always remember whatever it was that he saw. But I've been known to be full of shit before."

"Maybe we should just go home."

"No, I think he'll be okay now."

Timmy sat beside the front door and counted the cars on the passing train. Ninety-seven... ninety-eight... caboose. A relatively short one tonight. Clouds were blowing in pretty fast. It would probably rain before he went to bed tonight. A flash of lightning (One thousand-one, one thousand-two, one thousand-three), a roll of thunder. Yeah, Timmy would be okay, but right now he wasn't worried about himself.

"Mr. Thornhill, do you have a telephone I can borrow?"

"Yes, I do. Right behind the desk there."

"Thanks."

"Sure thing. Are you okay? You know, you gave us quite a scare."

Timmy was dialing the number from memory. "Yes, sir. I'm fine."

Mr. Thornhill wandered back into the viewing room as Timmy began talking.

"Is Charles there?" There was a long pause. "Charles? This is Timmy. When are you coming to the funeral home? Listen, when you get here, don't look in the coffin. I can't tell you now; I'll explain it all later. Just don't look in the coffin."

He felt some better as he hung up the phone. He had warned his friend.

But of course, Charles would look. He wouldn't see what Timmy saw, but he would look.

9

Ma sat at the table with Captain Jack beside her. In front of them was the conjure board.

"What happent to Jim?" she asked, and waited for the slow spelling-out process.

Jim is dead. Eat shit old bitch.

"Is it dem what got Jim?"

Jim is dead. Eat shit old bitch.

"Are dey done yet?"

Fuck you fuck you fuck you

"Who dey be after now?"

Fuck the gun bitch

"Dey after Timmy?"

Fuck you fuck you fuck you

"Are dey ready for a fight?"

The planchette stopped dead still. For a full minute, nothing happened. Then, as if an earthquake struck suddenly, the table began to shake and the planchette flew across the room. It was followed by the conjure board. As soon as the board hit the floor, the shaking stopped, and the room was quiet.

"Dey be ready, Jack-boy. Are we?"

10

Cleaning the gun had a calming effect on Michael. He no longer paced the floor but sat quietly on the sofa and pushed the cleaning rod slowly through the long barrel. Once in a while, he would stop the cleaning and stare for minutes at a time at one or another of the animal trophies on the wall.

Michael picked up the telephone and dialed the number again. He had done it so many times in the last couple of hours that he almost had it memorized. He had the 892; that's what all numbers in Crystal Springs began with. The next three numbers he got, but it was the 8 at the end that gave him trouble. He kept wanting to dial a 6 for some unknown reason. His call was answered on the third ring.

"Hello?"

Michael just sat there staring into the colored-glass eyes of one of the deer.

"Hello? Is anybody there?" The voice on the other end of the line was starting to sound agitated.

Michael looked at the receiver.

"Okay, whoever this is, I'm getting more than a little tired of this game. Either talk to me or let me eat my supper."

Michael broke his silence. "Hello, Brother Milford."

"Who is this?"

"It's me. Mike."

"Mike Ingram?"

"Yessir."

There was a long pause.

"Are you the one who's been calling me all night?" Milford asked, trying to keep Michael talking.

"Maybe. I mean, I think so. I'm not real sure." Michael pinched the receiver between his cheek and his shoulder and stretched the cord all the way to the gun cabinet. He put the cleaning kit back on its shelf and took two shotgun shells from the little drawer underneath. "See, I wadn't feelin' so good, so I found some of my Mom's pills -- muscle relaxers I think she calls 'em -- and I took me about four of 'em. I wadn't real sure what they was supposed to do, but boy, I sure found out in a hurry. I bet I've walked a hunderd miles around the room tryin' t'stay awake." Michael pushed a shell into each barrel of the shotgun and snapped it closed.

Milford didn't know how to react to what he had just heard. Four pills were hardly enough to consider as a suicide attempt, but he had been told about people who lost count and really didn't know how many pills they had taken. Maybe he should just take it one step at a time.

"Mike, are you sure you only took four pills?"

"I don't know. I think so. But I don't give a sh... I don't care none about that." Michael started to laugh and it made Milford feel like cold fingers had clamped around his throat. "Brother Milford, do you know what it feels like to kill somebody?"

"No, Mike." Milford couldn't bring himself to tell Michael the truth. "No, I don't."

"Yeah, well, neither do I. But there's some folks around town who think I do. You know that?"

"I don't know what you're talking about, Mike." Another lie. He had heard the rumors just like damn near everybody else in town. "Listen, Mike, I really need to find out some things. Do you have the bottle those pills were in?"

"It's around here someplace."

"Can you get it and tell me what kind of pills those were?"

"I guess so, but why do... Oh, shit! I know what you're doin'! Well I ain't killin' myself with no fuckin' pills! I ain't that much of a pussy, just like I ain't no murderer. I ain't no murderer!" Michael started to cry. "I ain't no murderer, damnit."

"Nobody said you were."

"Bullshit! It's all over fuckin' town! I hear 'em whisperin' when I go by, and I heard what they was sayin'. 'There he goes, the fuckin' kid killer.' Well I didn't do nothin'!"

"Mike, are you alone?"

"Yeah, I'm alone. Mom and Dad are down at the funeral home an' they didn't want no kid killer taggin' along with 'em."

"Michael, stop it."

"No, *you* stop it! Just stop it and listen t'me! I seen Jim get shot, you know that? I was right there an' I seen th' gun go off. I seen the whole side o'his face just... just blow up. A piece o'his skull bounced off my chin. Part o'his brains hit me right in th' face. Did anybody tell ya that? It was just like in slow motion. I even got t'see what pulled the trigger."

"Michael..."

"I didn't really see all of it, just a arm. I think it was a arm. It was kinda green and bony and it just picked up that shotgun and pulled th' trigger."

"Michael, let me call somebody who can help you."

Michael didn't hear him. Michael was beyond hearing anybody.

"I just stood there lookin' at that thing while it pointed th' shotgun at me. Then I heard this voice -- I didn't see no face, but I heard a voice -- an' it said, 'You're next, asshole,' an' then it pulled the trigger. Th' gun was empty, I guess. It just clicked. Then th' gun fell an' th thing just disappeared. I was scared shitless, but that's not th' kind o'thing ya tell th' sheriff when he comes around askin' questions. No, sir, then they'd haul me off to th' funny farm. Well, I ain't gonna let that happen. An' you know somethin'? I think that thing meant what it said. I think it's gonna come after me. An' I ain't gonna let that happen either."

There were two distinct clicks as Michael cocked both of the shotgun's hammers.

"You gotta tell 'em for me, Brother Milford."

"Michael, what are you doing?"

"I ain't waitin' around here for that little green fucker to come get me."

"Michael, answer me!"

"If it wants me, it's gotta chase me to hell. But you tell 'em for me, okay? You tell 'em..."

"Listen to me..."

"You tell 'em I ain't crazy..."

"Mike, wait..."

"An' you tell 'em I ain't no kid killer..."

"Oh, my dear God, don't..."

"You make sure they know."

"Mike, noooo!"

Michael put the twin barrels into his mouth and pulled both triggers at once.

The blast sounded like it was right beside Milford's ear. He held the phone receiver at arm's length and stared at it like it was some kind of snake about to attack him. He was shaking his head and moving his mouth but there was no sound coming from between his lips. His throat became suddenly very dry. He slowly hung up the phone and sat staring at the wall. Finally, with huge tears welling in his eyes, he dialed the emergency number and asked for an ambulance.

11

Milford got to the Ingram house at about the same time as the police. He went in with them and saw the mess. Blood. Blood everywhere. He went back outside and sat on the front porch and cried into his hands.

After the ambulance had gone with the body, one of the officers sat beside Milford and started asking him questions about Mike. The officer noticed the faint smell of whiskey on the preacher's breath.

12

"Dearly beloved, we are gathered here to pay our last respects to James Ingram, a young soul who now rests in eternal peace with God."

News of last night's tragic suicide had spread through town like an out-of-control brush fire. It took everyone completely by surprise. When the chief of police went to the funeral home to break the news to the Ingrams, Mrs. Ingram fainted dead away and Mr. Ingram ran out of the building screaming. He ran all the way home calling Michael's name between sobs. When he reached the house, Reverend Milford was sitting on the porch steps. He grabbed Mr. Ingram's arm as he ran by.

"Don't go in there. Please."

Mr. Ingram jerked away from Milford and rushed through the front door. A moment later he came back out of the house and sat beside Milford. He looked at the preacher and wiped at his tears with his shirt sleeve. "Why?" he asked, and then he put his head on Milford's shoulder and cried. Milford spent the rest of the night trying to comfort the Ingrams, but what is there to say to a mother and father who just lost all their children?

The townspeople had some very mixed reactions to Mike's death. Some said it was a shame and had the same feeling that Milford had. Others said it was good riddance and it saved the taxpayers the cost of a murder trial. Some people could be pretty damned cold blooded at times.

Michael's death wasn't the only news that spread quickly. Milford's whiskey breath raised quite a few eyebrows around town.

Now Milford was conducting the graveside service, and he was well aware that many of the people there were looking at him instead of the flower-laden coffin. It was only ten o'clock in the morning and he already looked hammered. He had already gone about twenty-eight hours without sleep, and it would probably be several more hours before he saw his bed again. Then he had to make another visit to the funeral home tonight to again express his condolences to the Ingrams. And there was Michael's funeral tomorrow morning.

"As much as our hearts grieve for this departed child, we must console ourselves for he is in a new world of peace and love. He is sitting at the very footstool of our Lord, Jesus Christ."

The Ingrams had a lot of friends, and all of them were there for the funeral. There were relatives from out of town and employees from the grocery store where Jim's father worked. All three of the fifth-grade classes were dismissed for the funeral (but it took a direct order from the principal before Lena Green would let her class out). All in all, there were probably three hundred people at the cemetery to see Jim off.

Charles and Timmy were there with their parents. They had managed to get near the front of the crowd so they could see the coffin... and Brother Milford. They glanced at each other occasionally and finally nodded, ever so slightly, so that only they could tell the secret.

"Let us pray. Our Father, we offer now the mortal remains of our brother, James Ingram, back to the ground from whence he came. Hold his soul in Thy hand until the time when Thou shalt come again, and he shall come at Thy right side. For we ask it in the name of the Father and of the Son and of the Holy Spirit. Amen."

Slowly the crowd began to disperse. Milford stayed at the head of the grave; he would stay there until all the spectators were gone. He would offer another word of comfort to the parents before they left. Then he would say a private blessing over the coffin before giving the order for burial. Not all the ministers he knew did that, it was just one of his own personal quirks.

Timmy made his way to Charles as they were carried along by the flow of the people. He grabbed Charles' coat and whispered, "You weren't lyin' to me, were you? Did you really look in the coffin?"

"Yeah, I looked."

"And you didn't see anything... strange?"

"Nothin'. Now will you tell me what it's all about?"

"Naw, I guess it doesn't matter. What did you think about

Brother Milford?"

"You were right. He looks like hell."

"I think we ought to do it, you know what we talked about."

"When?"

"Today. After school."

Charles felt a wave of panic rush through him. "Not after dark!"

"Shit, no! Right after school."

They were interrupted by a woman's high-pitched scream. They turned to see Reverend Milford holding both of Mrs. Ingram's hands. She was crying and shaking her head. Then, all of a sudden, she was silent and limp in her husband's arms. Her husband picked her up and carried her away from the grave site.

"Damn, she's taking this pretty bad." Timmy turned back to Charles and caught him wiping his eyes with his fists. Charles was embarrassed, but Timmy looked down at his feet to show Charles that he didn't really mean to see him. "So, are you with me?"

"Yeah, I'm with you."

"Good. Meet me out front as soon as school's out."

The two boys split up to find their parents. As they left the cemetery, they both saw Milford at the grave with his head bowed. And they felt sorry for him.

13

He didn't have one particular blessing to say at the grave site. Each one was different from any other, just as different as all the people under the granite markers. He never planned his private blessing ahead of time; he just stood at the grave and said what was in his heart. It was never easy, and it was always harder when the body in the coffin was that of a child.

He stood very still and listened to the low rumble of thunder from the approaching storm. The rain of last night had stopped just in time for the funeral today, but there would be more rain in just a little while. Was this supposed to be an omen of some kind? He didn't care. He would welcome the rain. It matched the way he felt lately.

He tossed his Bible onto one of the folding chairs where the family had been during the service. Then, with his hands stuffed deep in his pockets, he walked around and around the grave. He had never done that before, and he didn't know why he did it today. But not only did he walk, he *counted.* Seven times he went around the grave, just like some ancient religious ritual. Just like when "Joshua fit de battle ob Jericho."

Well, how 'bout it, Josh, old boy. Are the walls gonna come tumblin' down this time, too?"

"Nope, I think this wall's just a little too... permanent."

Then maybe you should give your old cow horn a toot, just like in the Good Book.

The Good Book. The Ritual. Even though it was a spur of the moment thing, Milford found that there was some comfort, some feeling of security in following that ritual. Maybe that's why Francis enjoyed being a priest, for the rituals. He would have to remember to ask Francis about that.

Somewhere in the distance a bolt of lightning struck a

transformer and it exploded in a shower of sparks. By the time the sound reached the cemetery, it was nothing more than a small *pop!*, like a tiny Fourth of July firecracker. That small *pop!* probably plunged a third of the town into a midmorning blackout. Milford chuckled. He remembered hearing once about a power failure in a big department store and how one woman went into a panic because she was trapped on the escalator. He shook his head and chuckled again, but the humor didn't last very long. He had some serious business to carry out, and he was only running on two of his four cylinders. The lack of sleep was catching up with him. He needed a drink.

Milford took his hands out of his pockets and clasped them in front of him. He looked up at the dark clouds.

"God, I've only known Jim for just a short time, but he seemed to be a nice boy. He had a lot of friends; we saw that today. That must say something about him. I would recommend that Jim be welcomed into Heaven with open arms."

There was a rumble of thunder from the depths of the clouds. Milford felt the tears welling in his eyes.

"But You don't give a damn what I recommend, do You? You don't give a damn because You aren't listening to me. You stopped listening to me weeks ago, didn't You? Why? What the hell did I ever do to deserve that? Huh?"

He let his arms drop to his sides. The clouds stirred and rolled above him, and he just stared at them, past them. "Are You listening to me?" he shouted as loudly as he could.

Tears ran down his cheeks and he dragged the back of his hand across his eyes.

"Will You please listen to me," he shouted to the sky. "Please. It hurts and I don't know what to do. Jim's dead and he was so young. And Michael's dead. And I'm losing my mind. Why won't You help me?"

Thunder and lightning were almost simultaneous now and the first drops of rain fell on Milford's upturned face.

"They were so young, God. Why did You take them? Huh? Why? Why couldn't You take me instead?"

Milford fell to his knees in the mud that would later fill the grave. His hands were fists pressed against the sides of his head. He was sobbing now and crying out to God.

"Why couldn't You take me?"

Fifteen minutes went by, and Milford finally pulled himself up out of the mud. He was breathing heavily. Fatigue caused every movement to be a major exertion. Slowly, he made his way back to the seats and retrieved his Bible. He nodded to the two men who were waiting to fill the grave and then he walked toward his car, the only one left at the funeral site.

When Father Francis answered the knock on his door, he was wiping his mouth with a napkin. "Good God Almighty, Jimmy! What happened to you?"

Milford stood with his shoulders hunched forward and his head leaning to the right. His black suit was soaked and there was mud all the way up to his thighs. Francis took Milford by the arm and led him into the house. "You look like somebody tried to beat you to death."

"Does it show that bad?" Milford said and tried to smile.

"Don't start that crap. Are you okay?"

"Yeah. Yeah, I'm fine." There was a long silence. Milford looked at Francis and knew right away that he wasn't buying any of that. "Well, actually, no, I'm not doing so good. That's why I wanted to talk to you."

"Well, come on in and sit down."

Milford saw the napkin in Francis' hand and the plate on the table. "Are you eating? I don't want to interrupt your dinner."

"It can wait. Sit down."

"I can't get mud all over..."

"Will you just sit down before I knock you down!"

Milford sat on the edge of the sofa being very careful not to let his muddy legs touch anything. He closed his eyes and let a sigh escape from deep in his throat. It felt good to sit down.

Francis was watching him closely. This was not the Jimmy Milford he knew and loved. "Do you want some coffee?"

"Yeah, that'd be nice."

From the kitchen, Francis could see Milford's lips moving. He was talking to himself. Every few seconds, Milford's lips would twitch and he would jerk his hand up toward his face as if to cover the twitch. *Maybe the rumors are true*, Francis thought, and he brought the coffee pot into the living room. "Now, what's the problem here?"

"Damn, Francis, I wish I knew. A lot of things have been going on... going *wrong* lately. I don't know where to start to tell you all of it."

"Then let me start. Have you been drinking?"

"Today? Not a drop... not since breakfast, anyway. Why?"

"I haven't seen it myself, but I heard you've been drinking quite a bit lately."

Milford laughed and shook his head. "My, my. Good news sure travels fast around here. The rumor mills must be working overtime."

"Maybe so, but you're my friend and I want to help you. Is it true?"

Milford looked down into the coffee cup he held tightly in both hands. He nodded slightly and then said, "Yeah, I guess it is. But I think I've had some pretty damn good reasons."

"Like what?"

"Like a kid named Michael. You know that kid who killed himself last night? Well, I heard it happen. He was talking to me on the phone and then he blew his brains out while I was sitting there yelling for him not to do it. Isn't that a hoot? I thought I could stop him over the telephone."

"There wasn't much else you could do."

"Sure there was. I could have told him the truth."

Milford sucked the hot coffee through his pursed lips. It burned, and he welcomed the pain as some sort of deserved punishment. He swallowed and felt the heat drop into his stomach.

A dramatist couldn't have done a better job of placing this pause. A "pregnant pause" they call it in the business. A pause so full... so *pregnant* with mystery or with suspense or with fear or with anger or with any of the hundreds of emotions... so full that it *must* give birth to a continuation. It is used to grab an audience, to get their full attention focused on that eerie silence, and then to drag that audience kicking and screaming if necessary, right on through to the end of the story. Francis was hooked. Milford probably wasn't even aware of what he was doing, but Francis was ready to hang on to every word that came next. But the silence dragged on and on and Milford just sat and stared at the floor and took two more long sips of his coffee. Finally, when Francis couldn't stand it any longer and opened his mouth to ask what the hell that meant, Milford continued.

"He asked me, sometime during that phone call, if I knew what it felt like to kill somebody, and I lied to him."

"You told him yes? Jimmy, why the hell did you d..."

"I told him no."

Francis felt his mouth falling open but was helpless to stop it. This pause was mercifully short.

"I didn't have guts enough to tell him yeah, I've killed a man, I squashed his skull with a sledgehammer, and it shook me up so bad that I felt like somebody was ripping my insides out and I spent the next five years wishing to God that I had died in the ambulance on the way to the hospital. Yep, if I had had the guts to tell him that, maybe I could've talked him out of doing what he did."

"You never told me you killed a man."

"It's not the kind of thing I like to brag about."

"You want to tell me about it? Maybe it'll help to talk."

Milford looked up and stared into his friend's eyes. "Shouldn't we be in the confessional or something?"

Francis smiled. "This'll do."

"It was my boss, a long time ago. He had a gun and I had a dog that only lasted through one bullet."

"That's where you got your war wound, huh?"

"Yep. One in the leg, and one to match it right here." He tapped his chest. "Did you know people were accusing him of killing his little brother?"

"Who?"

"Michael. And if I had told him what I just told you, maybe it would have helped."

"But you didn't tell him, so you started drinking. That explains last night, but what about before that?"

"Before that? Before that the preacher started going crazy." And Milford spent the next half hour describing in detail the mists in the church and the grinning idiots and the pain and the giggling. He placed his cup on the coffee table and stared at it the whole time. He would squeeze his hands together tightly and then he would rub them on his legs. He would crack his knuckles and then he would bite at his fingernails. It was hard for him to be telling this, even to his closest friend. But he kept on. He told about sneaking bottles into his desk drawer and he even slipped in the story of getting drunk with Melanie (but, of course, he didn't mention her name). And through it all, Francis sat sipping occasionally from his coffee cup but never taking his eyes off Milford.

"And that's about all there is." Milford took a deep breath and let it out slowly through his mouth. There was silence... a very long silence. When Milford looked up, Francis was still watching him. "Well, what do you think?"

Francis set his coffee cup down and refilled it. He put in the three teaspoons of sugar and the generous amount of milk and stirred the mixture slowly. "A psychiatrist would probably say that you're suffering from hallucinations brought on by anxiety and a feeling of inadequacy in your role as religious leader since the hallucinations only occur while you're in the pulpit."

"And what do you think about that?"

"I think that's all horseshit." There was another long silence. "I think I know what the problem is, but it's going to sound kind of strange."

"Stranger than what I just told you?"

"Well, maybe it won't sound that strange. Let me ask you a question. Has your church ever been consecrated?"

Milford shrugged. "I don't know. I'm sure there was a big dedication ceremony when it was first built."

"No, that's not the same thing. Do the Baptists have some kind of... some special ritual for consecrating a church or for reconciling a church that's been desecrated?"

"I don't understand."

"Okay, let me see if I can explain this. I think it's possible that something has defiled your sanctuary, like kids sneaking in and screwing in the baptistry or something like that. The evil deed, whatever it is, is manifesting itself where it can do the most good, or harm, depending on your point of view. It is distracting the leader of the congregation and making him less effective."

"That's an understatement."

"If a church has never been consecrated, it's just that much easier for the evil to take hold. A Catholic church can't be used until it's been consecrated."

"Do it for me."

This caught Francis off guard, and he choked on his coffee. "Now, wait just a minute. I only wanted to find out what kind of ceremonies you Baptists used and suggest you go to the head of the Church to get it resolved."

"But we don't have anything like that. And if I went to anybody else, they'd probably lock me away. You've got to help me."

"I can't do that kind of thing. I can't even bless the holy water to do that ceremony."

"Why not?"

"Only a bishop can do those things."

"Says who?"

"The Code of Canon Law, that's who."

"Canon Law? But we're talking about a Baptist church, not a Catholic church, so Canon Law doesn't apply."

"Don't start playing logic games with me, Jimmy. It won't work. I can't do it. I'm a priest, for Christ's sake! I can't go into a Baptist church and start going through a consecration ceremony."

"Not even to preserve a fellow minister's sanity?"

"Oh, yeah, that's great, Jimmy. Go straight for the heart. You have no scruples, you know that?"

"Will you do it?"

"If you don't have somebody higher in the Baptist Church you can go to, you should do it yourself."

"There's not anybody else. And I don't know the ritual, but you do."

"But I'm not a bishop."

"So what? Does that mean your prayers don't get answered?"

"Shit, that's not the point. The ceremony's in the Roman Ritual and that's sacred stuff."

"Sacred to who? To you? Great. Well, my church was sacred to me, too, and now I'm about to lose it."

"Damnit, Jimmy, you really put me on the spot."

"Please, Francis. I need your help."

Francis put his coffee cup down and, with his elbows on his knees, leaned forward until his face was only a few inches away from Milford's. "Why, Jimmy?"

"What?"

"Why me? Why do you want me there, really?"

Milford reached out and took both of Francis' hands in his own. "Because I'm afraid to go back into that church alone."

For a long minute, the two men of God looked into each other's eyes; one was searching desperately for a glimmer of hope to hang on to, and the other was trying to reconcile in his mind the mixture of two totally different dogmas. Finally, Francis leaned back in his chair and covered his face with his hands.

"How do I get myself into these things? I'm gonna be excommunicated. I know it. I just know it."

"Will you help?"

"I refuse to use the Roman Ritual."

"I don't care. Make something up."

"Okay, okay. Just don't tell anybody. This could cause some big trouble for at least one of us."

"I understand. When can we do it? Right now?"

"No, no, no! There're a lot of things I have to do to get ready. And I have to make up a ritual. Why don't you go on home and get cleaned up? I'll come over about six or so and we'll start."

Milford leaned back on the sofa, took a deep breath and closed his eyes. For just a second, he thought about not opening his eyes and just waiting right there for Francis. Francis could wake him up when he was ready to go. Then he felt his suit, still wet, sticking to his skin and he forced his eyes open. When he stood, his knees popped loudly. He stretched and felt his neck and back crack in several spots.

"Maybe you should take a nap before I get there," Francis suggested as he walked Milford to the door.

"No. If I go to sleep now, you'll never get me awake. I can make it." As he stepped out the front door, Milford turned to Francis. "There's no way you can know how much this means to me."

Francis smiled and winked. "You own me one."

A frown came to Francis' face and his brow pulled together forming deep furrows in his forehead. As he watched Milford walk to the car, Francis couldn't help having an uneasy feeling about the whole mess. He wasn't real sure how God would feel about his inventing a new ritual for purifying a Baptist church. Even though there was nothing specific that he knew of in the Canon Law to forbid what he was doing, it just felt like the whole thing was bordering on sacrilege. But how could it be? His friend was in trouble, and that friend had dedicated his life to serving God just like Francis had. How could it be wrong to help? Was the barrier between religions so great that it couldn't be crossed to benefit a friend, a brother? What would have happened if Christ had felt that way?

When Milford drove away, Francis went into his bedroom to pray before preparing for the evening.

14

After school, Timmy and Charles climbed onto their bicycles and rode all the way through town. They went the long way around so that they wouldn't have to pass either of their houses. They flew past their corner and the old oak tree. They were headed east, toward the gravel pit.

In the daylight, Charles wasn't afraid of the gravel pit; it was nothing but a big hole in the ground. But at night, he knew there was something out there just waiting for him to screw up and be alone, even for just a second. He had mentioned this to Timmy once, and Timmy said that was horse shit because he had been out in the gravel pit alone a lot of times and there was nothing out there but rocks, sand, and rusty old machinery. That might be true, but he knew for a fact that Timmy slept under the covers every night, including the hottest night of the summer. Everybody has his own quirks.

They left their bicycles on the dirt road where the cars had stopped on the night of the ceremony. The two boys stood at the edge of the road and looked first at the clump of trees and then at each other.

Charles felt his throat go dry. He wasn't afraid of the gravel pit, but *this* was a little different. "Are you sure this is a good idea?"

"I don't know, but it's all I can think of to do."

"You really think they did something to Jim?"

"I don't know, but if they did, I want to let them know that they didn't get away with it."

"But that's stupid! What if they find out it's us?"

"They won't... unless one of us tells somebody else."

"Well, don't look at me!"

Timmy knew he could trust Charles to keep his mouth shut. Charles was scared shitless. Of course, so was Timmy but he would never admit that to anyone. He knew there was a definite possibility that the witches would find out who was there today. After all, how had they found out that Jim had been there that night watching the offering? For all he knew, the witches could be hiding in the bushes right now spying on them the way they had spied on the ceremony. Hell, maybe the witches already *knew* who it was and were just playing a little waiting game. If that were the case, then the boys had nothing to lose.

Picking their way carefully through the brush, they found the paths leading into the clearing. Charles reached out and took hold of Timmy's shirt tail.

Everything was still just the way it had been abandoned that night. Altar, gold bowl, black candles burned completely down to the holder, and two charred spots on the ground. The fires had evidently burned themselves out without spreading. There was no way the afternoon sun could penetrate the thickness of the grove. The shadows added a sinister dimension to the already frightening stillness and silence of the clearing.

Neither of the two boys knew how long they stood and stared at the meeting place, but when Timmy felt a cold shiver start at the base of his spine and shoot straight up his back, he suddenly wanted this to all be over.

"Let's do it."

They approached the altar quickly but cautiously, never taking their eyes off the old orange crate. They weren't so sure that it wouldn't just jump right out and grab them and they would never be seen or heard from again. Timmy kicked it and jerked away. Nothing happened. He kicked it again.

"I think it's okay. Let's go."

Each of the boys picked up one end of the crate and they hauled it, gold bowl and candlesticks and all, out of the center of the clearing.

"What're we gonna do with it?"

Timmy thought for a second. "Out the back. It drops off back there."

On the opposite side of the clearing, they had to make their own path. There was nothing but trees and vines and thick bushes. Timmy was walking backwards forcing his way through.

"Be careful, Timmy. Don't step off the edge."

And Timmy was careful. About two feet from where they broke out of the thicket, the ground dropped away. Without even pausing to look over the edge, they swung the crate back and forth toward the cliff.

"One, two, THREE!"

They let go and the altar sailed out into the gravel pit. Melted wax glued the candlesticks onto the top of the crate, but the golden bowl flipped off neatly and took its own path to the bottom. It took several seconds for them to hear the wood splintering on the rocks below. It was gone. Maybe that would end it all.

Satisfied that they had done the right thing, Timmy and Charles turned to go. From somewhere deep in the caves and sand mountains of the gravel pit came the low howling of a dog. The sorrowful moan echoed off the walls of the pit and seemed to come from all sides. Timmy and Charles stopped only long enough to look at the expression of horror on one another's faces.

15

The sun had disappeared, and the dim light of dusk was fading to darkness before Father Francis decided that he was as ready as he would ever be. He felt very uncomfortable with the whole idea of what was about to happen. The consecration of a church was serious stuff, not something to be taken lightly.

He shook his head. No, that's not what was bothering him. Neither one of them were taking this lightly, certainly not Francis and from the way Jimmy Milford looked a few hours ago, it was possible that he was even more serious than the priest. He couldn't really put his finger on what bothered him about the whole thing. It seemed to be a collection of things, fears and excuses and cold steel fingers clamping tightly on his guts.

This is a bishop's job. What am I doing? I'm not qualified to do this kind of thing yet. I can't even bless the water for ritual. Ritual, ha! I must have some really big balls to think I can make up my own sacred rituals.

He shivered, closed his eyes, and let go a long deep sigh. His stomach churned and the low rumbling noises reminded him that he hadn't eaten yet. He had only eaten half of his lunch when Milford came calling, and after their conversation the rest of his lunch had been forgotten. But he told himself that was all right. He would eat a good dinner after they finished their night's work. Besides, a little fasting before the proceedings was probably in order.

But what if I'm wrong? What if it's not the consecration at all? What if it's something more serious? What if Jimmy Milford has taken a swan dive off the deep end?

Francis closed his Bible and stared at it for a long time. An intricate pattern of wrinkles, some of them worn smooth from use, fanned out over the *Genuine Cowhide* cover. On the front, the big gold letters of Holy Bible were fading. The gold on the edges of the pages was nearly gone, rubbed off by more than fifteen years of flipping through with his thumb. The thin satin bookmark sewn into the binding had started to fray on the loose end. A small rip had started along the binding and it wouldn't be long before the whole front cover would fall off in his hands. Soon it would outlive its usefulness, and another would replace it. Curiously prophetic? Possibly.

On the table was a short stack of notebook paper, the fruits of Father Francis's afternoon and evening labors. A great new addition to the Vatican library. The new Catholic ritual for consecrating a Baptist (or Methodist or Presbyterian) church. Boy, those Catholics can do anything, can't they?

Francis took the last page of the stack and paused with his pen over the paper. Then he added one more *In nominee Patris, et Filii, et Spiritus Sancti. Amen.* and put the page back in its place.

About that time his mind started to rationalize the whole situation. Jimmy was sick. *That's it. Jimmy's sick and he's tired and he's scared and he needs my help. If I can ease his mind by going through a simple ritual, what harm can it do? Right, God? I'm just helping out a friend. Christ would have done the same thing in my place, right, God? Sure He would. That settles it, right, God? Right.*

On the table with the ritual were the other implements Francis had gathered for the consecration. Small jars held the specially blessed Holy Water and Holy Oil which were, until a couple of hours ago, plain tap water and pure virgin olive oil. An ivory rosary rested beside a larger silver crucifix. A copy of the Roman Ritual (just in case) lay on top of two long pieces of purple silk he had purchased at the local fabric store. Francis put his battered Bible with these other things and then turned his attention to the leather case at the opposite end of the table. He had debated long and hard about taking the case and the debate was not over. Inside the case were two pieces of linen and the pyx which held the thin wafer of the Holy Eucharist. Now he really was bordering on sacrilege and blasphemy and anything else the bishop could possibly come up with. Even though he planned to use it only in the most extreme emergency, Canon Law was very explicit in forbidding a priest to share the Eucharist with a minister of any church which was not approved by the Catholic Church. And, let's face it, that definitely did not include the Baptist church. Was his friend worth the risk? That was a pretty stupid question considering how deeply he had already committed himself. Maybe he could compromise.

In the refrigerator were three or four flour tortillas, the remains of a not-too-distant dinner. He took two of the tortillas and wrapped them in a blue cotton napkin. They should work, at least as well as his bogus ritual. The pyx would stay at home.

With a heart full of mixed emotions, Francis unscrewed the lid from the jar of Holy Oil. He crossed himself and read briefly from the first page of his ritual. Very carefully he dipped just the tip of his right thumb into the oil. For just a moment he looked at his thumb and watched the drop of oil run down toward his wrist. Closing his eyes, he touched his thumb to the center of his forehead and drew it straight down to the tip of his nose, and then made another line across his forehead from left to right. He felt tiny drops from the oil cross begin to slide on his face.

"*In nominee Patris, et Filii, et Spiritus Sancti…*"

He swallowed hard.

"God our Father, I come to cleanse and purify and dedicate my spirit to the work which must follow."

He looked at his paper again. It was going to be a long night.

16

Timmy was still shaking when he got home. He let his bicycle fall to the ground and just stood there for a minute taking deep breaths and waiting for his heartbeat to slow to a normal pace. He heard the shouting before he even started up the steps to the front door. They were doing it again. There was no telling what started this one. It could have been anything. Timmy shook his head, amazed that not even a funeral could make them be nice to each other. One thing was for sure; after what he had been through in the last few days, the last thing he wanted to do was sit and listen to his mother and father hack away at each other.

As he walked away from his own house toward the certain shelter of Ma's next door, he was met by Doobie running around from the back yard and wagging his tail. With two fingers, Timmy scratched his faithful companion on top of the head and together they crossed the yard. At Ma's front door, he knocked and then heard Jack invite them in.

"Do you mind if I stay over here for a little while? I don't feel much like going home right now."

Ma was sitting at the table staring at the conjure board. She looked as if she hadn't slept for days. The wrinkled skin of her face was showing more than the normal signs of wear. Jack was on the table beside the board doing his familiar sidestep.

"Sure, Timmy boy. C'mon in."

There was none of the old friendliness in her voice. A slow, weary monotone was all she could muster. Doobie followed Timmy to the table and raised his muzzle to sniff the air around Captain Jack. In return, Jack lowered his head and cocked it sideways to get a good look at the dog. He spread his wings and flapped them once. Then he pulled his wings back in close and Doobie lay on the floor under the table. These two were good friends, almost as close as Timmy and Ma.

"You weren't at Jim's funeral." His comment was not a question but a mere statement of what they obviously both knew. Just a way to start the conversation.

"No."

"I wish I hadn't been there. I mean, I wish there hadn't been a funeral."

"I know, boy. Me, too."

Ma never looked up from the board in front of her. There was a look in her eyes that Timmy couldn't remember ever seeing there before. It wasn't the same tired look that the rest of her face showed. This was the look of hurt and concern. The look of someone who was deeply worried about something. The look of someone who had been betrayed by their best friend. Timmy saw this but didn't understand what he was seeing. He reached out to touch the old woman's hand, and Jack lowered his great beak to be within striking distance if the touch looked the least bit threatening. They were friends, but…

"Ma? Are you okay?"

She looked at Timmy and smiled a small smile, but it wasn't a happy smile.

"Yeah, Timmy boy. I be okay. How 'bout you?"

"Yeah. I guess."

Ma took the conjure board and planchette and returned them to their tattered box. Timmy was fascinated by the conjure board and all the mystery surrounding it. She had told him about it more than a year ago, when they first started talking seriously about supernatural things. It began with movies. They would sit and talk for hours about the horror movies they watched on late night television, and Ma, with her vast knowledge of such occult subjects, would tell him if they were accurate or not. Mostly they weren't. One day, when the discussion turned to ghosts and spirits, Ma told Timmy that she knew all kinds of spirits, good and bad, and that she used to talk to them once in a while. That was when she told him about the conjure board. She told him how she used it to talk to her spirit friends and how they talked back to her. They told her things that were about to happen or explained the things that were going on at the time. Naturally, he was excited and wanted a demonstration, but she put him off by saying that she didn't use it much anymore and was out of practice. So, he never saw the conjure board out of its box. Until today. The worn edges and the antique look of the board and the box added to the mystery and stirred up the old curiosity inside him. But she was putting it away. It looked as if he still wasn't going to get his demonstration.

"Did you find out anything good?" he asked, pointing to the board.

"No, boy, nothin' no good. So, how was de foon'ral?"

Changing the subject. Okay, so she didn't want to talk about it. He would talk about the funeral.

"Pretty sad. Everybody was crying and stuff. Jim's mother started screaming at the end. And Brother Milford looked bad. I heard somebody saying that he was drunk when Michael… well, when he died. Some people were even saying that he was drunk today at the funeral."

"Was he?"

Timmy shrugged. "I don't know. And so what if he was?" In

his mind, Timmy was not seeing a poor pathetic preacher tipping a bottle of whiskey to his lips. Oh, no. That would have made the whole thing a neat tidy little package that he could stash away and pull out whenever, in years to come, someone would mention *poor Brother Milford*. Too easy. Too clean. What Timmy was seeing in his mind was a photograph being burned at midnight in a golden bowl.

"So what if he was? I think there were some others there drunk today. It was sad. Real sad. And then after…"

He stopped cold. He had almost let it slip out about what he and Charles had done just a little while ago. It was really going to be a hard secret to keep.

"After? After what, boy?"

"Nothing. It was just sad, that's all."

"An' how you be feelin', boy? You be feelin' sad, too?"

Timmy shrugged again. "He was my friend." That was all he could find to say without spilling his guts about the witches in the gravel pits and the thing he had seen in Jim's coffin and about tossing the altar over the cliff. Now it was his turn to change the subject.

"You told me the other day that we needed to have a talk."

"Not now."

"But you said you knew who killed Jim."

"I *t'ink* I know who kill him. I gots to be real sure b'fore we talk 'bout it."

"Well, what did the conjure board tell you?"

"I tole you, boy, it ain't tell me nothin'. Nothin' no good. When it do tell me sumthin', I tell you. Later. Right now, dis ole lady is tired an' her brain need to rest."

There was a long silence. From where they sat at the table, Timmy could see the living room window of his own house. After a minute, his mother sat in the big chair beside the window. Timmy and Ma both watched as Pamela sat staring out the window and, every once in a while, wiping her eyes with her handkerchief.

"How dey doin'?" Ma asked, nodding her head toward Timmy's house.

"Not good."

"An' dat's why you ober here?"

"Well, yeah… but that's not the only reason I come over here."

Ma laughed a little. She was starting to perk up. "Yeah. Dat's what you say now."

"It's true."

"Well, boy, I know what it is dat you really needs."

"What's that?"

"You needs for me to teach you a good lessin, dat's what. You needs for me to kick you ass at gin rummy."

"I thought your brain was tired and needed to rest."

"It don't take no brain to beat you."

"Oh, yeah? I bet you really think you can beat me, don't you?"

"I don't has to t'ink dat. I *knows* dat."

"Get the cards."

"You on." She opened a little drawer on one of her end tables and took out a well-worn deck of playing cards held together by an equally well-worn rubber band. The band broke before she could get it off the deck and the cards scattered on the floor. "Shit!"

Timmy laughed, truly laughed, and it felt good for a change.

"You t'ink it so funny, you pick 'em up. You still young; my ole knees don't bent dat far no mo'."

He picked up the cards quickly and placed them on the table. "Okay. They ought to be plenty shuffled."

"You t'ink you purdy funny, don't ya? Well, you be laughin' out de udder side o'yo ass real soon." She was just about to sit and pick up the cards when a thought came into her mind. "Wait. Wait a minit. I got sumpthin' to give you. Does yo folks know where you are?"

"I don't think so. I came over here right after we got back fr… right after school."

"Den, you let dem know. I be right back. An' don't you mess none wid dem cards while I'm gone."

Ma disappeared into her room and Timmy went to the window. For just a second, he watched his mother with mixed feelings of love and pity. He felt the same for his dad. There was no hate, only sadness and anger that they fought all the time. Timmy called out the window and his mother looked up and waved. Even across the distance of the two side yards, he could see the tears on her cheeks. He sat back at the table, and when he heard Ma coming out of the bedroom, he reached out his hand toward the cards. Just as she walked through the doorway, he jerked his hand away.

"Caught ya, di'nt I?" She laughed and went to Timmy with something clutched in her small fist. She took Timmy's hand and pressed the object firmly into his palm.

"Here. You keep dis wid you."

It was a small silver crucifix on a chain.

"I can't take this."

"No, no, no. You take it. I got my own." She reached into her blouse and tugged on the chain around her neck. A crucifix, identical to the one Timmy held, dangled under her chin. "See? Dis one is mine. I buy dat one for you. It be real silber, boy, powerful stuff. Keep it wid you."

"Wow, thanks." He slipped the chain over his head and for one brief, fleeting second, he saw a fire flash in Ma's eyes; a fire of cold, deadly determination…

"Good. Good. You gonna need all de help you can git…"

… and then that second was gone and a grin covered her face.

"… startin' right now. Okay, boy. Deal de cards."

17

Just as the last remnants of daylight were fading and Ma was adding up the score of the last gin rummy hand (Timmy was preoccupied, and no matter how hard she tried to let him win, in the end he didn't have a prayer), Father Francis closed and locked the rectory door. It took all the self-control he could muster to make his feet carry him to the car. Off and on all afternoon, he had changed his mind about tonight and then reconsidered and then changed his mind again and then reconsidered again and even as he turned the key in the ignition, he felt the doubts coming on just as strongly as ever.

He reached to switch off the radio before he backed out of the drive. Any other time he would have welcomed the music as a pleasant diversion. Strong medicine for attitude adjustment. One goodly dose of rock and roll, please, heavy on the bass. But not tonight. Tonight there was some very serious biz going down and he needed to keep his mind clear. The last thing he needed was to have some simple idiotic lyric running through his head. *Oh, God, our Father, bless me now I pray because my baby is a lovin' fool, do wop and amen.*

"Stop it." *A clear mind. Got to keep a clear mind.*

He drove in absolute silence, his eyes fixed on the road ahead.

Milford was waiting for him on the front porch of the parsonage and ran to meet the car as it rolled to a stop at the curb. He hadn't slept, just as he had told Francis he wouldn't. Instead, he had spent all afternoon long drinking coffee, at least three pots full. As a result, he was completely wired. His face was white as ash and there were huge dark circles under his eyes. The thin veins in his eyeballs were shining bright red. His hands and knees were shaking as if any time now they were going to just lay down and die and let the rest of his body shiver helplessly on the ground in a caffein induced twitch-a-thon. Still, this man who was suffering from exhaustion and lack of sleep, this man who was nothing more than a walking pile of spare parts, this man found the energy to actually run to the car. Part of it came from the encouragement of a single ray of hope, and part of it came from the caffeine kicking his ass.

He ran to the driver's side and leaned in the window. "Are we ready?"

Francis nodded and stared at the steering wheel for several very, very long seconds. When he turned to look at Milford, he saw the sheer exhaustion in the man's eyes. He felt tears starting in his own. "Are you sure?"

"Please."

Francis nodded again and put his own hand over one of Milford's shaking ones. "Okay." They looked into one another's eyes and Milford moved his hand to grip the priest's. "Okay."

Francis turned off the engine and set the parking brake. He retrieved his implements from the seat beside him and then walked beside Milford to the small door at the side of the church. He was very nervous and very unsure of what was going to happen.

He would have shit if he had known they were being watched.

18

Ma didn't bother setting up the conjure board again. She had been at it all day and was pretty sure that the only message she was going to be able to get for a while was *eat shit old bitch*. She wished to God she knew what was going on. She had the gut feeling that somebody was fucking with her board, and that was not good. Not good at all.

There was a light tapping on the front door. Jack called out his usual invitation, but the door did not open. Ma got up to answer and the tapping came again. When she opened the door just a crack, she saw the familiar shape in the dark.

"Timmy boy, what you doin' back ober here? Is de house locked up?" Timmy had only been gone five or ten minutes. She glanced toward his house and saw the lights on in several of the rooms. She opened the door wider and light from the room spilled out onto the porch.

Timmy stood there with his hands in his pockets and looked down at his shoes.

"Timmy?"

He was acting awfully strange. It woke up the old butterflies in her stomach. Very slowly, he raised his head, and Ma clutched at her heart with one hand, threw the other up to her mouth, and staggered two steps backward.

It was Timmy… but it wasn't Timmy. His eyebrows were pulled together in the center and twisted up into points at the ends. His eyes were blood red. The mouth was ugly and spread into a wide grin revealing a full set of small, pointed teeth. A green warty tongue pushed its way slowly out from between those teeth and slid all the way across the thick lips from one side to the other.

Ma stumbled into her living room and turned to look out her window just in time to see Timmy sitting in his own house where his mother had been earlier. She tried to swallow, and a lump stuck in her throat. The thing that tried to look like Timmy stepped through her front door and just stood there grinning at her.

Suddenly, a loud swishing sound came from the other side of the room and filled the house. Captain Jack had stayed perfectly still and had been completely quiet until now. In what must have been quite an effort for him, he stretched out his great blue wings and flew for the first time in who knew how many years. He flew directly over Ma's head toward their guest who looked like Timmy but who wasn't Timmy, and as he did he let out an ear shattering *squaaaaawk!* He swung his claws forward and kept his beak open, ready for a fight. His main advantage was surprise, and he certainly caught Ma by surprise. But not the Timmy-thing. The Timmy-thing just slapped him aside like swatting a pesky mosquito. Jack crashed into the wall and fell to the floor. He twitched a couple of times and then lay still.

Ma opened her mouth to speak or to scream or something, but the thing pointed a finger at her, and an invisible hand closed around her neck. The thing stepped closer and spoke in a fingernail-on-glass voice.

"Now, old bitch, we're gonna have a little talk."

19

The sanctuary of the Baptist Church was almost completely dark. A little light from the streetlights outside filtered in through the stained-glass windows, but not enough to actually be able to see anything in any detail, just an occasional shape that was darker than the dark background. And in that darkness, the room seemed incredibly large, even to Milford who had been in there practically every day for the last two years. They stood and listened, straining to hear even the faintest of sounds, but the air was still as if the whole world had stopped dead still except for these two men. Looking, but not seeing; listening, but not hearing; momentarily paralyzed by the feeling of awe that rumbled around in their stomachs and the feeling of fear at not knowing what they might run into if they moved.

They might have just stood there all night, until the morning sun broke up the darkness, if the town's fire alarm hadn't sounded.

The siren itself was mounted on a telephone pole near the school, but it was loud enough that it could be heard clearly from any place in town and from a lot of places far out of town. Milford had almost gotten used to its sound calling the volunteer firemen away from his sermons. When the siren sounded tonight, he expected to hear the *rustle, rustle* of the men leaving their pews. But instead, he heard Father Francis shift in the blackness.

"Lights?" That single word that Francis thought he had whispered reverberated in the empty room and caused both of them to jump a little. Milford took a couple of steps to the side with his hand out searching for the wall. He moved his hand across the wall in an up and down pattern until he found the small bank of six light switches.

Milford had to admit that one of the things he really liked about this auditorium was the lighting. All the switches were rheostats so that he could have the lights as dim or as bright as he liked. The first two switches controlled the rows of lights over the congregation, no big deal. But with the rest of the switches, he had the opportunity for some theatrical creativity. The third switch controlled two bright spotlights focused directly on the pulpit. He used these a lot. The fourth brought up the lights over the choir. These came in handy for the Christmas and Easter cantatas – cue one, house to half, go; cue two, house lights out, go; cue three, choir lights up, go; cue four, music, maestro. It was a wonderful thing to behold. The fifth switch turned on the lights in the baptistry, which was directly behind the choir, but it was only used when they were "gwan have a babtis'n." The last switch was to light up the huge stained glass that formed the back of the baptistry. It was an absolutely beautiful picture of Jesus standing in the Jordan River. He had just come up out of the water and stood there alone (we can only assume that John the Baptist was camera shy or didn't want to spoil the picture) while a white dove hovered over him. The stained glass spent most of its time hidden behind a red velvet curtain, so the congregation wouldn't get too used to seeing it. Then, every once in a while, for a special occasion or sometimes just on a whim, Milford would pull the curtain, turn on the lights behind the picture, and have a truly religious experience (and hope it had the same effect on the congregation). Yep, whoever designed the lighting in this church had him in mind. But best of all, they had installed an identical set of switches right on the pulpit. He could have all sorts of fun and never stop preaching.

He pushed the first three switches up with one hand and held them as the rheostats hummed into action. As the lights intensified and slowly filled the room, making it seem a lot smaller than the darkness did, Francis raised his hand to Milford.

"Keep them low. We only need enough light to see by."

"Where are we going to be?"

"Just around the pulpit."

Milford held the first two switches down until the congregation lights were completely out and dimmed the pulpit spotlights until only a soft yellow glow remained.

"Perfect." Francis was impressed. Milford returned to his spot at Francis's side and Francis put a hand on his shoulder and squeezed it softly. "How's your faith?"

"Hanging in there."

"Good."

Together they walked to the communion table in front of the pulpit and spread out all the things that Francis had brought with them. Milford's first thought was that there wasn't very much stuff here for what they were about to do. Then he thought, what the hell do I know, Francis is the expert.

And Francis's thoughts were almost identical. Almost. I sure didn't bring much stuff, but what the hell do I know – this is all new to me.

Milford took in a deep breath and blew it out slowly through pursed lips. "Okay, Francis, what do we do first?"

"Well, I guess we're ready to start. Let's sit down over here." They sat on the first pew and Francis looked at the sheet of notebook paper that was now on the top of the stack. In his close slanted handwriting, he had numbered this one page 12. He had already gone through the first eleven before he even left his own home. He read aloud.

"We are here for the purpose of consecrating this building to be used solely for the work of the Lord Jesus Christ, God incarnate, Son of Mary."

Milford flinched, then shrugged. You can't take the Catholic out of the priest. So the church would be just a teensy bit Catholic. So what? After all, Francis was doing him a *huge* favor.

"We do not know if the building was never consecrated or if it has been desecrated at some time. But the presence of an evil force has been felt and the specters of unholy beings have been witnessed.

The comings and goings of these evil ones within these walls have begun to destroy the effectiveness of the worker chosen by God to minister in this place. Are we in agreement on these things?" He looked at Milford.

"Yes. Yes, we are."

"Then let us proceed with the preparations. Reverend Milford, please stay at my side. There are times during the ritual when you will be called upon to participate by responding to the things being said. At those times, I will point to the page and you will read your response. Is that clear to you?"

"Yes."

Then Francis began the ritual.

An hour later they were still in the middle of it. Milford wasn't really sure about a lot of the things that were going on. Francis had done some of it in Latin, and Latin had been more like Greek when Milford was in school. Still, he paid as close attention as he possibly could, but he was awfully tired.

The first part of the ritual had been pretty straightforward. Francis had blessed two silk cloths and draped one of them around Milford's neck and the other around his own. Then he opened one of the jars, said another blessing, dipped in his finger, and smeared a big oily cross on Milford's forehead. After that, things slowed down considerably. There were a lot of blessings and a lot of sprinkling what Milford assumed was holy water on various pieces of furniture in the auditorium, including the chair that Milford sat in every Sunday morning. They had worked their way up to the pulpit and, as far as

Milford could tell, it was the last thing before they moved on to the next part of the ritual.

Francis pulled out his handkerchief and wiped a thin bead of sweat off his upper lip. He looked at Milford who was rubbing savagely at his eyes. “You okay?”

“Yeah. Yeah, I’m fine.”

Francis flipped to the next page. Page 34. By this page, his handwriting was not longer close and neat. His hand had gotten tired and some of the lines consisted of only three or four words written in big sprawling letters, most of which he was having some difficulty deciphering. It was a sorry state of affairs when a man couldn’t read his own writing.

“Now is the consecration of this pulpit. Lord God of Abraham, look down on us.” He pointed to the next line and turned the page to Milford.

“Lord, hear our prayer.”

“Lord God of Isaac, look down on us.”

“Lord, hear our prayer.”

“Lord God of Joseph, look down on us.”

“Lord, hear our prayer.”

“With clear mind and heart, we are come. Lord God of Ages, look down on us and smile.”

“Amen.”

Francis unscrewed the lid from the jar of holy water and the grating sound echoed in the dim distance off the empty pews. For just a fleeting second, Milford thought it sounded like the congregation shifting when they started to get restless. Francis dipped his index finger into the cloudy water and crossed himself. He held the jar out to Milford who copied his actions. He dipped is finger in again and made a large cross on the top of the pulpit as he spoke.

"*In nominee Patris, et Filii, et Spiritus Sancti.*"

"Amen."

Everything was going right on schedule. There would now be a short intermission while Father Francis screwed the lid back on the jar of holy water and then consulted his stack of notes. Milford put his hand to his mouth to cover a yawn.

"*Ssar'ti sho mushii lupzshu.*"

Milford shot a glance at Francis. That was a completely new phrase; they hadn't used that one at all, and it didn't sound very much like Latin. Francis was busy putting away the holy water, acting as if nothing had happened.

"What did you say?"

Francis looked at him, honestly puzzled. "I didn't say anything."

"Oh. I guess I must be hearing things."

"What kind of things?"

"Words… I guess that's what they were. It's probably just the coffee and fatigue starting to work on me."

"We can stop if you want…"

"No! No, don't stop. Please."

With a loud *clunk!* Francis placed the silver crucifix on the pulpit. The spotlights reflected off the shiny legs of Christ in brilliant starbursts. Underneath, on the pulpit itself, was a gleaming wet cross. Milford heard the restless shifting again and immediately shoved it out of his mind to focus his attention on the silver figure of Jesus.

"Jesus Christ, Son of Almighty God, touch us now…"

"*Rabbutaii ssar'ti…*"

Milford again looked at Francis, this time straight at the priest's mouth. But even as he did, he knew that Francis hadn't said the words. They came from somewhere beyond their little glow of yellow light.

"… Enter this, Your blessed sanctuary, and grant us Your peace…"

"*Sho mass slikati.*"

"… Grant, we pray, a blessing on us and on all who enter here…"

"*Izzianimati r'butti.*"

Milford felt his jaw start to tremble. A drop of sweat ran into his eye. His legs turned to rubber and he leaned on the pulpit for support.

"… Jesus Christ, Everlasting Father, sit in judgement, we pray…"

"*Azth'thtu fomias.*"

"… and judge our hearts to be…"

"*Marthzhas ik…*"

Milford raised his eyes to the dark room, and saw his congregation waiting for him. They were vague and misty. And the auditorium was full of them.

"… and pure and clean…"

"*Ghaasha…*"

"Francis, make them stop!"

"*Sa'sh…*"

"What?"

"Make them stop!"

"*Shin talsa Kaspha…*"

"Who?"

"*Shin talsa Kaspha…*"

"Please! Make them stop!" He covered his ears with his hands and tears poured from his eyes.

"*Shin talsa Kaspha…*"

"Who? Make who stop?"

"Oh, God, please!" He fell against the pulpit and his elbow hit the fancy row of light switches.

"*Foli mekum…*"

The rheostats hummed…

"*Foli mekum…*"

… and the pulpit was engulfed in darkness…

"*Shamashu!*"

… and Milford screamed.

20

The Timmy-thing stayed at Ma's house for a very long time. He had quite a few things to say to her, and through it all he kept his invisible death grip on her throat. Then, suddenly, he said that he was being summoned elsewhere. He tightened the grip until Ma slipped into unconsciousness and then he left. As he passed Captain Jack, the parrot opened his great beak and snapped at the thing's ankle. With a smile that looked nothing like Timmy's smile, it kicked Jack against the wall.

The old lady was still, the pesky bird was still. And the Timmy disguise dissolved as the thing passed through the closed front door.

21

"Did you see them? Did you?"

"I didn't see anything, Jimmy. Nothing at all."

They were back on the front pew; Milford was shaking all over and Francis was doing his best to calm him down. Francis felt a throb of pain in his bottom lip and ran the back of his hand across it. It came away red.

Francis was a little surprised when the lights went out, but when Milford screamed it scared the hell out of him. He fumbled around the pulpit until he found the switches and got some light on. The first thing he saw was his friend curled up on the floor with his hands over his ears and his eyes shut tight. Milford was crying and shouting, "Make them stop! Please, God, make them stop!" Francis grabbed Milford's shoulders and shook them gently. Without opening his eyes, Milford closed his right hand into a fist and swung, connecting solidly with the priest's mouth. As much out of reflex as anything else, Francis slapped Milford twice, once on each side of his face. Milford was stunned into silence and lay perfectly still for several long seconds. When he finally opened his eyes and saw Francis kneeling over him, he sobbed from deep within his chest.

Francis looked at the blood on his hand and wished to God he knew what to do next. This thing was getting totally out of hand.

"Come on, Jimmy. It's time to go home."

"No! Oh, God, we can't stop now, Francis! Didn't you see them? Didn't you hear them?"

"I didn't see or hear anything except you turning into a vegetable on the floor. Now it's time to stop."

"Francis, please listen to me…"

Francis sprang to his feet and pointed his finger at a spot directly between Milford's eyes. "No, you listen to me. I stuck my neck way out for you on this one, and to be real honest I'm starting to get worried. First of all, if anybody finds out about this it'll be my ass. You know it and I know it. But what *really* worries me is you. You're falling apart, Jimmy, and I'm afraid I may be doing more harm than good."

"No, Francis…"

"What is it, Jimmy? Is it the booze? Is that it? Is it the pressure? Is it the helpless feeling of listening over the telephone to some tormented teenager blowing his brains out? Is that it? Whatever it is, Jimmy, you've got to get it straight or I'm afraid that one day it may be *me* on the phone begging *you* not to do it."

Francis stopped and was suddenly furious with himself. In less than a minute he had managed to shatter every rule of counseling that had been drummed into his head in seminary. Even if he hadn't been making things worse before, he was now. He shook his head sadly and sat on the floor beside Milford. He leaned forward and propped his head on his hands.

"I'm sorry."

This was followed by a long, long silence. Francis kept his head in his hands, ashamed to look up… until he heard Milford start to giggle.

"No, Francis, *I'm* sorry."

He giggled again, and Francis was now certain that he had helped push his closest friend over the edge. He touched Milford's shoulder.

"Jimmy, don't…"

"No, no, no. You've finished, now it's my turn to talk. I'm sorry for dragging you into all this. It just occurred to me what this must look like to you. A promising young preacher struck down at the height of his career, very much like another young man from Nazareth some years ago. But this one was not the victim of an angry mob crying out in righteous indignation. Oh, no. This one was driven insane by hallucinations which may or may not have been caused by what may or may not have been a drinking problem. You think I've gone off my nut, don't you? Well, I haven't. I don't have any way to prove it to you, you're just going to have to trust me. Right now I'm wired, I'm tired, and I'm sleepy, but I am not – I repeat, *not* – wack-o."

"Then why do you keep seeing those… those things?"

"Because they're here, damnit! I know that if I were to turn around right now and look behind me, I'd probably wet my pants, because this place is full. I mean, absolutely *full*."

"Then why can't I see them!" Francis shouted, and his voice boomed through the building.

"I don't know, I don't know, I don't know. But I do know that whatever you're doing must be working because they're all here. There's never been this many of them before, but for some reason they're all gathered here now."

"And what are they doing?"

Milford stood and carefully avoided looking out into the pews while he paced back and forth and thought about his answer.

"Waiting, I think. Waiting for… for a preacher, I guess. Sure. Why not? It's a church. Waiting for a preacher… or something… somebody they called while you were praying."

Francis noticed that Milford had developed a slight limp. A limp that became more pronounced as he continued to pace. Milford looked at the floor and pounded his fist into his other palm while he talked. It was almost as if he were putting himself into some kind of trance.

"And I think… I'm not sure, but I think that whoever they called may turn out to be very dangerous... even to someone who can't see him."

Milford sat and took both of Francis's hands in his own, and Francis saw a dreadful urgency in his eyes.

"Please, we can't stop. Not now. My God, Francis, they're right behind us!"

Francis looked at Milford for a moment and then shifted his gaze to the far wall. Milford sighed loudly.

"Shit! How can I convince you? What will it take?" He suddenly became aware of the pain that was growing in his chest and was struck with an inspiration. Ripping open his shirt, he exposed an ugly scar which was almost hidden by the curly hair around it. Any other time, it would have been difficult to find except that tonight it had turned a bright burning red against the pale skin of his chest. "Here! Take a look at this! Are my hallucinations doing this to me? Come on, Francis. At least let's finish what we've started. That's all I'm asking."

Francis looked at the preacher's scar and then into his eyes. "Okay. But we're going to change things a little."

Undoubtedly, Milford would think that his cheap theatrics had turned the trick. It was a ploy he had probably picked up from television where one picture of the bloated belly of a tiny black child in Africa was worth several thousand American dollars. Show them something to evoke pity, and you can name your price. There's nothing really wrong with that; in fact, that's probably the only way to get to the hardened hearts of today's society. So, that's what Milford would think, that pity had saved the day. That's okay, let him think that. It was better than the truth. Francis wasn't about to tell him what had really changed his mind. He wasn't about to tell what he had seen over against the far wall.

He wasn't about to mention the hand reaching for the light switch.

"Close your eyes. Tight."

Milford did as he was told so he didn't see the lights go out. And Francis would never tell him that the lights went out.

"Sit very still, keep your eyes closed, and repeat the Lord's Prayer aloud."

"Our Father which art in Heaven, Hallowed be thy name…"

Francis stepped forward cautiously, waving his hands in front of him and sticking his right leg out with each step until he felt the edge of the platform. His heart was thumping wildly and his only thought was to get the lights back on.

"... Thy kingdom come. Thy will be done on earth as it is in Heaven..."

He climbed up on the platform and crawled along on his hands and knees, groping in front of him, searching desperately for the pulpit. He finally bumped it with his right shoulder.

"... Give us this day our daily bread. And forgive us our trespasses as we forgive those who trespass against us. Lead us not into temptation, but deliver us from evil..."

But deliver us from evil... deliver us from evil... deliver us...

Francis grasped the edge of the platform and pulled himself up. The light switches were right on the edge. Somewhere.

"... For Thine is the kingdom, and the power..."

He pushed the switches, all of them with both hands, as hard as he could. He felt the electrical current surging in there somewhere. He squinted as the room was flooded with light.

"... and the glory forever. Amen."

"Amen."

Francis held his breath as he looked toward the wall. No hand. He looked out at the rows of pews. No ghostly congregation. He looked down at Milford. Milford sat patiently with his eyes closed. It did happen, didn't it? The lights did go out, didn't they? Or was this a case of contagious hysteria? Not bloody likely.

"Okay, Jimmy, come up here with me."

Milford opened his eyes and then closed them to narrow slits. "Jesus, Francis, I thought we didn't need much light."

"I changed my mind. I want you to look out into the room and tell me what you see."

He climbed up onto the platform and looked out into his church. What he had told Francis was true. The room was still full, and just a few seconds before he had been sitting out there with his back to them. The thought sent a shudder through him. They were out there. They didn't look like the clouds that haunted his sermons, not exactly. These were more definitely shaped, more in the form of people, but not completely. They were… vague was the only word he could think of. And they were just sitting there. Waiting. He told Francis.

"I still don't see them, but that doesn't matter. We're going to make some changes in the ritual."

"Is it okay to do that?"

"Of course it is. I made the damned thing up, remember? You just tell me what's happening as we go along. Okay?"

"Sure."

Francis jumped down off the platform and went to the communion table. He picked up the cotton napkin that held the tortilla and found himself wishing that he had brought the pyx with the real wafer. But it was too late for wishing. This would have to do. Suddenly the air went cold. He felt it blast through his clothes and he knew that something had happened even before Milford spoke.

"Francis, I think he's here."

He came in through the double doors at the back of the

auditorium. *Through* the double doors. They never opened. He just materialized there. If Milford had thought about it for a moment, he would have realized that the doors didn't open for any of the other things when they came in either, but he didn't and it wouldn't have made any difference if he had. Milford's complete attention was now focused on the specter that floated just above the floor at the back of the room.

"I know. I felt it."

"You did?" Was that surprise in the preacher's voice?

"Just keep watching. I'm almost ready." Francis spread the napkin on the communion table and placed the tortilla in the middle of it. To the right he placed a small silver whiskey flask and a plastic Dixie cup. He kissed the crucifix on the rosary and hung the beads around his neck. He put his hand over his heart thinking maybe that would slow it down some. It didn't. He crossed himself and whispered, "God help us."

"He's just sitting there. What's he waiting for?"

"I don't know, but we're not waiting for him to make the first move. Come on down here. And bring that crucifix with you."

Milford hesitated, thinking it might not be a good idea to turn his back on them again.

"Come on!"

Milford grabbed the crucifix that Francis had left on the pulpit and jumped down. He hurried to Francis's side.

"Just turn around and face them and hold the crucifix up in front of you. We're not afraid of them…" *liar, liar, pants on fire!* "… but you have to be my eyes. You have to tell me what's going on. I'll take care of the rest."

"Okay."

How's your faith?

He remembered asking Milford that question earlier in the evening, and now it was coming back to haunt him, no pun intended.

"Now, as we prepare for communion, let us call to mind our sins. Okay, Jimmy, think about your sins."

"All of them?"

"Just the big ones. You can do the rest on your own time. And once we have brought them to mind, we will spend a few moments in silence to make our peace with God."

Milford spent the moments of silence mentally racing through bits and pieces of prayers he had heard over the years. He didn't make it through any of them all the way. He was finding it very difficult to concentrate on anything except the faceless apparition he was told to watch. He wasn't even aware that the knuckles of both his hands had gone white from squeezing the crucifix.

"Almighty God, we confess to You our sins. Grant us now Your mercy, forgive our sins, and lead us into everlasting life. Amen."

"Amen."

"What's it doing?"

"I don't know if it's moving or not. I mean, I can't tell. But it seems to be closer than before."

Francis opened his Bible and flipped viciously through the thin pages. "Where is it… where is it… where…" He stopped, read a couple of verses, and turned another page. He was ready. He looked at Milford and then out to his invisible audience. "Our Lord, Himself, instituted the sacrament of communion when He went into the upper room with His chosen twelve to celebrate the Passover." Then, from the Bible, "And as they were eating, Jesus took bread, and blessed it, and brake it, and gave it to the disciples, and said, Take, eat; this is my body." Francis took the tortilla from the napkin, whispered a prayer, crossed himself, broke a small piece off the tortilla, and handed the piece to Milford. Then he broke off a piece for himself and put the rest back on the napkin. From the Bible again, "This is my body which is given for you: this do in remembrance of me." Both men put their piece of Christ's body into their mouths.

"Francis, it's definitely getting closer."

But Francis had already moved on to the second part. From the Bible, "Likewise also the cup after supper, saying, This cup is the new testament in my blood, which is shed for you." With hardly a pause, he sloshed some of the wine from the whiskey flask into the plastic cup, handed the cup to Milford, and turned back to the Bible. "And he took the cup, and gave thanks, and gave it to them, saying, Drink ye all of it; For this is my blood of the new testament, which is shed for many for the remission of sins." Milford drank. Francis drank. The specter moved closer. Francis found another verse and read again. "For as often as ye eat this bread, and drink this cup, ye do shew the Lord's death till he come. Amen."

"Amen."

Francis was completely ignoring his stack of notes. There was not time to read them now, and besides, everything had changed. He hadn't expected any of this when he made up his neat little ritual.

Then, there hadn't been a need to rush. But now, he was rushing. He opened his jar of holy water and poured about half of it into the now-empty Dixie cup which he then shoved into Milford's hand. "Jimmy, I want you to do exactly what I do. Put that crucifix in your pocket or in your shirt or somewhere but *keep it with you*. Listen very carefully to what I'm saying, and every time I say "amen," you shout it back at me as loud as you can. But most important, keep your eyes on that demon. You got that?"

Milford nodded, and his mind replayed one word: *Demon*. The priest's choice of that particular word wasn't wasted on Milford. He had already decided that's what they were. *Demon's*, just like in his sermons. He would keep his eyes on the *demon*, and the *demon* was already halfway down the aisle.

"Okay, Jimmy, I'll take this side and you take the other. Just go to the aisle and wait."

The two split up and Milford suddenly felt very vulnerable. The pains were shooting like fireballs through his leg and chest. His hands started to shake badly, and he spilled some of his water. Francis yelled into the silence.

"The consecration of a church is a sacred ritual to seal that church to a purpose, and that purpose is to be the center for God's work. Amen."

"Amen!"

Francis dipped two of his fingers into his holy water and flicked small droplets onto the pew on his left and then on his right. Milford did the same.

"Save this church from the demons of Satan. Seal it to Your

work. Amen."

"Amen!"

They took two steps up the aisle and stopped at the next row of pews. There they repeated their actions and their invocation. Then they went to the third row, and the fourth, and at each one they sprinkled their holy water, Francis said his few words, and Milford shouted "Amen!" As they moved to the fifth row, Milford saw that the first four rows were empty. Completely empty. When he looked to the back of the auditorium, he thought he could see some of the cloudy-vague-human forms passing back out through the wall. And he noticed that the demon had stopped moving forward.

"It's working! They're leaving!"

"Save this church from the demons of Satan. Seal it to Your work. Amen."

"Amen!"

Milford dipped his fingers to sprinkle the next pews, about halfway to the back of the room, and his fingers hit the bottom of the cup. He was running out of water, and there was still a long way to go. Then he found out that he wasn't the only one who noticed his short supply. When he looked up again, he saw the demon and a large number of the crew shifting to his side of the auditorium.

"Amen!" he shouted and stepped forward. All kinds of things began to race through his head. What would happen if he ran out of holy water? Would they just overrun him?

"Amen!" Step, step, dip, sprinkle, sprinkle. Could he pull the crucifix out of his pocket and chase them away, or does that only work on vampires?

"Amen!" Step, step, dip/*clunk*, sprinkle, sprinkle. He cursed himself for getting scared and spilling those precious few drops at the start. Maybe Francis would have some left over and sneak up behind them.

"Amen!" Step, step, *clunk/clunk*, sprinkle, sprinkle. He thought about Christ feeding five thousand people with five loaves of bread and two little fishes. If Christ could do that, surely God would stretch his few drops of water over just a few more pews.

"Amen!" Step, step, *clunk*, sprinkle, *clunk*, sprinkle. *Oh, God please don't let it run out please don't let it run out please don't let it...*

"Amen!" Step, step, *clunk*, sprinkle, *scrape*, sprinkle. *Oh, God, please don't let it run out please...*

He looked up, and the demon was at him, reaching for him, but never quite making contact. Milford swallowed hard and took another step forward. The demon pointed a long misty finger at Milford and growled, "You scumsucker! You!" It raised its misty arms as if to engulf the preacher. That was when Milford felt the cup begin to pulsate and tremble in his hand. It was a rhythmic throbbing that sent electric vibrations up his arm. He wanted to look down at the cup in his hand but dared not take his eyes off the demon. With his two fingers, he dipped back into the cup. His fingers hit water at the brim. In one sweeping gesture, Milford slung holy water into the face of the demon and onto the remaining pews. The demon turned and disappeared into the wall.

They had made it. Francis dipped his fingers and made a large cross on the doors. The consecration was done, and it hadn't been anything like he had expected. *How's your faith?* He turned to Milford.

"What do you see now?"

The tired young man turned slowly to look toward his pulpit. As he did, he studied each pew with great care to make sure that nothing had slipped by them. He looked up to the arched ceiling just in case some of them had flown up there. Finally, after several long minutes, he looked back at his friend.

"Nothing." He felt a smile come over his face, his first real smile in weeks. "I don't see anything at all."

He reached out his arms and managed to take two faltering steps toward Francis before fatigue overtook him. A great blackness flooded his brain and he fell forward onto the carpet.

22

The ordeal in the church was already over before Timmy and Doobie went to bed. It had been a very long day – a very long week – and it wasn't over yet. There was still Michael's funeral in the morning.

Timmy didn't really want to go, but Mother insisted. After all, she said, he was Jim's brother. But Jim was dead too, and didn't Michael try to blow their heads off that night at the lake? Okay, so Michael didn't know it was them… at least that's what he said. Timmy was never really convinced of that. Anyway, Michael was nothing more to Timmy than the brother of one of his best friends. But Mother insisted.

Between Timmy's feet, Doobie started to snore, and his front paws twitched slightly. Earlier, just a few minutes after Timmy got home from Ma's house, Doobie started to act strangely. He followed Timmy into the house and then paced back and forth in front of the door, barking and whining. Twice, Pamela opened the door thinking that Doobie needed to go out, even though he had been out all day. Finally, Gerald couldn't stand it anymore. He stomped to the door, held it open, and shouted for Doobie to get the hell out. Always anxious to avoid trouble, Doobie tucked his tail between his legs and hung his head in repentance. Gerald didn't buy it and slapped Doobie hard on the rump. Doobie ran just in case Gerald decided that once was not enough. He headed toward Timmy's room, his old sanctuary, but before he reached the doorway, he started to back pedal for all he was worth. His claws skidded on the hardwood floor, but he managed to stop just inside the bedroom. Well, maybe not *stop* exactly. Somehow, he managed to twist his body around and head back in the opposite direction before he ever came to a standstill. He cowered behind the sofa while Pamela yelled something about cruelty to animals and Gerald answered her with something about the fucking dog pound and Timmy sat quietly in one of the living room chairs. After nearly a half hour of this, Doobie sneaked quietly out from behind the sofa and climbed into the big chair beside the window. He stared out at Ma's house and whined softly.

Timmy lay in bed with the sheet pulled up to his chin and Doobie sleeping between his feet. He still had to physically carry Doobie into the bedroom every night. At first, he thought that it wasn't worth it, but he had come to find that he was more comfortable when Doobie was in the room with him.

Suddenly, Doobie came awake with a jerk and looked all around the dark room. He whined and in a matter of seconds he was at Timmy's pillow pushing his nose under the edge of the sheet. When he was completely covered, he lay at Timmy's side and panted like he had just been chasing field mice in the Davis's pasture.

Doobie whined again, and Timmy knew what was happening. The noises were an every night occurrence now. And every night they got a little louder and a little louder. If they were really mice (which he personally had begun to doubt) then they were about the size of his uncle Fred's '64 Buick Electra. At least that's how they sounded. A couple of nights ago he thought he caught a quick glimpse of something pretty big (well, maybe not Electra size) moving in one of the dark corners of his room, but since then he had convinced himself that it was just his scared-as-hell imagination playing tricks on him.

With one hand he stroked Doobie's head and with the other he clutched the sheet at his throat.

"It's okay, Doob. It's okay, boy."

But Doobie didn't think it was okay and he clawed at the mattress.

Digging a tunnel for the Great Escape? Good job!

But you're digging in the wrong direction! You're going to come out UNDER THE BED!

Oh, shit!

"Oh, shit!" He whispered the words and the sound of his own voice embarrassed him a little. He patted Doobie's head again. "It's okay, Doob. Really."

After a few minutes, the noises stopped – suddenly. Timmy kept very still, straining his ears to pick up the slightest sound, but there was nothing. Even Doobie ceased his tunneling and laid his head on Timmy's leg. He was sure that everything was indeed going to be okay.

And it would have been, too. He and Doobie would have just drifted off and slept like the proverbial little logs. They would have both gotten eight, maybe nine, hours of sleep and been refreshed for the hard day that was coming. But it just wasn't to be.

Something at the foot of the bed tugged on the sheet, and neither of them closed their eyes for the rest of the night.

23

The preacher regained consciousness and was coherent just long enough for Father Francis to get him back to his home and into bed.

Then he dreamed…

It was a chilly night in downtown Atlanta. That type of night the old back-woods hunters used to call a pricknipper. On this particular late January pricknipper there was a sixty percent chance of snow, and at the moment it looked as if all sixty percent was falling outside the little service station just off I-20. Behind the desk in the office, seventeen-year-old Jimmy Milford rocked back and forth debating the merits of keeping a service station open until midnight on a Saturday night. It's not like there was a lot of traffic. In fact, he hadn't pumped a gallon of gas, cleaned one windshield, or even checked the air in one tire for almost an hour and a half, and there was still a full hour left until closing. On a Saturday night, church going people would be at home (or *should* be at home) getting plenty of rest so that they could stay awake during church services in the morning. And on a *cold* Saturday night, with the wind whipping across the interstate and the snow swirling in massive clouds, even the heathens had enough sense to stay off the roads. So what was the point? Everybody was at home. Well, not quite everybody. Right about now and two states over, a woman in labor and her unconscious husband were trapped inside a wrecked automobile and the deputy sheriff who would eventually find them wouldn't be going off duty for more than three hours. But they didn't really count because they were too far away, and he wouldn't meet any of them for quite a few years yet. For all intents and purposes, everybody was at home. Everybody, that is, except Jimmy Milford.

In the service bay, Jake let out a low growl. Jake was the watch dog, or watch wolf. Whatever he was, Jake knew what his job was, and he was damned good at it. After the doors were locked at night, Jake was turned loose in the station to guard the motor oil, the antifreeze, and the new tires lining the walls of the bay. In fact, Jake was so good at his job that Jimmy had to be there every night to lock up and let Jake out, and he had to be there again every morning before school or church to open the doors and put Jake into his cage for the day. It was a shame because poor Jake never got to see the sunlight except when Jimmy worked the occasional day shift on Saturday. But nobody else, not even Ben (the station owner and Jake's master), dared to swing open the front door while Jake was on duty. Ironically, it was Ben who "trained" Jake, mixing a little gunpowder with his food and beating him with a thick leather strap. And now Jake hated Ben and distrusted every other human except Jimmy. Jimmy had always had a special way with animals, and after he took the job at the station it had only taken him two days to win Jake over. Some soft friendly words spoken through the wire of the cage, a small piece of beef jerky four or five times a day, and in no time at all Jimmy had the cage open. But Jimmy was very careful to renew the friendship daily. He had heard all the horror stories about lion tamers and their pets.

"What is it, Jake? You hear something out there?"

Jake let out a half-hearted bark, a signal to Jimmy that it was nothing serious.

"You wanna come out here and sit with me a while?" Jimmy went through the door leading to the service bay and saw Jake in a low crouch with his ears laid back against his head. Another low growl rumbled in his throat. He was ready to attack.

"Come on, Jake. Do we have to go through this every night?" Jimmy walked straight toward Jake, never wavering and never losing eye contact with the animal. That was <u>very</u> important. "I've told you a hundred times, the boogie man ain't gonna get you while I'm here." He reached out one hand and playfully ruffled the hair on the dog's head and pulled one ear lightly. Still the low rumbling growl. "Whatcha gonna do? Bite my arm off?" Suddenly, Jake threw his head back and left a long, wet trail with his tongue up Jimmy's arm. "That's better. Come on, let's go." Jimmy gave his heavy leather collar a tug and Jake walked right along at his side.

Jimmy took his seat at the desk and Jake lay beside him. Together they sat for about five minutes watching the snow swirl past the windows and pile into small drifts against the wooden fence outside. Out on the highway, a set of headlights approached. Jake snapped his head up and pointed his ears. *Maybe this is somebody I can kill.* The car slowed at the long drive in front of the station, but then drove another twenty-five yards and turned onto the highway on-ramp.

Jake was still gazing out the front window with his ears pointed forward when Jimmy whispered, "Where's the rabbit, Jake?" Jake jumped to his feet and began his deep growl, "Wanna rabbit, Jake?"

Jake barked and lunged toward the front window. No rabbit there. "Get the rabbit! Go get it!" He ran to the side window, barking loudly enough that the glass shook. No rabbit there either. He ran through the service bay and clawed at the garage door. He was becoming frantic. *Gotta find that rabbit!*

By now, Jimmy was laughing so hard that he could barely see Jake bounding off the walls. "Get the rabbit! Get him, Jake!" Jimmy opened his eyes just in time to see Jake racing toward him with his bare teeth flashing. Before Jimmy had time to react, Jake grabbed Jimmy's shirt sleeve with those teeth and pulled him toward the front door. He wanted out. Gotta find the damned rabbit!

"No, Jake. There's not a rabbit." Jimmy was laughing again, and Jake was thumping the cigarette machine with his massive tail. "You know I can't let you out. You might chew up somebody's car, and then we'd both be in trouble." Jake reared up and planted his huge paws on Jimmy's shoulders. Jimmy rubbed his sides vigorously. "You know, boy, there's really nothing wrong with you, is there? You're a good dog, y'know that?" Jake dutifully licked Jimmy in the ear.

That was when Jimmy saw the flashing red lights coming toward the station. As soon as they turned into the drive, Jimmy pushed Jake down and led him back to the service bay, closing the glass door between them. "You wait in there, Jake."

The red lights belonged to Ben. Not only was he a part-time service station owner and a part-time guard dog trainer, he was also the part-time constable of the district. And, this being Saturday night, he was probably drunk again. That was one of his favorite games. He would sit home Saturday evenings watching TV and drinking beer. Then, when he was on the verge of not being able to stand up, he would get in his constable car and go out looking for drunk drivers. That caused quite a stir in the district and gave him quite a reputation with the Fulton County Sheriff's Office. But it would all be over soon. Election time was coming.

Ben's car fishtailed down the drive and slid to a stop in front of one of the gas pumps. The minute Ben stepped out of the car, Jimmy knew that his assumption was correct: Ben was shitfaced.

Ben opened the front door and was followed inside by a rush of frigid air. "Put some gas in my car."

"Please."

"What'djew say?"

"Forget it. Jake's loose in the bay."

"I saw."

The only customer for two hours and it had to be Ben. Of course, Ben wouldn't pay for the gas. He never did. Tomorrow, if he even remembered that he stopped by, he would juggle the books so that there was no record of the fifteen or so missing gallons. Then he would make out a phony receipt and be reimbursed by the county for the gas he bought for his official vehicle. It was quite an operation. Very slick. And Jimmy wasn't supposed to know anything about it. But Jimmy did. Hell, even a mental midget could have figured it out. Jimmy even used it against old Ben once.

It was when the Jesus Movement was shaking Southern California. One afternoon an old beat-up Cadillac convertible pulled in at the station. The four young men in the car all had long, long hair and wore leather headbands. They had on sandals made of water buffalo hide and wore bell-bottom pants. When they pooled their monies, they had a combined total of $3.75. Jimmy struck up a conversation with the young men and discovered that they were new converts to Christianity, and they were on their way to Los Angeles to spread the Good News and have fellowship with their brothers and sisters on the West Coast. This struck a soft spot in Jimmy's heart and he filled the Caddy with gas, for free, and gave them $20 out of the cash register. He gave them his address and sure enough, about two weeks later, he got a post card from them – they were in L.A. and everything was fine. Jimmy kept the post card. Every time he looked at it, he remembered not only the four young men, but also what happened the day after they visited the station. Ben came in that next day and was going to try to balance the books. Before he started,

Jimmy said, "Don't forget the gas you got yesterday and the twenty dollars you took." Ben just looked at him dumbly and said, "Oh, yeah, right."

Yes, sirree, a slick operation. Ben didn't think Jimmy knew about it and Jimmy never told him otherwise. It made things easier.

While he pumped the gas, Jimmy watched Ben in the office. Even through the glass, he could hear Jake's barking above the howling wind. Ben walked over to the glass door and yelled something at Jake. Jake leaped against the door. Ben pounded on the door and Jake barked louder. Ben kicked at one side of the door and Jake clawed at the other. A master and his dog. A dog and his enemy.

Jimmy went back inside, and Jake began to settle down. "Car's gassed up." He hoped Ben would leave. Instead, Ben pounded on the door again.

"You was playin' wid th' muhfugger, wadn't ya? What'd I tell ya bout playin' wid th' muhfugger? Ya ain't s'pose t'play wid th' muhfugger. Gotta keep 'im mean."

"Yeah."

"What's that s'pose t'mean, 'yeah'?"

"Nothing."

"Don't tell me it didn't mean nothin', fuckwad. I can tell you was bein' a smartass. You don't like me no more, do ya?"

"Ben, you're drunk. Why don't you go home and get some sleep."

"I ain't drunk, ya little shithole. Now tell me why ya don't like me no more."

Jimmy sat at the desk and flipped through the few credit card receipts of the day. He would graduate from high school after this year, and Ben could take this service station and put it where the sun don't shine. Maybe Jake would tear Ben's rotten throat out. Or maybe Jimmy would take Jake with him when he left. Now there was a thought. "Why do you treat Jake like that?"

"That ain't none o'your fuckin' business."

"Damnit, Ben, God made dogs for a reason, and it wasn't so you could feed 'em gunpowder!"

"I said that ain't none o'your fuckin' business! Now stop changin' th' subject an' tell me why ya don't like me no more!"

"Good God, Ben! Look around you! It's not just me. There's not a single person in this whole city… in this whole damned *county* who likes you. And do you know why? That was a stupid question. Of course you don't. Well, I'll tell you. It's because there's not a decent bone in your body. You're an asshole, Ben. You're like a buzzard slurpin' up chipmunk guts off the highway. You sit in the bushes and wait for somebody to drive by with a busted taillight so you can write out that ticket and collect that percentage. You arrest people for drunk driving when you're so stewed you can't even see the road in front of you. You beat up black people just because you don't like their color. You didn't think I knew about that, did you? Well, I know a lot of things you didn't think I knew." Jimmy almost spilled the beans but then suddenly realized what he was saying. He was on a roll, and he almost blew it. Luckily, Ben was too drunk to notice.

"I don't need no shit from th' likes o'you." There was a touch of disgust in Ben's voice that went right over Jimmy's head.

"Then what do you need, Ben?"

"I don't need nothin' but this." Ben pulled a service .38 from the holster on his hip and rubbed his hand along the barrel. In the service bay, Jake was barking again. "Ya wanna know what this is, shithole?"

Jimmy sat quietly in the chair. This was the first time he had ever seen Ben take the gun out of its holster, and Ben's being drunk didn't make it a pleasant sight.

"Well, let me tell ya what it is." Ben proceeded with his piss-poor imitation of Clint Eastwood. "This is a .44 magnum, th' most pow'rful handgun in th' world…"

"It's not a .44."

"What'djew say?"

"I said it's not a .44. I may not know much, but I know that's not a .44."

"You may not know much? That ain't what you said just a minute ago, now is it? You said you knew a lot of things. Ain't that what you said?"

"Maybe I was wrong."

"Or maybe you're lyin'! Why don't you tell me some o'them things you know? Huh? D'you know 'bout me fixin the books? Huh? Is that what you know? Or maybe you know 'bout me bein' in th' Klan? Oh, I know what it is. You know 'bout me chasin' that nigger what raped little Susie Lyons. They still got half the law officers in th' state lookin' for that sonofabitch, but I'm the only one who knows where he is. I hung that motherfucker! One day next spring he's gonna thaw out an' get real ripe an' some poor hunter's gonna find his carcass hangin' from th' end of a rope out in th' woods. Is that what you know? Or did you know my ole lady's been fuckin' Buster Willis? Maybe that's what you knew, 'cause it seems like ever'body in this whole fuckin' town but me knew 'bout it up 'till t'day. An' you can bet I beat holy hell outta her. An' he's next."

Jimmy sat back and didn't say a word. Ben's eyes were glazing over, and he was waving the gun back and forth in front of Jimmy's face. Jake was scratching at the glass with his claws.

"Well, if you knew all o'that, maybe you was right. Maybe you do know a lot. But maybe you ain't the onliest one. Maybe I know a few things myself. Like maybe just before I heard my wife was a fuckin' whore, I heard you was a faggot queer-boy. Is that true? Do I got a queer-boy workin' for me?"

"No, it's not true. One of the guys on the football team made it up as a joke because he doesn't like me."

"It's not true?"

"No."

"I think you're lyin' t'me. I think it *is* true. An' I also think since my fuckin' whore wife got herself all busted up an's gonna be outta commission for a while, I think you're gonna have to take her place for a while. That's what I think." Ben moved forward until he was directly in front of Jimmy. With his thumb, he pulled back the hammer of the revolver and he placed the cold steel of the barrel against Jimmy's forehead. Jake was lunging at the glass door and gnawing at the handle.

"Okay, queer-boy, I'm gonna drop my pants and you're gonna take a long slow suck on my dick. An' if ya don't, I'm gonna blow th' whole inside o'your head out that window back there."

Ben started to laugh and with his free hand reached for the buckle of his belt. He had never been like this before, and Jimmy was scared. What Jimmy did next was out of sheer desperation, but from where he was sitting, he really didn't have anything to lose. As soon as Ben's pants fell around his ankles, Jimmy caught the gun barrel with both hands and pushed it toward the ceiling. It went off immediately and they were showered by pieces of ceiling tile. Jimmy's fingers were burned, but he couldn't let go of the gun. Not yet. With all the force he could muster, he brought both knees up into the soft spot of Ben's groin. Ben dropped to the floor, but he kept a death grip on the gun. Jimmy knew he only had a few seconds, so he jumped over Ben and ran to the door of the service bay. When he pulled it open, Jake leaped past him. Jimmy didn't stop to look back.

Ben was still on the floor when he saw Jake coming at him. He fired and the bullet tore through Jake's shoulder. He fired again and the top of Jake's head peeled away. The dog fell on top of Ben and died trying to sink his teeth into the man's throat.

Somehow, the garage door had jammed. Jimmy worked at the handle and lock. Several seconds had passed since the two shots were fired and he dared not waste any time finding out what happened. The most he could hope for was that Ben missed and Jake didn't. But he couldn't be sure. It was so quiet in there, and that probably wasn't a good sign. He put all his weight into pulling on the handle until he felt it bending in his hand.

Ice. It had to be ice. When he washed out the service bay this afternoon, the water that ran into the door track must have frozen the door shut. He glanced quickly along the floor and spotted a small sledgehammer. He snatched it up and pounded at the bottom of the door. One more jerk of the handle freed the door and it slid upward on its tracks. Jimmy turned just in time to see Ben standing across the room holding his pants up with one hand and pointing the gun with the other one.

The first shot caught Jimmy as he was turning to go out the bay door. The bullet skimmed his left arm and plowed into his chest. The impact knocked him out the door. Jimmy hit the cold pavement and the sledgehammer sailed over the low wooden fence. Another shot exploded into Jimmy's left thigh as he was stumbling to his feet. He fell again, this time into the soft snow around the corner of the building.

He wanted to just lay there and wake up from the dream he was having. It had to be a dream; none of this shit really happens in real life. He was really at home in bed. The pain in his chest was just the pepperoni pizza he had before he went to sleep, and he must have cut off the circulation in his leg because the blood was rushing back into it and causing it to sting. He must have made some noise, too. He could hear someone coming to wake him up.

Ben!

He could hear their footsteps getting closer. Closer.

Get up! It's Ben!

Sure. It'd all be over any time now. Just as soon as they… they… what?

Get up, you dumbass! Run! Hide! Do something!

Jimmy opened his eyes when he heard Ben's voice echoing in

the service bay. "Where you at, shithole?" From the sound of the footsteps, Ben was close to the door.

Using what felt like his last ounce of strength, Jimmy dragged himself to the fence and managed to stand. He thought he was breathing heavily, but it felt as if no oxygen was going in. Like one of his lungs might not be working. He was light-headed and weak in the knees.

So this is how it's going to end, eh? Up against the wall, Redneck Mother. Propped up here on one good leg, holding one worthless arm with one so-so arm, waiting for a drunk with a gun to make your head five pounds lighter. Wanna lose five pounds of ugly fat? Ha, ha.

Ben would be around the corner any minute. Jimmy had just one chance. Clawing and scrambling as best he could, he pulled himself over the top of the fence and fell to the ground on the other side. He landed on the leg with the hole in it and stifled the scream that he felt building in his throat. The hammer had gone over the fence somewhere in the vicinity of his mad climb. He had to find it. His life depended on it.

"Hey, muhfugger, where you at? Huh?"

Jimmy groped in the dim light that managed to escape through the grease-caked windows of the service bay. The snow around him was tinted by a spreading red stain. His warm blood, when it met the cold air, created streams of artificial fog that rose from his leg and chest.

"You made me shoot my dog, shithole!"

As his hand closed around the handle of the hammer, Jimmy

peeked through a crack between the boards of the fence. He couldn't have climbed over the fence without leaving some sort of sign, a blood smear on the fence, footprints that just mysteriously ended, something. He just prayed to God that Ben wouldn't look over the fence.

Please, God. Not yet!

Drunken footsteps shuffled across the cement. The oil drums stacked behind the station rattled, then boomed as the stack was overturned. Fifty-gallon drums rolled empty onto the tarmac.

"Don't nobody fuck with my dog an' get away with it. Now you gonna pay."

Ben was past him now, with his back turned. Jimmy stood up quietly and looked over the chest-high fence.

"Where you at, goddamnit!"

"Ben…"

Ben whirled and the sledgehammer caved in the top of his skull. His last shot sailed deep into the woods behind the station. Ben died instantly, without ever knowing what hit him.

Jimmy rested for only a moment. He knew that he was losing blood much too quickly. Every movement threatened to drain him of his last remaining strength. After what seemed to be an eternity, he made his way back over the fence and into the station leaving a trail of large, bright red drops on the tile floor. He reached into his pocket for a dime to put into the pay phone which happened to be the only phone in the building. No dimes in his pocket. For a moment, he was stumped. His mind wasn't functioning. He was blacking out. Struggle. Think.

The cash register. There were dimes in the cash register. As he pulled the handle on the old cash box, he remembered thinking, "Sure. Why not? Old Ben won't need these where he's going, not unless they've started selling ice water there."

He rested the receiver on his shoulder and tilted his head to hold it in place. In the corner beside the desk, he saw Jake's body. Poor Jake. He couldn't help what he'd been turned into. The sight of him lying there, unmoving and blood soaked, made Jimmy want to throw up.

"Atlanta Police Department. Sergeant Williams speaking."

"I need help."

"What's the problem?"

"I've been shot, and I need help." Everything was going gray.

"Okay. Can you tell me where you are?"

"At the service station." Getting dizzy.

"Which service station?"

"Please hurry. I'm bleeding all over…" Jimmy dropped to the floor and the receiver dangled at the end of the cord with a small voice squeaking through its holes…

… and when it was finished, he woke up. But what he had just seen wasn't a dream. Not a real dream. It wasn't unreal or disjointed like dreams always are. It was flowing and coherent. And it was true. It was a bit of history replayed for his own personal benefit. All except the part at the beginning about the pregnant woman and the wreck. He knew the story of the miraculous birth – the whole town did – but did it really happen on the same night as the shooting? He would have to remember to check that out.

He drifted back into sleep, and he didn't dream again that night.

24

Timmy and Doobie were still awake to hear the first stirrings of life outside the bedroom. It was finally safe to get up, but now he didn't want to. What he really wanted to do was go to sleep. He was exhausted. Doobie had already lay his head down and closed his eyes and was now licking his chops in anticipation of a good day's rest. Timmy suddenly understood where the phrase *lucky dog* came from. Timmy knew that he would have to get up soon, so he might as well not even try to get any sleep. But even as these thoughts went through his mind, his eyelids slid shut. He was just dozing off when the argument started in the kitchen.

Gerald was pouring his first cup of coffee. He had come right out of the bedroom. He was dressed in only his pajama bottoms and his hair was standing straight out all over his head. Pamela's pink cotton dressing gown was open, and the sash hung limply in the loops. Her fuzzy slippers were a slightly darker shade of pink and came very close to clashing with her gown. She tried not to look at Gerald when he sat at the table.

"What's for breakfast?" he asked and sipped at the steaming coffee.

"French toast. Any objections?" Cold.

"Goddamn. I just got up. Have I fucked up already?"

"Watch your mouth." She sniffed, took a handkerchief from the big pocket of her gown, and blew her nose as quietly as possible. She stuffed the handkerchief back into her pocket and cracked four eggs into a shallow bowl.

"Look, let's don't start again…"

"I'm not starting anything. Timmy! Time to get up!" Still cold.

"Come on, Pam, gimme a break, okay? What's the problem?"

She poured a little milk on top of the eggs, a little salt, a little pepper. With a slight touch of viciousness, she whipped the mixture with a fork. *Tink, tink, tink, tink…*

"Will you stop that and answer me!"

Pamela slammed the bowl down onto the counter, hoping deep in her heart that it would shatter and send slimy egg shit flying, and threw the fork across the kitchen. The bowl didn't shatter, so she had to settle for a snotty smear on the kitchen wall. "What do you want?"

"Are you still pissed off about yesterday?"

He had *really* fucked up yesterday. The funeral had been a real gut wrencher. Hell, funerals were bad enough, but the coffin for this one was so *small.* The body was just a kid. Little Jim, for Christ's sake! It wouldn't have surprised him at all if ole Jim had just flipped up the coffin lid right in the middle of everything, grinned a shiteatin' grin, and told everybody it was all a joke. But he couldn't sit up, he was dead. And there wasn't enough of his real face left to make up a whole grin. And he was just a kid, little Jim, for Christ's sake! The funeral was sad, and everybody was crying and blubbering and leaning on each other. He even had to wipe a couple of tears on his own sleeve. But goddamn, life goes on, right? As much as he hated his job, he had to go back to work after the funeral. He didn't get paid to sit at home and comfort his wife.

Strike One!

When he had gotten home from work and Timmy had finally wandered in from next door, Pamela started making plans for them to go to Michael's funeral the next day (today). He had said, very plainly and simply, that he couldn't take any more time off from work and he didn't think it was such a great idea for Timmy to go either. Pamela started in on him about how it was important for Jim and Michael's parents. *How would you feel if it were Timmy and no one showed up for the funeral*, she had said, *just because they didn't think it was a great idea? You can do what you like, Timmy and I are going.* Well, it wasn't Timmy, and it was pretty damned morbid of her to be saying that shit while Timmy was sitting right there listening. Right?

Strike Two!

And on top of all that, Doobie was running through the house and barking and generally being a nuisance. Finally, Gerald smacked him on the ass. Pamela said there were laws against cruelty to animals and he said, *So would you rather me take him to the fucking dog pound so they can sell him to some lab where they'll torture him to death so you can live a longer and healthier life? Is that what you want?*

Strike Three! You're outta there, Big Fella!

Yep, the major fuckup. With Gerald that usually came from one of two things: Either he couldn't tell when enough was enough, or he didn't have enough sense not to start anything in the first place.

"I think I have a pretty damned good reason to still be pissed off!"

Gerald threw up his hands. "Hey, look, I don't want to start anyth…"

"Then shut your damned mouth! Timmy! Come on!"

"Okay. Okay, if that's the way it's gonna be, I'd like to get a few things off my chest here. First of all, I don't like the way I'm being treated around here! I pay for the goddamn groceries, I pay the goddamn bills, I pay the goddamn taxes, and all you do is sit on your ass…"

"What!"

"… all day while I have to go to a goddamn job that I hate!"

Pamela's eyebrows pulled together and her eyes filled with hate. When she spoke, her words were quiet and lethal. "Then get another fucking job or shut up. I'm sick of hearing it, and I'll leave if I have to."

"You wouldn't dare."

"Try me."

Déjà vu. His mind flashed back to the night she had threatened to go to the hospital without him. It all started that night. That was the first time she ever mentioned leaving him, and even though "leaving" didn't mean quite the same thing then as it did now, that was the first time. And she'd talked about leaving quite a lot since that night. Maybe yesterday wasn't the only thing she was still pissed off about. She had never come right out and said it, but it was possible that she was still pissed that she was awake and suffering when Timmy was born, and he wasn't. But that was silly. Right?

For a long time, they just stared at each other. When they

heard the door to Timmy's bedroom open, Gerald leaned back in his chair and Pamela took another fork from the drawer.

Timmy plopped himself in the chair opposite Gerald and crossed his arms on the table. Slowly and carefully, he lowered his head to rest on his arms. He looked like hell.

"You look like hell, sport." Even as he spoke to Timmy, Gerald kept his gaze fixed on Pamela. He just knew that someday all of this would make sense.

"I didn't sleep too good." Timmy yawned and closed his eyes. He felt himself drifting away into sleep and he didn't want to stop. It felt so good to doze… so good to slip away… so good… soooo goooooo…

"Timmy?"

It was Lena! He had fallen asleep at his desk again and she had asked him a question only he didn't hear it and he didn't answer and maybe he had even snored out loud and now she was standing over him with the meter stick in her hand and a guillotine behind her!

His head jerked up off his arms and his eyes shot open.

"Whoa, son! I didn't mean to scare you!"

There was a hand on his shoulder. He pulled away from it and shrank back in his chair. His face took on a look of horror and fearful dread. He stared at the person in front of him.

"Timmy, are you alright?"

The room around him shifted and swirled. Walls crumbled and rebuilt themselves. The face peering down at him faded into a soft blur, changing and refocusing itself as he looked on.

It was his father. It took a few seconds for his brain to pull it together, and his first thought was *what the hell is he doing here?*

But *here* was no longer exactly where he thought it was. It wasn't a schoolroom; it was a kitchen. A familiar kitchen. His kitchen. There was his refrigerator that held his two six-packs of Coke, there was his microwave where he made his own nuclear melted cheese and butter on soggy white bread sandwiches, there was his mother beating the hell out of a bowl full of raw eggs, there was his father staring at him as if he were some curious looking animal that just crawled out of a hole. He was at home, and he was officially awake.

"Timmy?"

"Huh?"

"I said, are you alright?"

"Yeah."

The *tink, tink, tink* of the fork on the bowl stopped abruptly and his mother's voice replaced it. "Yeah?"

"I mean, yessir."

"That's better." She went back to her French toast. The slice of bread made a sickening *plop!* as it dropped into the eggs.

"What's the matter? You have a nightmare that woke you up?" Gerald shot occasional glances toward Pam hoping to see some sign of change in her attitude. No such luck.

"No sir. I didn't sleep long enough to have a nightmare."

"You feel sick?"

There was a sharp sizzling sound from the stove and the smell of cooking eggs drifted across the room to the table. On any other day, that smell alone would send Timmy's tastebuds on a memory trip through thick French bread dipped in egg batter, grilled in real butter, coated with powdered sugar, and served piping hot, and he would be drooling all over himself before his plate even got to the table. But this morning his stomach did one flip, kicked up its legs and quivered inside his belly like a small animal in the throes of death. He was already feeling the effects of an entire night with no sleep, and it was going to be a looooong day, boys and girls, you could bet your ass on that.

"No sir, I feel okay. It's just…" Just what? Just that there are boogie mens hiding out under the bed and waiting for the right moment to grab him and do all the horrible things that nobody ever sees because they happen during the commercials? That should go over just dandy. But he couldn't go through many more nights like last night. In fact, one more in a row would just about do him in. But how should he go about telling them what happened last night?

Flat out, that's the best way. He remembered that from somewhere, and at the time he heard it, it sounded like pretty good advice.

"There's something in my room." Whew! It was out, and it wasn't so bad.

"Something in your room? Like what? A mouse? Pam, I thought we were going to get traps and set them out." Pamela put Timmy's plate on the table and set a glass of milk beside it. She looked flatly at Gerald and returned to the kitchen.

"No, sir. Not a mouse. It's…" a ghoulie, a goblin, a gremlin, a haint, a ghost, a vampire, a zombie, a werewolf, maybe more than one, werewolves, mummies, a monster, monsters, something…"

something that's trying to get me."

If Gerald had been drinking from his coffee cup, he would have choked. But he wasn't, and he didn't. He did, however, have to hold back a burst of giggles that he felt was about to surface. "And what does this something look like?"

"I don't know. I haven't seen it, but last night it started pulling the covers, and I'm getting scared. There's no rule about anything like that."

"Rule?"

"Yes, sir. You know the rules, don't you?"

"I'm afraid I don't."

"You know, the monster rules."

"Are you telling me there's a monster in your closet?"

"No, sir. Under my bed."

That was all Gerald could stand. The laughter came in a sudden burst, and once it started it had to run its course. Pamela brought Gerald's French toast (slightly burned, of course, as a continuing reminder of her malice toward him) and slammed it in front of him. Under her breath, she muttered, "Shit! Real sensitive, asshole."

Timmy felt his face flush. It was always embarrassing to be laughed at, but when it was your own father and you were being serious, well, that went beyond embarrassing and into… whatever was beyond embarrassing. And he knew that the only reason his mom wasn't laughing was because his father *was* laughing, and she was pissed at him. He took a big mouthful of his toast and looked down at his plate so they couldn't see his face.

Pamela put her own plate on the table beside Timmy's and ran her fingers lightly through his hair. "It was probably just a bad dream, sweetie. When you're under a lot of pressure, like with Jim and Mike dying, your mind can play some pretty mean tricks on you."

That's okay, Mom, you don't have to pretend. You can go ahead and laugh too.

"That's okay, Mom. I knew y'all wouldn't believe me." He shrugged his shoulders but was careful not to move his head from under his mother's hand. There was something comforting about the rubbing and the slight pulling in his hair.

"It's not that we don't believe you, son. When you get older, you'll start to understand more about what's going on around you. You'll have a whole new set of things to worry about and your monsters won't seem quite so important or real to you anymore."

Timmy pushed his plate away and slid his chair back from the table. Maybe they didn't believe him, but he knew somebody who would. "I'm not very hungry anymore."

"Then get your clothes on. I think we should get to the church as early as we can." Gerald opened his mouth to say something, probably something stupid to start the whole argument all over again, but a glance from Pamela stopped him.

"I was going to Ma's house for a few minutes."

"You can go after school."

"School? Do I have to go to school?"

"Right after the funeral." That, at least, should make Gerald feel a little better.

Timmy stood up. It was a major effort. Every muscle in his

body was crying out for some genuine sleep. As he dragged himself toward his room, he saw Doobie standing in the living room chair and staring out the window toward Ma's house. Just like last night, he was whining. But this morning it was a quiet whine.

Flat out, that's the best way.

Bullshit.

25

The smell of freshly brewed coffee was the first thing James Milford was aware of when he awoke. Then the sizzle of hot grease and the distinct aroma of eggs being fried. He was still groggy and blurry-eyed when he peeked around the corner into the kitchen.

"Hello, sleepy head." Father Francis was at his post in front of the stove with an apron tied around his waist and a spatula in his hand. From the looks of all the pans in use, Francis was cooking up a hell of a meal. "You ready for breakfast?"

"What are we having, or should I be afraid to ask?"

"Grits and eggs, over medium, country style pork sausage loaded with sage and crushed red peppers, pan fried hash browns, buttered toast with a paper-thin layer of melted cheddar cheese on top, orange juice, and a big pot of Father Francis's Killer Coffee. Did I leave anything out?"

"Good God, I hope not!" Milford laughed. It was an honest laugh, the first one for, oh, quite a long time, and it felt very, <u>very</u> good.

"You're feeling better, I assume."

Yes, Milford was feeling better. For the time being, he wanted to just forget about the things that had been happening to him. He wanted to forget all about last night. He wanted to forget about the upcoming funeral that it was his duty to preside over. It felt good to laugh, and at this very moment he wanted to laugh forever.

"By the way, what are you doing in my house?" Milford used a tone of mock indignation and shot a piercing glare toward Francis.

"Well, I came to make sure you didn't oversleep." Very delicately stated. Francis had that gift of tact that so many people never seem to be able to develop in themselves. "I knocked on the door, and when you didn't answer I just came on in. I knew the door wasn't locked because after you passed out last night, I couldn't find your house keys to lock up."

"That's okay. I never lock it anyway."

Francis pointed the spatula at Milford and shook it lightly. "That's going to get you in big trouble one day. Just mark my words."

Milford laughed again. "Consider them marked."

Together the two men sat at the table and ate until they couldn't move. They laughed some more.

Big trouble.

But trouble couldn't find them here. They were in that special place where friends hide out and nothing can get in. Even though Francis wasn't really sure what had happened, they had beaten all of Milford's troubles last night. They had driven them right through the very walls of the church. And Milford felt good. He laughed and talked just like he used to, and that made Francis feel good. Together they could whip any problem that could possibly come up.

Together.

Big Trouble.

If they only knew.

26

Not many people showed up for the funeral. Of course, the very close friends were there. Those were the ones who would show up no matter what the circumstances. It wouldn't make any difference to them if Mike *did* murder his brother. Yes, the big M word had already reached the ears of Rev. Milford three times this morning. Well, three that he could actually pin to real people. Several times he heard talk of killing, and when he turned to see who was perpetuating the rumors, he discovered that it was Michael's own voice zipping through the telephone lines of his memory.

"There he goes, th' fuckin' kid killer..."

Milford looked at the faces of the mourners, and they looked truly sad. Timmy White and his mother were there. He wasn't crying, but that was okay. Pamela was spilling enough tears for both of them. To Timmy's right were Charles and his mother. That made sense: Charles and Timmy went practically everywhere together. They rode to school together, they went bicycle riding together, they sat together in church, they even went to the lake and almost got shot together. Like the rest of the town, he had heard the story of the nighttime raid. As much as anything else, that one story was responsible for the funeral he was conducting today.

"Friends, we are here this morning to pay our final respects to

Michael Ingram, a young man known and loved by everyone here."

And what a crowd we have. Boy, oh, boy. Mrs. Larson could get more people than this together on any given weekend for a Tupperware party. There were some real assholes in this town, and it was becoming more and more apparent who they were.

There was some sniffling and muffled sobs from in front of the coffin. It was Sandra Taylor. She was sitting beside Mrs. Ingram, her boyfriend's mother, and trying to be strong, but the sobs and sniffles were coming. Poor Sandra. In three more weeks, she would find out that she was pregnant.

"It's a sad state of affairs when a person so young feels the necessity of taking his own life by whatever means."

"I found some of my mom's pills – muscle relaxers, I think she calls 'em – and I took me about four of 'em."

If only it had been pills. That would have been easier to deal with. Not that it was ever easy. Knowing that the person you were talking to had suddenly joined the ranks of the deceased was always bad. But walking into a room and seeing bits and pieces of that human being scattered over a wide area was… well, it would have been easier to handle a whole body with a stomach full of pills.

"This isn't going to be one of those funerals where the preacher stands beside the grave and says a lot of wonderful things about the dead person. Everyone here knows… knew Mike, and we all know what kind of person he was. But what about those people who aren't here? What about those people who decided not to join us because of the rumors that have been spreading through town?"

"Do you know what it feels like to kill somebody?"

"Yes, Michael. Yes, I do." There. It was out. He said it out loud in front of all those people. But nobody had time to react because he kept right on talking.

"There are some things that I have to get off my chest, and the people who really should hear them are the very ones who saw fit to not show up today. But that's okay. Maybe you should know these things, too. And maybe you'll repeat them to somebody who wasn't here. Anyway, Michael, I owe you this much. These are my final respects to you."

Milford felt tears welling in his own eyes. He wiped at them with his coat sleeve, not ashamed to let anyone know that he was being emotional. He opened his mouth to continue but paused. Someone was walking across the cemetery toward the gravesite. He was pleased and waited for that person to join the rest of the company.

It was Gerald White. He stepped quietly beside Pamela and she turned to face him. There was a brief moment and then he put his arm around her. She buried her face in his chest and sobbed deeply.

"As most of you know, I was talking to Mike on the telephone when he... well, when he shot himself. I'm sorry, Mr. and Mrs. Ingram, but that's what he did and there's no sense trying to candy coat it. There was no candy coating on what the good people around here did to Michael. Nobody tried to spare his feelings, so I'm just returning the favor for him.

"Michael loved his brother. I know he had a strange way of showing it at times, but he was completely devastated when Jim got killed. Then to hear the rumors that he shot his own brother. And, yes, he heard them just like I did, from people who were supposed to be his friends. That's all it took to push him over the edge.

"I wish everyone here... no, I wish everyone in the whole damned town could have heard what Mike told me on the phone that night. I wish everyone could have heard the desperation in his voice, the pleading and the crying out and the need for everyone to understand."

"I seen Jim get shot. I even got to see what pulled the trigger."

"He told me things that he saw..."

"You're next, asshole."

"... things that he heard..."

"I ain't waitin' around here for that little green fucker to come get me."

"... things that were going on in his mind. Things that he knew nobody else would believe. I'm not sure he actually thought *I* would believe him, but I did. And I do. And there are two things that have to be cleared up, once and for all."

"You tell 'em I ain't crazy..."

"Mike wasn't crazy..."

"... And you tell 'em I ain't no kid killer."

"... and he wasn't a kid killer."

KABLOOMBLOOM!

The rapid explosions were so real in his mind that he stopped and grasped his head. Several seconds went by, and the funeral party just stared at him. He had been right. This wasn't your everyday run-of-the-mill funeral. Finally, Milford stepped closer to the coffin and put his hand on the closed lid. "It's done, Mike. Rest easy."

Then he walked away.

27

Timmy found Ma right after school.

When he knocked on her door, he expected to hear the high-pitched "Come in" that Captain Jack always called out, but it didn't come. From across the yard, he heard Doobie barking. He could see Doobie standing in the living room chair with his paws on the windowsill, and he wasn't exactly crazy about what he saw. The bark was not the oh-boy-am-I-glad-to-see-you bark. Not at all. The dog had his ears laid back and he was shouting out a warning to his master.

Timmy knocked on the door again, and then he turned the doorknob… just a little. The door wasn't locked. Cautiously, he pushed the door open just enough to get his head in. If he *wanted* to put his head in. That might have to wait a minute or two.

"Ma?" Silence.

"Ma? Are you here?" Dead silence.

"Jack? Hey, Jack. Where's Ma?" Really dead silence.

"Oh, well, I guess nobody's home." He was just about to close the door when he spotted the little pile of blue feathers on the floor. He knew that Jack lost an occasional feather or two, but this looked a bit excessive. He pushed the door open a bit more and looked in.

Jack was there, sitting on the perch in his cage. He wasn't moving. He looked like he had been stuffed and mounted. Timmy went in to see if he could tell what was wrong. Before he even got halfway to the cage, he saw Ma sprawled on the floor.

"Ma?" His first thought was that she had fallen and hurt

herself. Then the idea crept in that she had had a heart attack and was dead. She was dead and he was in the house with her. He was *alone* in the house with her. Timmy's devious little mind conjured up a vision of Jim in his coffin, complete with rapidly collapsing face and eyelid fluttering open, and when Ma drew in a long, shallow, raspy breath, Timmy ran out of the house.

In the fresh air, is head cleared and his heart stopped trying to crawl up his throat long enough for him to realize that Ma needed help. Doobie was still barking, and it flashed into Timmy's mind that somehow the dog had known what was happening. Then it flashed right back out again, and he was suddenly wondering what was wrong with Jack. That thought fled and his immediate concern was finding his mother.

In less than fifteen minutes, Ma was on her way to the hospital.

Chapter Three

1

FEAR THE DARK

by

Timmy White

It was getting close to midnight
When Abby heard the noise,
But she paid it not attention and
Kept playing with her toys.

Then suddenly a man in black
Jumped across her bed.
He scared her so, she couldn't move,
Then hit her on the head.

When she awoke, the light was dim
And she wasn't in her room.
Instead the place was cold and damp
Like a cave, or maybe a tomb.

Her hands and feet were tied up tight,
Her head swam ‘round and ‘round,
And in the shadows in the corners
She heard a shuffling sound,

Then another, and another; there were
Lots of people there,
But she couldn’t really see them
Through the darkness everywhere.

Suddenly, there was a flash
And her heart inside her froze.
She had seen this place before,
In a hundred horror shows.

The candles all around were black,
There were pentagrams, and crosses
Hung upside-down to make a joke
Of all the Christian losses;

A ram’s head overlooked the scene
With a frozen sneer,
The man in black who hit her
Called the others to come near.

He had a long knife which he passed
From one hand to another,

Then poor Abby saw in horror
On the altar was her mother!

With one swift thrust the man in black
Stabbed her mother's chest,
And with a slash he opened her and
Showed her to the rest.

He drained her blood into a cup
And passed it all around,
And all the people drank from it
With sickening slurping sounds,

Except those in the shadows (those
Whom Abby had not yet seen),
They shuffled and they moaned and
Enjoyed the gruesome scene.

Then softly, very softly,
Abby heard somebody say,
"Now it's little Abby's turn.
Don't let her turn away."

And those "people" in the shadows
Moved much closer, and she saw
That they were not people after all
As she was stroked by a fleshy claw.

It looked much more like an animal
With it's slimey, scaley skin
And its tongue that flickered from its mouth
And its eyes as black as sin.

It rubbed her cheek, and suddenly,
It gripped her face and chin,
And the things that must have been its lips
Stretched into an evil grin.

The cup of blood was brought to her,
The shadow creatures gathered 'round.
She clenched her teeth as they tipped the cup
And the warm drops trickled down

Across her lips and off her chin.
Then someone pinched her nose
And from the shadow creatures
A spooky chant arose.

She opened up her mouth to breathe
And she tasted the hot sticky blood
As it poured between her teeth in
A thick and lumpy flood.

Then she felt the claw upon her

As they ripped away her gown.
And she never knew what happened next
Because her memories shut down.

That was twenty years ago,
And sometimes they come back
To little Abby without warning
To pick her up and take her back.

For years her heart was heavy
With the all-consuming fear,
Each night a time of waiting
For the footsteps to draw near.

And nighttime was a time of terror
In the moonlight cold and stark,
And a time of cruel testing as
She learned to fear the dark.

But all the years have changed things,
She no longer lives in fear.
She lies naked on the bed tonight
Hoping someone will come near.

But what if they don't come for her?
Then she'll have to go alone
To find the blood she's learned to crave

And drink it on her own.

(This is how it was supposed to be, but I
had to read a shorter version for class.)
Timmy

2

The organ music was soft, barely audible, a series of long, low notes in a minor key. Mood music to create suspense, tingle the spine.

Overhead, the moon hung like a silver serving tray suspended over a dark and forbidding world. A full moon. A werewolf moon. Clouds blown by the howling wind whipped quickly past causing the moonlight to flicker briefly.

Below was the forest with all its dreadful dark spooky-night sounds: The deafening chirp of cricket; the near silent swissssh! *of an owl swooping past; the whistling of the wind through the high branches, invisible in the darkness; rustling of leaves as they were shaken on their stems, sometimes losing their grip and falling in crazy spirals to the ground; the snapping of dried twigs under the foot of some animal too deep in the woods to be seen; the crash of a diseased tree as it collapsed under its own weight. And underneath it all, the constant rhythm, the steady beat, the gradual crescendo of the organ.*

"Robert?"

A new sound in the night. The voice of a young woman stepping cautiously through the undergrowth.

Stupid girl! She was alone! Why? Didn't she know something was going to happen? Couldn't she tell? Couldn't she feel *it?*

COULDN'T SHE HEAR THE MUSIC!!!

Obviously she couldn't hear the music or she wouldn't be wandering around there in the dark. Deeper into the forest she went where the blackness was thicker, the night noises were closer, and the organ music was louder.

"Robert?"

She called again, tentatively, but Robert didn't answer her. A little further on, she pushed aside a bush and stepped right in the middle of the mangled mass that had been Robert. Her hand went to her mouth and she turned to run. That was when the scaley claws clamped around her throat and she screamed.

"Eeeeeeeeeeeeeek!"

Timmy reached up and turned the TV volume down just a little more. It was another session of afterhours viewing, and it wouldn't do to have a loud scream wake up Mom and Dad.

It was one of those Italian-Spanish horror movies that came out in the late 60's. "Succubus Lover." Timmy looked up "succubus" in the dictionary. Interesting concept, but not very appealing in the light of what was going on in his life right now. Things were getting all screwed up. First there was all the weirdness at the gravel pit, then Jim got wasted, then Mike scattering his brains all over the house, and Brother Milford was acting really strange.

That's what really bothered him the most. For all these years, he had been sneaking out of his room at night and watching the horror movies on TV, and for all these years he had been saying to his friends and to himself, "Yes, I believe all this stuff, I believe in ghosts, I believe in werewolves, I believe in witches and spells and all that other shit, and yes, I believe in all things supernatural and scary," but did he really? Up until now, did he really believe all the stuff in the movies, or did he just enjoy being scared for a few minutes and then knowing that when the end credits ran everything would be back to normal and life would go on as usual? That must have been it. He just enjoyed that rush of adrenalin that came with being terrified. He wasn't really a believer… up until now. Now, in real life, he was watching people being killed and a man's life being totally destroyed, all because of a stupid witch's curse, one of those things that only really happened in the movies.

"Aaaarrrrrrrrrgh!"

The girl bit the big one, done in by the same vile demon that had just (during the commercial break, of course) screwed Robert's brains out, literally, and spread them on the ground for all the cute little forest creatures to nibble on. Now the girl's mangled mass fell across Robert's mangled mass, and during the next few days their mangled masses would mesh and merge into one massive mound of moldering maggot munchies. God, that's good!

Shit, I can write this stuff.

Timmy always thought it was a shame that all the really good neat gross scenes got cut out of the movies before they were shown on TV. Who decided what to cut, anyway? Adults, obviously. Probably well-meaning adults who were trying to shelter innocents like Timmy from the horrible world of make believe so that they wouldn't be afraid to face the real world. Well, Timmy had seen the real world, was *seeing* the real world, and had decided that those adults would make better use of their time finding a way to protect him from whatever was under his bed.

Speaking of which…

Timmy felt Doobie shift under the blanket that was covering them. Rule Number One: Cover. Timmy lifted the blanket into a tent and saw Doobie turn toward the bedroom door, his ears perked forward. He heard something. The only time a dog ever acted that way was when he heard something.

There it was. Timmy heard it, too, very faintly, and he knew it was the same thing Doobie was hearing because Doobie started a low rumbling growl deep in his throat. There it was again, louder this time. And it sounded like footsteps, like someone walking back and forth across the hardwood floor, but they must have had very tiny feet.

The organ music seemed to fill the darkened living room as Timmy slowly peeked from under the blanket. A crescendo culminating in a loud long hold on a high-pitched minor chord, and then… silence.

Timmy's bedroom door became a big ugly gaping black hole made to look even more sinister by the flickering blue-gray glow of the TV.

Clomp, clomp, clomp, clomp…

It was there. No doubt about it. And it was coming toward the doorway. Doobie growled again and jumped when Timmy touched him.

"Shhh! Doobie, we can't wake up Dad or Mom or we'll get in trouble!" Timmy wasn't really surprised at how dry his throat suddenly was, but he was surprised at how dry his underwear still was.

Clomp, clomp, clomp…

It had to be right at the entrance, but the light was so dim that Timmy couldn't see anything.

Clomp, clomp.

Wherever it was, that was where it wanted to be because the footsteps stopped. For several seconds Timmy stared at the open blackness and Doobie continued his low growl. Then, very suddenly, a small shiny object flew out of the bedroom, landed on the floor about two feet past the doorway, and rolled toward the edge of the blanket. The tiny feet ran back into the depths of the bedroom and the receding footsteps were accompanied by a burst of giggling and then the dead silence.

It took Timmy ten or fifteen minutes to get up enough nerve to reach toward the edge of the blanket and quickly snatch up the small object. When he opened his hand, he stared at it with his mouth hanging open. Then, the whole world was engulfed in a huge white light as Timmy passed out and Jim's silver bullet fell to the floor.

3

"I'm worried about Timmy." Pamela was at the stove cooking breakfast. The smell of frying bacon filled the room and the sizzling sounded like static from a TV station that had gone off the air.

Gerald sat at the table reading the newspaper. "Why? What's he done now?"

"Nothing. That's what worries me."

"Sure, he's done something. He sneaked back into the living room last night to watch television and fell asleep on the floor. I found him at three o'clock this morning and hauled him back into his bedroom, just like I've had to do damn near every night for the last three years. That sounds pretty normal to me." He found the comics page and folded the paper back to get his daily dose of intelligence.

"I guess so. But don't you think it's kinda strange that he hasn't mentioned Ma once? I mean, my God, he found her half dead on her living room floor. He thinks the world of that woman; he spends more time with her than he does with us. Don't you think he'd want to talk about it?"

"Beats me. Maybe it is strange. Kids can be pretty strange when they want to be. My mother used to say I was strange."

"You still are. Timmy, breakfast is ready."

From deep within the bowels of the house, she heard a small sleepy voice say, "Coming," followed a few moments later by the shuffling of bare feet on the hardwood floor. When the footsteps stopped short of the kitchen, she peeked into the living room to make sure he hadn't taken a detour to snooze on the sofa. He had been known to do that on occasion. What she saw was her son on his hands and knees searching the floor in front of the television.

"What are you looking for?"

He caught a glimpse of the shiny object hiding just under the edge of a chair. Carefully closing his hand around it, he said, "Nothing. I found it," and continued his shuffle into the dining room. He sat at the table in silence, his eyes half closed.

Gerald folded the newspaper and looked at Timmy. He felt a

smile touching his lips and, try as he might, he couldn't stop it. His son was feeling like early morning shit, and he was enjoying every minute of it. He decided to enjoy it even more. Make the kid talk. "So, tomorrow's the last day of school, huh?"

"Yes, sir."

"Well, you don't seem very excited about it."

"I'm excited."

"You sure have a funny way of showing it. You look tired. Did you sleep okay?"

"I dunno. I guess so."

"You know, you'd probably sleep a lot better in bed than on the floor."

"I don't think so."

"Still got monsters, huh?"

What Timmy said next caught both of them completely off guard. "Can we go see Ma tonight?"

Pamela looked at her husband with a mixture of relief and confusion. He was talking about her; that was a good sign, but she had never imagined that he would want to go to the hospital to visit her. They had taken him to visit people there before, and every time he got sick to his stomach. He said it was the smell. And he would start to hyperventilate. In all the times they had taken him to the family doctor, Timmy had never shown any sign of being afraid of him. But in the hospital, whenever a doctor would approach, Timmy's body would tense, and he would start breathing very rapidly. Once, he even passed out. After their last visit to the hospital, he told his parents that he never wanted to go back there, even if it meant he had to die. Now, it was his suggestion that they go. Pamela looked to her husband for some indication of what she should say, but he looked just as confused as she was. Finally, she looked at Timmy.

"Well, I don't know that that's such a good idea, son. We don't really know what happened to her, and they might not be letting her have visitors yet."

"Please?" He turned to Gerald. "Please, Dad?"

"I tend to agree with your mother on this one. Ma's an old woman and she needs time to get well."

"But it's real important."

"Now, what could be so important that it can't wait until she comes home?"

"What if she doesn't come home?"

"Timothy Peter White!" Her voice had that incredible tone of shock that only a mother's voice can have. "What a horrible thing to say! Of course she'll come home!"

"You don't know that."

Pamela's mouth dropped open, and she could not, for the life of her, find a reply. She stared at him dumbly, not believing what she had just heard.

Gerald reached across the table and put his hand on Timmy's arm. "Okay, son. If that's what you want, we'll go as soon as I get home from work."

"Thanks."

Nothing else was said, and Timmy ate his eggs and bacon with his right hand while clutching the silver bullet in his left.

The hospital was relatively quiet that evening. There were no ambulances wheeling into the Emergency Room loading area, there were no doctors and nurses with patients in gurneys frantically racing toward the operating rooms, there were no cryptic messages booming from the hallway loudspeakers. There were only white-uniformed nurses moving casually from room to room distributing the nightly medications.

Still, the sterile hospital smell of alcohol permeated the air. The stark white of the overhead fluorescents reflected unmercifully off the glossy institutional green walls. Just the fact that a building so big and so well lighted and with so many people in it could be so incredibly quiet was a bit scary. Timmy felt his stomach begin to churn. When he started to feel lightheaded, he knew he was breathing too fast. He forced himself to slow down and take shallow, measured breaths. This was too important for him to screw it up. He had to tough it out.

He felt a little better in Ma's room. The smell was still there, but the light wasn't so bright. The TV was on and the old woman had her bed raised into position to watch it, but she looked as if she were asleep. Timmy and his parents approached her quietly and he whispered, "Ma?"

Without opening her eyes, Ma smiled and said, "I know if enybody was gonna come t'visit ole Ma, it be my buddy, Timmy. How you doin', boy?"

"I'm fine. Are you okay?"

"Dey say mebby I be goin' home in anudder day or two." She opened her eyes and looked at Timmy, then his parents. "I see you brung de folks wid you."

Gerald shuffled his feet a little. He had always felt somewhat uncomfortable around Ma. She was friendly enough, but there was something mysterious about her. She wasn't like all the other old people he knew. Even though she sounded like she was fresh off the turnip truck, something about her made Gerald feel like a babbling idiot; like she had already forgotten a lot more than he could ever hope to know. He opened his mouth to speak, but even her present ailment didn't diminish her effect on him. He found himself intellectually impotent. Pamela was the one who replied.

"Yes, he did. What in the world happened to you? You had us worried sick."

"Dey say mebby ole Ma fall down an' bonk herself on de haid."

"Well, we weren't sure that they'd be letting you have visitors, so we tried to talk Timmy out of coming for a couple of days. But he said it was important that he talk to you, so…"

"I'm glad you let him come. Dis place gets so quiet, it like t'dribe me crazy. Well, Timmy-boy, what is dis great impo'tency?"

"It's kinda private," he said, and he turned to look at his mother and father. After several awkward seconds, Pamela took Gerald's arm and led him toward the door saying, "Why don't we go downstairs and get some coffee and let these two talk things over."

"Sure. Coffee." Yeah, boy, coming up with that bit of conversation really taxed his mental abilities. Gerald was relieved to step out into the hallway.

As soon as the door closed behind Gerald and Pamela, Timmy

sat in the chair beside the hospital bed and leaned close to Ma. "What really happened to you?"

"I done tole you, boy..."

"No, you told me what *they* said."

"An' you don't b'lieve dat?"

"No, I don't think I do. What really happened?"

Ma was silent for quite a long time, her eyes focused on some place far away. In her mind were images from two days ago. The thing with the red eyes and the pointed teeth and the green tongue. The thing that had tried to look like Timmy. Captain Jack lying still on the floor. The grating voice warning her against interfering. The hand around her throat squeezing tighter... and tighter... and tighter...

She sucked in a raspy breath and said quietly, "I can't tell you, boy."

"It was whoever killed Jim, wasn't it?"

"What is it you sayin'?"

"You told me that you knew who killed Jim. Well, I thought I knew, too, until last night... when this flew out of my room." He extended his fist and let the silver bullet drop into her open hand. "This was Jim's."

She studied the bullet carefully, turning it over and over and over between her fingers. "You say dis come outta you room?"

"Yes'um."

She frowned and said softly, "Den it be awready started." She set her mind to work. It was time to tell him something, but how much? How much did he already know? How much more *should* he know? She had to be careful of what she said or the thing that had visited her before would do an encore. "You got de boogies in you room, doncha."

It wasn't a question. She already knew. "Yes'um."

"You eber seen 'em?"

"No, ma'am. I just heard noises."

"Tell me de rules."

"What?"

"De rules, boy, de rules. You know de rules, don'cha?"

Of course, he knew the rules, but he didn't know that *she* knew them. He had always thought they were some kind of secret.

"Yes'um, I know the rules."

"Den tell dem to me. What is de first rule?"

Timmy felt a little embarrassed. Even though he had known the rules all his life, he had never spoken them aloud before. Suddenly they seemed silly. But how had she known about them? He cleared his throat and said, "When the room's dark, you have to keep your feet under the covers."

"Right. Now tell me de rest ob dem."

"In the dark, any part of your body that's not covered up can be grabbed." Then he added quickly, "Except your face… you have to breathe."

"Keep goin'."

"After you turn out the lights, you have three seconds to get under the covers before they come out. They usually won't try to get you if you're with somebody else. They can only come out in the dark."

She waved her hand to stop him. "Dat's enuf. Who tole you de rules?"

Timmy tried to remember, but it suddenly occurred to him that *nobody* had taught them to him. He had just always known them. Ma answered the question for him.

"You was born wid dem, right?"

"Yes'um. I guess so."

"Dat means you was marked. You was marked right at de time you was born. Habe de rules been good so far?"

"Yes'um, up until just the other night. One of them tried to pull the covers off of me. I didn't think they could do that."

The old woman propped herself on one elbow and leaned as close as she could toward Timmy. On her face was a look of seriousness that he had never seen there before. "Now, I gonna tell you sumpthin', an' you lissen good t'what I say. You keep dem rules right up close in you mind. But you keep dis close, too: Dese ain't no frien'ly boogies, boy. I don't know t'tell you ev'rythin' right now, but I will tell you dat dey can do t'ings like you ain't neber seen in dem late night films we watch on telebision. Dey can make you see t'ings dat ain't real. Dey can even look like people dat you know." In her mind, she saw the evil thing standing at her door looking like Timmy. In *his* mind, Timmy saw Jim disintegrating in the coffin. "Dey is dang'rous, boy. But you keep doin' dem rules, you hear? If dey been goin' by de rules so far, mebbe dey will keep on for a while. Anyway, couldn't hurt none fer now. But de time is comin' when all de rules in de world ain't gonna help you none. You'll know when dat time come. Dere won't be no doubt. You feel it here, deep in you guts. An' when dat time come, boy, den you *better* be afraid."

Timmy was already afraid. He had come to Ma for reassurance, for comfort. But there wasn't any comfort for him in her face.

"But what about…"

There was a light tapping on the door and Pamela stuck her head in. "It's getting late. Are you ready to go?"

Timmy was about to shout, "Hell, no, I'm not ready to go," when Ma pressed the bullet back into his hand.

"Go now. We talk more later," she whispered.

Timmy left the hospital with one victory: Someone besides himself believed there were monsters in his room. But somehow that was very little consolation.

4

Of all the days in the school year, the last day was the day when the least amount of work was accomplished. The teaching was finished, at least until summer vacation was over (except for those unfortunate few who found themselves attending summer school). The tests had all been taken and graded. There were no more essays, no more book reports, no more math problems to be solved at the blackboard, no more historical dates to be memorized. All that remained was to check in textbooks and pass out report cards. For that, they made all the students come in at eight o'clock in the morning so that they could leave again at eight-thirty.

Well, not everyone got to leave at eight-thirty. The high

school seniors had graduation ceremony rehearsal for most of the morning. They marched, all eighty-three of them, up and down the aisles of the auditorium to the seemingly endless strains of "Pomp and Circumstance" played with somber majesty by one of the school's piano teachers. Then, when they were finally all on the stage, they would go back out the doors and do it again and again until everyone in the procession could execute the tricky hesitation step in time with the music. Finally, they would be released on their own recognizance until six o'clock that evening when they would return for the seven o'clock ceremony. The rest of the day would be spent in shopping, riding around town, acquiring booze for the graduation party, and generally raising hell.

Graduation day always invoked a variety of memories in everyone who had ever gone through it. For Gerald White, it was the only day of his whole educational career that he remembered, and he remembered it quite vividly. It was probably the hottest graduation day in the history of the school. For the whole week preceding it, the early evening temperatures had been in the mid-nineties. There had been talk of breaking with tradition and holding the ceremonies on the football field, but in the end, tradition won out. The graduating seniors were sent to a classroom down the hall from the auditorium where their caps and gowns had been laid out for them. Gerald and some of his cohorts had already planned to beat the heat by wearing Bermuda shorts under their gowns. They thought they were pretty clever until they looked across the room and watched in awe as about three-fourths of the girls in the room removed their underwear. They, too, had thought of a way to overcome the oppressive heat, and it sure beat the hell out of what the guys had come up with. For the males in the room, it was a dream come true. The very girls they had spent years mentally undressing were now standing before them in all their naked glory. The touchy-feely games they had played on dates in the dark suddenly paled in comparison to this overwhelming vision of so many beautiful, undressed females all in the same place at the same time. The girls closed their gowns around their nude bodies and, as they left the classroom, flashed seductive smiles, perhaps suggesting better things to come later in the evening. That image stayed with Gerald through the whole ceremony, and he had to bite his lip to keep from laughing as he watched those girls walk up to the principal one at a time to receive their diplomas. That night, at the party, the suggestions of those wickedly delicious smiles proved true.

Even now, Gerald smiled at the memory. He couldn't help but wonder if Timmy would have a similar experience in another seven years. And speaking of Timmy…

"Come on, son. You don't want to be late for the last day of school."

"This is stupid. We're not gonna do anything. Why can't they mail the report card?"

"Because that's not how it's done. Come on or you're not going to have time to eat breakfast."

"Can't I eat when I get home?"

This time it was Pamela who answered. "No, you cannot. Your eggs'll be ice cold by then, and I'm not throwing out perfectly good food just because you're too lazy to get out of bed on time. Now eat."

Timmy sat at the table and picked at his eggs with his fork. A thought suddenly struck him. "I have to go to Ma's house and feed Jack before I go!"

"He can wait."

"But I promised Ma!"

"I said, he can wait."

Timmy mumbled, "Oh, sure, he can wait and I can't."

Pamela heard him. The ever-present Ears. "What did you say, young man?"

"Nothing."

"Yeah. Right."

Gerald watched Timmy push the food around on his plate. "Why aren't you eating?"

"I don't know. I don't feel real good."

"I'll bet you didn't get enough sleep."

It was true. Timmy had spent most of the night sitting in bed, rubbing Doobie's head and thinking about what Ma had told him. In a way, he wished they hadn't gone to the hospital. Having a few answers was sometimes worse than being completely ignorant. In the early morning hours, he had finally fallen asleep with his light on.

They can only come out in the dark.

Pamela joined them at the table. "How is Jack doing? Is he still acting strange?"

"Yes, ma'am. He just sits in his cage and stares at the wall. I tried to get him to come out yesterday and he almost bit me."

"He probably just misses Ma. But you be careful. Those birds can bite awfully hard."

"Yes, ma'am."

Timmy's energy level started to pick up as soon as he was out of the house and on his bicycle pedaling his way to school. He had already taken his textbooks back yesterday, so the basket hanging on the front of his handlebars was empty. As soon as he got home this afternoon, the basket was coming off to be stored in the closet until the start of the next school year. He looked at the empty basket and grinned. Down the street, Charles waited for him. As soon as Timmy got close, Charles set his own bike in motion and the two rode side by side the rest of the way.

"Jesus, I was starting to wonder if you were coming! I thought maybe you had gone on early." Charles was shouting above the early morning street noise.

"Naw, I was just taking my time today," Timmy shouted back.

"How do you think you did? On your grades, I mean."

"I dunno. Okay, I guess. How about you?"

Charles didn't get a chance to answer. In the distance, the first bell was ringing, and they were still a full block from the school. In another five minutes, when the second bell rang, Lena would close her door and begin her roll call. That was a shitty thing to do on the last day of school, but Lena would do it anyway. That was her way. Never let up. Keep pushing. Don't cut anybody any slack. Hopefully, today would be the last time Timmy would hear Lena call out his name in class.

The two boys pumped their legs as fast as they would go. When they got to the school grounds, they slammed their bikes into the parking rack and ran to the building. "I'll meet you out front,"

Charles shouted, and then disappeared down the hall. Timmy burst into the classroom just as the last bell started to ring. Lena stared at him over the top of her glasses.

5

Charles was at the bicycle rack for almost a half hour before Timmy and his classmates came out of the building. His own teacher had kept her class just long enough to check in textbooks and pass out report cards, about five minutes; she did the two simultaneously to speed things along. Lena, on the other hand, kept her class the full thirty minutes that the principal had allowed. As the boys rode away from the school, Timmy relayed the events of the morning.

First came the roll call. Not only did she call out each and every name and wait for an answer, she then looked up from her book to make sure that the person whose name she called was indeed in the room. It was painfully slow. Next was the textbook check-in. Starting with the first name in her grade book, she called each student up to her desk. The student would stand there while Lena verified the name in the front of every book. Then the student would take the books and place them in neat little stacks on the floor under neat little signs that Lena had tacked to the chalk tray of the blackboard: "Math", "English", "Spelling" … When that exercise in stupidity was finished, she looked at her watch. She saw that she still had plenty of time, so she gave her class one final lecture on the value of education, how extremely fortunate they were to have had her for a teacher, and how they had failed miserably to live up to her expectations. She sat at her desk, looked at her watch, and then remained absolutely silent for two whole minutes. Just when the room full of youngsters thought they couldn't stand it any longer, she opened her grade book and, starting with the first name, again called each student to her desk where they were handed a sealed envelope containing their report card and then individually dismissed. Since Timmy's last name started with a "W," he was one of the very last to be allowed to leave. In essence, Lena had managed to cram three roll calls into a thirty-minute day. That had to be some kind of record.

"Well, what did you get?"

"I don't know. I haven't even opened the damned envelope."

"Let's see."

They stopped their bikes and Timmy ripped one end off the envelope. His grades were worse than he expected: Two B's, three C's, and one D. The D was in English. Things never had cooled off after the book report incident. Even though he thought the *Scarlet Pimpernel* report was the best he had ever done, Lena said it was obvious he had spent his time reading other trash and not his assigned book, so she gave him an F on it. At the time, he had thought about arguing with her, but had then decided it wasn't worth it. The D didn't really surprise him. But how was he going to explain the grades to his parents? Up until the last term he had been doing so well. Up until the last few weeks, when the monsters showed up, his report card carried a lot of A's. The shit would really hit the fan when he showed his folks this.

"What'd you get?" Timmy asked, stuffing the card into his back pocket.

"Four A's and two B's."

"You lyin' sack of shit."

"I did! Here, look." Charles held out his card to Timmy who looked at it briefly and then gave it back.

"Well, your teacher wasn't as good as mine. Just ask Lena."

There was a split-second of silence before the two boys burst into laughter. Then, they rode off to Ma's house. Timmy still had to feed Jack.

6

That night was much the same as every other Friday night.

Midnight.

"Friday Frightmares" on Channel 3: *Invasion of the Body Snatchers*.

Low volume, dark picture.

A blanket for cover.

Doobie whining.

Giggling in the bedroom.

7

Saturday morning, Ma got the news that she could go home. Her doctor, Doctor Coleman, the only doctor from Crystal Springs who was on the staff of the hospital, broke the news to her during his morning rounds. He came down the hallway, whistling some happy tune, swung open the door to her room, and said, "We've got to get you out of here. We need this bed for sick people. Now, you've got two choices: You can leave under your own power, or you can croak. Which do you prefer?"

She grinned and said, "I t'ink I druther leave myse'f."

"I thought you might."

She made a phone call to Pamela and within an hour she was on her way home in the White family's station wagon. In the back seat, Timmy silently wished that he knew how to drive so that he could have gone by himself to pick Ma up. Then he could have talked to her all the way home. There were a lot of things he had to ask her.

Pamela and Timmy escorted Ma into her house, just to make sure she was going to be all right. Doobie ran from next door to meet them and followed them in. At the first sight of Ma, Jack stepped out of his cage and stood on his perch. Ma was back; everything was normal again. She petted the great bird, and he gave her hand a gentle peck. He was, however, soon distracted by Doobie, who was sitting on the floor under the cage, wagging his tail and looking up at him. The two animals stared at one another for a long time, occasionally making whatever noises they thought were appropriate for the moment.

Ma sat back heavily in her chair and let out a long sigh. "It good to be back home. I don' care none fer de hosspiddle."

Pamela went to her side and knelt by the chair. "Well, you've got to be more careful, or you'll end up in there again."

The old woman smiled. "Yes'um, Mudder."

Pamela stood and walked toward the door. "We'll be going

now, but if you need anything just let us know. Okay?"

"Mom, can I stay just a little longer?"

"I don't think so, son. Ma's probably tired and wants to rest."

"Please?"

Ma saw what he wanted to do, but she wasn't quite ready for that yet. "You mudder be right, Timmy-boy. You go on home. We got plenty time fer chit-chat some udder day."

Reluctantly, Timmy agreed. "Okay. Come on, Doobie. Let's go."

Doobie sat very still, staring at Captain Jack for several long seconds. Then, he jumped up and ran out the front door behind Timmy.

8

Sunday morning, James Milford sat in his study mentally preparing himself for the coming sermon. This would be the true test.

How's your faith?

"Not worth a damn right now, but it'll get better." It *had* to get better.

He had spent the last hour checking and rechecking his scripture references. He had stood in front of the mirror reciting bits and pieces of the more powerful sections of the sermon. He had rewritten several of his notes. The sermon was ready. Now, the big question: Was *he* ready?

He thought for a moment about the dream he had last night. He couldn't remember many of the details, but it was another strange one. He was preaching in a pit when acid began to fall from the sky and eat away his skin. He was joined by a boy with a sword, and together, amid shouts and evil laughter, they fought off lightning bolts and fireballs. That was about all he could remember about the dream… except the end: He and the boy lost the fight. He woke up this morning with a very uneasy feeling.

He was getting nervous. His stomach was doing cartwheels on his intestines. He had just put one of his fingers into his mouth to chew on a fingernail when the phone rang. It was Father Francis.

"I just wanted to call and wish you luck."

Milford chuckled. "We're religious men; we're not supposed to believe in luck."

"Whatever. How are you doing?"

"Oh, I'm doing fine. Great."

"Jimmy, this is me you're talking to. How are you doing?"

Francis was right. After what they had been through together, the least Milford could do was be honest with him. "Truthfully? I'm scared."

"Scared, huh?" There was a pause, and Milford heard a rustling of paper before Francis spoke again. "Well, being scared's not so bad. At least you're in good company."

"What do you mean?"

"Open your Bible. Matthew. Chapter twenty-two, verse forty-four."

"Are you going to preach to me?"

"Just do it."

Milford flipped the pages of his well-worn Bible. When he

found the passage, he read it. "And being in agony he prayed more earnestly: and his sweat was as it were great drops of blood falling down to the ground."

"Even Christ was scared, Jimmy. But He didn't let it stop Him. Don't let it stop you."

"I won't. Thank you."

"Look at the bright side. At least you're not on your way to be crucified."

The two men laughed, but neither of them had any way of knowing what was about to happen during that church service.

It was ten-thirty, time for the Sunday School teachers to be letting their classes out. The call from Francis had definitely boosted Milford's spirits. He actually found himself whistling softly as he gathered his notes to go into the auditorium. He was just ready to leave the office when there was a solid knocking on his door.

"Come in."

One by one, the deacons filed into the room led by chairman Roy Wilson. He wasted no time in getting right to the point.

"We just had a little meeting, and we think there may be a big problem here. We've been hearing some talk lately and if there's any truth to it, it could turn out to be real serious."

Milford leaned back in his padded office chair and tried to appear as composed as possible. "And what talk is that?"

Mr. Wilson glanced over his shoulder at the others in the room and then looked again at Milford. "Word has it that when the Ingram boy shot himself, you were there, and you were drunk. Is that true?"

Milford clasped his hands in front of him and rested his chin on his intertwined fingers, shaking his head slowly. He had wondered how long it would take for somebody to say something to him. If Father Francis had heard about it days ago, obviously everybody in town had heard. He knew it was just a matter of time, but why did they have to pick today to confront him? He had enough on his mind right now.

"Yes, I was there. And yes, I had had a drink. I wasn't drunk, but I had had a drink."

"Drunk or not, you know that doesn't look very good to the rest of the community, not to mention to your own congregation."

"Quite frankly, I don't really care what the rest of the community thinks. And as for my own congregation, I would hope that they knew me well enough to understand that I was upset. I had just listened on the telephone while a very disturbed young man took his own life. I was upset, and I took a drink."

The deacon shifted his weight nervously. "That's not exactly what bothers us. You had a bad experience and I'd venture to say that some of us would have probably done the same thing if we'd been in your shoes." The other deacons silently nodded their agreement. "But what bothers us is where did you get the whiskey to begin with? This is a dry county, you know. Are you telling us that after you talked to that boy on the phone you had enough time to drive clear into Hinds county, buy a bottle, have a drink, and then get to the Ingram house at the same time as the police? Is that what you're trying to say? I know the police are a little slow sometimes, but…"

"No, that's not what I'm saying at all."

"Then did somebody give it to you?"

"No."

"Well, what exactly are you trying so hard to not tell us?"

Milford leaned forward on the edge of his chair and crossed his arms on the desk. He thought about reaching into his desk drawer and showing them the bottle he had there, but he knew that wouldn't be appropriate. So he did the next best thing. "I have a bottle at home. I keep it in the kitchen cabinet, right next to the corn flakes and the instant rice. Is that what you wanted to know?"

Mr. Wilson nodded slowly and looked down at his feet. "Yes, sir, I guess it is. And I guess we need to have another meeting." Then he looked at the preacher and pointed a finger at him. "But we want *you* to know something, too. Until we decide what to do, we're going to be keeping an eye on you. We pay you to be an example for the people here, and, quite frankly, we haven't been real pleased with what we've seen lately."

Milford stood and picked up his Bible and notes. "You do whatever you have to do. In the meantime, there is a building full of those people who are waiting for a sermon. Unless one of you men wants to deliver it, I would suggest we go now."

The deacons left the room and Milford stood there behind his desk wondering why all of the deacons had come in when only one of them was going to speak. Security in numbers? Possibly. Intimidation in numbers? That was more likely. Well, it didn't work. He wasn't intimidated at all. He was angry. He was going to go out there and show those people what preaching was all about. As he walked toward the door, he had never been more ready for a church service in all his life.

9

Milford wasn't the only one who was ready for the church service that day. Young Bobby Fuller had a surprise to show some of his friends, and he was going to do it during the sermon when everybody would think they were looking at their Bibles.

Bobby's older brother had come home from college just a few days ago and Bobby, while nosing through some of the college notebooks, had discovered a stash of photographs of his brother's girlfriend. And she was naked. Boy, would the guys on the back pew be surprised.

Boy, would James Milford be surprised.

10

When Milford stepped up to the pulpit, he kept his head down and flipped through the pages of his Bible for a long time. He stalled as long as he possibly could, giving his nerves time to settle, letting his anger at the deacons cool just a little, building his courage to look up at the congregation. Finally, the time came.

He almost cried for joy at the sight that greeted his eyes. The day was clear and warm. Sunlight flooded the room in long, multicolored rays filtered through the stained-glass windows. The large room was filled with real people who had real faces. Very few of them were smiling, but he didn't care; at least they were familiar faces. His whole body relaxed. He took a deep breath and began his sermon.

"Will you take your Bibles now and turn with me to the book of Matthew. Matthew, chapter four. Today we are continuing our series of sermons on Satan and his powers. I know there is some concern among you about why I feel this series is even necessary. Some of you have asked, 'When are you going to preach normal sermons again?' or 'Why is all this stuff about the devil so important?' or 'When are you going to preach about Jesus?' Well, I'll answer those questions for you right now.

"I have come to realize that a 'normal sermon' has absolutely nothing to do with reality. It is what the people *want* to hear, not what they *need* to hear. Any pastor whose sermons can be called 'normal' is doing his people a great injustice. He is not making them aware of the ever-present dangers that are all around them. Satan is important for only one reason: He is a very real danger. He is more dangerous than any of you can possibly imagine. In answer to the third question, I am going to preach about Jesus right now.

"Matthew, chapter four, verse one. 'Then was Jesus led up of the Spirit into the wilderness to be tempted of the devil.'

"That one verse is the subject of today's sermon. The temptation of Christ. But we're not going to look at it from the 'normal' standpoint. We've done that before, over and over. We've all heard the story of how Christ was tempted and how He overcame the temptations and what a great example that set for the rest of us. No, today we're going to look at the temptation from another point of view. From Satan's point of view."

Milford unbuttoned his coat and threw it across his chair.

In the very back of the auditorium, Bobby Fuller took some

photographs out of the inside pocket of his suit coat and passed them to the friend sitting next to him.

Milford continued. "What could Satan have possibly been thinking about? He knew who Jesus was. Later in the Scriptures we find that all the demons in hell knew who Jesus was. What could Satan have possibly hoped to accomplish with this temptation?"

It wasn't until his leg began to throb that Milford realized that the room was growing dark. The sunbeams that had been streaming through the windows were being replaced by shadows. A strong wind was beginning to pound against the outside of the church building. Milford's heart sank.

Concentrate!

"At this particular time, Satan had a lot at stake. He had tried for centuries to find some revenge for his banishment, his expulsion from Heaven. With the arrival of Christ in human form, he saw his opportunity. He knew that when a spirit takes on a physical body, it also takes on the limitations and weaknesses of that body: the need for food and water for example. He knew that Jesus had been fasting and was weakened and hungry. He also knew that if he could persuade Jesus to do even one of the things that he suggested, he could screw up…"

Oops!

"… God's whole plan."

A slip of the tongue. The sermon was sliding toward the back of Milford's mind and was being replaced by the old fear. The wind was louder. The pain struck his chest.

"Control of the universe was at stake. By striking at the very essence of God in His most vulnerable form, Satan saw a chance to…"

Something warm rolled down Milford's leg and his mouth hung open in disbelief when he saw the blood seeping through his pants leg. A small red stain appeared on his white shirt and spread rapidly.

"Desecrated," he whispered, and tried to step away from the pulpit but he felt his leg going numb. He grasped the top of the podium and held on for dear life. The wind outside sounded like a hurricane. Gusts struck the windows and rattled them in their frames. The preacher looked out at his bewildered congregation and shouted above the wind, "Why is this happening!"

Suddenly, the doors at the back of the room blew open and slammed into the walls. The strong wind whipped through the sanctuary, distracting the crowd but only momentarily. Their attention soon returned to their babbling preacher. He was on his hands and knees now, crawling away from the pulpit.

Roy Wilson had seen enough. He stood to address the congregation, but was stopped by high, piercing screams.

The preacher was screaming at the top of his lungs. *They* were back. In hordes they floated through the open doors. Hundreds of them, thousands, millions. They had bodies now, and faces. Horrible, evil faces. He saw them clearly, and he screamed.

Closer they came, at a slow steady pace. Milford forced himself to his feet and limped toward the side door, but they were there waiting for him. He turned to go the other way, but they were there, too. He was trapped, and they were coming closer, and closer, and closer.

He tried to muster his courage. "They can't hurt me," he said softly to himself.

Closer…

"You can't hurt me!" he shouted.

… and closer…

"You can't hurt me!"

… and closer…

"You can't hurt me you can't hurt me you can't hurt me you can't…"

Milford's mind shut down. His eyes rolled back in their sockets and he fell forward onto his face.

11

"Ma! Ma!" Timmy burst into the old woman's house without knocking or waiting for Jack to answer. He was excited, but it wasn't like the excitement of a young boy who gets a bicycle for his birthday. It was like the excitement of a young boy who suddenly realizes that he has witnessed a murder. The excitement was translated into fear on his face, and Ma saw it immediately.

"What is it, Timmy-boy? What happent?"

"Ma, I gotta talk to you! This is bad! Really bad! I gotta talk to you right now!"

"You gots to seddle youse'f down some is what you gots t'do. You gonna blow de brain right outta you haid."

"I can't settle down! This is… this is *bad*!"

"Den I guess you should tell me all 'bout it."

Timmy sat on the sofa beside Ma's chair, and in less than five minutes he relayed to her the whole incident of the morning church service. His hands were shaking, and he would never look up to face her. He looked at Jack, he looked at the door, he looked at the walls, but he would not look at Ma's face. That wasn't like him. Ma would find out the reason, but she would let him finish having his say first.

"... and as soon as he hit the floor, a bunch of men ran up there. My dad was one of them who helped haul him into his office, and he said the deacons said it was because of his drinking and that they thought they should probably fire him. But it wasn't because of his drinking."

"An' how you know dat?"

"I... I just know."

That was the problem. There was something he wasn't telling her; something that, from the very start, he had had no intention of revealing. That's why he wouldn't look at her. That's why he wasn't answering her questions. A little nudge might help.

"Is dat all de story?"

Timmy sat silently for a moment. Then, quietly, "I guess so."

"Well, you right, Timmy-boy. Dat is bad. It is a terr'ble t'ing fer de preacher. But why is it dat you be in such a state?" Timmy didn't answer, he just looked at his shoes. "Is it dat mebbe you know sumpthin' else dat you ain't tellin'?"

"Yes, ma'am," he said, sounding a little bit ashamed.

"An' what might dat be?"

Timmy opened his mouth and then hesitated. Goddamn it. Why had he even come here? He knew there were some things that he couldn't say, and he should have known that it would come down to this. He was so shaken by the church service that he just didn't think about what he was doing… until it was too late. Asking Ma for help had been the only thing in his mind, but now he was stuck. "I can't tell you," was all he could find to say.

"Why not?"

"I took an oath not to tell anybody, and I can't break that."

Ma leaned her head back to gaze at the ceiling and for a long time she and Timmy sat there in silence. An oath was a serious thing, not something to be taken lightly. But in the giant jigsaw puzzle that was forming in her mind, a lot of pieces were missing, and she figured that at least some of them were locked away in Timmy's oath. She had to have those pieces.

"You lookin' fer de truff, ain't you son?"

"What d'you mean? What kind of truth?"

"Oh, 'bout lots of t'ings. 'Bout how you frien' Jim die, 'bout what happent to de preacher, 'bout dem t'ings under you bed. Ain't dat right?"

"Yes, ma'am."

"You go t'church damn near ev'ry Sund'y, don't you?"

"Just about."

"An' why is dat?"

"I don't know. Because my mom and dad make me, I guess."

She rubbed her eyes and thought for a minute. The was going to be much harder than she imagined.

"Dat's de wrong reason for a truff seeker to be goin' t'church. Just goin' t'church ain't seekin' de truff, dat's play-actin'. Seekin' de truff is what you does here…" she tapped her chest, "… deep in de soul. Now I got me a feelin' dat de preacher was tryin' t'tell you a whole lot ob truff an' you didn't hear it 'cause you was dere fer de wrong reason."

"He didn't have to tell me. I know why Jim died… I think… but I *do* know what happened to Brother Milford."

"An' I got me some idears, too, but if you don't tell me what you t'inks den we'll neber know if we t'inkin' de same t'ings. You gots t'help me, Timmy-boy, or I can't help you."

He spent several minutes weighing what she had said. It seemed to make sense, in a warped sort of way. After all, he hadn't come rushing over here just to tell her about Milford; he came to get help. But what about the oath? Yeah, what about the oath? Keeping the oath hadn't helped Jim at all because the witches didn't know they had made an oath. When Timmy finally looked at it that way, the decision wasn't very difficult.

"Okay. But you've got to promise that you won't tell anybody."

"If it be anyt'ing like I t'ink it is, who gonna b'lieve me anyway?"

And so, he spilled his guts. As soon as he started, the words flowed like a river out of his mouth. Of course, he sort of skimmed over all the sex stuff, but when he got down to the real ceremony he went into great detail. Through it all, Ma listened carefully, making mental notes of things to discuss when he finished. That turned out to be quite a while.

He ended with the story of he and Charles destroying the altar.

By then he was drained, and he just melted back into the sofa. Now it was Ma's turn.

"Let's go back to sumpt'ing. When dat woman start talkin', what was it dat she said, 'zactly?"

"Well, I don't remember exactly what she said." The notebook popped into his mind. "But I wrote it all down! As soon as I got home, I wrote down as much of it as I could! Just a minute and I'll go get my notebook."

Timmy raced out the door and across the yard to his own home. He threw open the front door and was greeted by Doobie, waging his tail and leaping in short hops as he tried to keep pace with the running boy.

"No running in the house." The voice belonged to his mother and came from the kitchen where she was, once again, cooking the family's meal.

"Yes, ma'am." He slowed to a fast walk until he got to his bedroom door. That's where Doobie hesitated. "Come on, boy. It's daytime." Doobie followed, and when the door was closed behind them, Timmy leaped across the foot of his bed to the side where he had stashed the notebook. He didn't take the time to lift the mattress; he just slid his hand under and moved it back and forth until his fingers touched the hard edge of the cardboard cover. When he had the precious notebook in his hands, he paused. How was he going to get it out of the house? It might look like an ordinary notebook, but what was inside bordered on pornography. What if his mom or dad wanted to look at it? He couldn't risk that. He pulled the tail of his pressed white shirt from inside his suit pants (left over from church) and pushed the notebook as far under as it would go. When he retucked his shirt, he saw that the notebook made a definite impression as it stuck out from his chest, but he figured that if he went fast enough no one would notice it. "Okay, Doobie. Let's go."

"I'm going back to Ma's house," he shouted as he fast-walked through the living room.

"Don't be long. Dinner's going to be ready in just a few minutes."

"I won't," and he was out the door and running across the lawn with Doobie at his heels.

When they got back to Ma's house, Doobie went immediately to his spot under Jack's cage to watch the huge bird. Timmy found Ma sitting at her table with an ancient looking, leather bound book opened in front of her. He pulled the notebook from under his shirt.

"Why you keep de book dere?"

"I didn't want my folks to see it."

"Good t'inkin'."

While Ma searched through her book, Timmy sat and flipped through the pages of his own book; past the part that told about their plan for the night, past the drunken party, past the sexual orgy (he turned those pages quickly). "Here it is. When they started their spell, this woman said, 'Father Darkness, we have a petition.' I'm pretty sure that's what she said. I know she started with 'Father Darkness'."

Ma carefully turned the yellowed pages, which were probably older than she was, and muttered, "Fodder Darkness... Fodder Darkness..." After a minute of reading and scratching at her thin gray hair, she asked, "Is dat all she say?"

"No, ma'am. She said they had some of his blood and a picture."

"Did she eber say sumpt'in' like 'Agu Mass Sarratuu' or 'Rabbutaii ssar'ti'? Did she eber say dose t'ing?"

"No, she never said anything like that. She didn't use any strange words. It was all stuff that I could understand."

Ma closed the book, and for the first time Timmy saw how old it really was. The leather binding was cracked and big chunks of it had peeled away. The title, if it ever had one, was completely gone. It looked like the pictures he had seen of books that were kept inside glass cases in museums. He wanted to get his hands on it, but he knew that would never be allowed.

"Dem witches, you say dey run when de t'ings start happ'nin'?"

"Yes, ma'am. And so did we."

"Den dey ain't done nothin', boy. Dey ain't real witches; dey be only playin' at it. Dey couldn't conjure a balomey samitch outta de 'frigerator."

"Then what happened to Brother Milford? And what happened to Jim? I don't understand."

Ma got up slowly and tottered back to her more comfortable padded chair. "Dem witches ain't call nothin' up. All dey done was piss sumpthin' off." She looked at Timmy and he had a look of total confusion on his face. "You still wants to know de truff?"

"Yes, ma'am."

"Dat could be good, dat could be not so good; dat's not fer me t'say. But I will tell you one t'ing. Dem what seeks de truff us'ly gets more dan dey bargains fer. Mos' people can stop wheneber dey gets too much. But some people, like you an' me an' you preacher-man, we ain't got much say in it. Fer some reason, we was chose special.

"Now, what I got t'say ain't pleasant, boy. I ain't got all de why's figgered out yet, but dose t'ings I do know will scare de shit right outta you. I didn't t'ink you was ready t'hear all dis, but time seem t'be gettin' mighty short all ob a sudden. So lissen good."

Timmy swallowed hard. If what Ma had to say was even more scary than the story he had told her, he wasn't really sure that he wanted to hear it. But, ready or not, she plunged right in.

"You got dem monsters under you bed, right?"

He nodded.

"All you life, you knowed dey was dere, but you neber see or hear dem 'til just recent. De preacher got de monsters, too, but he don't know what dey are. He know sumpthin', but he ain't quite sure what it is dat he know. I got dem, too, boy. But dey ain't monsters; dey be debils. Dey be *bad* debils. I got me a visit from one ob dem. Dat's why ole Ma got in de hosspiddle, not 'cause she fall an' bonk her haid.

"Sumpthin' is happenin' aroun' here, son. Sumpthin' real import'nt. An' I gots a feelin' dat de t'ree ob us is a part ob it."

Timmy went to the sofa and sat heavily. "I don't understand. What about the witches?"

"I tole you, boy, de witches ain't witches an' dey ain't done nothin'. I 'member one Sund'y you come in here an' you tell me 'bout de preacher bein' strange. If my rec'lection is right, dat was b'fore de witches done de spell on him. De debils was awready comin' to him.

Dey didn't need no witches to conjure dem up. All de witches done was t'stumble on de debils' restin' place, an de debils jus' d'cide t'habe some fun so dey jump up an' scare de play-witches. Dat's all dere is t'dat. But dat ain't all dere is to de debils. Dey seen you dere, you an' you frien's, an' dey seen a way t'get to you. Jim. After Jim was dead, did you look at him?"

Timmy looked away from the old woman and nodded.

"You seen sumpthin' bad, didn't you?"

He nodded again, but it was so slight that she almost didn't see it.

"Dat was de debils usin' Jim t'get to you. Den dey throwed his bullet at you." Suddenly, in her own mind, she saw the thing that had visited her, the thing that had tried to disguise itself as Timmy. She felt the hair on the back of her neck prickle. "An' mebbe dey gonna use you t'get to somebody else, like de preacher. Or me. Dey'll use whateber an' whoeber dey want when dey d'cides t'get to somebody. But dere ain't nothin' we can do 'bout any ob dat, 'cept be ready. 'Cause when de time come, it gonna be a mighty battle."

That was all she had to say. That was all she knew to say because she still didn't have all the pieces of the puzzle. And she never would.

An eerie silence filled the room. Ma looked at Timmy. Timmy looked at the floor. Captain Jack and Doobie stared at each other. During the last few minutes, a multitude of information had been conveyed, and not just between Ma and Timmy.

12

It was the middle of the afternoon when the knock came on James Milford's door. He got up from where he had been lying on the sofa and immediately reached out for something to steady himself. He was groggy and the room was spinning around him. The doctor had pumped him full of tranquilizers and it was a struggle just to stay awake. Finally, he sat back down and said, "Come in."

Father Francis entered with a look of genuine concern. "Jimmy, are you all right?"

"Do I look all right?"

"You look like hell."

"Well, there you have it."

Francis sat with Milford and placed the books he carried on the coffee table. "I just heard what happened this morning. At least I heard what the people in town think. Now, you tell me what really happened."

Milford leaned forward and held his face in his hands. He took a deep breath and let it out with a loud sigh. "They came back. The church doors flew open, and they just blew in with the wind."

"How many of them?"

"God, I don't know. Hundreds, maybe thousands. The whole damned room was full of them." He turned to look at Francis and felt a tear roll down his cheek. "I can't go back in there, Francis. I just can't. Then he began to sob.

The priest put his arm around his friend and felt the depth of the pain through the heaving of Milford's shoulders. "I'm really sorry, Jimmy. I guess it's my fault. I should have known better than to try screwing around with the rituals. I was afraid it wouldn't work."

"But it did work! I saw them leave when we did the ritual!" Milford pulled away and looked at Francis. There was a sadness in the priest's eyes. "But you didn't see them, did you?"

No, Francis hadn't seen the church full of demons being driven out through the walls of the building. But what was the hand he saw at the light switch? An hallucination? A figment of his imagination? No, it was a hand. "That doesn't mean they weren't there."

"When I stepped up to the pulpit this morning, that place was clean. I could feel it. And then… something… happened."

"Maybe consecration wasn't the answer. Maybe we should have done an exorcism."

"Don't make fun of me."

"I'm not, Jimmy. I'm deadly serious. But it's too late for that now. There are rumors about you all over town. I think maybe you've outlived your usefulness here. And I've outlived mine. At least that's what the Church feels."

"What are you talking about?"

Francis hesitated, then cleared his throat. "I'm being transferred."

"What?"

"They told me just a couple of hours ago. I'm being transferred. Well, actually, they're sending me back to school for some 'readjusting.' Then I go to some small parish up in New Hampshire."

"When?"

"I leave tomorrow morning."

"Tomorrow morning! Jesus Christ! Don't they have to give you some warning or something?"

Francis shifted uncomfortably in his seat. He didn't want to say what he had to say; it would only make Milford feel worse. "Well, when you screw up, the wheels of bureaucracy can turn awfully fast."

Milford could see the rest of the story in Francis' eyes, but he asked anyway. "They found out?"

Francis nodded.

"How? I didn't tell anybody."

"It was one of my parishioners. Evidently, he saw us going into the church and got suspicious. He peeked in while we were performing the ritual. I don't know how much of it he saw, but it was enough to convince the bishop that something had to be done. Immediately."

Milford was dumbfounded. He had never expected something like this to happen. All he did was ask a friend for help, and now the friend was on the firing line. Somehow that just didn't seem fair. He wanted to become hysterical, but the tranquilizers wouldn't let him. He struggled to find something to say, but a feeble, "I'm sorry," was all he could come up with.

"Jimmy, it's not your fault. I don't want you to think that, not ever. It's not anybody's *fault.* It's just one of those things… coincidence, fate, will of God, something. Whatever it is, it's over and done. Let's just leave it at that."

"But you can't go!"

"I don't have any choice."

"Francis, I need your help!"

The priest was trying to remain as calm and unemotional as possible, but Milford was making it very hard for him. "I can't help you any more. I've done all I can do."

"No! No, you haven't! The ritual! We can do it again! It worked before, and this time…"

"There's no time. I have to leave."

"Call them! Tell them something's come up. Tell them you have some things to finish before you go."

"Stop it, Jimmy! You don't understand. I'm breaking the rules just by being here right now. I was specifically ordered to not have any further contact with you. They would have my ass if they knew I was here." There it was, the whole truth blurted out in a moment of angry frustration. Yes, sir, that should really make his friend feel better, right? Francis stopped for a moment to let his feeling of shame pass. "I can't do any more. I have to leave. Face it, Jimmy. It's over." His emotions caused his voice to crack, and, once again, Francis had to stop.

Milford was devastated. His last ray of hope had just vanished. The drugs were all that kept him from completely breaking down.

Francis cleared his throat to regain control of his voice. "I brought you some books. Read them. Maybe they can help."

Milford stared dumbly into space. Francis took him by the shoulders and turned him so that they were face to face. "Jimmy, listen to me. I'm going to give you a piece of friendly advice. After the rumors I heard about you, I think you should leave, too. Think about it." Then, he put his arms around Milford, hugged him tightly, and whispered, "God bless you, James Milford."

Francis walked away, and Milford let him go without a word.

It would be many years before the two men met again, and when they did, it wouldn't be a pleasant reunion.

For a full half hour, Milford sat staring. For most of that time, he didn't really think about anything. There was so much he *needed* to think about that his mind couldn't find a place to start. So, he sat.

Finally, his gaze fell upon the books that Francis had left. On the top of the stack was the Roman Ritual.

Ritual.

One step at a time. That was the key. One step at a time. That's how rituals were performed; that's how he would proceed.

One step at a time.

Milford stood on uneasy legs and made his way to the writing desk. He fed a new sheet of paper into the typewriter, thought for a moment, and then began.

Dear beloved friends, it is with a heavy heart that I write these words. They do not come easy for me, but they must be said. I have done a great injustice to you...

13

"... but they must be said. I have done a great injustice to you in my striving to be your spiritual leader. Certain events have shown me clearly that I am not properly prepared for this calling. It is a more serious responsibility than I ever dared to imagine.

"The time has come for me to explore my beliefs and renew

my faith. I know not what course this exploration will take, nor the amount of time involved. Only God can ascertain the answer. I feel, however, that I would be doing a further injustice by continuing any attempt to guide you when I, myself, am unsure of the path.

"It is, therefore, necessary that I submit to you my resignation, effective immediately.

"God bless you.

"Sincerely, Reverend James Milford."

Roy Wilson, Chairman of the Board of Deacons, looked out at the evening congregation from the pulpit. He folded the single-page letter and stuffed it into his inside coat pocket.

"The letter is dated today. Brother Milford handed it to me in the hall just a few minutes ago. At this time, I would like for it to be noted that the deacons met right after the incident in this morning's service and voted to grant Brother Milford a Leave of Absence; some time to straighten out what we considered to be some personal problems. But it seems that Brother Milford has something else in mind. Do I hear a motion that we accept Brother Milford's resignation as stated in his letter?"

One of the front row deacons raised his hand and said, "So moved."

Another raised a hand and said, "Second."

Roy Wilson continued with the formalities. "The motion has been made and seconded. Is there any discussion?"

There was none.

"Okay, all in favor say 'aye'."

"Aye."

"All opposed?"

There was no opposition.

14

School was out, and Monday was officially the first day of summer vacation. Suddenly, the town was swarming with young people who had a lot of time on their hands. And there would be more of them in a couple of weeks. It seems that on Friday night, right after the graduation bash, most of the high school seniors left for Fort Lauderdale on a little excursion before beginning the temporary jobs that would keep them busy until it was time for them to start college. Those who stayed behind were now cruising the streets in their own, or in their parents', cars. The younger kids took to their bicycles or played in their yards in small groups. None of the students, from the very youngest to the very oldest, needed much time to adjust to their new schedule. After all, they had been waiting nine whole months for this day.

Gerald White was a little envious of the young people and their new freedom. It just didn't seem quite fair that while they were out shopping or cruising or lying on the beach, he had to be stuck inside the shirt factory all day. On a whim, he called in sick.

Any other day he would probably have felt guilty about doing that, but not today. And, if he were to be completely honest, envy had very little to do with his decision to call in. The truth was that he didn't plan to be at the shirt factory much longer anyway. A few weeks ago, he had put together a resume that made him sound like the greatest thing since sliced bread and he had sent a copy of it to every institution of higher learning that he could think of in the state. It was just a matter of time.

Gerald stepped out of the house and into the dazzling sunlight and the sweltering heat of the summer morning. He breathed in the clean, fresh air and remembered once more why he didn't regret moving back here from Los Angeles all those years ago. With no particular plan in mind, he decided to walk around the yard and look things over. He hadn't done that for a long time.

The family lot had grown smaller over the years. Gerald remembered a time, probably thirty years ago, when his parents owned practically the whole block; probably more. They had a couple of cows, some chickens, and a goat, too, if memory served. There was a nice, big garden on the south side of the property, and when he was just a small boy, Gerald used to stand beside one of the tomato plants and eat fresh tomatoes until his mouth was raw. But most of that acreage was gone now, sold off in small portions to various people. The last to go was the small lot where Ma's house now stood. What was once a substantial, self-sustaining farm was now reduced to a typical middle-class subdivision lot.

The family house once stood in the north-west corner of the lot. When his parents finally had a new house built further back on the property, Gerald and his father tore down the fine old house, board by board, all by themselves. It must have taken them two years, working on weekends and late in the afternoons, but they managed to get it all down. All except the cement slab that was the front porch. They left that, and it still remained, along with all the rose bushes that his mother had so painstakingly planted around it. They called it a patio and decorated it with several pieces of lawn furniture, but it always looked so lonely just sitting there in its little corner of the yard.

The whole lot was a miniature botanical garden, and Gerald was constantly amazed at how many different types of trees and plants his parents had managed to cram into that small space. There were oak trees and pecan trees and mimosa trees and redbud trees and silver-leaf maple trees; these were all in the front yard. In the back and side yards were the fruit trees; peach, quince, pear, crabapple, fig, pomegranate, and three types of plum. In between all the trees, wherever there was room to dig a hole, were the azalea bushes, the roses, the honeysuckles, the muscadine vines, and a host of others with such exotic names that no one ever dared an attempt at pronouncing them. And there was even a bit of poison ivy that crept in from somewhere. All of this, plus lovely, colorful flower beds; and Gerald's mother had one of the worst cases of hay fever known to mankind. But she absolutely refused to give up her plants.

Everything was still there, all the things that Gerald remembered from his childhood, including the gravel driveway where he had spent countless hours sifting through the rocks to find the tiny fossils that were brought up from the gravel pits. Everything was basically the same, but everything had changed. The small trees that he remembered helping his father plant were now fully grown and stood like giants over the lawn. The branches of the older trees, where he played as a boy, were rotting and breaking away. The whole yard had lost the crisp beauty that was so vivid in his memory. The years were taking their toll.

As Gerald came into the front yard from behind the house, he saw Doobie snoozing peacefully under one of the maple trees. He smiled and thought about his own dog who, on hot summer days, used to lie just about in that same spot. Fluffy was her name, and a boy couldn't have asked for a finer dog. She would have probably been a good hunting dog; she was definitely a good tracker. One day, while he was at school, Fluffy got out of the house and followed his scent all the way down the street, into the school building, and right into his classroom. Everyone thought it was really cute. Well, *almost* everyone. His teacher was Lena Green, and she didn't think it was cute at all.

In the tree above Doobie, Timmy and Charles were hard at work on the tree house they had been planning for months. This wasn't a first for this old tree. Gerald and one of his friends had built their own tree house in it years ago, just before Hurricane Betsy ripped through. While they were working on it, Gerald's dad climbed the ladder that was leaning against the tree and, in his deep Southern country drawl, asked, "Y'all need a hand?" They didn't quite know what to think, but to satisfy a middle-aged man who needed to feel useful, they said "yes" and put him to work cutting the lumber for them. He turned out to be more helpful than they expected, and the tree house was great. It even survived old Hurricane Betsy.

Thinking about his father brought a sudden heaviness to Gerald's heart. He walked slowly across the lawn to one of the bushes and ran his foot across the grass there. That was where his father died, right on that very spot. He was mowing the lawn and he just dropped. The doctor said he was probably dead before he even hit the ground.

Dad was quite a guy. He was quiet and smiling and strong as an ox. Just about everybody in town knew him, and they also knew that if they ever needed help with anything at all, they just had to ask and he would do whatever he could. There wasn't a better man in the world.

That was the Dad that Gerald remembered, but there was another side to him that Gerald wished he knew more about: The Dad in the old family photo box. Some of the pictures were taken during World War II, some even earlier. They showed a much younger man, short, with lots of dark wavy hair and laughing eyes. A man who worked hard, even early in his life, but never regretted a minute of it.

One of Gerald's favorite photographs in the box was taken on board a ship during the war. In the background was some port, France or Russia or somewhere, and on the ship's deck were two men. One was wearing only a towel with his shoes and socks. The other man, Gerald's dad, was not wearing a shirt, but he *was* wearing a .45 automatic on his hip. For some reason, that photograph always fascinated Gerald. When he was a boy, he would look at that picture and then look at his father and try to imagine that quiet, gentle man carrying a gun. It boggled his mind.

The last time Gerald saw his father alive was when the parents flew out to Los Angeles right after he and Pamela were married. That visit was quite an event. His mother had never been to California and his father had never been on an airplane. They stayed for two weeks and had the time of their lives. At the end of their stay, Gerald drove them to John Wayne Airport and watched as they walked across the tarmac toward the plane. For the first time, Gerald noticed the forward slump of his father's shoulders and how his steps were more shuffling than they used to be. Gerald whispered, "God, he looks old." *I'll never see him again.* The thought was in and out of his head in a flash, but it was true. A few months later, his father was dead.

After the funeral, Gerald's mother decided to move to Jacksonville to live with one of her sisters, so Gerald brought Pamela back to Crystal Springs to keep up the family homestead. And they had kept it up as best they could, but somehow it just wasn't the same; it could *never* be the same as he remembered. He wasn't seeing it through the eyes of a child anymore.

As he walked toward the maple tree, he sighed and snapped a dry twig off one of the bushes he passed. He really loved this old place. It was going to be hard to leave when the time came.

Gerald climbed the makeshift ladder that led to Timmy's tree house where the two boys were trying desperately to drive nails into an old, weather-hardened oak two-by-four.

"You boys need a hand?"

Charles and Timmy looked at each other for a moment. Then, Timmy shrugged and said, "Sure," and Gerald knew exactly what his son was thinking.

15

The letter came in the Tuesday afternoon mail delivery. It was on official University of Southern Mississippi letterhead and was addressed to "Mr. Gerald L. White." Keeping it unopened until Gerald got home from work was almost more than Pamela could handle.

She held her breath as Gerald ripped open the envelope and read the one paragraph letter. Short letter. That usually wasn't a good sign. When he finished reading, Gerald's face revealed nothing; no excitement, no disappointment, nothing. He just folded the paper and stuffed it back into the envelope.

"Well? What did it say?"

"They want to talk to me as soon as possible."

"That's great!"

"That's not great; it could mean anything."

"Well, aren't we Mr. Optimism today? What, they want to call you all the way down there to congratulate you on the wonderful resume you wrote? They're *interested* in you, dumbass!"

"I'll call them and see what they have to say."

Pamela gave up on him. He was the only person she knew who could turn good news into gloom without ever knowing exactly what the good news was. But she knew that if he went into an interview with that same attitude, he would never get a job. Still, she kept her mouth shut.

He called the school the next day to set up an appointment, and when they said, "as soon as possible," they weren't kidding. The dean of the department wanted him there at ten o'clock Thursday morning.

Hattiesburg was a ninety-mile drive from Crystal Springs, so Gerald, being unfamiliar with the early morning traffic patterns along the route, allowed two hours for the drive and a half hour to find the building and compose himself. He should leave home no later than seven-thirty A.M.

When he came out of the bedroom at six-thirty, on his way to the bathroom, he had to step over Timmy and Doobie who were asleep on the living room floor. The TV wasn't on, so Gerald leaned down and whispered, "Nothing good on last night, huh?" He ruffled Timmy's hair and went for his shower. A light breakfast of toast and coffee would hold him until after his meeting, then he could stop for a burger on the way home.

Seven-thirty A.M. He left right on schedule.

16

"Mom, we're gonna camp out at Charles's house, okay?"

Before Pamela could say, "Yes, please, get out of here, just let me have some time in peace, and oh, by the way, have fun," the two boys were out the door and racing down the street toward Charles's house lugging Timmy's camping gear on their backs. She breathed a deep sigh of relief. With Gerald gone for the day and Timmy gone until tomorrow, she could finally get out of the goddamned kitchen. She poured a cup of coffee and sat in the living room with her feet propped on the footstool. It was ten-thirty on a Thursday morning, and with her two men out on their own, she wasn't going to do anything all day long.

Well, maybe she would do *one* thing. If it took her the rest of the day, she was going to figure out what had gone wrong with her marriage. It hadn't always been bad, and to be quite honest, it wasn't really bad now. At least it hadn't gone completely sour like those of so many of her friends. No, she and Gerald just had some rough times now and then. What really bothered her was that lately "now and then" was coming more and more often.

She tried to think of all the things that Gerald did that would infuriate her, and the list was pretty long. He would take off his shoes and socks and leave them laying where they fell, usually on the living room floor. He did the same in the bedroom with the rest of his clothes; he left little piles of dirty clothes everywhere *except* in the clothes basket. Heaven forbid that he should help her gather them up to wash, much less wash some of them himself. After a meal, he would just walk away from the table and leave his dishes there. When he would insist upon cutting his own hair, he would leave the trimmings in the bathroom sink. He did the same when he shaved. Etcetera, etcetera, etcetera.

Then he expected her to fix it all. What did he want, a wife or a fucking maid?

No, not a maid.

It suddenly occurred to her that she was even one step below a maid; she was a *housewife.* She wasn't hired to do all the cooking and cleaning and household chores; she was *expected* to do them.

That was the root of the whole problem. She hated being a housewife. She had never wanted to be a housewife and had never planned to be one; it just sort of happened while she wasn't looking. What she really wanted was to be a career woman, but Crystal Springs was a small town. Jobs weren't that easy to find, especially in her field of commercial design, and the idea of driving to Jackson every day wasn't exactly appealing. Hattiesburg, on the other hand, was more like a small city. If Gerald got a teaching job at the university, and that was a big if, she would have a better chance of finding work and getting her career started. And getting out of the goddamned house.

There it was. In ten minutes, she had come up with a solution to all her personal problems. She would go to work... if Gerald got a university job. Hell, no, she'd go to work anyway, even if it did mean driving the twenty-five miles into Jackson. What the hell, all she had to lose was her sanity, and it was on its way out the door already.

Look out world; Pamela White was on the move.

17

"Mom, we're gonna camp out at Timmy's house, okay?"

That was the scam; Timmy's parents thought they were at Charles's house and Charles's parents thought they were at Timmy's house. In reality, their campsite would be in one of the numerous open fields on the outskirts of town. The two boys had pulled it off a hundred times and nobody was ever the wiser. Of course, it never occurred to either of them that one of the parents might call the other to check up on them. It had never happened, therefore it was never something to be considered.

It was now mid-afternoon. When his mother gave her approval, Charles took Timmy into the kitchen where they made sixteen peanut butter and banana sandwiches; that would be enough for supper that night and breakfast in the morning with one each left over for a midnight snack. They put the sandwiches in a grocery bag along with two six-packs of Coke, a box of beef jerky, two large cans of Vienna sausages, a pack of saltine crackers, and four candy bars. That should hold them over until tomorrow.

With Timmy hauling the grocery bag and Charles carrying his own camping gear, the two boys walked to the drainage ditch where they had hidden Timmy's stuff earlier. It took quite a bit of organizing, but they finally managed to arrange all the bundles into carriable sizes. Then, looking like a pair of Andean pack llamas, Timmy and Charles set out to find their place for the night.

They followed Dallas Street until it dead-ended at an open field that was overgrown with uncut grass, ragweed, and goldenrod. At the far end of the field was a thick clump of trees and bushes; in the middle of this was a small pond. That's where they would set up camp.

Timmy and Charles were no strangers to the pond. It had become their own isolated playground and favorite overnight camping site. There were several large trees for them to climb, one of which was an old pecan and it supplied them with some of the best nuts they had ever tasted. The trees were connected by a tangle of bushes and undergrowth that made anything inside practically invisible to the outside world. The pond itself was, for all intents and purposes, stagnant, but it was a near-perfect example of ecological balance.

There was no stream running into nor out of the pond, but the water level remained pretty constant. Evaporation during the day and a parade of wild animals drinking at night should have gradually exhausted the pond's water supply, but along its edge were tiny springs which constantly fed trickles of fresh water up through the mud. Throughout the pond, and in various stages of development, were tadpoles. Those which did not fall prey to the other inhabitants of the murky water eventually grew into heavy, deep voiced bullfrogs. While small turtles swam in the shallow water among the dense aquatic plants, their larger counterparts sunned themselves on downed tree trunks that lay half-submerged. At night and during the cooler hours of the day, snakes could be seen slithering along the ground or swimming in their characteristic back and forth rhythm just under the pond's surface. Scores of minnows in the shallows gave evidence of larger cousins that lurked in the darker depths. Occasionally, the stillness of the water was broken by the mouth of one of the larger fish as it gulped water bugs or mosquito larvae and then disappeared leaving only a widening ring of ripples to tell what had happened.

Survival of the fittest.

Left to work on its own, Nature had managed to keep the delicate balance for many years. From their days and nights spent here, Timmy and Charles had come to recognize and appreciate the balance, and they did nothing to interfere with it. They would camp here, and they would watch in awe as the cycle continued around them. This was a special place, and they wanted to absorb as much of it as possible before somebody got the bright idea to turn it into a new subdivision.

Under the pecan tree, the boys spread their tarpaulin, unrolled their sleeping bags, and ate the first of the sandwiches. They knew the scent of the bread would probably attract some animals later in the dark, but that didn't bother them. They had seen most of the night creatures already; the wild dogs, the cats, a chipmunk once in a while.

One night they had even been visited by a curious skunk. As with all the other animals, they stayed quiet, and the skunk just very casually passed on through. All in all, the local animals were a friendly bunch. The only thing that really concerned either of the boys was the possibility of a snake deciding to curl up in the sleeping bag with one of them. But, just like getting caught by their parents, it was something that had never happened.

By the time the sun started to disappear, Timmy and Charles had polished off six sandwiches and four Cokes and they had reexplored their whole little world around the pond. It was going to be a glorious night.

18

Dear Timmy,

My time is here. He is calling His saints home. But my job ain't done yet. Look for me again, but not in the coffin. Don't look in the coffin, boy.

Ma

19

Pamela was going to repair her marriage, no matter what it took. Starting tonight.

Gerald didn't roll in until almost eight-thirty, but Pamela, wearing her bathrobe, met him at the door. The house was dark except for the flickering light of a single candle on the coffee table in the middle of the room. All the furniture was pushed back against the walls to clear a space for the quilt that had been spread on the floor.

"Did the electricity go off?"

"No," she answered, taking his hand and leading him into the room. She pulled at the knot of his necktie until the loose end slid free.

"What are you doing?"

"Shhhh." She put a finger on his lips for a moment, and then she kissed him gently. Using both hands, she unbuttoned his shirt and let it drop to floor. When she reached for his belt buckle, he stopped her hand.

"Where's Timmy?"

"Camping."

"Oh, yeah?"

"Yeah." The look in her eyes and the smile on her lips could have melted a glacier. It was something that he hadn't seen for years, and the warm fluttery feeling in his stomach made him grin. He released her hand and she finished undressing him, slowly and deliberately.

He reached for the tie belt of her robe, but she stepped away and slapped his hand. "Lie down on your stomach," she said, and disappeared into the bathroom. Water began splashing into the bathtub, and a moment later Gerald felt Pamela's hand on his back.

"Now, just close your eyes and relax." She poured a small puddle of baby oil into her palm and rubbed her hands together until the oil was warm. When she spread the oil across his shoulders and squeezed softly, he moaned. Down his spine and out over his ribs she rubbed, replenishing the oil as his skin soaked it in. Back and forth, over and over. Rub and squeeze, rub and squeeze. *Moan.* Rub and squeeze. When his whole back side, from the nape of his neck to the bottoms of his feet, was glistening with oil, she rolled him over and started on the front. That was the part she liked best, so she really took her time. The massage continued for, oh, a long time, and she stopped only once to turn off the bath water. For several minutes she just sat and watched him, letting the oil soak in and giving his muscles time to savor what had just happened to them. Then, she held out her hand.

"Come with me." He took her hand and she led him into the bathroom where another candle was burning. "In you go."

"Aren't you getting in?"

"Not this time."

The water was hot enough to sting just a little when he sat down, but it felt like heaven. Pamela rolled up her sleeves and knelt beside the tub. She placed one hand behind Gerald's head and said, "Lean back." With a coffee cup, she scooped up some water and poured it in a steady trickle over his head. She rubbed shampoo into his hair with her fingertips, making small circles on his scalp and scratching lightly with her nails. While she stroked, she leaned over to breathe her warm breath into his ear and to kiss his neck. She rinsed away the lather with the cup, and then did it all over again.

Using soap and a sponge, she started at his neck and bathed him. Her touch was purposely sensual, and he started to move his body with the rhythm of her motions. He was aroused. Good. Neck and chest, play with the hair there. Down, down, past the stomach, but not too far, not yet. Keep him squirming, keep him anticipating.

"Okay, stand up."

"Do I have to?"

"Yes, you have to."

She toweled him dry using short, slow strokes. Her finishing touch was to wrap the towel around his waist.

"Come on," she said, and took his hand again.

When they reached the front door, he asked, "Where are we going?"

"Just come on."

The night air was warm and quickly evaporated the few droplets of water that remained on him. Pamela led him across the yard to a secluded spot that was sheltered by small shrubs. There, another blanket had been spread. Gerald grinned at his wife.

As she pulled the towel away, she said, "Since Timmy's camping out, I thought we would, too." She untied her robe and let it drop to the ground. In the moonlight, her naked body shined white against the darkness behind her. She stepped closer to him, until her breasts lightly touched his chest. For just a few moments, she swayed back and forth, letting her nipples rub against him. With both hands on her behind, he pulled her to him, and she wrapped her arms around his neck and kissed him deeply.

Then, they made love.

20

About the time that Pamela was meeting Gerald at the front door, Timmy was deciding what he and Charles should do that night.

"Let's go," Timmy said and jumped up.

Charles was right behind him. "Where we going?"

"To the gravel pit."

Charles stopped dead in his tracks. "Are you shittin' me? This is a joke, right?"

"No, it's not a joke."

"Timmy, you're outta your mind! We can't go back there!"

"We're not going back *there.* We're going down into the bottom, where we always go."

"I don't think that's such a good idea."

"It's never been a good idea, but that's what makes it so much fun."

From his backpack, Timmy pulled a belt that held a hunting knife on one side, a canteen of water on the other side, and an empty pouch on the back which he filled with beef jerky. He dug a little deeper in the pack and found a pair of long jeans. "You brought some long pants, didn't you?"

Charles looked in his own pack. "Sure, I did. I don't want to freeze my ass off."

The two boys traded their short pants for long ones and Timmy strapped on the belt. "You ready?"

Charles hesitated. "Are you sure about this?"

"Sure, I'm sure. It'll be great."

They started walking across the field toward the gravel pit and into another night of adventure.

21

Ma had a very busy evening. By the light of a three-quarter moon, she dug a deep hole in her back yard and dropped in her conjure board and the ancient leather book. Those had to be gone; they could be very dangerous in the wrong hands. At first, she had thought about burning them, but somewhere in the back of her mind she remembered hearing something about how fire often did strange things to magical objects. In the end, she decided that burying them would be okay. She planted a small azalea bush on top of them so that the freshly turned earth wouldn't draw any undue attention.

She put the letter addressed to Timmy inside her purse. It would be easily found there and delivered to him. Standing beside Jack's cage, she ran her hand lovingly down his long back. "I can't stop dem, Jack, an' we can't run no mo'." She sat in her chair and waited.

It was only a matter of minutes before the front door burst open and a cold voice screeched, "You couldn't do it, could you, bitch? You couldn't keep your fucking mouth shut."

Ma stood and held out her arm to Jack who jumped from his perch to take his place beside her. Then, they turned to face their adversary. They were old and they were slow, but they were determined to fight with everything they had left.

22

Even if there had been a quicker way to get to the gravel pit, the boys probably wouldn't have taken it. A certain amount of thrill was involved in successfully sneaking through old man Hill's peach orchard. He had become somewhat a legend among the kids in town. To hear all the horror stories about him, a person would think that "Old Man Hill" was listed right under "Satan" in the Evil category. And every time somebody had a close brush with him in the orchard or almost got caught stealing one of is precious peaches, another story was added to the "Did you hear about old man Hill" anthology.

Timmy climbed through the rusty barbed wire fence and held the strands apart as Charles followed. Then, keeping an ever-watchful eye for the wicked man with the big shotgun, they made their way through the trees. Fortunately, their familiar path led them away from the dreaded "place." In the distance, through the neat rows of peach trees, they could see the gravel road and beyond that they could see the dark, faint outline of the grove surrounding the witches' meeting place. The scary place. The evil place. They had passed it many times before without ever knowing what went on inside. Now that they knew, passing wasn't quite so easy.

At the far end of the orchard, they felt safe; safe from old man Hill and safe from the place. The only thing separating them from friendly ground was the sagging fence. It wasn't until they had crawled through the strands of barbed wire and breathed a sigh of relief that they heard the howling, and they froze in their tracks. From deep within the belly of the pit it came, carried higher and higher by the night breeze. The cry of the wild dogs. A long, sorrowful cry that touched the back of Timmy's neck like an icy finger. His mind skipped back to the night by the lake when they had all heard the howling; the night Michael almost shot them in the woods. The night before the evil happened. The night they were all still alive.

"Let's go," Timmy said. He could tell by the look on Charles' face that if they didn't start moving forward right away, they would have to turn and go back. "It's just those stupid dogs again. It sounds like they're at the other end of the pit."

"How can you tell?"

"I just can. Come on." But he couldn't tell, not really. He was just trying to lighten things up a little. Damn near every time they came to the pits, they heard the dogs and they usually laughed and made some shitty comment about it. This time shouldn't be any different.

But it was.

The climb down into the pit wasn't treacherous. They were on the north side where huge mounds of presorted gravel rose from the bottom all the way to the rim. All they had to do was pick a mound and decide how they wanted to go down. They could slide on their butts and wear the seats out of their pants, they could roll on their sides and get dizzier than hell, or they could run straight down and hope they could stop before they bought it at the bottom.

Tonight was a running night. Timmy went first. Peering over the edge into the dark shadows of the pit, he made sure that none of the old rusting equipment had been left at the bottom of the mound. That stuff could be pretty deadly. The moon wasn't directly overhead, and it was dark at the bottom, but he didn't see any great looming black things down there so he decided that all was clear. He backed away from the edge. Three steps. Six steps, twelve. Finally, he stopped, hesitated for a moment, and then ran as fast as he could. At the very last instant, before the hill sloped away beneath his feet, he leaped as far and as high as he could. Pumping his feet wildly, Timmy fell for nearly five seconds before he sank to mid-calf in the loose rocks of the mound. But he couldn't stop there. His momentum pulled him forward and down. He had to pull his feet free and start taking gigantic leaps unless he wanted to go over on his face and slide the rest of the way on his stomach. He leaped, again and again, gaining speed as he descended. The flat, solid bottom of the pit was rising fast to meet him. Stopping was always the tricky part. The timing had to be absolutely perfect or some real damage might be done. When his vast experience told him it was time, Timmy began to lean backwards, a little further with each leap, until he felt the rocks of the mound sliding along his back. The he stopped moving his feet, locked his knees and elbows, and buried his feet and hands in the gravel. If he was right, he would slow to a stop; if he was wrong, the force would rip his arms right out of their sockets.

But, just like getting caught by his parents or sleeping with a snake, it had never happened.

He stopped about two feet from the bottom of the hill. "Hey, Charles! Come on down!"

"I'm coming!"

There were a few seconds of silence and then Timmy saw Charles vault from the top of the mound, just like a pro. It was a thing of beauty, even in the dark. He made contact with the hill and began his long, running leaps. He was doing fine until he got about half-way down.

"Timmy! I can't stop!"

"Lean back! Lean back!"

"I caaaaaaaan't!"

And, like a fool, Timmy stepped out to try to catch him.

In a brief second, Timmy thought *he must be going nine hundred miles an hour.*

It ain't the fall that kills you, it's the sudden stop at the end.

And Charles stopped... hard. They collided, standing up, face to face, chest to chest, and hit the ground at nine hundred miles an hour. Timmy didn't slow him down a bit. All he did was give Charles something soft to land on.

For several seconds, Timmy could only lie there with his eyes closed trying to gather his wits. He was dazed; he didn't know where he was, and he really didn't give a shit. He just knew that his brains felt like scrambled eggs inside his skull. It didn't take long for everything to come back to him. Camping out, the gravel pit, the run down the hill, the tremendous weight on his chest.

He opened his eyes, and Charles was still on top of him. But Charles looked strange. His eyes were wide, like he was afraid, and his mouth was opening and closing like some sort of weird fish. And he wasn't breathing.

"What's wrong?"

All Charles could do was wave his hands wildly and look helpless.

Timmy flipped Charles onto the ground and grabbed the front of his pants at the belt buckle. Pulling as hard as he could, he lifted Charles by the belt, then let him down. He lifted, then let him down.

Over and over. He had seen the football coach do this to players who had gotten the wind knocked out of them. He hoped that was all that had happened to Charles.

Lift, release; lift, release; lift, release.

When Charles began to gasp and wheeze, Timmy let go of his belt and lay beside him on the cold, hard rocks. Soon, Charles was taking deep breaths and letting them out noisily through his mouth. Timmy started to giggle. His giggles turned to outright laughter, and Charles joined him. Once again, they had beaten the Reaper.

Finally, Charles managed to say, "What the hell are we laughing about? I coulda died!"

"But you didn't."

"Yeah, but if you hadn't been here, I coulda died right there in the rocks."

"True. But if I hadn't been out here, neither would you."

That was true, too. Charles never went into the gravel pits alone.

Rule Number Four: They won't try to get you if you're with somebody else.

Timmy sat up and looked around. There was lots to do and the night was still young. "You ready?"

"I guess so."

The gravel pits looked much different from the inside than they did from the top, and in moonlight they were absolutely beautiful. Shadows were long and deep and every surface, from the smallest mound to the steepest wall, glowed with pale blue light, a miniature lunar landscape. The possibilities of games to be played here were endless.

"Let's go to the water."

"Okay."

And they were off.

The water was actually a lake in the deepest part of the pits. It hadn't always been there. In fact, it started out as a small puddle when one of the digging machines got too close to the water table. Over the years, it gradually grew to its present size. There was still flat ground all the way around, so to the gravel pit workers it was more an inconvenience than anything else. But the water was still coming in. In a few more years, the lake would completely cover the bottom and the excavation of this particular hole would cease. Nature would reclaim its ground.

At the edge of the lake, the sand was soft and appeared to be dry. However, as they lifted their feet, their footprints filled with water and quickly disappeared. There was a lot more water under the sand just waiting for an opportunity to come out.

Or to grab a little kid.

Timmy and Charles had heard the story about the pit worker who had accidentally fallen near the edge of the water and the sand just sucked him under and he was never seen or heard from again. (Of course, nobody knew his name or his family or anything else about him.) There were rumors that the center of the lake had collapsed into a gigantic, bottomless water cavern. There were rumors of catfish in this lake that were completely white, had no eyes, and could swallow a man whole. There were rumors, and there were rumors, and there were rumors, and all the rumors just made the lake that much more tempting.

"Let's make some waves," Charles shouted, and he started to jump up and down. Timmy joined him and the ground began to ripple like a sheet in the wind. When the sand started to fall away from under their feet, they ran backward and watched the water surge a few feet closer to them. A simple thing, but at night, in the dark, away from home, it was great fun.

They moved to another spot and did the same thing, then another, faster and faster, and each time the sand fell, they would laugh and scream and run to another spot, working their way deeper and deeper into the pit. Until Timmy started to sink. This time, the sand didn't crumble like before; it just vanished, and Timmy was up to his knees before he knew what was happening.

"Oh, shit!" In a panic, he reached out and grabbed Charles' legs. Charles fell on his back.

"What the hell are you doing?"

Timmy was up to his waist. "Help me, you butthead!"

Charles managed to twist and turn until he could catch one of Timmy's hands. He pulled as hard as he could, and the cold water swept over them. They scrambled backwards until they were on firm ground again.

"'Butthead?' What do you mean, 'butthead?' I shoulda let you drown."

"I wasn't drowning. It was a joke. My feet were on the bottom the whole time. Come on, let's explore."

Maybe Timmy was joking, but the sudden change in games didn't go unnoticed.

They had only gone about ten yards when Charles started to shiver. "Damn, Timmy. Now I'm cold."

"Let's build a fire."

"With what?" Charles reached into his pants pocket and pulled out a soggy box of matches.

"Is that all you have?"

"It doesn't matter. Even if I did have more, they'd be wet, too."

"Shit." Timmy thought for a moment and then pulled his wet shirt off over his head.

"What are you doing?"

Timmy took off his tennis shoes and tied them together by the laces. "I'm just doing what my mom would tell me to do. I'm getting out of my wet clothes."

"But you don't have any dry ones to put on."

Timmy grinned. "Then I guess I'll have to go naked."

In a matter of seconds, both boys were completely nude except for the wet clothes which hung tied around their shoulders like super-hero capes. After Timmy had strapped the belt with the hunting knife around his waist, they continued their exploration.

Further and further they went, playing games and skipping flat rocks across the surface of the lake. Deeper and deeper into the pit. Before they realized it, they were at the foot of one of the sheer cliff walls.

"Timmy."

There was something in the tone of Charles' voice that Timmy found to be very unsettling.

"Timmy, come here."

"What is it?"

Charles pointed to the ground. It was the witches' altar, still in pieces. But something new had been added. The pieces now lay in the middle of a large circle and a five-pointed star.

"Jesus Christ! They found it!"

"Timmy, let's get out of here!"

And then the growling began.

It came from behind them, and they spun around to face the pack of wild dogs that had followed them all the way across the gravel pit. In the darkness, it was impossible to tell how many there were, but their eyes seemed to glow like burning embers and their teeth, dripping with saliva, reflected the moonlight like the blades of a million moving knives. The air in the pit was filled with the sounds of snarling, growling, and snapping jaws. The boys were trapped against the stone wall and the army of deadly canines advanced slowly, toying with their prey as they moved in for the kill.

"Shit, Timmy! What are we gonna do?" Charles was screaming, and his voice quickly bounced back from the opposite wall. In desperation, Timmy waved his arms high in the air and shouted at the dogs.

"Get out of here! Go on! Get!"

Charles copied him, and for just a moment the dogs stopped, unsure of what was going on. But only for a moment. When it was obvious that the flailing arms were no real threat, the dogs continued their slow march.

"Charles, where are your shoes?"

"Right here."

"When I give the word, throw them at those dogs right over there." Timmy pointed to the right. He took his own shoes from around his shoulders and untied the laces so that he held one in each hand.

"Ready?"

Charles nodded.

"Now!"

With all their might, they hurled the wet shoes at the dogs. Contact was made. Several of the animals yelped as the shoes bounced off their backs or their noses. Then, as if blown by an invisible breeze, the entire pack shifted toward the left.

"Run!"

The boys bolted through the opening the dogs had left, and as they ran Timmy slid the knife out of its sheath.

Don't drop it don't drop it don't drop it don't drop it don't drop it...

With almost no hesitation, the dogs took up the pursuit. The growls and snarls had turned to vicious barking. It was the time for killing.

The boys were halfway across the pit and they had no idea where they were going. They were just running blindly.

"Timmy, what now?" Charles was finding it harder and harder to breathe and his side was beginning to burn with pain. He also felt himself slowing down; he knew he couldn't hold out much longer.

Timmy quickly scanned the area in front of them. Sand, gravel, walls, water, conveyor belts... Conveyor belts from the bottom of the pit to the top.

"The conveyor belt! Go up the conveyor belt!"

They were almost there; just a few dozen more yards to go. That should be easy enough. Hell, on a football field guys ran that far in four or five seconds, and they didn't even have wild animals chasing them. Not literally, anyway.

Charles jumped onto the conveyor belt and began scrambling toward the top. Timmy felt hot breath on his heels and heard teeth clicking together as jaws snapped at his legs. Without looking back, he swung the knife behind him and felt it hit something soft. The cries of the injured dog reached his ears just as he, too, made the leap onto the conveyor belt.

But they were far from safe. The dew had settled and going up the wet belt was much like trying to climb a greased flagpole. Even though they could hold on to the metal framework on either side and pull themselves up, there was nothing for them to push on with their feet. They had no traction. And Timmy was having a hell of a time because he still had the knife in one hand. But he refused to let it drop. His father would kill him.

Timmy stole a glance behind them, and, to his relief, he saw that the dogs were having the same problem. Maybe they had a chance after all.

Maybe not.

"Timmy! I'm slipping!"

The warning came too late. In fact, it came just as Charles collided with Timmy. Timmy couldn't hold them both. His hands slid on the rough rusty metal of the frame until his fingers hit one of the reinforcement bars that ran underneath the conveyor. He gripped and held on tight. He had to.

The two boys spent the longest fifteen minutes of their lives hanging on that wet conveyor belt while the dogs barked and leaped not ten feet below them. They dared not move for fear that they would screw up and slide feet-first into the waiting jaws of death. Good incentive to keep still.

Finally, the dogs had had enough and went in search of easier game. It was only then that the boys resumed the long struggle to the top of the pit. And it was a struggle. Slipping, sliding, and pulling with their arms, they were completely exhausted when they managed to reach the top. They collapsed on the sand and lay still and quiet for a long, long time.

"Goddamnit, Timmy! Don't ever try to get me out here again! I hate these goddamn gravel pits! I've always hated them! And now I've lost my best pair of tennis shoes! I'm not ever coming back here, so don't even suggest it!"

Timmy didn't argue. He just slid the knife back into its sheath, wiped the sand from his bare butt, and said, "Let's go back."

They had to walk almost all the way around the whole rim of the gravel pit to get back to the path through old man Hill's peach orchard. They were in no hurry. They had already had a long night; what difference would another half-hour make?

In the middle of the orchard, the smell of fresh, ripe peaches became irresistible. Timmy figured that old man Hill would never miss a peach or two and he reached up to pluck one from a branch above his head.

There was a click. Then another.

Charles and Timmy looked at each other and their mouths dropped open. When the old man shouted, "Thieving fuckers!", they ran. Two shotgun blasts shattered the quiet of the night.

There is no feeling in the world quite like the feeling of rock salt and bacon rinds, fired from a shotgun, hitting a bare ass. Charles and Timmy now knew that feeling, and they didn't think they would soon forget it.

They didn't.

23

The best guess that anybody could come up with was that she had been dead between twelve and eighteen hours. The doctor suspected a stroke; that's what the death certificate would say. He figured it had to have happened very quickly because she fell on top of her bird and crushed it. It was still underneath her when she was found.

Foul play was immediately ruled out. There was no evidence of a struggle, no markings on the body. By all appearances, it was a quick and quiet death.

There was not a trace of the three hours of hell that Ma and Captain Jack went through before they were finally allowed to die.

Chapter Four

1

The TV was on, and Timmy, wrapped in his blanket, sat on the floor in front of it. But he wasn't watching or listening. He was thinking, and his thoughts were of death.

In his hand was a crumpled note. Doctor Coleman had delivered it to him earlier in the day, just after they had taken Ma's body away. He had read it at least twenty times, and it still didn't make any sense to him.

They said it was quick and she probably never knew what hit her. But that's not what the note said. The note said that she *knew* something was about to happen. The note said that she was expecting it and that she was ready for it. What had really happened to her?

They got her, too.

Or did they? Old people were supposed to die, weren't they? That's sorta how things worked. People got old and their bodies just stopped working. Ma was old.

But what about the note?

Timmy ran his hand across Doobie's head and the dog looked up with his tongue hanging out one side of his mouth. "Sometimes I wish I were a dog. I could just be dumb and happy all the time and not have to think about all this shit." Doobie just snorted a couple of times and then closed his eyes to dream of the big blue bird that had told him so many things. The big blue bird that was now buried in their back yard.

Timmy had done that. From the living room window, he had seen one of the ambulance drivers drop Captain Jack into the garbage can at the end of Ma's driveway. When everyone had gone, Timmy took Jack out of the can to give him a proper burial. Ma would have wanted it that way.

Timmy opened the note and read it again. What was it like to die? Jim knew. Michael knew. Now, Ma knew. He rubbed his eyes and looked at the TV, past the TV, focusing his gaze on something a million miles away. It was more than he was able to comprehend. His mind slipped quietly into neutral and cleared itself.

He had almost drifted off to sleep when the noises started in his bedroom. He glanced toward the great black hole that was his bedroom door and said, "Shove it." Then, he let his eyes close again.

Doobie, too, looked at the door and snorted once as if to reinforce his master's feelings. He didn't have time to waste on those stupid things that hid in the dark. His mind was at work on something much more important. He was replaying all his meetings with Captain Jack; going over all the things the bird had told him in the last few weeks. Strange things; scary things. Things that had already happened; things that might still happen.

Doobie opened his eyes and looked at his sleeping master. He wished there were some way for him to tell Timmy that things might not turn out very well. He touched the end of his cold wet nose to Timmy's arm and the boy, still asleep, rubbed the dog's head. There was still comfort in the touch.

2

It was hard for Timmy to believe that only one week had passed since James Milford had gone berserk in the pulpit. So much had happened; so much had changed.

"Turn with me now to the tenth chapter of the Gospel of John..."

There was a new man on the stage today. A substitute preacher had been called to fill in until a permanent replacement could be found. He was an older man and not nearly as friendly looking as Brother Milford. He also used all the long, obscure, important sounding words that Milford had somehow managed to avoid. His monotonic delivery of the sermon made it awfully difficult for a ten-year-old to sit still for forty-five minutes.

And the blisters on his butt didn't help any. Rock salt and bacon rinds, what an incredible discovery. All Timmy could hope for was that a curse had been placed on the man who first thought of it. He shifted slightly on the hard wood of the pew; Charles did the same. Misery loved company, or so they said. Comfort was obviously out of the question. The boys would have to live with the pain until they could stand up again. As the preacher spoke and the hurt got worse, the minutes got longer and longer.

We are part of a plan, boy.

Timmy jumped in his back-row seat. Where had that voice come from? Not from the preacher; he was still droning away at his chosen sermon. Timmy looked at Charles and Charles gave him a questioning stare.

"Did you say something?" Timmy whispered.

Charles shook his head.

"Oh." Maybe he had dozed off. Or maybe his mind was playing tricks on him. He shifted again and prayed for the sermon to be over soon.

3

"We're moving to Hattiesburg."

"What?"

"We're moving to Hattiesburg."

The news hit Charles like a splash of cold water in the face. That was probably the last thing he expected to hear coming from Timmy's mouth. For a moment he was silent, his jaw hanging slack. Then he started to grin. "Says who?"

"My dad."

"You're full of shit." Charles let out a short laugh but stopped when he saw Timmy slowly shaking his head. "You're not kidding, are you?"

"They called him yesterday from the university. They gave him a teaching job."

"Well, shit." Charles let out a deep sigh and lay back on the grass, his head resting on his intertwined fingers. He looked up through the branches of their favorite oak tree on their favorite street corner and he was silent. What do you say when you find out that your very best friend in the whole world is leaving? He and Timmy had been best friends all their lives. Their mothers were pregnant together. The baby boys learned how to crawl and walk and talk together. They were practically joined at the hip. They knew everything there was to know about each other... well, almost. Charles had never told Timmy about the monster rules. He had thought about it once or twice, but he had decided that it was stupid, and he didn't want Timmy to think that he was a baby. But other than that, they were almost like two boys living one life. What would they do without each other?

"When are you leaving?"

"I don't know. A week, I think."

"That sucks." Charles looked at Doobie on the grass between them. Doobie wasn't sleeping like he usually did; Doobie was staring at Timmy. Charles reached out and touched his back and Doobie jumped. "Sorry, boy. I didn't mean to scare you."

"That's okay. He's been real jumpy lately." Timmy rubbed the dog's head and Doobie licked him in return.

"Is he going with you?"

"Shit yeah! If he can't go, I'm not going!"

"I don't blame you."

And then there was silence again. There was no reason to say anything else; a week was plenty of time for them to say all the things they could find to say to one another. Of course, there would always be things that they would *wish* they had said, and those things would invariably come to mind when it was too late to say them. But the boys were still too young to know anything about that. As far as they were concerned, a week was plenty of time to talk.

But time was shorter than they thought. They didn't even have a week, and there were many things, simple trivial mundane things, that would never be said.

And so, on this lazy summer day, Timmy and Charles spent in sad friendly silence the last Sunday afternoon they would have together.

4

Sunday night was Old Fashioned Hymn Sing night at the church. Those were usually pretty fun. The entire service was spent with people calling out the names of their favorite hymns and the whole congregation singing them. Every once in a while, someone would throw in one of those obscure ones that hadn't been sung for a zillion years and Matt Wilson, the Minister of Music, would get flustered because he had never heard it before. After stumbling through two or three verses of it, he would laugh, the congregation would laugh, and life would go on. But for the most part, people would just love to sing those old familiar favorites that they never got tired of; *To God be the Glory* and *Since Jesus Came Into My Heart* and the somber, majestic *Old Rugged Cross*. Those were the ones that they knew by heart. They could leave their hymnals on their laps and just throw back their heads and sing.

Hymn Sing nights were welcome diversions. The young people liked them because they weren't boring; the old people liked them because they were more like the church services they remembered from long ago. But tonight, Hymn Sing night was a weak attempt to cover the fact that there was no preacher, not even a substitute, to fill the pulpit.

On his back row seat, Timmy sat very still. He wasn't singing and he wasn't even listening while everybody else sang. A moral battle raged in his head.

You took an oath.

But you've already broken it.

Does that make it right?

"Milford, Milford, Milford..."

They burned his picture.

"Dey ain't real witches..."

Brother Milford's going crazy.

And you know why.

But you took an oath.

One week

"Milford, Milford, Milford..."

One week and you'll be gone.

"Dey be debils."

You took an oath!

"I'll be right back," Timmy whispered to Charles and started to stand, but Charles grabbed his arm.

"Where you going?"

"Timmy shook his head and repeated, "I'll be back," and in the middle of the second verse of *Love Lifted Me*, Timmy slipped quietly out the back door of the auditorium.

The night air was filled with the heavy sweet smell of

magnolia blossoms. Crickets chirped in the holly bushes growing along the sides of the church building. Across the street a dog barked, and a stray cat ran for its life. A car door slammed somewhere down the block. High overhead, the moon was getting smaller, and each passing night was a little bit darker than the one before. Clouds gathered; a storm was approaching.

Timmy glanced across the church lawn. The lights were on in the parsonage and James Milford's car was in the driveway. That was good. He was still here; there was still time. With one hand, Timmy dug in his pants pocket and pulled out the silver bullet. With the fingers of his other hand, he traced the chain around his neck until he felt the crucifix that Ma had given him. The bullet and the crucifix. Werewolves and vampires. That's what he had always told Jim. He remembered that night at the lake and how he had laughed at Jim for carrying the bullet and the crucifix. My, my, how things had changed. Shit, as they say, had happened.

But the bullet and the crucifix hadn't helped Jim, had they?

Maybe Jim hadn't known how to use them. Maybe Timmy didn't know how to use them either.

Clenching the bullet in his fist, Timmy walked down the church steps and across the yard to the parsonage. It was time to have a little chat with the preacher.

At the door, Timmy hesitated and for a fleeting moment he was almost overcome by a desire to turn and run and pretend that the whole thing had never happened and that everything would be just fine if he would keep his mouth shut. But that's what the oath was all about, and everything wasn't just fine. It wasn't going away. But

Brother Milford was going away, and so was he. This might be his last chance to help the poor man understand what the hell was happening to him.

He knocked.

When James Milford came to the door, he looked worn, but he managed to smile at Timmy. "What are you doing here? You should be in there singing with the rest of them."

"It sounds better from out here." Timmy was right. The distance blended the voices into a nicely balanced harmony that somehow got lost inside the cavernous auditorium. The boy and the minister listened for several seconds, then Milford broke the silence.

"So, what brings you over here? I know you didn't come to listen to the singing."

"No, sir." Timmy shuffled his feet on the *WELCOME* mat. "I need to talk to you."

"Sounds serious."

"Yes, sir. It is serious."

"Then maybe you'd better come inside."

Well, he was there, he was inside, and he was sitting face to face with the preacher. Now, how should he go about telling what he came to tell?

Flat out, that's the best way.

Yeah, right.

"Dad, I have monsters under my bed."

That really worked like a charm, didn't it? But what was his alternative? He wasn't nearly as prepared for this as he should have been.

"Okay, Timmy, what's on your mind?"

The moment of truth.

"I know what's happened to you."

The preacher just looked at him for a long, long time. His icy blue eyes never wavered, as if he were trying to read Timmy's mind. If he could, that would be a great relief to Timmy. Why was Milford just sitting there? What was going on in his brain?

"Can I get you something to drink?"

That's it? That's what that monumental concentration was all about?

"Uh... maybe a Coke if you have any."

"I think I might." A few moments later, Milford returned from the kitchen with two open Coke bottles, one of which he placed on the coffee table in front of Timmy. "Now, tell me what you think happened to me."

"It's kind of a long story."

"I've got a lot of time."

Timmy sipped from the Coke bottle and thought about how he should begin his story. "You remember that Sunday when you preached about the witches in the gravel pits? Well, right after that, me and some other guys went out there to see if we could find them."

"That could have been dangerous. Why would you want to do something like that?"

"I don't know. Just curious, I guess. Anyway, we found them, and they did this really strange ceremony and some weird stuff started to happen."

"And you were there to see it?"

"Yes, sir."

"Was that the night that the smoke came down out of the sky and started attacking people?"

Timmy's eyes got wide. "Yeah. How did you know about that?"

He knew about that night. It was the same night that Melanie Davis had come to him in a panic and spilled her guts. "Never mind. Go ahead."

"Well, before all that, the witches... they did this... well, they did this thing where they burned some stuff and they... they sort of..."

Spit it out, son!

"They put a curse on you."

Now it was the preacher's turn to be surprised. "They did what?"

"They put a curse on you. At least that's what I thought. I mean, they took some tissues that had blood on them and put them in a bowl and set them on fire. Then they burned a picture; I think it was a picture of you. And all the time they were chanting your name over and over. It was real creepy." He was speaking faster. Unconsciously, he tightened his grip on the bullet. "Right after that, all the weird stuff started happening and we ran away."

"So, you think I've been cursed."

"No, no, no, that's what I thought *then*."

"You don't think that any more?"

Timmy shook his head. "See, we started to think that maybe they'd seen us there and put a curse on us, too, because a few days later Jim got killed and Michael shot himself and I got..."

Should he tell him about the things under the bed? Probably not; they were Timmy's problem and didn't really have anything to do with Milford.

"... well, I got scared and told Ma what had happened. You know Ma, don't you?"

Milford nodded.

"She said the witches weren't real and they didn't really do anything. Then she started talking about devils and saying that the witches found the place where the devils were hiding out and they pis... made them mad. That's who's doing all the bad stuff. It's not witches, it's devils!"

"Whoa, whoa, whoa! Slow down some. You're not making any sense. Just stop for a minute and calm down. Okay?"

Timmy nodded and took several deep breaths.

Milford was intrigued. "You said they found the place where the devils were hiding. Do you mean there are demons in the gravel pits?"

"I sure do!"

And they look a lot like wild dogs.

"What else did Ma say?"

"Well, she said a whole bunch of stuff that I didn't understand, and she said she didn't really understand all of it either. But then she said that all the things that were happening to you were caused by the devils."

Milford already knew that, but now he had some more very important pieces of information. Information that he could possibly put to good use. But on top of that, and even more important to him personally, there was another living breathing human being who knew about the demons. Even if that human being was only a ten-year-old boy, that one simple fact put to rest any doubt that he was having about his sanity.

"Is that all?"

"Well... yes, sir, I guess so. You believe me, don't you?"

Milford laughed a little. "Yes, I believe you. And I could tell you things that would scare you to death."

"Me too."

"I'll bet you could." That confirmed Milford's suspicion: Timmy knew a lot more than he was telling. "But what about Ma? She knew about the demons, or devils, or whatever, but did she say what to do about them?"

"No, sir. I don't think she knew either. I think..." His voice trembled. "I think they got her." His eyes filled with tears and he reached up to wipe them on his sleeve.

Milford put his hand on Timmy's shoulder. "You okay?"

Timmy nodded.

"Why do you think they got her?"

From his coat pocket Timmy took the crumpled note that Ma had written to him and he handed it to Milford. The preacher read the note twice and handed it back to Timmy.

"Where did you get this?"

"They found it in her stuff when they took her away. It was all sealed up in an envelope with my name on it."

"So she knew what was about to happen to her." It was more to himself than to Timmy.

"Brother Milford, I'm scared."

And the preacher could see from the look on his face that it was true. "Me, too, son. Me, too."

On an impulse, Timmy pulled the crucifix out of his shirt, lifted the chain from around his neck, and held the small cross out to the preacher. "Here. Ma gave me this. I think maybe you should have it."

Instead of taking it, Milford shook his head and pulled at the chain that hung around his own neck. "You keep that one; I have my own." He smiled at Timmy and Timmy returned the smile.

"Good. That's good." He hadn't really wanted to give up his crucifix, but it was all he could think of to do. With a great feeling of relief, he let the chain drop over his head and he tucked the cross back into his shirt. "What are we going to do, Brother Milford?"

Milford stood and ruffled Timmy's hair. "Well, I'm not sure what I'm going to do. But you'd probably better get back to the church. The service is going to be over soon."

"Oh, yeah. I forgot about that."

Milford led Timmy to the front door. "Timmy, thanks for coming and telling me all this. You've been a big help. And as soon as I figure something out, I'll let you know, okay?"

"Okay. But we're going to be moving away pretty soon."

"Really?"

"Yes, sir."

"So am I. I guess I'll have to work fast, huh?"

"I guess so."

When Timmy stepped out of the house, he felt better. He just knew that if anybody could make some sense out of what was going on, it was probably the preacher.

The parsonage door closed behind him and he took two or three steps toward the church. Then the voice boomed into his skull like thunder.

Be strong, boy. We are part of a plan.

5

The music from the church drifted through Milford's open windows and he listened in silence to the songs that he had heard so often. A sadness crept over him and settled on his heart. Why had all this happened to him? What could he have possibly done to deserve it?

Thou shalt have no other gods before me.

Thou shalt not make unto thee any graven image.

Thou shalt not take the name of the Lord thy God in vain.

Remember the Sabbath day to keep it holy.

Honor thy father and thy mother.

Thou shalt not kill...

"Thou shalt not kill?" He whispered the question and then waited.

"Brother Milford, do you know what it feels like to kill somebody?"

"No, Mike. No, I don't."

"Yes, I do." He did. He had killed. With his own hands, he had eliminated another human being and he had thought about it every day since. That act of violence, self-defense or not, haunted him without mercy. It hung in his mind during the day and slid slickly into his dreams at night. There were times when he wanted to run down the street screaming at the top of his lungs, "Yes! I have killed a man! I have killed a man, and it isn't fun, it isn't glamorous, and it isn't any of those other things that the movies show. It feels like shit!"

"That's how it feels, Michael. It feels like shit and it eats away at your guts until you think that the only way to get away from it is to take a shotgun and blow it the hell right out of your mind. So how about that, Mikey? Even if you had killed your little brother, you'd have probably ended up the same way. You never had a snowball's chance in hell, you know that?"

Is that what this was all about? Killing?

Across the yard, they sang. "At the cross, at the cross, where I first saw the light, and the burden of my heart rolled away..."

Milford closed his eyes and let the sound of the old hymn flow over him. He breathed in deeply through his nose, held it for a second, and then let it out slowly through his mouth. He felt a little better, a little cleaner. He took another breath, then another. The singing from the church seemed to fade away as he let his mind go blank. He hovered there, in that limbo of consciousness.

Snap!

A connection was made. Deep in his subconscious, a seed that was planted years ago suddenly sprouted. Something that was buried in his past awoke and linked with something... something new. Something big. Something that had remained quietly hidden from Milford until now.

Words formed in his mind, words and images and feelings, but there was no voice to express them. They were communicated in silence, and Milford had no control over them. Stunned, he sat back and listened as the eerie conversation took place somewhere just behind his eyes.

The killing is gone; it is to be put aside. You have been forgiven; you have not forgiven yourself.

Mercy, Father. Show me how absolla.

Mercy is with you. Corrabon absolla now, for the time draws near when the spirit must be free basunda gondrema.

Ondo matia to grant colome.

Iam tos Iam, corremega. Finiess do cora domment a, corremega. Wontro mieget a tonofie. Iam tos Iam, corabasunda.

It went on for a long time, and all Milford could do was wait for it to be over. The words were strange to him, but something inside him knew what was being said and his body reacted accordingly. Sometimes he would feel a warm tingle of happiness, sometimes an icy chill would grip his heart; sometimes he would find himself smiling, sometimes his brow would wrinkle with concern. Whatever was being said, it was taking him through the gamut of emotions.

Then it stopped. As abruptly as it began, the conversation was over, and Milford was left sitting on his sofa feeling somewhat drained and not really knowing why. There was a long silence, and then his head-voice saying, "Now, James Milford, you must prepare." After that, the voice was gone.

But he didn't need the voice. He stood and found that he knew exactly what he had to do. For the next hour, he performed one ritual after another. He poured water into a jar, said some words that he did not understand, and sealed the jar with candle wax. He poured olive oil into a small jar, repeated the words, and sealed the jar. He said prayers; some of them he understood, others he didn't. He blessed communion bread, he blessed juice glasses, he blessed everything he could get his hands on. He was doing it all precisely the way it had to be done... until he started thinking about it.

"Is this the way Francis did it?"

And Jesus saith unto him, you gotta have the faith if you're gonna walk on the water, Peter.

"I don't remember this at all."

Don't look down, Peter! Don't look down!

"Maybe I should..."

You're gonna sink!

And he didn't know what to do next.

Oh thou of little faith.

The certainty with which he had been functioning gave way to indecision and doubt. The goal that he had been working toward became a blurred, out of focus image in his head; finally, it, too, was gone.

At least he was prepared, he knew that much. He just didn't know what he was prepared for. He knew earlier... he *thought* he knew earlier. He wished the voice would come back and give him a refresher course on what was going on. This was a lot like being all dressed up with no place to go; but he *did* have some place to go, he just couldn't remember where.

Like Peter who tried to walk on the water, Milford had looked away and lost the blind faith which had been driving him. But Peter eventually got the faith back. Would he ever get it back? He didn't know. When Peter began to sink beneath the waves, Jesus took his hand and pulled him into the boat. Was someone also waiting to haul Milford in? He didn't know that either. All he knew was that he should wait.

He waited until he finally fell asleep on the sofa.

6

At ten o'clock, Timmy and Doobie curled up in front of the sofa with their favorite blanket pulled over them. They never slept in the bedroom anymore; it was too hard.

Gerald and Pamela had gone into their room and closed the door as soon as they got home from church. Something had changed between them, and Timmy was glad to see it. They didn't fight like they used to. Now they actually held hands and even said, "I love you," to each other. They also went to bed a lot earlier than they used to, so Timmy and Doobie didn't have to stay up so late to sneak out of the bedroom.

No TV tonight; nothing good on. Just close the eyes and go to sleep.

Be strong, boy.

Timmy and Doobie both jumped at the same time.

It's all clear to me now. Be strong. We are for someone else.

Doobie whined softly and Timmy leaned up on his elbow. "Ma? Is that you?"

But there was no answer.

7

In the deep recesses of the human mind, hidden from the light of day and well beyond the realm of confession; in the mystical shadows of the darkest night, lurking like a phantom on the prowl; in those forever dim and secret places, Fear resides and is absolute monarch. Fear of the unknown, fear of the unexplained, fear of dying, fear of death. Fear of Evil.

Since the beginning of time, Evil has been personified and given names. The Serpent, the Dragon, the Goat; Lucifer, Beelzebub, Baal; the Prince of Liars, the Prince of Sinners, the Prince of Darkness; the Evil One, the Wicked One.

The Devil.

Satan.

Throughout the ages and by whatever name, it has made itself known to man by screwing into the very fiber of human existence and growing there like a malignant tumor.

The Devil.

Satan.

Evil.

In a desolate gravel pit just outside Crystal Springs, the mist waited. The mist itself was no more than a finger on the hand of the greater Evil, but it had proved its power, its superiority over the frail, insignificant beings that were its earthbound prey. Now, as the first light of dawn began to creep across the dunes, the mist swirled and seethed impatiently, waiting for the cover of night to hide its movement. Yes, it had all day to wait, and it would be a long day, but tonight it would move. Tonight, it would complete its assignment.

The Chosen Ones were almost gone; the demons of the mist were doing their job well. The old woman was out of the way and the preacher, that pitiful pulpiteer, was reduced to a babbling idiot. Soon it would be finished in this dreary little town and they could all move on. There was still much to do; this town, these people, this assignment, was just a small part of something big. Bigger than had ever been seen before. Every part, every assignment was important.

The mist boiled with eager anticipation. It was ready. Tonight would be glorious. Tonight would be exciting. Tonight... tonight would be a celebration of death.

Iss mass ssarati...

It would be glorious...

Sha mushi lipshuru...

... exciting...

Ruxisha Limnuti!

What if someone tried to interfere?

Fuck 'em.

8

There were very few people at Ma's funeral. As far as anyone could tell, she had no next of kin. She had no life insurance policy naming a beneficiary, she had no address book, she had no old letters from relatives (or from anyone else for that matter). It was as if she had just dropped out of the sky.

Pamela White had asked Mr. Thornhill, the funeral director, if he would conduct a short grave side service -- for Timmy's benefit, he and Ma had been so close. When Mr. Thornhill had asked what Ma's full name was, it suddenly occurred to Pamela that she didn't have the faintest idea. He said, "That's okay, Doctor Coleman will know," but for some reason, the very fact that she had known the old woman for so long and didn't even know her first name bothered Pamela greatly.

So, she had thought, *this is what our society is reduced to? We're so caught up in our own tiny little worlds that we can't even take the time to find out the names of the people we call our friends. That really stinks.* And she went home that day wondering, not what Ma's name was, but why she didn't know what Ma's name was.

They had decided on a morning funeral. Not that it really mattered. No more than a handful of people showed up at the funeral home to view the body in the whole two days she was there. That was quite a statement on the old woman's life. Except for Timmy and his parents and a very few of the town's old timers, Ma and Captain Jack were pretty much alone in the world.

"Don't look in the coffin, boy."

Timmy kept Ma's warning right in the front of his mind, and he was one of the many who did not go to the funeral home. It had nothing to do with wanting to remember her the way she was or not being able to face the death of a close friend; it had to do with what he had seen

Don't look in the coffin, boy.

in Jim's coffin. And so, he stayed at home while his mother and father made their obligatory visit. He stayed home, and he and Doobie sat staring out the living room window and wondering just what the hell was going on and what the hell could possibly happen next. That was on Saturday night. He was still wondering on Sunday night when he had his talk with Brother Milford and he was still wondering on Monday morning as the small group of mourners stood around the freshly dug grave. But no one seemed to have any answers so he would probably go on wondering for the rest of his life.

Yep. The rest of his life.

They used to say that rain during a funeral meant that God was crying. If that was true, then God must have liked Ma, at least a little. The night before, Sunday night, thunder and lightning had begun and had eventually given way to a steady downpour of rain. By early morning, it had slowed to a drizzle, but that drizzle showed no sign of letting up during the funeral. God was crying... a little.

Sometime in the wee hours of the morning, after the backhoe had dug the deep narrow hole, the funeral elves had appeared to set up an open-sided tent over the gravesite. As it turned out, the tent was large enough to serve as shelter not only for the casket, but also for the entire group of mourners who came to pay their last respects. There were Mr. Thornhill and his three assistants (who also served as pallbearers), Timmy White and his mother Pamela, Mrs. Prewitt, a fine Christian woman from down the street, and Mrs. Barlow, one of those seemingly ancient people who made it a point to go to every funeral, whether she knew them or not, just to see who she had outlived that day. Some said she was just morbid; others said that when you got to be her age, that kind of thing probably became pretty important. It didn't really matter; she was there.

As Mr. Thornhill opened his Bible and began to read, Timmy let his eyes wander across the cemetery. In the center was a huge mound topped by a gazebo and a monument which read "Our Confederate Dead 1861-1865". Timmy had rolled down that mound on many a hot summer day while his folks visited one relative or another that was buried nearby. North of the Confederate mound was the old part of the cemetery with row after row of tombstones unlike anything that was made today. There was a tall one that looked like the Washington Monument; the date on its base read March 15, 1847. Right beside it was a granite pedestal on top of which stood a marble woman wearing an old-fashioned dress with a draped overskirt and a high collar, her hair pulled back into a bun and a bouquet of flowers in her hands; the date was October 15, 1852. There were several angels with folded hands and outstretched wings, there were scrolls with the important information carved in Old English lettering, there were cement tree trunks graced with ferns and birds. But probably the most impressive, and certainly the only one of its kind in the cemetery, was the cube of white marble which held the life-sized statue of a man wearing a suit and hat and sitting cross-legged with his dog lying in front of him. That was the tombstone that really fascinated Timmy and the one that always drew his attention. Today he looked and behind it he saw James Milford, bareheaded in the rain, watching the funeral service.

Milford wasn't quite sure why he was there, but he knew he

was supposed to be there. He knew it in the same way he had known all the rituals the night before; something deep in his guts directed him. If he hadn't lost contact with it, maybe he would know what he was looking for out here in the rain. He watched the small group of people under the tent. Out of everyone there, Ma was probably the only one who had any information that could be of use to him, but she wasn't really in a position to relay that information to him. He knew immediately when Timmy spotted him because their eyes met, and Timmy gave him a sort of half smile. Milford returned the smile and was just about to raise his hand in greeting when the wave of dizziness swept over him.

It came suddenly and without warning. He reached out for support and his hand landed on the stone dog's tail. Nausea overcame him and he felt the liquid, bitter and acidic, rising into his throat. He held his stomach with his free hand and tried desperately to not throw up. The world spun crazily beneath his feet. He looked across the cemetery to Timmy in the faint hope that there might be an answer there, but his eyes were met by an incredibly brilliant light flashing rapidly like a strobe. He turned his head and covered his eyes until the flashing stopped. With his eyes drawn into a squint, he looked again at Timmy. What he saw took his breath.

A thin misty fog, like steam, was rising from the ground. The whole cemetery glowed with an eerie light; a light that had no visible source. Timmy stepped away from the funeral party. One step, two steps, three. He raised one hand toward heaven and a bolt of lightning came down to meet it. There was a flash, and Timmy became a warrior in shimmering white armor and wielding a sword of blue flame. He took two more steps and looked directly at Milford. With a smile, he raised the sword in a salute to the preacher.

Suddenly, the strobing began again, forcing Milford to look away. When it stopped, the nausea was gone. As quickly as it had come, it disappeared. The dizziness, gone. Milford rubbed his eyes trying to make them focus. The mist and the strange glow became a drizzling rain once more. The warrior was gone, and in his place was a ten-year-old attending a funeral and looking curiously at the preacher.

For no particular reason, Timmy pulled at the chain around his neck and, grasping the crucifix at the bottom of Jesus's tiny feet, held the cross up for Milford to see.

"A salute?" Milford thought, and he smiled. He returned Timmy's gesture with his own silver cross, and for just a second he could have sworn that it began to pulse in his hand.

9

"Maybe we should have done an exorcism."

Those words, spoken by Father Francis not so very long ago, kept forcing themselves into Milford's mind. "Maybe you were right."

He glanced at his watch. 9:00 pm. It would be completely dark in just a few more minutes. Then he would make his move; in the dark, when there was no danger of anyone else seeing; in the dark, because that was the time when magic worked best; in the dark, because that was the time for sending demons back to Hell.

Picking up the telephone, he dialed the number that was

scribbled on his note pad. There was the *click, click, click* of connections being made, a moment of silence, and then the sound of ringing.

"Hello?"

"Hello, Melanie."

"Hi, Brother Milford! How are you?"

"I'm fine." *But I don't want to waste time on pleasantries.* "Melanie, I need to see you."

"You do?"

It would take Melanie about fifteen minutes to put on her clothes, make up an excuse to get out of the house, and drive across town to the rendezvous. (They had decided to meet at the Dog 'N Suds so no one would see her car at the parsonage late at night; someone spreading rumors of statutory rape was all he needed on top of everything else.) She would probably be there before Milford was because he had a couple of things to do before he left. First, he hauled three battered suitcases, which held approximately ninety-nine percent of his worldly possessions, to his car and tossed them into the trunk. Then he walked across the lawn to the rear entrance of the Pastor's study. On the desk were two cardboard boxes of books and papers; they were the rest of his possessions. He placed his ring of keys on the desk, picked up the two boxes, one stacked on top of the other, and left the office. He stood beside his car for a moment and looked at the parsonage and the church; then, he drove away. He would never return.

The Dog 'N Suds was a small burger stand beside the old

highway. It was a popular teenage gathering spot on weekend nights, but tonight, Monday night, it would more than likely be deserted except for Mrs. Crowley, the owner.

As Milford turned off the highway and into the parking lot, he saw Melanie in her car waiting for him. Even in the glow of neon lights, she was beautiful. Her hair was pulled back out of her face... out of the way. She chewed softly on one long fingernail as she stared toward the building. When Milford stopped his car beside her, she smiled broadly and went to meet him. However, when she saw the concern on his face, her smile disappeared.

"What's the matter, Brother Milford?"

"Melanie, I found out about the ceremony that went on in the gravel pit. You didn't tell me all of it, did you?"

"Oh." She looked down at her shoes.

"Why didn't you tell me about the curse?"

She shrugged her shoulders without looking up.

"Didn't you think it was important?"

"I don't know."

"Where did the photograph and the bloody tissues come from?"

She said softly, "From your office. I found them when I took the list."

"So it was my picture and my blood, right?"

She looked up at him and tears rolled down her cheeks. "Please don't hate me! I just couldn't tell you all that! I never in a million years thought it would work."

"Maybe it didn't, but something sure as hell did."

"Brother Milford... I'm so sorry." She buried her face in his shoulder and began to sob. He took her in his arms and held her close until her crying was reduced to sniffles and a hitch in the chest.

"It's okay, Melanie. I don't hate you. But I need your help."

"What... what can I... do?" *Sniff.*

"I have to go to the gravel pit, and I need you to take me there."

"No!" She looked at him in utter horror. "I can't go back there! I... I... can't!"

"You have to, Melanie. Please. You don't have to do anything; just show me where the meetings were. I'll do the rest."

She started to shake her head.

"Please."

There was a long, *long* silence before Melanie asked, "When do you want to go?"

"Tonight. Right now."

"Oh, Jesus!" Why not tomorrow? Next week? Next month? Next year, for Christ's sake! Tonight? Right now? That wasn't at all what she wanted to hear. "What are you going to do?"

"I'm not sure. I'm hoping I find out before we get there."

She hugged him tightly and whispered, "I'm scared."

"I know. There's a lot of that going around lately. Will you take me there?"

He felt her head nod against his shoulder, and they held each other for a long time before he opened the car door for her.

10

It had been a very long day for Timmy White. After the funeral, he went to Charles' house, but Charles and his mother had gone out of town. He climbed into his tree house to watch the rain but a bolt of lightning that struck nearby changed his mind about that. Besides, he suddenly felt that he didn't want to be away from Doobie. He spent the rest of the day sitting in the living room and talking to the ever-faithful dog who was a very good listener. He didn't have a particular subject in mind when he started talking; he just opened his mouth and let whatever was in there come out. As it turned out, he talked mostly about Ma and Captain Jack. There were a lot of "Do you remember...?" stories and "Wasn't it funny when...?" tales. The only conscious effort he made was to not talk about what had happened to Ma and Jack. He didn't have any answers so there was no need to talk about it.

The day just sort of passed.

Now the boy and his dog were under their blanket in front of the sofa waiting for the Ten O'clock News to come and go so they could watch whatever was on the late movie. Outside, the thunder and lightning were putting on quite a show and rain was pounding on the metal awning over the porch. Timmy liked stormy nights; they were so... sinister.

Through the fabric of his short pants, Timmy felt the lump of the bullet in his pocket. It dawned upon him that he had never asked Jim if it was a live bullet or a fake. He imagined the headlines and laughed:

EXTRA! EXTRA!

BOY BLOWS OWN DICK OFF WITH SILVER BULLET

Claims Werewolf in Pocket Got Away

By the time the TV news was half over, Timmy was staring numbly at the screen. He didn't know what the coming movie would be, and it didn't matter anyway. Doobie's eyes were already closed, and Timmy felt his own getting heavy. Screw the late movie. At that very moment, he would have given his left nut for a remote control.

After he crawled to the TV and pushed the power button, he pulled the blanket up to his chin and was asleep in seconds. It was a very good sleep while it lasted.

11

"It's right over there." Melanie pointed to the clump of trees. "There's a path that leads to the inside."

Milford peered through the windshield of the car but couldn't really see anything. "It was inside the trees?"

"Yeah."

He reached into the glove box for his flashlight. "Okay. You can wait here if you want to."

"No! I don't want to be out here by myself!"

From the back seat Milford took the small bag that contained the items he thought he might need. He had tried to duplicate the things that Father Francis had taken to the church that night. Even though the ritual hadn't been entirely successful, it was the only point of reference that Milford had to work from. He tried to remember all the things Francis had said, all the gestures he had used, but most of that night was just a blur. The only copy of the homemade ritual went with Francis when he left. Milford had no idea how to turn tap water into holy water, how to turn taco shells into Holy Communion wafers, or even how to bless the crucifix that was around his neck. So what the hell was he doing out here?

Winging it, that's what. He had absolutely nothing to lose.

Milford pushed his door open, and a breeze blew rain into his face. He opened the umbrella as quickly as he could and went to the passenger's side to open the door for Melanie. When she got out, she leaned stiffly against the side of the car. The cold water on the car soaked into her clothes, but she didn't seem to care. It was obvious that she wanted no part of this night. Milford put one arm around her shoulders. "Are you sure you don't want to wait in the car?"

"No, no! I'm sure! Come on, I'll show you where the path is." She led the way, and even though she walked slowly, she was never unsure of her footing. She knew this path very well, even in the rain.

As the path opened onto the clearing, Melanie stopped and looked a bit puzzled. "Boy, things must have gotten real strange after we left that night. There was an altar here, and candles, and a bowl. Do you see them anywhere around?" Milford did a quick sweep of the ground with the flashlight but there was no sign of the altar. Overhead, lightning streaked through the sky and was followed by the *crack!* of thunder. "Brother Milford, how long is this going to take? This place gives me the creeps."

"I hope it only takes a few minutes."

"So do I," Melanie muttered and reached out to hold his arm.

The wind pushed through the leaves of the trees and all the water that had collected there dropped, pelting the umbrella that sheltered Milford and Melanie. Lightning flashed, slicing through the layer of clouds that hung close to the ground. Another blast of thunder followed. This would have been a perfect evening to sit in an old rocker on the front porch, rocking slowly, drinking iced tea or something stronger, and watching the storm rage. It was the kind of night that brought butterflies of excitement to the stomachs of many people.

Milford had butterflies, too. Big ones. Suddenly, he was struck with an overwhelming desire to get the job done and get the hell out of there. He looked at Melanie; she was huddled close to him like a child. "If you're going to be here, you have to do what I tell you. Okay?"

"What are we doing here?"

Milford hesitated. He could do this stuff in the dark, but he wasn't sure that he could talk about it out loud. It would probably sound stupid. But look who he was talking to; she described some pretty weird shit to him once. Oh, well.

"There is the possibility that the curse that was placed on me didn't work. It's hard to know for sure -- blood is pretty powerful in spells. What *I* think happened is that there were some demons hiding somewhere around here and the witchcraft activity woke them up or set them free or something like that. At least that's what a friend told me, and I think he may be right. I decided..." He stopped. That was exactly what had happened: He decided. He hadn't been led here; he hadn't been told to come here. It was his decision, based on careful consideration. Was it a good decision? Hell, he didn't know. "... I decided to come here and get rid of the demons."

She looked at him with deep concern. "Do you know how to do that?"

She really wasn't thrilled about being out here in the rain with somebody else who was about to try another bit of hocus pocus; not after what happened last time. Milford just smiled at her. From his bag he took a handful of small dry communion bread squares that he had gotten from the church. He held them out to Melanie.

"What is it?"

"Just take one." Then he spoke from memory the words that he had so often said to a much larger congregation. "And He took bread and gave thanks and broke it and gave it to them, saying, This is my body which is given for you: this do in remembrance of me." He placed one of the wafers in his mouth and chewed it. He nodded to Melanie and she ate hers. He gave Melanie the handle of the umbrella and held the rest of the bread squares at arm's length, saying, "May the flesh of Christ seal and sanctify this place." He took a deep breath and prepared himself for whatever was about to happen; the explosion, the blinding flash of light, whatever the reaction would be when a sacred holy object met another object that was saturated with evil. He let one of the wafers drop to the ground.

Nothing.

No *boom!*, no *flash!*, not even a spark or a sizzle. Maybe he'd watched too many movies. However, he didn't dwell on the lack of spectacle. Ignoring the rain, he stepped from under the umbrella and walked in a wide circle, dropping one of the bread squares every two feet or so. Melanie shivered and chewed on one of her fingernails. When all the bread had been distributed, he went back to the umbrella, took a bottle of red wine from his bag, and opened it.

"And He took the cup and gave thanks and gave it to them, saying, This is my blood of the new testament, which is shed for many for the remission of sins." He handed the bottle to Melanie and she took a sip. He took a big mouthful himself and felt the alcohol start to warm his body as it went down his throat. He held the bottle up and said, "May the blood of Christ purify the ground and drive the demons of evil from this place." Following the same route as before, he poured the wine onto the ground a few drops at a time until it was all gone. He tossed the bottle aside and reached into his bag again. The small glass jar he took out was sealed with wax. It was the water he had sealed earlier.

He unscrewed the lid and stuck his finger into the water. He turned to Melanie and drew a wet cross in the center of her forehead. He dipped his finger again and made the same mark on his own head. It was unnoticeable because of the small stream of rainwater rolling off his hair.

"Protect us, oh God, from the evil of this place. Look down upon us now and send your guardian to shield us as we..."

He stopped abruptly and stared questioningly at the jar in his hand. For a full minute, he didn't move, he didn't speak, he barely breathed.

"Brother Milford?" Melanie was frightened and her voice betrayed her. "Are you all right?"

He didn't look at her; he just stared at the jar.

"Brother Milford?" Her lip quivered and she started to cry. "Brother Milford, you're scaring me! Say something!"

He turned to face her, but his eyes retained the strange stare. "They're not here." His voice was so soft that the rain covered the sound.

"What?"

"They're not here."

"You mean, this worked? They're gone?"

"No. They're gone, but they were gone before we got here."

"How do you know?"

"I'm not sure. I just know. I know they aren't here, and I know they were gone before we got here. Where could they be?"

"How would I know?"

"Shit! Where the hell are they?" He screwed the lid back on the jar of water and shoved it into his pants pocket. Then he began to pace around the clearing. He started slowly but soon worked himself into a frenzy. He was waving his arms, running his hands through the wet tangles of his hair, taking giant steps that sent sheets of water into the air when he hit a puddle. When the lightning would flash, he looked like Victor Frankenstein impatiently waiting for his monster to be given life. And all the while he was shouting, "Where the hell are they?"

Melanie stood to one side and watched him. She didn't understand any of what had happened tonight; she just knew that she was very frightened. Finally, she rushed to Milford and grabbed his shoulders, interrupting his pacing. "Brother Milford, I'm scared! I want to get out of here! Let's go! Please!"

"You're right, Melanie. I'm sorry; I don't know what I was thinking. I'll take you back to your car."

In the safety of Milford's automobile and moving well away from the gravel pits, Melanie's fears went away, and she watched Milford, his face illuminated by the lights of the dashboard. He was a troubled man, there was no doubt about that, but he was very handsome. He was also kind and gentle, good and honest, caring and giving. And she was in love with him.

Milford turned the car onto the Dog 'N Suds parking lot and stopped beside Melanie's car. He turned to face her. "Thank you for helping me tonight."

"But if they weren't there, then we really didn't do anything, did we?"

"That doesn't matter. You helped and I appreciate it."

She leaned toward him and touched his face. "I'll help you any time you need me." Then she kissed him.

From the front seat of her car, Melanie watched Milford as he drove down the street and out of sight. She loved him, and now he knew it. And when she kissed him, he kissed her, too. If she had her way, they would be together very soon. And so, with thoughts of love and romance and wonderful sex coursing through her head and her body, she went home.

But Milford's thoughts were of something completely different.

Where the hell are they?

12

For the first time in nearly twenty years, Gerald White had to get up in the middle of the night to go to the john. Chances were that he would have gone into the bathroom, taken a leak, and gone all the way back to bed without ever really waking up. Chances were that he would have done all that if he hadn't stepped on Doobie's tail.

The dog yelped and Gerald stumbled forward, smashing his shins on the coffee table.

"Goddamnit!" He was awake now, and boy was he pissed. He looked at the dog who was licking his injured tail and then he looked at his son asleep on the floor. "This is stupid," he whispered, and he leaned down to pick Timmy up. He grunted. Timmy was getting too big to be carried to bed. Tomorrow morning, they were going to have it out, and Gerald planned to win.

As they neared Timmy's bedroom, Doobie realized what was about to happen and made a mad dash at Gerald's bare leg. He nipped lightly and Gerald brushed him back with his foot. Finally, one step away from the door, Doobie clamped his jaws around the calf of Gerald's right leg.

"Shit! Goddamnit! What the fuck are you doing!" Gerald kicked and sent Doobie flying into the sofa. Then he disappeared with Timmy into the bedroom. Doobie ran back and forth across the room, whining loudly and watching the door. When Gerald reappeared in the opening, Doobie started to bark.

"Doobie! Shut up! Shut up, or I'll throw your ass out in the rain!" Doobie stopped and sat very still until Gerald went, shaking his head, into the bathroom, and then he was running back and forth again, still whining but no longer barking. At the sound of the toilet flushing, Doobie sat again and was staring at Gerald when he came back into the room.

Relieving himself had not done much to change Gerald's disposition. He went straight to Doobie, squatted, and grabbed the dog by the ears. "What is your fucking problem?" The dog just glared up at him, and there was not a trace of the usual please-don't-be-pissed look in the canine's eyes. In fact, there might even have been a touch of defiance there. But none of that quite registered with Gerald. "Whatever it is, you better get over it because if you ever bite me again, your ass is outta here. You got it?" When Gerald let go of Doobie's ears, the dog went to the bedroom door and paced back and forth in front of it, looking alternately at Gerald and the dark doorway.

Gerald rubbed his face with his hands and shook his head again. "No, I'm not gonna carry you. If you want to go in the damned bedroom, then drag your lazy ass in there. The damned door's open." Then Gerald went back to his bed, mumbling along the way that he couldn't believe he was trying to converse with a stupid dog at whatever o'clock in the morning it was...

Doobie looked at the door and Gerald was right; it was open, but not as much as it was a minute ago. It only took a few more seconds for Doobie to see that the door was slowly -- very slowly -- closing. He had a choice to make, and he had to make it soon. He should be in there with Timmy; that was one thing he learned from Captain Jack, stay with the master if at all possible. But THEY were in there. If he went in right now, could he even make it to where Timmy was? The door closed a little more and one of the hinges let out a faint *squeak.*

His muscles tensed and he lurched forward, but he stopped himself before he even took one step. He whined, and the door kept moving; half closed now. He lurched again, stopped again. He was afraid. His whine was becoming a pitiful plea for help but there was no one to help; Gerald obviously didn't understand what was going on. It was up to him. He had to decide. Was he going in, or was he hiding behind the sofa?

Suddenly, he let out a bark and bolted through the shrinking opening, and the door closed silently behind him.

"Where the hell are they?"

He was obsessed. He had screwed up somehow and now things were a mess, and he didn't know what to do to straighten it out.

Milford screamed at the top of his lungs, "SHIT! Where are they?"

He stopped the car and rested his head on the steering wheel. His thoughts were a jumble of ideas; there was no rhyme or reason. He closed his eyes. "God, I can't do it. You've got to help me with this one." He took a deep breath, counted to ten, let it out.

A house.

The images were starting to come... slowly.

Trees. A yard.

There was a flash of light. Was it lightning? Could have been. On the other hand...

"Stop thinking," he scolded himself.

There was another flash, and another, and another. Faster,

faster, strobing now like... like in the cemetery.

A young man in shimmering armour.

A sword of blue flame.

A silver crucifix.

"Oh, my God! Timmy!"

Timmy!

Timmy's eyes shot open, and he knew immediately that it was time. There was no messenger, no neon sign flashing *It's time... It's time... It's time.* Just a feeling, like a sixth sense; a tingle in his stomach, a shiver at the base of his spine. It was time, all right. He didn't know what it was time for, but it was time, and he knew it and he was scared.

"Oh, no! No, no, no, no, no!" He was in his bedroom! How could that have happened? That's not where he was when he went to sleep and that's definitely not where he wanted to be right now! Something moved under the covers beside him and he almost shit until he realized that it was Doobie. He ran his hand down Doobie's head and felt the dog's whole body trembling. Maybe fear was contagious.

"It's okay, boy," he lied. "It's okay."

Doobie heard the noises before Timmy did and he started to growl deep in his throat. "What is it, Doobie? You hear something?" And then Timmy heard it, too; the scuffling and scurrying of feet in the dark shadows of the room. "They're here, aren't they?"

Scraaaaape!

The window at the head of the bed started to open itself and

Timmy felt the splattering of raindrops on his face. He swallowed hard and clenched his hands into fists.

"Keep your feet under the covers," he whispered, and Doobie kept growling. "Any part of your body that's not covered can be grabbed. Three seconds to get under the covers. They can't get you when you're with somebody else..." He reached out and dug his fingers deep into Doobie's fur. "...They can only come out in the dark... Oh, shit!" Timmy snatched the covers over his head as the lightning split the darkness. Not only was he startled, he suddenly realized that Ma had been right. The rules weren't working any more. Tonight, not even the light could make them go away.

The scurrying sound continued. The lightning flashed, the scurrying continued, and Timmy's heart felt as if it would jump right out of his chest. In the total darkness he could feel his senses sharpening. He felt every spring in his usually smooth mattress; he felt them until they were like spears in his back. Every sound was magnified a million times. The thunder crashed like cannon blasts, the wind whipped and howled, the scurrying sound got louder and louder. It got more intense, more terrifying. There were more of them, many more of the things than there had ever been before. There must have been a whole army of them. It got louder and louder and louder...

Then it stopped, and Timmy's heart sank.

Milford stopped his car a couple of blocks from the Whites' house. He gathered his materials from the back seat and stepped out into the rain. He left his umbrella; it would only get in the way. He walked quickly down the sidewalk and under the sounds of the storm he heard his own footsteps echoing off the houses he passed. It was then that he realized that most of the sounds of the storm were coming from just ahead of him... from Timmy's house.

Another bolt of lightning zipped through the sky, but it didn't originate in the clouds. It came out one of the windows of the White house. Milford stopped to watch for a minute and another lightning bolt went *into* the window. Out and in they went, back and forth, like a laser light show. "That must be Timmy's room," he said to himself. As he stepped onto the lawn, he immediately felt the electricity in the air crackle on the ends of his hair.

Where are they?

The whole room had gone silent, and Timmy heard nothing but the sound of his own blood throbbing in his ears.

Damn it! Where are they?

There was a gentle tug on the blanket at the foot of the bed, then another and another, each one considerably stronger than the last. In his fear and nervousness, Timmy almost giggled. In his mind he pictured a little green monster with coal black eyes and great long fangs standing at the door asking, "Can Timmy come out and play?"

"Timmy?"

The picture quickly faded.

"Timmy, it's me..."

The hair bristled on the back of his neck. Jim was calling him.

"Come on out, Timmy..."

His mind raced. He had to think this thing out. Jim was here, in his room, and those things were in here somewhere. Maybe Jim scared them away when he came in. Maybe they were gone. But if they weren't gone, Jim shouldn't be in here with them. If they were hiding, Jim was in danger.

But Jim was dead.

Something grabbed his foot; something like vines or fingers. Something cold. It made its way between the sheets and tightened around his foot. The game was over.

Timmy jumped, but the fingervines held fast. He pulled, trying to break free, but the vines began coiling up his leg. He couldn't stand it any longer. He threw the blanket off his face.

Outside the window, Milford set up his station. He completely ignored the pouring rain; it was of no importance. The certainty had returned. He knew what he had to do. He opened his black bag and arranged his supplies on the ground in front of him. Everything was there, all the things that had been chosen for him; all the things he would need and more.

With a twist, he broke the wax seal on the jar of oil. As he dipped his thumb into the oil, his whole hand began to shake as if some great idling motor were inside waiting to be revved up. He touched the thumb to his forehead and the spot began to tingle. He touched his chest, his left shoulder, and then his right shoulder, and even though the oil touched cloth and not skin, those spots also began to tingle. His whole body picked up the vibration of his shaking hand. It was working now. He felt the power growing, anticipating release.

He heard some activity within the room. Holding his right

hand in front of him, he made the sign of the cross in the direction of the open window. Lightning bolts crackled and popped as they flew past him, some coming so close that he could feel the heat they produced. He didn't flinch from his work.

"Our Father, which art in heaven, Hallowed by thy name..." Even though he spoke them softly, the words rang out like the chiming of church bells. They rose above the noise of the wind and thunder and resounded in the sky.

"Thy kingdom come. Thy will be done in earth, as it is in Heaven..."

Thunder *crack!*ed right beside the preacher's head. They were here, his enemies, and they were trying to distract him. But he did not hesitate in his prayer.

"Give us this day our daily bread. And forgive us our debts, as we forgive our debtors. And lead us not into temptation, but deliver us from evil..."

Bolt after bolt of lightning struck the ground at his feet and sent clouds of steam rising from the wet grass.

"For thine is the kingdom, and the power, and the glory, forever. Amen."

From deep in his soul and from the very gates of Heaven, a chorus of voices responded, "Amen!"

His bedroom was gone. At least the walls were, and so was the floor. They had been replaced by a seemingly endless black void, much like Timmy thought outer space must be. He and Doobie and the bed floated in the void. They were surrounded by darkness, but he could see clearly.

His window hung suspended in space with the curtains flapping in the wind. Long forks of electricity shot through the void, paused in places, and then streaked through the curtains. Where his closet had been, his clothes floated and did a strange, eerie kind of dance. His shirts reached toward him and small clawlike hands emerged from the sleeves. His dresser had disappeared also, leaving his pants, folding and unfolding themselves in some sort of ritual, and his socks, unrolling and filling themselves.

Jim stood at the foot of the bed with his own head cradled in the crook of his arm. The head grinned, but the grin did not reach its eyes, which were wide and menacing, glaring and reaching out to suck Timmy into their depths. There were hideous gashes on the face. The hands, gouged and gashed like the face, were outstretched, beckoning. The fingernails, which were sharpened to points, were caked with dirt and sand.

"Come on, Timmy. It's fun."

The voice belonged to Jim, but not the rest. When Timmy shook his head, the grin turned into a snarl. The thing that pretended to be Jim hissed its anger.

"Then I'll see you in hell!"

It put its ugly head on top of its shoulders and came toward Timmy with slow, faltering steps, gnashing its long yellow teeth and opening and closing its gnarly claws.

"Stay away from me!" Timmy screamed. "Leave me alone!" He struggled to move away, but he was held firmly by the fingervines. In desperation, he shoved his hand into his pocket and brought out the silver bullet. "Here. This belongs to you."

He threw the bullet as hard as he could and the blast that followed rocked the entire void. Pieces of the Jim-thing were hurled as far as Timmy could see. Breathing deeply, Timmy felt under the covers until he touched Doobie's back. Comfort in the touch.

The fingervines reached his knees and Timmy finally got brave enough to look at what was holding him. There were three or four or five of them wrapping their way up his leg. They were dark, almost black, with deep green fingernail-like claws on the ends and a blob at the base which could have been a hand. A spiny arm disappeared under the bed.

Timmy reached over his head to pull on the window frame. He had to get away from the vines. Maybe with the frame for support he could pull free. He reached, and the window dropped. As it fell, the shiny glass changed into razor sharp steel which cleanly severed his left hand.

Where is the Scarlet Pimpernel when you need him?

Timmy jerked his arm back and stared at it dumbly for a few seconds. His hand was gone. There was no pain, there was no blood, there was no hand. He watched in disbelief as the blade slowly raised itself and waited.

"Doobie," he shouted, his voice betraying his fear, "help me!" But Doobie was already at work. He dug at the fingervines with his claws and chewed at them with his teeth. His ears were laid back on his head and he growled viciously. When he would get a grip with his teeth, he would shake his head vigorously trying to tear the vines apart. The battle was fast and furious and soon all the covers had been thrown from the bed. Even though it had already failed them, Timmy felt that with the covers gone the last remaining façade of sanctuary was also gone and he suddenly felt naked in the fight.

He tried to kick, but his legs would not move so he twisted and turned as much as he could. Doobie continued untiringly in his attack, but, though they had slowed somewhat, the vines were gaining ground. And in the fierceness of the fight, neither Timmy nor Doobie noticed the one vine that crept up the opposite side of the bed.

With incredible swiftness, the new vine lashed out and wrapped itself around Doobie. It easily picked the startled dog up and tossed him at the open window. As Doobie went through, the blade dropped again.

"Doobie!" Timmy screamed.

From outside the window a familiar voice called out, "Hold on, Timmy! Hold on!"

Then they came for him. Slowly, around the edge of the bed, they appeared. Red eyes, yellow eyes, no eyes; claws and bony fingers; skeletal grins that bared vicious canine teeth. They were worse than anything he had ever seen in movies or even dared to imagine, and they were coming for him.

"Hold on, Timmy! Hold on!"

When the dog had come flying through the window, it caught Milford off guard, but he had somehow managed to break the dog's fall. When he had heard Timmy's scream, he knew, and his guiding force knew, that time was of the essence. The Voice took over.

"*Assolla bon materrs materrs, common irr mator, Iam.*"

Milford felt the pain begin in his chest. It didn't surprise him; he knew that it would come. He just wasn't prepared for it to explode. It was as if everything inside him was struggling to get out. The front of his shirt shredded, and blood gushed out. Doobie, who had been watching the preacher, tucked his tail and hid under a fig tree. Milford was startled, but only momentarily. With only the slightest pause, he regained his composure and reached for the jar of blessed water. He doused some on the open wound. There was a blinding flash and the pungent smell of burning flesh, and as he watched, the wound healed itself.

"*In nomine Patris, et Filii, et Spiritus Sancti...*" He was under control; he could continue.

"Almighty God and Father, take away my sins that I may enter the most holy place and the power may flow through me. Almighty God, creator of the universe and all things..."

There was another explosion, this one in his leg. Without any warning, Milford found himself on the ground, his left leg a useless mass of torn and bleeding flesh. He poured more of the water on his leg and, as before, the flesh mended itself. He stood to face the window once more and Doobie ventured out of hiding.

"Almighty God and Father of our Savior Jesus Christ, I humbly ask thy favor in granting to me aid against the evil at work in this place..." He picked up a handful of communion wafers, now a soggy mass, and rubbed them on the side of the house. The bread hummed and vibrated under his hand and blue-white sparks danced between his fingers. Doobie looked up to the sky, whining and flinching from the falling rain. Milford began to feel heat from the raindrops that fell on him.

"Grant me power over the Evil One which thou hast cast out from Heaven and who now torments thy Chosen Ones created in thine image." Pouring oil from his jar, he formed a crude cross on the side of the house. As the oil touched the wood, it began to sizzle and smoke and spit out sparks. Something was wrong with the rain. Doobie cried and again sought shelter under the broad leaves of the fig tree. The rain ate into Milford's skin, burning and destroying the flesh. He tried to ignore the pain.

"Lift thy hand toward me and give me... grant me strength to serve... to guard..." He was in agony. He found himself wanting to leave this place, but he had a job to do. He reached for the bottle of holy water and turned it upside down over one of his new wounds. It was empty. In despair, he threw it against the side of the house where it shattered in an explosion of light. He raised his hands to shield his eyes and saw that there was no skin on his fingers. He cried to Heaven.

"The spirit is willing, but the flesh is weak."

Raising his gnarled hands toward the sky, he had to scream his prayer above the noise of the thunder.

"Father God, grant thy protection to this thy servant as he continues to fight against the Evil One. Grant thy safety and secure the victory..."

A bolt of lightning struck his upraised hands and drove him to his knees.

"God of ages, who sent thine only Son to crush the foes of Heaven, bless the work of thy servant and elevate the name of Jesus

Christ our Lord..."

Another bolt of lightning forced him backward until he lay flat on the ground looking up at the sky and watching the acid-rain fall into his eyes. He felt that he had been abandoned...

"In the holy name of my Lord and Master, Jesus Christ, God, hear my prayer!"

... but he didn't know the plan.

And the chorus of voices shouted down from Heaven, "Amen!"

Timmy cried, but there were no tears. He hurt, but there was no blood. He screamed, but now there was only the hollow rush of air from his lungs. The voice outside told him to hold on, but he had just about reached his limit. The fingervines were wrapping around his body now. He wanted to struggle but he could barely move. Sharp claws began to tear his flesh. The air was filled with a menagerie of sounds: Thunder behind the flapping curtains, gnashing of horrible fangs, ripping of flesh, a squawk...

A familiar squawk.

Captain Jack!

He struggled harder; he had to find Captain Jack. As he turned, he caught only a glimpse, but that was enough to tell him that everything would be all right. Ma was coming. It didn't look like Ma, but he knew it was her and she was coming to help. She was dressed in white, bright white, and she glowed like a painting of an angel. In one hand she carried a shiny golden snake and in the other, a flaming sword. Timmy tried to call to her, but no sound would come from his lips. Still, she raised her sword to him.

The golden snake left Ma's hand to fly toward Timmy and somewhere between the two it changed. Hovering over the bed was a golden Captain Jack with the long whip tail of the snake. Jack swooped and with his great beak snatched the crucifix from around Timmy's neck. Timmy reached with his one hand and grasped the tail as Ma brandished her sword against the creatures. Limbs were severed, headless bodies staggered and fell only to rise again. They could not be killed; they could only be held back, but that was all that was necessary.

As Timmy held his tail, Jack began a backward flight and Timmy felt the pull. For a moment there was nothing, only a strain like walking against a strong wind. Then he felt a sliding sensation, like taking off his pants. Suddenly he was free; free from the world, free from the pain, free from himself. And in that instant, he touched eternity.

From somewhere over the bed, he watched as his own limp body was torn and mutilated by the demons, but that had become unimportant. What was important was to join the man outside the window. Everything was clear to him now, just like Ma had said. Plans had been made, bigger plans than anyone could have possibly imagined. There were strategies and sub strategies, plots and counterplots. The opponents were millennia old enemies, and this battle was nothing compared to the war that was brewing. James Milford had been appointed; he had to be protected.

Captain Jack and Timmy, still clutching Jack's tail, sailed out between the curtains leaving Ma to fight for the moment. Outside, the preacher lay on the ground and when Timmy and Jack appeared in the air he began to cry. "God, forgive me! I have failed!"

"No, Brother Milford, you haven't failed. It was never meant that you save me, only that you try. It is in the trying that you will learn."

Timmy took the silver crucifix from Jack's beak and held it high into the air. It began to pulse in his hand and grow longer and longer until it became a sword of bright blue flame. A ring of light formed at the point and began to flash until it was a brilliant strobe in the darkness. When it stopped, Timmy was transformed. He wore the shining armor of Milford's vision.

When Ma came through the curtains, she was followed closely by the demons. She joined Timmy and the preacher, taking a position that placed Milford between them, while the demons stood in rows facing the three. Milford recognized most of these monsters; he had seen them before in his own church. Now he had to face them again. He hoped this would be the last time.

But he didn't know the plan.

For a long time, the two enemy camps stood unmoving, appraising the situation and reckoning the strength of their opponents. Finally, a smile spread across Timmy's face and he tipped his sword in a salute to Milford. Milford returned the smile and nodded slightly. With Jack circling overhead, Timmy looked at Ma, they raised their swords, and the battle was on.

The demons came in waves, attacking without mercy. They clawed and slashed, trying desperately to get to Milford, but Ma and Timmy kept them away. Milford was their goal now; he was the

Appointed One. If they could get past the immortals and get to him, the coming war would be all but over before it even began. They should have gotten Milford in his own church while they had the chance, but things just didn't work out that way. Shit kept happening. And they had fucked getting rid of the mortals, too; they had let them become *immortals.* Now they had to deal with them, too. The new shitstorm made them more determined, and they pressed harder.

After what seemed to be hours of fighting, Ma and Timmy both knew that they alone could not defeat the energy of their attackers. They needed help. Moving as close together as possible, they joined their free hands over Milford's head and held them up toward Heaven.

The power came to them in a blue spiral of light, coming straight down from the clouds until it touched their hands and surged through their beings. Their swords became focal points for the energy. With grand sweeping gestures, they pointed their swords at the enemy demons and balls of throbbing sparking blue-flame energy shot forward. When a ball hit its mark, the explosion rocked the foundation of the earth and sent a shower of white-hot sparkles into the air. Not even the demons could stand against the power coming from the swords. They fought as long as they could, but as explosion after explosion shook them, they were quickly driven away and back to the places they haunted.

The battle was over. Ma and Timmy stood at either side of the preacher and watched as he reached a hand toward each of them. Then he closed his eyes and collapsed.

Jack let out a *squawk!* and Ma nodded up to him. "We must

go, Timmy. There is still much for you to see."

"What about Brother Milford?"

"You take one hand, I'll take the other."

"Just a minute." Timmy went to the fig tree and lifted one of the low broad leaves. Doobie looked up from where he was hiding. When he saw Timmy, he barked and wagged his tail. "You've got to come, too, Doobie. You know I can't go anywhere without you." Doobie barked once more and trotted out from under the tree. Captain Jack led the way with Ma and Timmy floating low above the ground carrying Milford between them and Doobie chasing along on the ground. Ma and Timmy, Doobie and Jack; they were almost together again, and they were very happy.

The night had grown relatively quiet. There was still the occasional peal of thunder and streak of lightning and the rain was still a steady downpour, but all was normal again and the wind had just about disappeared. The only sounds that broke the quiet rainy serenity of the night were the screech of tires and the dull thud of a dog being hit by a car.

James Milford awoke behind the wheel of his car. He didn't know how long he had been there, but it was still dark outside. His first thought was that he had fallen asleep and dreamed the whole thing, but the blood on his shirt and pants told him differently. He closed his eyes and cleared his mind.

"It is in the trying that you will learn."

"What did I learn?"

"You have learned of your enemy; now you must learn of your

allies."

And the chorus from Heaven shouted, "Amen!"

Milford smiled, started his car, and drove away from town.

13

Tuesday morning, Gerald White had wanted to sleep late. He didn't have to go to work; the shirt factory was history. Even so, he still awoke just before seven o'clock. Old habits were hard to break. Pamela slept peacefully beside him. She must have gotten warm during the night. She had kicked the covers away and her nightshirt was bunched up around her waist. Gerald felt a rush of early morning desire and he reached out to hold one of her breasts. When she exhaled loudly and rolled over onto her side, he decided it was time to get up.

As soon as the smell of coffee drifted through the house, Pamela shuffled out of the bedroom and sat with her husband at the kitchen table.

"How'd you sleep?" he asked as she propped her head in her hands.

"Fine up until just a few minutes ago. I had the weirdest dream about a monster that collects tits." Gerald broke into laughter and Pamela looked at him with a trace of irritation. "What's so funny?"

"Oh, nothing," he managed to say between snorts. "I guess you had to be there. The coffee'll be ready in just a minute." He left the table, still chuckling, and went to the front door.

It was still raining, and the clouds didn't appear to be breaking up at all. It looked like it would be another dreary day inside. Gerald looked with some dismay at the lawn. The morning newspaper lay a good twenty-five feet from the front porch and it had landed in the largest puddle in the whole yard. It was in a plastic bag, but Gerald knew in his heart that the paper was beyond salvaging. Still, he had to try.

Holding an umbrella over his head, he walked barefoot across the lawn to retrieve his paper. By the time he reached it, water had already soaked the bottom eight or nine inches of his pants legs, but he didn't care; they would dry a lot faster than the soggy newsprint.

As he turned to go back to the house, he caught a glimpse of a drenched mass in the middle of the street. He had to go a few steps closer before he could tell what it was.

"Oh, no." He dropped the newspaper and the umbrella and went into the street to pick up Doobie's body.

When Pamela heard the front door open, she went toward the living room. "Do you want some eggs or..." And then she saw Gerald, dripping, at the door, his entire front covered with mud and blood. "Jesus Christ! What happened?"

"It's Doobie. He got run over."

"Is he hurt bad?" When Gerald didn't answer, she knew. "Oh, shit. Where is he?"

"On the porch. He's a mess. I don't know how he got out, but I guess it's a little too late to worry about that now." He looked at his hands in disgust. "I gotta clean this shit off me."

As Gerald went into the bathroom to wash up, Pamela went in to wake Timmy. A minute later, she screamed.

14

From the

Crystal Springs *TIMES*

Timothy Peter White, son of Mr. and Mrs. Gerald D. White of Crystal Springs, passed away Monday night at the age of ten. Cause of death was diagnosed as intracranial aneurysm. There were no prior signs of serious illness. He died quietly in his sleep. He is survived by his mother and father.

Funeral services will be held Thursday at 10:00 A.M. at the Baptist Church. The body rests at Copiah Funeral Home. Interment will be in the Old Crystal Springs Cemetery.

15

Someone, somewhere, sometime coined the phrase, "Life goes on." It was true. Life went on in the sleepy little town of Crystal Springs, even after the strange events of that summer in 1983.

Sandra Taylor had Michel Ingram's baby, and it was a fine strong son. Against the advice of friends and relatives, she decided to keep the child. It was all she had left of Michel. No one could argue with that.

Melanie Davis left town about two weeks after Timmy White died. She told her parents that she wanted to do some traveling before she had to go off to college. They tried to dissuade her but, as usual, Melanie got her way. The small-town rumor mill had a somewhat different story, several of them, in fact. One was that she was pregnant and went away to have the kid so she could give it up for adoption and nobody would ever know. Another story said that she was a sex-starved slut and after she had done every available man in town, she went to get some outside excitement. But a few of her closest friends told a few of their closest friends that she had gotten a postcard from James Milford and that she had gone off to find him. At any rate, she was gone, and nobody knew when she would be back, if ever.

Timmy's funeral had been painful and exhausting for Gerald and Pamela, but through it all they had remained strong and silent. The ride home had lasted forever, but still they were strong and silent. All along the street, rose gardens were in bloom, children played in yards and pets romped with them, and neighbors went about their daily chores. But these went unnoticed. Gerald and Pamela were being strong. Neither spoke; what was there to say? Their only child was gone. Dead. Buried. When the car pulled into the drive, Pamela saw Timmy's bicycle parked beside the house. The tears flowed. They sat in the car for a long time, Pamela crying and Gerald holding her and stroking her hair.

They made the move to Hattiesburg. They decided that even though their son was buried in Crystal Springs, they could still come back to visit the grave. Hattiesburg wasn't that far away. But Gerald couldn't bring himself to sell the house. It had too many memories for him. He would rent it out instead. As they packed their belongings, Pamela found a notebook under the mattress of Timmy's bed. She hesitated before opening it, afraid that reading something of her son's might be more than she could handle. She was right.

And so it went in Crystal Springs, just one day leading into the next, on and on, nothing really changing, nothing really staying the same.

Until one night near the end of summer.

Darkness came quickly and quietly and covered the world like a skin-tight black glove. The fingernail moon shed very little light, but it was there to watch over the night. Somewhere a dog barked, probably at some unfortunate tomcat that wandered into his yard. On the northern horizon storm clouds gathered but they wouldn't come this far south. Not tonight. All Crystal Springs would get tonight would be the wind that moved on the outer edge of the cold front.

It started slowly, coming in whisps until it built to a steady breeze. And for a moment... for one brief, fleeting moment... the wind that whispered through the pine needles sounded like a hoarse voice saying, *"It's time... It's time..."* In one of the houses on one of the streets in this small town, a young boy heard a tapping at his window and a voice calling out to him.

"Hey, Charles! Let's go to the gravel pits!"

"Timmy?"

END

Made in the USA
Coppell, TX
22 October 2022